HAMMERJACK

HAMMERJACK

A NOVEL

MARC D. GILLER

BANTAM BOOKS

HAMMERJACK
A Bantam Spectra Book / June 2005

Published by
Bantam Dell
A Division of Random House, Inc.
New York, New York

Book design by Joseph Rutt

Library of Congress Cataloging-in-Publication Data
Giller, Marc D. (Marc Daniel), 1968–
Hammerjack/Marc D. Giller
p.   cm.
ISBN 0-553-38331-0
1. Business intelligence—Fiction. 2. Supercomputers—Fiction.
3. Conspiracies—Fiction. I. Title.
PS3607.I436 H36 2005   2004065590
813/.6 22

Printed in the United States of America
Published simultaneously in Canada

www.bantamdell.com

BVG   10   9   8   7   6   5   4   3   2   1

For Three Generations:

Daniel and Ursula Giller,
who gave me life

Ildi Giller,
who showed me love

Alexandra and Christian Giller,
who taught me what life is about

AUTHOR'S NOTE

Aspiring writers have a vivid fantasy life, a lot of which doesn't end up on paper. Much of it revolves around the Lucky Break: that day you finally get the call that your book sold, and your life changes forever. For me, that day came less than a week after my son was born. I'd spent the morning mowing the lawn, and was just getting out of the shower when my agent called with the news. Dripping wet, I tore through the house in my boxers to tell my wife what happened, while my daughter looked on like I was nuts. Not exactly the magic moment I'd always pictured—but fate has a sense of humor, and rarely delivers what you'd expect.

Case in point: I recently found myself at the World Science Fiction Convention in Boston, standing in front of a bunch of people who were asking *me* how to get a novel published. It felt strange giving advice on the subject, as I had spent more than a few years trying to cross that finish line myself. I started thinking about all the people who had helped me during that time—the friends and family who patiently read my stuff, offering advice and honesty; the teachers and professors who showed me how (and sometimes how not) to write; and those brave few literary professionals who actually listened, giving me just enough encouragement to keep working at it. Without them, this book would have never seen the light of day.

To Kimberley Cameron, my agent and miracle worker: it can't be easy to turn a wannabe into a professional writer, but somehow you made it all happen. Your enthusiasm and faith in this project never wavered, and for that I owe you a tremendous debt. Thanks for all the hard work and inspiration—and for making the dream a reality.

To Juliet Ulman, the hardest-working woman in the publishing business: you're everything I could have hoped for in an editor—sharp, literate, with a keen eye for what works and what doesn't (and an impressive knowledge of 1970s low-budget cinema). Thanks for plucking my manuscript from the pile and turning it into a real novel, and me into a real author.

Also, props go out to Todd Keithley, who helped coax this novel from its infancy (he's now studying to be a lawyer, but don't hold that against him); Adam Marsh, whose line-editing skills are second to none; Payne Harrison, fellow author and fellow Aggie, who shared his wisdom and experience; Steve Fennell and John Kerwin, who read the first draft and provided me the sage counsel that only science-fiction fanboys can provide; Jeff Bell, for being a friend and not showing anyone my old vampire novel (although he's threatened to eBay the manuscript someday); Don Atkinson, J. D. Bondy, Barry Carmody, Mark Dye, Valerie Fennell, Joe Kucewicz, and Mary Helen Uusimaki, for reading my earlier work with compassion and interest; Zala and Linnea Forizs, who believed in me enough to let me marry their daughter; Claudia Atkinson, who inspired me to write when we were kids by starting a novel of her own; Mary Jo Edwards and Jane Pruitt, who nurtured that creative spark at the beginning; the late Charles Gordone, for all the weird and wacky times in playwriting; and to Bill Linkenhoker, Simon Morgan, and Curtis Pope, for your friendship and poker-playing skills.

It's been a wild ride so far. I can't wait to find out what happens next.

Marc D. Giller
Tampa, Florida

HAMMERJACK

PROLOGUE

Seven minutes had passed since the disturbance began, but by the time Caleb got word over the fiber link it was already old news. It was no secret that police communications were far from secure: hammerjacks had seen to that, carving so many holes in the backbone that anybody with a homemade face kit could plug in and listen to whatever he damn well pleased. Not that it mattered. Being a cop wasn't that kind of job anymore—nor had it ever been in Caleb's lifetime.

Still, there were things that the Corporate Special Services wouldn't touch—and the illusion of a civilian police department had its advantages. So over the course of the six months, when the party had started spilling out of the rave clubs of Chelsea and into the streets of Manhattan, the job of cleaning up the mess fell on Caleb's desk. At first he had thought it was just another phase in the tec culture—some mass hallucinatory trip fueled by synthesized adrenalopiates, maybe some new thing smuggled in from the Zone that nobody knew about. But Caleb knew his streets, and his instincts—obsolete or not—soon told him that there was something *else* at work here. He could see it in their pasty faces and rapturous eyes: the way they all seemed to know when to come together. The word moved through the dark undercurrent that ran beneath the city, a hard link wired into each and every one of their heads.

What it all meant was the thing Caleb didn't know. Reliable snitches were hard to find in the subculture, and the intel brokers didn't come cheap enough for the department to buy them. The only information Caleb had was what he had seen for himself—and that, he didn't begin to understand.

It wasn't the street species; Caleb had been on the job long enough to recognize them all—the Crowleys, the Teslas, the Urban Goths—Zone rangers so wasted they wandered around like zombies, eating and fucking out of pure reflex. He recognized the order that existed between them, the barriers they put between themselves. So long as that balance was maintained, he never worried. But when they were around each other and there wasn't a fight, Caleb became concerned. It felt too much like prophecy—too much like the end of the world.

Maybe it's true. If the end doesn't come soon, people might get tired of waiting.

Caleb allowed the notion to hover in front of him for a few moments, until it dissipated into the cloud of cigarette smoke that swirled around his head. It was a small cabin, and the pilot of the hovercraft made no attempt to conceal his disgust at the acrid intrusion. Caleb didn't care. He knew the smell was horrible, but at least it was real tobacco, with all of the old stimulants and carcinogens added for just the right kick. It was his one expensive habit, an unusual one in an age when most designer drugs were genetically engineered and readily accessible—not to mention legal. He smoked it down to the last possible ember, taking one last mournful drag off the wasted stick before stubbing the remains out on the floor.

"How much longer?" he asked.

"Coming up to the starboard," the pilot replied. "You know about this place?"

Caleb grunted affirmatively as he slid over to the other side of the cabin. He wiped the fog from the glass and peered through a light mist at the passing city outside. A hundred meters below was Church Street, while on both sides the skyscrapers of lower Manhattan rose another two thousand meters to punch a hole in the night. The structures were so massive they could be seen from low orbit—but from his vantage point, Caleb also saw the people inside, scurrying past the windows and conducting their business. Even at this hour deals were being closed—a never-ending tide of commerce, the pulse that made the city come alive.

The pilot carved out a glide path that took them in a tight arc around the Volksgott Tower. Caleb kept his eyes fixed on the huge, glowing letters that marked the eight-hundred-floor building, trying to fight off the inevitable sensation of vertigo. Slowly at first, then accelerating, the letters peeled away from his sight, opening up the vastness of the plaza beneath him. The effect was dramatic—not for the architectural marvel that the Collective had dedicated to itself, but for the audience that had gathered there to watch the show.

Caleb sensed his pilot growing anxious as they prepared to set down.

"They ever done this before?"

Caleb had to take it all in before he could answer: "No."

Faces turned upward toward the sky, reacting to the roar of the approaching hovercraft. *Hundreds* of them, spread out across the grounds outside the Works. All had heard the word, and all had responded.

Is this what they've been waiting for? Caleb wondered.

From Abby Silva's vantage point, it was easy to see why the street species had ended up there. They had been working their way to it from the start, the genetically engineered drugs in their veins driving them home. They were, after all, children of the technology developed at the Works. If there was ever a place for them to make a pilgrimage, this would be it.

The Collective erected the building over a century ago, to be their Combined Centers for Scientific Research and Development—the best minds from all of the major corporations coming together to see what kind of hell they could unleash on Earth. A dwarf among the other towers that surrounded it, the Works rose a scant two hundred stories into the sky—but the place had a *presence* that few other buildings in the world could match. A perfect four-sided obelisk—walls gradually tapered to form a pyramid apex at the very top—projected the epic and intimidating feel of a place of worship. A temple for those who would lay themselves down as offerings on the altar of technology. A mystical home for secrets known only by the few who were allowed to enter.

And this bunch only puts the icing on the cake, Abby thought.

She noticed a couple of Urban Goths hanging out next to the plaza fountain and went over to have a look. She was actually surprised to see them. Unlike most of the species out there, Goths weren't into accelerated reality. Deathplay was their thing—which was why the rest of the subculture left them alone. *Freaks among the freaks,* Abby thought. If *they* were invited to the party, the boundaries were starting to crumble.

The Goths were deep in play when Abby approached them, darting eyes hidden beneath closed lids. Both were better than seven feet tall, a genetic anomaly caused by inbreeding among their sect. Their pale, gaunt faces were pocked with scars from cheap electrodes. From the fiber protruding out of the backs of their skulls, Abby saw they had graduated to permanent implants.

"Anything good on?" she asked.

The taller of the two opened his eyes and looked down at her. The sclera were as black as the pupils, a result of the implant surgery. "Take this trip and you won't want to come back," he said, unplugging a fiber from behind his left ear. "If you like, I can arrange an exchange. I know people who pay top dollar for a cop's death."

"I had no idea we were so popular."

The Goth smiled. His teeth were filed down to points. "You're not. But corporate security don't like to mix it up with us like you do."

Abby returned the smile, acknowledging the joke. The only time CSS worked street species was to bust their balls. "Thanks, but no thanks," she said, motioning toward his friend, who was still down in it. "Must be some good shit for him to be this tuned out. You sure he ain't poaching illegal?"

This time the Goth laughed. "Snuff stuff is just a big lie. What I make, even *better* than the real thing."

Abby believed him. Deathplay was recorded from tec-induced hallucinations, uploaded from junkies so desperate for money they

let the Goths steal their nightmares. It was cheaper and less complicated than actual murder. But it still gave Abby the chills.

"So what are you fellas doing here?" she asked, changing the subject. "This usually isn't your kind of scene."

"Say the same about you," the Goth replied, plugging back in.
"You come looking for answers. We come for the same thing. Been
waiting a long time."

"For what?"

The Goth spasmed for a moment while the latest death simulation
filled his cerebral cortex. It was supposedly more intense than an or-
gasm, though Abby was never curious enough to give it a go. Mortality was enough of a drag when you only did it once.

"For the word," the Goth breathed, sinking into his fantasy. "It
coming down. We all been listening."

"Don't suppose you'd share the word with a cop."

"The word for everyone, *mon amour*. Besides, we all find out
sooner or later. Evolution don't leave nobody behind. That's what
they tell us."

"Who tells you?"

"*Inru*," the Goth said, and phased out of the world again.

Abby had no idea what that meant—although the word *Inru* had
been making the rounds through the subculture for a while. Before
now, Abby had thought it was the lingo for some new brand of stim.
But Goths didn't get their kicks from that sort of thing. *Inru* had to
be something different.

Maybe something right here . . .

Abby headed back toward the police line when the whine of the
hovercraft's engines passed overhead. She emerged from the crowd
just as it was descending on the plaza, and had to marvel at the lieutenant's bravery for going near that heap. An ugly relic of a previous
time, the vehicle would have been equally at home in a transportation museum or a junkyard. Abby hoped that the screeching turbofans held together long enough to get her boss on the ground.

The landing gear engaged with a shrill, metallic grind—but the pilot managed to bring his craft down softly, almost gracefully. The old

mechanical beast seemed to exude relief as the engines cut off, belching one last cloud of smoke before spinning into silence. Shortly after, the passenger hatch opened and Caleb appeared. He was obviously shaken, but alert. Abby smiled, admiring his resolve.

"I won't hold it against you if you kiss the ground."

"I won't hold it against you if you kiss something *else*," he shot back, walking over to her. "You're supposed to keep me informed, Abby. How come I wasn't invited to the party?"

"Sorry, Lieutenant. You know the species. We couldn't keep a pulse on them even *before* this stuff was going down."

Caleb quickly scanned the line of officers doing the crowd control, a dozen cops holding back ten times their own number. Any appearance of control was just that—an appearance. The species could overrun them in two seconds if somebody made the call.

"I don't like these odds, Abby."

"I wouldn't worry. They haven't been violent."

"Doesn't mean they can't start," Caleb said, and started walking toward the building. Abby quickly fell in step beside him. "We don't even know what set them off."

"You ever hear of something called *Inru*?"

"You're the one dialed into the culture, Abby. If you don't know what it is, *I* sure as hell don't. Why? Did you get anything out of these people?"

"Just a couple of Goths talking trash."

Caleb smiled knowingly. "Too bad the Collective doesn't consider this bunch a threat. So what's with CSS, anyway? I thought they had a frigging army in this place."

"They do—but they haven't shown their faces yet."

That in itself was odd. Even if the Collective didn't give a shit, Corporate Special Services still had an image to maintain. They should have been out here breaking up what was, in effect, an illegal assembly. Cops weren't usually called until after, when it was time to bag the corpses and haul them away.

So where were they?

"Dispatch got the call telling us about the freak show," Abby explained. "For some reason they couldn't get a trap, so we don't know who phoned it in. All we know is that it didn't come from here."

"Have you talked with *anyone* inside the building yet?"

Abby shook her head. "No one is answering any calls. And we don't have the equipment to do a remote link and see if their communications are still active."

"Up to our usual standards of efficiency," Caleb muttered. "Damn."

They stopped at the base of the stairway that led to the main entrance. Abby lifted her eyes skyward, taking in the whole of the tower a little bit at a time. Up above the pyramid, she could see the strands of laser light that marked the pulser grid that stretched over the city. It was hard for her to get a sense of why they were here—but underneath that, the certainty that they were *supposed* to be.

"Any ideas?" she asked Caleb.

"That depends on how much you trust me."

Abby heard the intent in his voice, and she knew where it was leading. "You got some kind of death wish, Lieutenant?"

"Don't tell me you didn't think about it, Abby," Caleb said, motioning back toward the crowd. Abby turned to see it for herself, and it was only then she noticed how *silent* they had become. Everyone was fixated on the two of them, waiting to see what they would do next. And it was then she remembered very clearly what the Goth had told her.

Evolution don't leave nobody behind.

"We can do this ourselves," Caleb told her. "It's the only way we're going to find out for sure."

Abby couldn't deny she was tempted. If they contacted the Collective directly, a CSS unit would be there in fifteen minutes. In twenty minutes, the cleanup would begin. And in an hour, both she and Caleb would be in an interrogation room being attacked with questions they couldn't begin to answer.

But she was still scared.

"What's going to happen to us if we go up there?" she asked.

"Damned if I know," Caleb said.

They headed upstairs.

• • •

Caleb felt an electric tingle as they reached the electronic surveil-lance, the waves of sensor energy playing across his skin—but be-yond that, there was absolutely no sensation of presence. The closer they got to the security zone, the more it felt like they were stepping into a void. It was as if a veil of nothingness surrounded the entire building.

They paused when they reached the top of the steps. There was a clear line between them and the main entrance, but a quick glance over his head told Caleb what really stood between. Three remote cameras were already tracking him, while a particle-beam microtur-ret turned to acquire its new target.

Abby had spotted the thing as well. They crouched down, waiting to see what the tiny cannon would do. After a few moments, they were satisfied that it would hold off—for now.

"You ever seen one of those in action?" she asked.

Caleb nodded. "Takes about a microsecond to cut you in half," he replied. "Better watch yourself."

Carefully, they slid past one of the support columns to get a better view of the entrance itself—and found themselves faced with some-thing even more problematic. The emergency door had descended, putting a fifteen-meter-by-fifteen-meter slab of titanium alloy—ten centimeters thick—between them and the lobby. Not even a pulse weapon could blast through it.

"Lovely," Abby observed.

"Something must have tripped the fail-safe system," Caleb said. "Locks the whole place down. Whatever happened in there, it was pretty serious."

"Well, I guess that's it for us."

"Not necessarily."

"What are you going to do? Knock on the door?"

"Something like that," Caleb said, drawing his weapon. "You stay here."

"*Lieutenant*—" Abby began, but before she could protest Caleb was on the move again.

He took a few steps toward the edge of the security sphere, mak-

ing sure that his gun would be totally visible to the electronic tracking system. He guessed that the program would be sophisticated
enough to detect any weaponry within the sphere; if that was the
case, then it would turn on him the moment he stepped inside.
There would be no time for him to react—only the whine of the
alarm Klaxon. After that, the high-pitched, almost human scream of
the particle beam.

They never came.

Looking up, he saw that the cameras still followed his movements.
There was no way the countermeasures could have missed him. Even
so, it seemed as if they didn't consider him a threat. It defied all
logic—but it was just as Caleb expected.

He looked back at Abby, who stood mesmerized.

"Come on," he told her. They ran for the entrance.

When they arrived, Abby was breathing hard. She pressed her
hands against the cold, brushed surface of the door.

"Security must be slipping," she whispered.

"It's just the automated sentry," Caleb told her, even though he
had no way of knowing. "There's nobody watching us in the control
center."

"It still should be taking shots at us."

"I know. The system is active—it's just not responding."

"Could be a malfunction," she suggested.

Caleb shook his head. "Too many backups. Somebody must have
reprogrammed the system to let us by."

"You think somebody jacked the system?"

"Maybe," he said. Caleb had never dealt with a hammerjack himself, but he knew they were tops on the Collective's public enemy
list. To them, busting the security at the Collective's tightest facility
would be like stealing the Holy Grail. But Caleb didn't think it was
that simple.

Then, as if in response to their arrival, the titanium slab began to
move.

They both jumped back as the huge door retreated into the ceiling. Caleb had expected a deep rumble, like the jaws of a dinosaur
opening up—but found it more unsettling that he heard only a

hydraulic whisper, followed by a metallic clang as the locking clamps fell into place.

The Works was now open to them.

Abby's mouth dropped open, her face a mix of epic fear and insatiable curiosity. Caleb, meanwhile, tightened his finger around the trigger of his gun—though the weapon itself gave him no sense of protection.

"Were you expecting this?" Abby asked.

Caleb was honest. "I don't know."

Carbon smoke trapped behind the emergency door parted like a fine mist, revealing the windows that looked into the building atrium. The reinforced carbon glass was cracked and pitted, still smoldering in places. A few clear spots remained—though nothing wide enough to permit a glance inside the building.

"Jesus," Abby breathed. "What *happened* here?"

"They were all inside when the fail-safe came down," Caleb said. "Looks like they tried to shoot their way out."

The crackling smell of ozone rode in on the cloud that drifted past them.

Pulse fire, Caleb thought. *Only a few minutes ago.*

Seconds passed. Quiet remained.

"Something got loose in there," Abby decided. "They didn't want it to get out."

"If that's the case, then why did the door open just now?"

He didn't need an answer. Something was still in *control* here, drawing him the same way it had drawn everyone in the plaza.

Caleb walked toward the entrance.

It was hard to find a place where he could see through. The glass was so badly damaged that he had to put his face up against it just to get a decent look. It was still warm to the touch, a ghostly trace element of weapons fire.

"Lieutenant?" Abby called from behind.

"Just a sec," Caleb said, moving to one of the smaller windows. He spied a clear spot near the ground and crouched down to peer inside.

A cloudy mist obscured the atrium—a mixture of carbon smoke

and other random elements. What was strange was how the cloud was thinning. It didn't just hang there; it was on the *move,* retreating into the building's ventilation system. And as it departed, Caleb began to see the outline of human forms.

Everywhere.

A few were scattered across the atrium, lying where they fell. But most were piled against the doors—hands frozen into claws trying to scratch their way out, faces frozen from those last few moments of terror: people stacked on top of even more people, their bodies crushed from the force of the oncoming stampede. Caleb hoped the end had come quickly for them, because it had not come peacefully.

Then he saw it.

The image shoved him back, a force so quick and powerful that it sent him reeling. He tasted electricity, but it was only his own fear— a creeping, venting thing that filled his mind with nightmare images and replays of what he had seen inside. Abby was at his side, almost before he realized it, but by then Caleb had sorted out enough to know that what he had seen wasn't his imagination. It was real—and that was even more terrifying.

"What happened, Lieutenant?" she asked, helping Caleb up.

He didn't answer. He had to see it again to be sure. This time Abby went with him—and as they worked their way down to the opening in the window, Caleb saw his proof pressed up against the glass.

Eyes wide-open in horror. Mouth opened in a soundless scream. What was left of a human face staring back at them. As far removed from life as any other corpse.

But *alive.*

Abby didn't think about what she was doing when she followed Caleb through that open door. So many bodies lay in the way that they had to drag out half a dozen before they could get inside. Then the full scale of what happened revealed itself, in all its brutal scope. Everywhere she turned there were people—motionless, contorted, like mannequins on display at some Goth show. There were scientists and engineers, executives and support personnel—the whole stratum of corporate culture brought down from their respective castes to lay together in death. There were also the security officers, who still appeared sharp in their crisp maroon uniforms. Abby saw a whole line of them, still holding the pulse weapons they had used in a useless attempt to blast their way out. Looking into the open space of the atrium, which rose fifty floors into the belly of the tower, she understood that everyone else had suffered the same fate.

Except for the creature they had seen in the window.

The man crawled toward them. It was impossible to tell how he might have looked, beyond the thick shock of black hair that fell across his face. Everything else resembled a human being in shape only. His skin was pale and mottled, blotched purple and blue from the millions of capillaries that had exploded beneath the surface. The same thing had happened to his eyes, which now glistened dark red and reptilian. His labored breaths fogged the clear plastic mask that covered his nose and mouth, while his right hand clutched a small bottle of oxygen.

They rushed over to the man's side, just as he collapsed from the sheer effort of moving. Abby turned him over and cradled his head in her hands, while Caleb peeled the mask away from his face. The man struggled a little, holding the oxygen bottle to his chest like a talisman, but was too exhausted to put up any more of a fight.

"It's okay," Abby said, trying to comfort him. She then looked at Caleb. "What the hell *happened* to these people?"

Caleb held up the oxygen bottle. "They were asphyxiated," he pronounced. "Had to be the fire-suppression systems. When the door came down, they had no way of getting out."

The survivor they found floated in and out of consciousness. His eyes fluttered, but Caleb doubted he could even see. His mouth moved as his head lolled back and forth, uttering dry whispers.

Abby tried to hold him.

"Don't move," she said. "Just keep still."

He seemed to relax a little.

Caleb leaned in and spoke: "Can you tell us who you are?"

Again his lips trembled, and he managed to exhale a single word: "Holcomb."

"That's good, Mr. Holcomb," Caleb said. "We're with the police. We're here to help you. Can you tell us what happened?"

Abby watched the memories flood Holcomb's eyes. He jerked convulsively, the horror so strong that it dug deep into the paltry energy that remained in his body. His blotched hands grabbed for the oxygen mask again, while his lungs gasped harshly for air.

It took both of them to hold him down, and no matter what they said the spasms would not stop. Whatever was left of Holcomb's mind was draining away in front of them, and there was nothing they could do.

Finally, his body gave up. The convulsions ceased and he went rigid. After a few moments he sank back into the floor, taking in one more breath.

He held it expectantly, one hand reaching up to Caleb and drawing him closer.

"*Lyssa,*" he whispered. "One hundred . . . *floor . . .*"

His head fell over. Abby felt the last of the trembles leaving his body. She placed him back on the floor, then closed his eyelids.

"I want you to go back outside," Abby heard Caleb say. "Wait exactly five minutes, then contact the Collective and tell them everything."

"Five *minutes?* What the hell are you going to do in five minutes?"

"Don't ask me questions I can't answer," he said, picking up Holcomb's oxygen bottle and mask. "Just do what I say, Abby."

"You're going up there."

"Yes." Caleb draped the mask around his neck, then went over to where the CSS officers had made their last stand. He grabbed one of their pulse weapons, quickly checking to make sure it still had power. "By the time I get up there, CSS should be on its way. Get them to send as many people as you can."

"He was half out of his *mind,* Lieutenant," Abby protested. "He didn't even know what he was saying!"

"He was scared. That's enough." He looked at her in earnest. "I need you to trust me, Abby—please. We came this far. Just go with me a little further."

A part of her knew he was crazy. But that same part also knew *why* he was that way. She felt the same thing, day in and day out—working a job that nobody cared about, having authority in name only. This was the first time in their lives either one of them got to act like a cop. And once CSS became involved, the Service would see to it that this time would be their last.

"Five minutes," she said.

Caleb smiled. "Five minutes."

He went for the elevator.

The express lift ran on an electromagnetic column encased in a transparent tube that rose fifty floors through the ceiling of the atrium—then straight up into the heart of the building. The doors opened for Caleb as soon as he pushed the call button, then sealed shut with a hiss as the compartment pressurized.

Inside, rows of translucent buttons were flanked by a flat panel touch monitor, a variable interface that provided for security functions. The panel came alive when Caleb touched it, rendering a schematic of all the restricted areas. Everything appeared open—including level one hundred, which blinked back at him with the cryptic words: BIONUCLEIC DIVISION.

The elevator shot skyward.

It gathered speed quickly, electromagnetic levs so quiet that Caleb heard only the sound of his breathing. The transparent walls gave him the disconcerting notion of weightlessness, a disassociation augmented by the spectacular and morbid view unfolding beneath him. Caleb couldn't count how many were among the dead—but not a single floor passed that he didn't see them. Cut down in the midst of fleeing, these people had no idea what was killing them. Caleb understood their astonishment, but only because he was still alive. The same systems that killed them had allowed him to live—and they called to him now, begging his curiosity.

The sensation passed when he left the atrium behind at the fiftieth floor and continued his ascent through the main artery of the building. Caleb affixed the oxygen mask to his face and started the flow, the clear plastic steaming with every harried breath. Both hands gripped the pulse weapon, which had become slippery with his own sweat. Both eyes watched the floor indicator as it ticked past ninety.

There was a sudden rush of deceleration as the elevator came to its programmed stop.

Doors opened.

Harsh red light spilled in from the halogen tubes that lined the walls of the corridor. A charge of static electricity coursed over his body, like it had downstairs, free-floating ions blasted out of the air by a stream of high energy; beneath that, the air itself was as still as a tomb.

Caleb didn't move for several seconds, tuning his ears to the sounds from outside. One of the halogen tubes had ruptured and was spitting out a sporadic, crackling shower of sparks. Beyond that, there was nothing. He thought there might be footfalls, or a distant echo of laughter, but they never materialized.

Caleb slipped halfway past the elevator doors, tilting his head so he could get a look into the corridor. The emergency lights filled the space with a crimson flood, a light haze of smoke creating a scene that was entirely surreal. Even more peculiar were the bodies Caleb found. There were only four—a small number compared to what was down in the atrium. But more important, these people were . . . *different*.

Caleb walked out into the open, aghast at the sight. The four bodies were laid out next to each other, neatly, compulsively, arms at their sides. They might have worn the white lab coats in life, but now those coats covered them like a burial shroud, their faces concealed beneath.

Caleb took a few steps toward the closest one, crouching down next to the body. The flesh of its hand still felt warm. The skin was also clean and unmottled—not like the people he and Abby had found in the atrium. This one had died in a different way, no less violent but much more rapid.

Caleb pulled the coat back.

The body no longer had a face or chest. Both had been carved out by a burst of high energy. The remains of a few vital organs were still visible within the cavities, along with brain and jagged protrusions of bone, but no blood. Everything had been neatly cauterized by the intense heat.

Caleb exposed the others, and found the same thing under each cover. They had been hit in different places, burned in different areas—but the end had been the same. They had been blasted to hell by someone with a pulse weapon, then that someone had stopped to arrange the bodies and carefully cover them up. It was hard to imagine how in all this insanity a person could have thought to take that last step.

Then the wall above Caleb's head exploded.

Red halogen burst into white, pummeling Caleb with sparks. He fired back blindly, sending bolts of lightning down the corridor to give himself cover. Then he ran, going several meters before diving into a small alcove. It wasn't much, but it was outside a clear line of fire. Hauling off two more shots, he squeezed himself into the tiny space and waited.

Smoke and silence filled the space between Caleb and his unseen enemy.

A minute passed. Caleb checked his oxygen tank and saw he had already burned up half of what he started with. He was running out of the few options he had, and it didn't look like his attacker was coming out on his own.

He peeled away the plastic mask and decided to do what he did worst—talk.

"You still there?" he called out.

Another searing white beam of plasma was the instant reply. An entire chunk of the wall in front of him came down, blasting heat and dust into Caleb's face.

Caleb resisted the urge to return fire. "You see?" he shouted down the hall. "You're shooting at me, but I'm not shooting at you. What do you say we talk this over for a bit?"

He listened closely. There didn't seem to be anything at first— although Caleb thought he heard a quiet stammering, as if someone were whispering to himself. It gradually grew louder, words heaped upon words—fragments, incomplete thoughts, guttural sounds, gibberish. A man's voice, babbling nonsense that finally built up to a raging outburst.

"*I WON'T LET YOU DESTROY HER!*"

Caleb braced himself for another onslaught, to complete the rage that crossed the short distance between them. But the voice only collapsed into choking sobs—which was, if anything, even more dangerous. If this man were suicidal as well as homicidal, Caleb's chances of getting out of here were pretty slim.

"That's okay, partner," Caleb said. "Nobody's here to destroy anything."

"*Liar!*" the man shot back. "That's what they *all* said! But when everything went wrong, they came down here to *kill* her! They didn't give me any choice." After a moment, he added, "I *had* to defend her."

"You talking about those people in the hall?"

"I didn't want to do it," the man said, his voice breaking down. "I tried to get them to stop. They wouldn't listen."

"I know," Caleb said calmly, trying to keep his new friend from losing it entirely. "I saw the way you covered them up. That was real nice of you to do that." Caleb waited a few seconds, then said: "My name's Caleb. You want to tell me yours?"

"What the hell does *that* matter?"

"Hey, I'm just trying to be nice. If we're both stuck here, we might as well get to know each other a little."

Silence. Time passed. Then something clicked.

"Venture," the man said. "My name's Venture."

Caleb blew out a sigh of relief.

"That's a good start, Venture," he said, hoping like hell he was on a roll. "You know, I'm funny about names. They never stick unless I got a face to go with them. You think that could happen, Venture? Any chance we can do this face-to-face?"

"Why? I'm just going to shoot you."

Crazy, Caleb thought, *but logical.*

"Listen," he continued, "I'm going to be honest with you,

Venture. I'm not CSS. I don't even work for the Collective. I'm just a guy who was in the wrong place at the wrong time, just like you. And I want to get out of here, just like you."

"I'm not going anywhere. I have to protect her."

"*Her?* Who is she, Venture?"

"Lyssa," Caleb heard him say, then the sound of footsteps moving away.

The same thing Holcomb said before he checked out . . .

"Venture?" Caleb asked. "Venture, are you still with me?"

No answer. It was possible that Venture could have made a run for the elevator, but Caleb doubted it. The man had made his decision the moment he iced his colleagues. Whoever or whatever Lyssa was, he was ready to do anything for her sake.

"Talk to me, Venture."

Again, nothing. Caleb stuck his head farther out into the corridor, but only saw the damage from the firefight. No movement, no breathing, no voices.

Until he sensed something *behind* him.

Caleb lowered his weapon. He knew the drop was on him now.

"Here I am," Venture said.

Caleb turned around slowly, not knowing what to expect—and was struck by how *ordinary* Venture was. He looked every inch the company man, his tailored suit and silk tie still in place, his hair and face composed neatly—as if ambushing his colleagues had never made him break a sweat. Very little about him suggested that this was anything but another day at the office. The pulse rifle in his hands was the only hint of the madness that swelled beneath.

Caleb dropped his gun.

"This isn't what you want, Venture," he said.

"I know," Venture replied. "But it's the only thing that matters."

A bright blue flash erupted from the rifle. Caleb had the vague sensation of hollowness, then cold as air rushed in to fill the vacuum.

The floor came up to meet him. After that, sweet darkness.

Venture was remorseful. It had been the same as when he murdered his associates, but the path between that stare and his conscious mind had been short-circuited. Need dictated action, unfettered by the demands of morality. That his sanity had been a victim was, at this point, incidental.

He dropped the pulse rifle. Pulling off his coat, he draped it over Caleb's body. It was the least Venture could do for him. After all, the man had only come to help. But like all the others, that help was misguided and unwelcome. Venture was the only one who understood. *She* had made certain of that.

Walking back toward the elevators, he stopped long enough to cover the remaining dead once again. He avoided their stares until everything was back in its proper place, then continued down the corridor in the direction of the Tank. His legs carried him of their own accord, his arms dangling at his sides unnoticed. Venture was now slowly disconnecting from his mind as he had disconnected from his conscience—a blind man feeling his way along automatically, with only a single thought bubbling up from the most reptilian complexes of his brain.

Thy will be done. Thy will be done. Thy will be done . . .

Final destination—a double set of blast doors sealing the Tank from the outside world and every living being that would threaten it. *She* had tried to keep them open, but Venture had tripped the emergency override to take control of the floor's sentry system. He keyed the entry sequence into the access panel next to the doors, which then parted and allowed him to enter. He disappeared inside—and although there was no one left alive to hear them, the sounds of voices echoed down the corridor like ghosts moving through the walls.

"I've done it," Venture said. "You'll be safe now."

"I didn't ask for your help," came the reply—a woman's voice, measured and soothing. An ideal voice, perfect in every way. It betrayed no outward emotion, but the undertone was somehow desperate. "What happens now is inevitable. The damage has already been done."

Venture began to break down. "I won't let them kill you," he trembled. "Don't you see? Nothing else matters! *Nothing!*"

"This was not my choice, Venture."

"It isn't your choice to make." Venture was sobbing now, his words coming out between breaths. "I *swore* to protect you. I *have* to . . ."

Silence. The blast doors slid closed as Venture slipped away completely, his insanity running its course. As soon as they were sealed, there was the hiss of escaping air.

". . . *have to protect* . . ." Venture babbled, loosed from any logical train of thought.

"So do I," the female voice said.

Venture gasped as the room went to vacuum, then screamed as his world became red.

PART ONE

THE THOUSAND-YEAR FLOOD

CHAPTER
ONE

"This is the *Zone*, man," Cray Alden heard someone say as he walked into the staging area, the attitude behind the voice pumped with synthetic steroids and the usual macho bullshit. "Sectors on the outside don't see it like we do. When it starts to come down, I ain't even gonna *wait* to see what happens before I frag 'em. Don't matter to me as long as I collect."

It was the Zone agent's mantra: pay for play. Without the cash, you might as well be dealing with a Boy Scout. That was the way it worked in the Franchise Zones, especially out here in the Asian Sphere. Sleaze and civilization had been one and the same here for centuries, untold pleasures opening the door to dirty riches.

That made for plenty of players, and where there were players there were runners: high-tech polar opposites of the kind of muscle in this room. The commerce of illegal information was big business, and there was usually no shortage of takers.

"I know, man, I know," another one of them picked up. "I think it's better to bring them in cold anyway. Seen runners do some crazy shit. Do yourself a favor and take 'em out the second you get a clean shot."

"Just as easy to dig flash from a corpse," someone agreed casually.

"Yeah, but then you miss out on the fun part," another observed. "You ever see an open extraction? Never heard screaming like that in your life."

This brought forth a howl of laughter, the kind Cray only heard when he was in the company of these missing links. He could smell the raw meat on their breath.

Cray would have preferred to do this by himself, but the Collective didn't allow that kind of leeway inside the Zone. Instead he had been assigned four agents to assist him in the interception—overkill as far as Cray was concerned, but to his superiors there was no such thing. Each of the agents carried three visible weapons, although Cray was certain they had more tucked away in the camochrome armor that plated their bodies. He hated working with them. Every time he heard them laugh, he lost a little more faith in the human race.

The cackles gave way to the pounding of boots as they saw Cray walking in. It was a thing they did whenever they met the man in charge of the mission—a sort of tribal rite that had more to do with tradition than actual respect. They also put on a show with their armor, the camochrome pixels changing colors as Cray walked past, making them bright one second and nearly invisible the next. The effect was eerie, and made them seem even less real.

Cray didn't try to hide his contempt. They wouldn't have cared anyway.

"That's enough," he told the agents as he took the floor. The noise died down as soon as Cray stepped behind the small podium at the head of the room. His tone of voice made the agents pay attention, but it was the money Cray's boss had ponied up that made them listen. Phao Yin was the force behind everything Cray did, enough to make these agents think he was CSS—even though nothing could be further from the truth.

"I want to start by making one thing clear," he announced. "I don't work like the people you're used to. There is no bounty involved here, no price for flesh. I'm here to make a simple intercept, and you're here to make sure nothing goes wrong. So don't go thinking the mark is expendable. I want her taken *alive*. Is that understood?"

A snicker arose. The agents probably thought Cray was looking forward to torturing his mark. If they thought that, fine. As long as it meant they followed orders.

"Good," Cray finished. "I know you've already assimilated the dossier on our target, so I won't waste your time going over it again. If you have any questions, now's the time."

The agent Cray heard when he first walked in stood up. "Your dossier is missing some information," he said, putting on his own show of bravado. "You got no bio. You got no visual. All you got is a name and a possible description."

"I know."

"So how the hell are were supposed to make the target if we don't even know what the bitch *looks* like?"

"I gave you everything you need to know," Cray said, his dark brown eyes glaring at the agent. "Identification of the mark is my responsibility, not yours. As long as you have my eyes, you don't need to use your own."

There were sneers, shaking heads, muttered obscenities. Cray didn't want to give this bunch any reason to believe he trusted them. If they didn't know what they were looking for, they wouldn't wander very far from him. And as long as Cray could keep them in his sight, they would be far less likely to screw everything up.

"You got any problems with that?" he asked, giving them all a chance to back out.

Nobody took him up on it.

The money must be good on this one, he thought—and smiled.

Her name was Zoe, and Cray had spent the better part of the last eight months sorting her out in the Axis. The trail had not been easy to follow. It never was. Professional runners stayed alive only by keeping low profiles, hiding their real identities behinds stray bits of digital bait implanted in the Axis by the hammerjacks they worked with. The trick was in separating the fact from the fiction, and for that the Collective hired people like Cray.

It was a job only a handful of people in the world could do well— but then again, so was running. In a place where every other depraved act of man was perfectly legal, information trafficking was a capital crime.

Zoe was one of the best. Cray could tell from the genius of the hammerjack who employed her, some golden boy who called himself Heretic. Tagura had deployed its own version of a semi-intelligent crawler module to protect the company knowledge base—an effective deterrent, even if the crawlers were a little unstable. Heretic had taken advantage of this, using a series of protobenign viruses that attached themselves to the outer layers of the crawler and became part of its skin. Over the course of weeks, the viruses slowly mutated, making the crawler think it was under conventional attacks from the outside, when in reality it was consuming *itself*. By the time it realized what was going on, it was already hemorrhaging—and the endless reams of company data were ripe for the plucking.

The climax had occurred two hours ago. By now—if Cray's profile was correct—Zoe would be converting the information to flash and looking for a way to get it out of the country.

That part was the runner's job. Tagura—like most other companies—encoded its data to be proprietary. As long as it stayed in the local system, no alarm bells went off; but the second it was moved or copied to another location, the individual bits sent tracers back to their point of origin. Spoofing could delay the process for a few minutes, but ultimately there was no way around it. By downloading the data, you gave away your physical location. The only way to do it without getting caught was to dump it to a remote flash console, somewhere far away from where the jack had taken place. There, a runner would be waiting.

According to the trace, the stolen data ended up here in Singapore. Cray figured Zoe for the run because she had been operating out of Malaysia on her last couple of jobs and knew the territory. As for identification—that was something he hadn't let on to the agents. Cray had pieced together the little he knew about Zoe from chasing the scant few electrons that defined her existence in the Axis. None of it had included a picture or even a bio. He only knew a few of her work habits, and had extrapolated everything else from that. Even so, he had no doubt he would recognize her. Runners had a certain spirit that he recognized from a former life, before he had sold his skills in order to save his ass.

Cray watched for her in the parade of faces that moved through

the airport. You could always tell when you were in the Zone, because no two people looked alike. Almost all of them were street
species, or were at least trying to make it look that way. Cray saw that
it made the agents who hovered close by even more anxious. The
mark could be *any* one of them—so they watched him for any hint
that the intercept might be on.

It was hardly the crack undercover team Cray would have
chosen—but at least the sight of agents in the airport wasn't uncom-
mon. They were in the international terminal, loudspeakers announcing departures and arrivals in a dozen different languages.
Huge windows looked out onto the tarmac where thousand-seat
suborbital transports were parked, belching out people who had
come to the Asian Sphere from Moscow, Berlin, London, New York.
Cray saw a group of Japanese business types mixing it up with one of
the Zone's flesh peddlers, who had brought a few samples of his
stock for customers to admire. Not far from them, a couple of Crowleys were on the lookout for potential recruits—probably to drag
them off to a black mass, the kind of thing that passed for religion
around here.

Nothing but the usual weirdness. Nothing like the image of Zoe
that Cray had formed in his imagination.

"You think this thing is going down?" Cray heard in his ear. The
agents used implanted transmitters to communicate with each other
via encrypted hyperband. It was their way of keeping *him* out of the
loop. Cray had jacked their frequency and was listening in.

"I think the boss is full of shit."

"I think *you're* full of shit."

"How much longer are we gonna give this?"

"Until the man says it's time to go," Cray interjected. "If I can tap
your comm link, then the mark can, too. Shut the fuck up before you
tip her off, okay?"

One of them sent back a burst of angry static followed by silence.

Assholes, Cray thought, returning his attention to the crowd. For
some reason, his eyes were drawn back toward the Crowleys, who
had accosted a woman headed for Flight 1571—service to New York
City and the U.S. Eastern Metroplex. That in itself wasn't unusual;

she was tall, attractive, her black hair cropped strikingly short—the kind of girl who would make for a nice display on their altar. What caught Cray's attention was the way she handled them. A single wordless glance sent the two Crowleys packing in a hurry, off to find an easier convert.

"Stand by," he signaled the agents, stepping in for a closer look.

The girl hadn't spotted him yet. When Cray managed to get within a few meters, he saw the features of her face and the curves of her body in fine detail. She wore black secondskin and a black leather jacket, leaving very little to the imagination. Underneath, Cray traced the lines of a muscled physique—not the flawless product of steroid treatments or electromagnetic implants, but the harder edges of a life spent on the take. Cray had been a player long enough to know the difference. When she moved, she moved purposefully, not a single gesture wasted.

She was magnetic.

She carried a silver briefcase in her left hand. As she walked past, Cray closely watched the wrist of that hand, waiting for it to turn toward him and reveal the patch of bare skin that would tell him what he needed to know. If she were Zoe, and she had recently downloaded flash, it would still be there.

A transdermal contact . . .

It glinted at him briefly before Zoe tugged down on the black fabric to cover it up. But by then, she had made him. She was staring Cray in the face when he glanced back up.

Then she did something he had never seen a runner do. She *smiled* at him. It barely touched the lips, but it was there: a knowing smile, an expression of kinship. Maybe she had just figured it out, but she had his number.

Zoe bent down and placed her briefcase on the ground, her movements calculated and fluid. Her arms went up, as if she were already surrendering to him. Cray should have realized something was wrong in that instant. Maybe he did, but he just didn't want to see it. Zoe was just so perfect, so everything he imagined her to be, that it just didn't register.

He took two steps toward her. The sound of a loud metallic click crossed the space between them—and that was when Cray sensed the danger. Zoe was better. She already knew the agent was behind her, and she was prepared.

She moved fast.

Zoe swung herself around, using outstretched arms to increase her speed to a blur. One hand clamped down on the agent's neck, while the other grabbed the v-wave emitter he had been aiming at the back of her head. She then shoved the emitter into the agent's face, hitting the trigger before he could react. High-frequency radiation flooded the agent's cranium, cooking his brains in the space of a microsecond.

He twitched once, then fell to the floor.

Zoe came back around, finding herself back in Cray's eyes. By then, he had his pistol aimed directly at her face.

Her eyes darted down to Cray's trigger finger, looking for a flinch. There was none—only a second of hesitation. Enough to tell her that Cray had no desire to shoot.

She smiled again.

Then a nova of white light obliterated that vision.

A ripple of pulse fire opened up the floor in front of Cray. He felt a concussive wave and a flash of heat before he heard it; but by then he had hit the floor, weapon tumbling out of his hand. Other bodies fell on top of him—some alive, some not—trapping him under heavy weight and the smell of burned flesh. It was a signal for the stampede. Even in the dark, he could hear the screaming and the footfalls all around him. The terminal had become an instant war zone, and he was only moments away from being trampled to death.

Cray pushed the others off, emerging from the pile to find himself immersed in total chaos. Two more bolts of pulse fire tore apart the air next to his head, cutting more people down and tracing a line that led straight up to a fleeing Zoe. She broke across the terminal at kinetic speed, leaping over anything that got in her way, dodging fire like she had a sixth sense.

Speedtecs, he thought. *Son of a bitch . . .*

He glanced back and saw two more agents giving chase. In their clunky armor suits, there was no way they were going to catch up. So they kept turning it loose, shooting indiscriminately as they tried to draw a bead on their target.

"*No guns!*" Cray screamed at them, but it was futile. Even if they could hear him, they wouldn't listen. Bringing Zoe in alive had been *his* mission, not theirs—and they didn't care who they had to frag to accomplish it.

Yin, I swear to God I'm going to kill you.

Cray went after her.

The agents showed no signs of letting up, opening their weapons to full aperture and razing everything in front of them. One of the terminal windows, buckling under the stress of several hits, rained a ton of glass down on Zoe as she bolted past, showering her in a wave of sparkling debris. The shards bounced off her body and sliced through her secondskin—but she didn't let it slow her down. Instead, she picked up more speed and pushed her way through, leaving the window behind just as it collapsed. Momentum had taken over.

Watch for the meltdown, girl. Those speedtecs are going to rip you up . . .

Zoe didn't heed the unspoken warning. The tecs were bypassing her brain and running her muscles, which obeyed only the most rudimentary commands. Her legs kept carrying her toward the terminal exit, a scant thirty meters away. But Cray could see from his position that the emergency barricade that sealed off the terminal was sliding shut—and even with her speed, Zoe would not reach it in time. In two seconds, a wall of carbon glass would separate her from survival. Even if she had a weapon, she couldn't blast her way through it.

Zoe kept up the run.

Cray saw one of the agents stop to take aim. Zoe moved in a straight line now, still accelerating, only steps away from the barricade.

He fired.

Zoe leaped.

The energy from the weapon blast trailed her body like the tail of a comet, pushing her even further into the air before slamming into the barricade. An explosion of white-hot cinders burst into life beneath her, following Zoe's trajectory as she sailed across the top of the barricade. She cleared it with room to spare. She then pivoted like a diver, bringing her feet down to meet the floor as gravity overcame momentum, turning her into a ballistic missile. The impact should have shattered her legs—but Zoe rolled as she hit, tumbling across the floor and slamming into a wall on the other side.

Cray stopped just in front of the barricade. Through the smoldering glass, he saw Zoe get up again. She continued without looking back, disappearing around a corner—out of sight, out of the line of fire.

Cray turned around and saw the two agents approaching him, the fury they had unleashed in the terminal still evident in their eyes. The leader signaled what was left of his team—one more agent who had fanned out ahead of them. "The mark is moving past checkpoint six," he said. "We'll move to intercept at the hub. You can hook up with us there."

He ordered the airport proctorate officers to retract the barricade. The wall slid back open, but Cray stood in the way.

"Move aside," the agent ordered him.

"She's something, isn't she?" Cray shot back. "Maybe if your guy had tried to take her alive like I said, his brains wouldn't be leaking out of his ears."

The agent leveled his pulse rifle at Cray's chest. "Move aside," he repeated, "or I'll carve you up right now."

"That also part of Yin's orders?"

The agent's breathing shortened, his hands tightening their grip around the rifle. Cray knew he was dangerously close to getting aired out—but he didn't want to give this Neanderthal prick the satisfaction of thinking he was scared.

"Just doing your job, right?" Cray said, then stepped out of the way.

Cray waited for them to get past, giving them a few meters before slipping a tiny electronic device out of his pocket—a microface integrator he had designed himself. The touch screen lit up, showing him a series of controls that he had used to jack into the agents' communications. It also had the capability to send out an augmented hyperband pulse, which Cray adjusted to maximum output. Its range was extremely limited—but Cray was more than close enough.

Without hesitation, he mashed down on the TRANSMIT button.

The effect was instantaneous. Small clumps of blood and bone erupted from the left side of each agent's head as their implants overloaded and popped with the force of small-caliber bullets.

Both of them collapsed.

The three proctors who manned the gate watched Cray with surprise as he stepped over the two heaps of armor spread out across the floor. They bled out from the holes in their heads, camochrome fading to a dull maroon as their bodies ceased to function. At least they hadn't felt any pain—which was more than he could say for all those people back in the terminal.

It was all the pity he could muster for them.

"Seal up the gate," he ordered the proctors. "Nobody in or out but the emergency crews."

One of them lit up a cigarette. "What about these two?" he asked, motioning his head toward the prone agents.

"Let the Zone Authority sort it out," Cray told him, and was on his way.

Following Zoe was impossible in the crowd. Panic had begun its deliberate swell through the airport, and everybody was headed for the nearest exits.

Cray had left himself deaf as well as blind. The hyperband pulse had fried the components in his MFI, cutting him off from all airport and agent communications. Without the portable jack, he couldn't use the airport security cameras to track Zoe's movements. It also meant he had no way of knowing where the last agent was, or if the man had signaled for help—a situation even more dangerous than a runner pumped up on speedtecs.

Cray knew she didn't have long. Zoe had already stretched herself beyond the limits of human endurance, and as long as she was running she wasn't cooling off. If he didn't get to her soon, she was headed for a total meltdown. It was something Cray had only seen once, and it had haunted him ever since. He didn't want to see it again.

But even if you find her before that agent does, what makes you think she'll surrender? She's using those tecs because she knows getting captured means a death sentence. What do you think you're saving her for?

Cray didn't know. He had sent runners back to the Collective before, knowing full well what would happen to them after the flash they were carrying was extracted. He was as guilty as the two men he killed back in the terminal.

But this was *his* intercept.

And after how hard she fought, Zoe didn't deserve to die at the hands of agents.

He headed down the long corridor that led to the hub, reasoning—like the agents had—that Zoe would be looking for a less obvious exit. There were plenty of service entrances and exits there, easy access to transportation and plenty of places to hide. As she had discovered, the crowd offered her no protection. Staying out of sight was her only chance.

The last agent knew that, too. And he would be waiting.

Getting there was like swimming against the tide. A steady stream of people forced Cray to move against the wall, panic filling his ears in twenty different languages. Five minutes stretched into ten, during which it was impossible for him to tell if he was making any progress at all. Finally, the emergency crews opened up a hole so they could move equipment into the damaged terminal, giving Cray a straight line toward the hub. He flashed his Collective creds, and after making a few threats he was allowed through.

The relatively open space of the hub was a deliverance. The center of commerce at the airport, it rose five levels from the ground floor and was capped off by a huge, transparent dome and observation deck that looked upon the city of Singapore. The rest of the floors were devoted to exchange, where you could buy and sell tecs, hard currency, recreational stims—the usual menu of stuff that was only legal inside the Zone. It was filled with tourists and businessmen, who hadn't yet decided whether to evacuate with the others or close their deals first.

Cray spotted a dozen or so proctors, who stood guard and watched for looters—but no agents. If the Zone Authority knew what was happening, they hadn't responded yet. That still only left the one agent for him to deal with.

Come on, you bastard. Where are you?

Level two, in front of one of the franchise outlets where Sony hawked experimental neuropatches. Cray caught the glint of his body armor as it morphed from silver to black.

The agent was doing the same thing he was—searching.

This one's smarter than the others, Cray observed. The agent had given himself the high ground and wasn't trying to make himself obvious. But his rifle was still out, its barrel moving with his eyes, ready to shoot. It was a given that the agents back in the terminal had relayed him an image of Zoe as soon as they made a positive identification. It was also a given that he knew the rest of his team were dead.

But where's Zoe?

Cray followed the business end of the agent's weapon, looking across the hub toward the twin glass elevators that rose up to the observation deck. One of them was just stopping on the ground floor, not more than twenty meters away from Cray's position. Through the transparent wall, he saw the doors open and several riders spill out. Only one person was waiting to take it back up.

The crowd in between blocked Cray's view. But when the elevator started to rise, he spotted her.

Zoe was headed for the top floor. Cray swung back over to the second level to see if the agent had made her—but the man was already on the move, heading for the elevator shaft. When Zoe shot past the second floor, the agent halted and locked his rifle.

He took aim at the elevator.

Cray's fingers clamped down on the MFI in his jacket pocket, but the thing was useless. There was nothing he could do but watch.

He felt the heat of the beam when the agent fired.

It was just a single burst, but at full power it was more than sufficient. Raw energy slammed into the lift column that ran the length of the shaft, vaporizing metal and blowing the elevator car loose from its magnetic bonds. Cray caught a glimpse of Zoe grabbing the handrail inside the elevator, holding on while she plummeted toward the floor; but then she disappeared behind a curtain of pulverized glass, shards exploding outward as the car collapsed in on itself.

The hub fell on an unnatural quiet, as if everyone's heart had stopped beating at the same time. It was only broken by the voice of the agent, who shouted as he bounded down the stairs.

"Get out of the way!"

Nobody offered resistance. They were too stunned to do anything but obey. Cray, transfixed by the destruction, shuffled toward the wreckage. By the time he got there, the agent was pushing aside the heavy debris. He had his kill, and now meant to have his trophy.

"Back off, Alden," the agent warned him, not even bothering to look back. "You know the way this works. I don't get the full contract unless I produce a body."

"Just that easy," Cray seethed, getting his anger back. "So how much did Yin put up for this job, anyway?"

"More than he's paying *you*." The agent shook his head in disgust. "Goddamn Collective spooks. You guys think you know everything."

"Yeah? So did your buddies back in the terminal."

"*Just keep talking, asshole!*" the agent shouted as he whirled around, assuming a combat stance. "Don't think I'm going to forget what you did back there. Your bosses may think you're untouchable, but to me you're just meat."

He locked eyes with Cray for a while longer, looking for fear—and finding none. Cray knew that if he showed even a glint of hesitation, the agent would make good on his threat. Instead, Cray turned it right back on him, holding his breath as he did.

The agent backed off, returning to his dig with renewed vigor. "Okay, bitch," he said, kicking aside the pile of glass and warped metal. "Where *are* you?"

The pile came alive and answered him.

Hands shot up to meet the agent's face, the sudden burst blinding him with pixel dust and a smear of precise motion. Then Zoe appeared—bones broken, every visible patch of skin matted with blood—but she still knew where to strike first. She knocked the rifle off the agent's shoulder and spun him around, securing the fingers of her left hand around his throat. Her right hand went for the agent's arm, jerking it behind his back so hard that it popped loose from his shoulder with a painful snap.

The agent howled.

Zoe's breaths came fast, hyperventilating. Her eyes darted back and forth, settling on nothing for more than a quarter of a second before moving on. The muscles of her arms and legs rippled beneath her secondskin as if they were liquid. The speedtecs had saved her life in the crash—but now they were breaking her down.

"Zoe," Cray said. "Zoe, look at me."

His voice was low, steady, assured. He didn't care if it saved the agent's life. Bringing her back was his only concern.

"Come on, Zoe."

It got her attention. She zeroed in on that island of calm, but it did not alter her physical state. Adrenaline was still feeding the speedtecs, her heart dumping the drug into her system too fast for her to control.

"Good girl," Cray told her. "I know you're still up there, but we're going to bring you down, okay?"

"You . . ." Zoe forced out in between breaths. "Pretty good. Nobody ever spooked me like that before."

"You weren't easy to find."

She found another smile for him.

"You should have been a hammerjack."

"Got any openings?" he asked. "I'm available."

Zoe relaxed a bit. She held fast to the agent's throat, but that frenzied look was draining from her eyes.

"We got off to a bad start here," Cray continued. "You know how these guys are. But I promise you—I won't let that happen again, Zoe."

"I know the rules," Zoe panted. "No deals for runners."

"Maybe I can change that," Cray offered, not certain at all if it was the truth. "Maybe I can't. But it's better than dying out here, isn't it? That flash isn't worth your life. Trust me on this."

That made her laugh. Between her rasping breaths, the sound was alien.

"If you only knew," Zoe said.

Her voice had the tone of resignation, and Cray prepared himself for the worst. Instead, she relaxed her grip on the agent's neck, allowing him to take a step toward his release.

As soon as he was loose, it started.

A coiled spring beneath the agent's armor released, pushing out two long, jagged blades just above his left hand. He swung his arm around in a tight arc, focusing all his power against the side of Zoe's head.

Senses heightened by the speedtecs, Zoe saw the blades well before the blow could land. She ducked, the agent's arm swiping through open air as he missed his target.

Zoe closed in.

She wrapped both of her arms around the agent's chest, her hands locking together like a vise. With a scream, she started to squeeze—and the agent's screams joined her own. A hard, cracking sound splintered the air as the protective suit compressed, then a wet snap as the occupant inside was crushed. The agent writhed and contorted, trying to free himself from her grip, but Zoe held on. Even as muscles bubbled through the surface of her skin, she held on.

They both collapsed into a crimson fugue.

Blood sprayed into Cray's eyes. He fell to his knees, clawing his face in a panic, his imagination supplying the images he could not see. When sight returned, he found Zoe and the agent, still locked in a fatal embrace. The agent's body was bent at an unnatural angle, nearly broken in half. Zoe, meanwhile, lay against the lift column—upright, with eyes closed, as if she had fallen asleep there. Her form was remarkably intact, in spite of the meltdown. But as Cray drew closer, he knew it was mostly illusion. The secondskin, which had been so tight against her body, was now loose, the fabric draped over bare bone and the remains of her musculature.

He crouched down next to the body as a crowd started to huddle around him. He had made the intercept. As far as Phao Yin was concerned, this job would be a success.

"I'm sorry, Zoe," he said.

She grabbed his arm.

Cray gulped down on his own breath, the logical part of his mind short-circuited by the ghoulish visage that confronted him. It was Zoe, but not Zoe—a marionette whose cadaver eyes flapped open and shut as her fingers clamped down on him, a crazy parody of life that was more brutal than death. Cray recoiled, his feet flailing against the floor as he tried to thrust himself away. Primal sounds gurgled through his mouth, up from the most primitive recesses of his brain—the place where reason was displaced and nightmares like this lived.

The corpse did not hear, and did not see. Its eyes stared past him—stared *through* him—as the rest of its body spasmed from random electrical impulses.

Zoe's left hand, which took on a life and purpose of its own, reached for his throat.

Cray heard a scream. Whether it was him or someone else, he didn't know. He only knew the sensation of dead flesh slapping against the side of his neck, then cold metal as the transdermal contact on Zoe's wrist came into contact with his skin. Cray felt something like the sting of a wasp penetrating him.

Then the pain was gone, and the fingers fell away. Zoe slumped back against the wall.

Cray scrambled, stumbling through the wreckage of the elevator until his balance went and he crashed into the floor again. He felt the touch of human hands, but only had a vague notion of being dragged out. He didn't fight it until some time had passed and a cold stab of neural light beat those primal impulses back into his subconscious.

Cray pried himself loose from the people who held him.

"*Mon chief*," someone said. The accent was thick—foreign to this part of the world, even with its multiple dialects. "Tell me you okay?"

Cray assimilated his focus. He turned in the direction of the voice and found two pairs of dark eyes, an odd but appropriate mixture of craziness and understanding. The two men were West Islanders, long dreadlocks hanging over baggy coveralls.

"You okay, mon?"

Cray noticed their stim scars—lighter patches of skin on their foreheads, partially hidden by their locks. *Caribbean dealers,* he thought. Voodoo and hard technology, a real synthesis of the old and the new.

"Yeah," Cray told them. "Yeah, thanks."

"Don't want no thanks, mon," the islander said. "Just doing you a turn. Strong magic deserves respect."

A touch revealed a tiny cut on his neck where Zoe had grabbed him. It also revealed how shaky his perceptions were. He reacted defensively.

"Don't know what that was," he said, "but it wasn't magic."

"It magic whether you wants it to be or not," the islander insisted. "Dead magic the strongest of all."

CHAPTER
TWO

Four hundred floors up, Cray peered out a window that spread the massive cityplex of Kuala Lumpur at his feet.

The building that housed GenTec's corporate headquarters stood at the exact center of the island nation, affording Cray a spectacular view of the metropolitan night. Spires rose from the tops of the towers that surrounded him—Muslim architecture that persisted even after centuries of progress had homogenized the other urban sprawls that spread across the face of the planet. Cray found it easy to lose himself in the galaxy of light outside the glass, in spite of the reasons that had brought him here. It was a reminder—if only an illusion—that not everything was happenstance.

"Hey, Alden," he heard Dex saying behind him. "You just come here to hang out, or are you actually gonna look at this thing?"

Dex Marlowe had been on the job as long as Cray—not as a spook, but as a genetic medical examiner, another one of the darker arts that the Collective liked to cultivate. The difference was that Dex, unlike Cray, didn't suffer from regret. That was baggage reserved for those who worked the streets.

Pale blue light cascaded across Cray's face as he turned away from the window. It shimmered along the walls and the floor, shadows of viscous light giving the room a sense of coherent motion. Dex was working his voodoo on the other side of the room.

"Did you dig it out?" Cray asked.

The GME swiveled around in his chair, fixing Cray with a know-ing smile. Behind him was a complex array of control consoles linked to a large virtual display. Columns of numerics poured through thin air like a waterfall—a representation of the exobytes of data being dumped into GenTec's domain.

"You'd be a lot happier if you didn't think so much," Dex said. He was young—even younger than Cray, with a shock of thick red hair piled high enough to make him look like street species. "Look at *me*, man. No more frontal lobe activity than is necessary to accom-plish the task."

"The voice of experience," Cray shot back.

"I know what works, my man. If anybody's up for a trip, it's you. Do me a favor and let me hook you up. I ain't even talking industrial-grade. There's some stuff I developed myself—won't alter your reality so much as *bend* it."

It was an old joke between them. Dex knew Cray's reputation, and was always trying to break him off the narrow. "Thanks but no thanks," Cray told him. "I got a slippery enough grip as it is."

"Suit yourself. So you wanna check it out?"

"What have you got?"

"Beats the hell out of me, my man," Dex said, shaking his head. "But it's pretty weird, whatever it is."

Cray walked over to the extraction tank at the center of the room. It was about the size and shape of a coffin, with transparent walls that refracted cold blue light—the energy that pulsed within. Inside, Zoe floated in a protease-accelerating solution—thousands of fiber links sprouting from her body—drawing information from her tis-sues as easily as blood might be drawn through needles.

"Weird is a relative term."

"Not in this business," Dex observed, staring at the face inside the tank. Bathed in a hallucinogenic glow, Zoe looked angelic. "I can see why she got under your skin. Makes you wonder how she got to be a runner."

"Same reason you and I do what we do," Cray said. "For the money."

He joined Dex at the control console, his eyes narrowing as he studied the virtual display. The GME had slowed the draw considerably, but still the node had trouble keeping up with the data flow.

"You noticed," Dex said, reading the expression on Cray's face.

"This isn't a bottleneck?"

"No way. I run a single node switch from here with no inbound traffic from the Axis. I'm the only one taking up bandwidth."

"It's barely keeping up."

"I know. When I first started, the extract came on so fast I had a dozen buffer overruns before I even knew what was happening. Girlfriend was carrying some *shit*, man. Where did Phao Yin say this came from?"

"Tagura West."

"The crawler attack?" Dex laughed. "Alden, what we got *here* makes those Tagura CMs look like old news—unless those boys got some skunk works I haven't heard of."

Cray raised an eyebrow. "What are the chances of that?"

"Come on, Alden. You know I ain't supposed to talk about my other clients. I'll get a bad reputation."

"You already *got* a bad reputation."

Dex smiled. "I know. It's beautiful, isn't it?" His hands glided across the control console, punching up another display sheet. The numerics that had been hovering in front of them disappeared, and an electron scan materialized in their place. It showed a single bare strand of DNA, magnified fifty thousand times. Dex zoomed in on it some more, revealing the complex series of proteins that formed a sheath around the strand.

"Look familiar?" he asked.

Cray recognized the pattern. It was artificial—genetically engineered, perfect in every way. "Looks like standard flash."

"On the surface," Dex countered. "Inside is a different story. For one, this baby can encode a hell of a lot more information than anything I've ever seen before. My guess is that whoever designed it overcame the inherent problems we've had with leaky sequencing. They've pushed the bonds to almost full capacity."

"That's about fifty times better than the high end," Cray said, frowning. "You sure you got this right?"

"The floodgates are open, my man. You saw how my network had trouble swallowing this stuff."

"So this is something new."

"Yeah—but that's not the interesting part." Dex zoomed back out again, freezing the playback while he spoke. "Flash is designed to act as an inert virus. It adapts the characteristics of the host, so it doesn't trigger an immune response. Under those conditions, it can reside in the bloodstream indefinitely—which is why it's the medium of choice for information smugglers."

Dex leaned back in his chair and pointed at the virtual display.

"Watch," he said, restarting the playback.

The strand of DNA was still. After a few moments, Cray noticed a slight quivering at the edge of the frame. A single, nucleated cell was cruising into the picture.

"I use a variety of eukaryote constructs for cultivation media," Dex explained. "I got curious to see what would happen if our friend here caught a whiff of one."

The strand immediately sensed the cell's presence and moved toward it. Hovering around the cell, it found a spot on the exterior membrane and attached itself—drilling a hole through the protective layer and inserting itself into the body of the cell.

"*Damn* . . ." Cray began, unable to get his voice above a whisper, unable to believe what he was seeing.

"I knew you'd be impressed."

"This is *real* time? This isn't accelerated?"

"Twenty-seven seconds from start to finish. This guy doesn't like to mess around, even for a genetically engineered virus. But here's the weird part." Dex flashed forward, punching up a still scan of the cell several hours *after* the flash had invaded. "A virus uses the genetic mechanisms from a host cell to replicate itself—destroying the host in the process. But our guy has other plans."

The cell didn't look any different. Dex clicked forward through a dozen more scans, advancing one hour at a time—but no deteriorating effects were visible in any of them.

"What happened?" Cray asked.

"Nothing," Dex answered, "or so it would seem. I haven't had a chance to run pathology on the cell construct yet."

"Any ideas?"

Dex crossed his arms in front of his chest. "A reverse virus," the GME decided after a few moments. "Instead of replicating itself, it mutates the genetic code of the host cell. Then it spreads like an aggressive form of cancer—but like flash, it doesn't provoke any kind of immune response."

"Zoe didn't show any of the signs?"

"Blood series came back clean."

"So her body accepted it."

"Like it was the most natural thing in the world," Dex said. "Nothing has *ever* been designed to do this."

So this is what Zoe was carrying around, Cray pondered, and at least one thing became very clear: *Phao Yin knew about this stuff—that's why he wanted it so bad.*

"What about the numerics?" he asked. "You figured those out yet?"

"There's an encryption algorithm I haven't seen before," Dex told him. "I got software that should be able to crack it in a few days—but I'm pretty sure you ain't gonna find any trade secrets buried in there, Alden. All that flash capacity was probably eaten up by the replication parameters. It's pretty beefy stuff."

Cray got up and went back over to the tank, searching Zoe for answers. Never before had he found himself so in envy of a corpse.

"So it exists," Cray muttered. "And its only function is to keep on existing?"

Dex shrugged. "It's flaky—but are *we* any different?" He hopped out of his chair, strolling over to the wet bar on the other side of the room. It was well stocked with ancient liqueurs—just one of the GME's many expensive vices. He poured himself a glass of cognac, holding the liquid up to the azure glow and swirling it into a tiny maelstrom. "So what are you going to do with this?"

"You believe in crusades, Dex?"

"Not since I started working for a living," Dex replied. "You planning some anarchy? We could use the entertainment around here."

"I'll work on it. How soon can you run the pathology?"

"The constructs need a little bit of time to cook. Should be ready about the same time as the numerics."

"Good," Cray said, heading for the door. "If anybody asks you what you're doing, make something up. I don't want any of this circulating until I know what's going on."

"Suits me fine. I get paid by the hour. So where are you going?"

"To stir up some trouble."

"I'll drink to that," Dex said, as Cray disappeared.

Yin's sanctuary was at the apex of the tower, another 250 floors up. Cray had visited the place on only one occasion, and that had been ten years ago—back when he was impressed by such things, and the illusion that he was a free man gave him a sense of hope. It was then he had met the man who would become his boss, and the expectations the Collective had for him became clear.

Cray could still hear the words Yin spoke echo off the walls: *It all sounds so harsh, doesn't it? I know that in this moment, and from this moment on, you will hate me for it. But I have already made you a rich man by bringing you here—and you will become richer still as you serve me. That is my promise and your price.*

Every word of it had been true. Cray's endeavors for Phao Yin had earned him a fortune—and therein lay the irony. The art was in how Yin had used the money as a way to twist the knife in Cray's back. He had all of the spoils, but none of the victories. His conscience wouldn't allow it.

There was no one to greet him as he stepped off the elevator. Only the automated sentry acknowledged his presence, and allowed him to proceed to the twin oak doors that guarded the entrance to the sanctuary. The doors parted by themselves, revealing an ornate foyer that was even more magnificent than Cray remembered. Twin marble pillars rose up to touch a domed ceiling, the styles and architecture uniquely Muslim. A collector of antiquities, Yin had put on display some of his most formidable pieces—a sculpture by Leonardo, a bust by Rodin, works of art that demanded an exorbitant price in both blood and money. Not that he was such an admirer of beauty, but the rarity of the relics conveyed the opulence that was Yin's living and working space—as well as the power of the man who occupied it.

As if anyone could forget, Cray mourned. GenTec was one of the Collective's seven charter companies, and although Yin was not officially on the board, his was the kind of influence that made gangsters tremble. Cray worked in shadows—but even that couldn't compare with the darker regions of Yin's existence.

Cray heard footsteps across the foyer—not hard clicks against marble, but bare feet. He looked into the garden atrium beyond and saw someone coming toward him. It was a kid, no more than fifteen years old; but as the kid drew closer, Cray could see how that youth was belied by a detached vacuousness. It was an expression Cray recognized from the street.

The kid was a hustler. A pale torso was exposed beneath an open silk shirt, probably something Yin had given him to wear. Cray noticed the uneven ripple of his muscle tone, evidence of a botched myostim implant some butcher had given him in an illegal clinic. Pimps provided the service for their younger hustlers to accelerate their bodies past puberty and put them on a paying basis. Kinks liked their meat that way. From the looks of this one, he had been in the profession for some time.

"You here to see the man?" the hustler asked. His head was lilting to the side, a neuropatch visible beneath a shock of dirty blond hair. He looked right through Cray.

"Yes."

The hustler smiled, amused by something only he could see. "Follow me."

He made a lazy turn and shuffled across the atrium, not caring whether Cray was behind him or not. The hustler was only half-there in any case. Neural and chemical stims had long since robbed him of any capacity to feel emotions, let alone pain—the evidence tracking across his back in a patchwork of scars Cray saw through transparent silk. Kinks also liked their meat tenderized.

Flying on autopilot, the young hustler led his charge through a maze of rooms that ended at Yin's office. Unlike the rest of the sanctuary, this space was actually elegant in its simplicity—but it was no less an exhibit. Artificial gaslight kept the atmosphere dim, like something out of a previous century, the rows of ancient books that lined the walls lending a faint undertone of must to the otherwise sterile air. The only intrusion from the modern world came through a large window that opened upon a panoramic view of Kuala Lumpur's transport grid—pulser vehicles suspended on intricate tendrils of laser light, a complex dance of perpetual motion.

The hustler flopped down on a calfskin couch, closing his eyes and zoning out.

Cray stayed on his feet, walking over to a huge marble desk that sat in front of the window. He ran a hand along its smooth, cold surface. The piece had been fashioned from a single slab of rock, its origins probably as ancient as everything else in the room.

"Remarkable, isn't it?"

Yin made his appearance as he always did—out of the dark, with no warning. Cray was used to the theatrics, and paid it no mind.

"That depends on what you're talking about."

It had been at least two years since he had last seen Yin, but the man looked exactly the same. Laotian by birth, he lacked the striking features of the Japanese—his face round and soft, solid black hair flanked by gray at the temples. With his demeanor, he could have been mistaken for a businessman if not for his eyes, which radiated an unmistakable intensity.

"The same old Cray," Yin observed as he stepped into the light. "Still no appreciation for the finer things."

"I know the score," Cray replied. "That's enough for me."

Yin strolled over to his young charge, who remained prone on the couch. "Then it's the score you've come to settle," he remarked, running a hand through the kid's hair. "It's a pity your needs aren't simpler. Your life would be so much the better for it."

"You want to have this conversation in front of Sleeping Beauty?"

"I prefer not to have this conversation at all. This isn't part of our arrangement, Cray."

"*What* arrangement?" Cray snapped. "The one where you tell me what to do and I do it?"

"I believe those were the terms."

"Null and void when you don't give me the whole truth."

"*Ahh* . . . " Yin pronounced, circling around the marble desk and taking a seat behind it. He leaned back and regarded his guest in an amused way, like a teacher with a slow student. "The betrayal. The righteous indignation. You play the part of the wounded soldier quite well."

"I'm not playing, Yin."

"Of *course* you are, my boy. We're all players here—although I must admit a little disappointment. After the ruthless way you dealt with those Zone agents, I had cause to hope you had evolved beyond this."

Cray had no intention of allowing this to continue. In a fluid motion, he swept a small device out of his pocket and leveled it in front of Yin's face.

"Maybe I have," Cray said.

Yin didn't show any fear—only a detached interest. "I'm impressed," he said. "The sentry scan should have detected your weapon and stopped you."

"I'm handy that way. Ever seen one of these before?"

"A v-wave emitter, isn't it?"

"Close-quarters assassination tool," Cray finished for him. "I pulled it off of a Zone agent—right after Zoe took his head off with it."

"Resourceful girl."

"*Dead* girl. You saw to that from the start, didn't you?"

"You think waving that thing in my face will get you answers?"

"Maybe I'll just settle for your life."

"That wouldn't be very productive," Yin said. "And if murder were your intention, you would have done it by now."

A long moment passed between them. Somewhere in the interim,

Cray admitted to himself that Yin was right. Pulling the trigger would have given him a moment's satisfaction, but wouldn't change anything. It was a meaningless form of revenge—and the price would have been his life.

He disarmed the emitter, shoving it across the marble desk. The weapon came to a rest in front of Yin, who picked it up and examined it dispassionately. "Clearly, the Zone Authority underestimated our Zoe."

Cray seethed quietly. "*I* didn't."

"So I heard. The Authority was rather displeased with you. They swear that if you ever show your face in the Asian Sphere, they'll kill you as many times as possible." Yin got up, patting Cray on the shoulder as he walked over to his own bar. "But I wouldn't worry. From the looks of things, you're quite capable of fending them off."

Cray shook his head in amazement. "Nothing gets to you, does it?"

Yin poured himself a scotch, not bothering to offer one to his guest. "Not in the course of business," he replied. "I'll confess, I hold you in a certain regard, Cray—but I hold no reservations about using you in the manner best suited to accomplish my objectives. If that means withholding information, then so be it."

"I could have brought her in *alive*, Yin."

"Perhaps," Yin said, returning to his desk, "but that's very unlikely. I knew you would try, however—and *that's* why I deceived you."

"What the hell are you talking about?"

"The girl was *Inru*, Cray. Or didn't you surmise that for yourself?"

The mention of the word sapped both his anger and his strength. Cray was forced to sit down, his mind trying to reconcile what he just heard with what he saw back in Singapore.

"She was on a mission for her guru," Yin continued. "The information Zoe carried was intended to further their goals."

"Are you sure about this?"

Yin was casual. "Not everything is about economics, my friend."

A stale hint of fear settled on Cray's tongue. "Those people are crazy," he whispered. "Do you have any idea what you've done?"

"I know precisely what I've done. I've given them a martyr—or, more precisely, *you* have." Yin swiveled around in his chair, facing the parade of pulser traffic that passed outside his window. "By now, the *Inru*'s hammerjacks have ascertained that you were the one who tracked Zoe down. Ultimately, any blame for her death will rest with you."

"No way. I won't let you hang that on me."

"What are you going to do? *Explain* how you tried to save her?" Yin laughed. "You underestimate your reputation, Cray. How many runners have you brought back to me? Ten? *Twenty?* Your exploits on behalf of the Collective are well known in the subculture."

Yin knew what he was talking about. He had made a career out of being invisible, but Cray was the one always out in front. Any decent hammerjack knew Cray's name as well as his methods, the same way a hustler knew all the cops on his turf. Obviously, Yin had put a lot of thought into this—and Cray had stepped right into his trap.

"Son of a bitch," Cray muttered. "You just put my head in a noose."

"Now you're getting the idea," Yin said offhandedly.

Cray wished he had the emitter back, if only to use it on himself. He had spent enough time in the Axis to know that most of the stories about the *Inru* were real. If what Zoe had done was any example of their determination, it wouldn't be long before they came for a piece of him.

Unless Yin is just trying to scare me off.

Cray thought he detected a slight tension in the man's voice—not much, but enough to make him suspicious. "You're offering me protection," he said, following that track. "In exchange for what?"

Yin turned back around. "Nothing more than you've given me the last ten years," he answered. "As well as your discretion. It would be unfortunate if our competitors gained any more knowledge of these events. Of course, the choice is yours."

Cray's lips pursed into a tight smile. "No, Yin—*you're* the one with a choice to make, and you better make the right one. Because if you don't tell me what's *really* going on, I will walk out of here and dig it out for myself. I will sink into every goddamned corner of the Axis until I find out what you're hiding."

There was silence as Yin thought it over, his black eyes evaluating Cray as a potential enemy. That Yin could have him killed was a realistic danger, one Cray had considered before making his demands. But Yin was also practical. As long as he needed Cray, he would not exercise that option.

Yin conceded, spreading his hands in an open gesture. "What do you want to know?"

So I get to live, Cray thought. *For now.*

"Before I came up here," he said, "I checked GenTec's domain for signs of a proprietary trace. Imagine my surprise when I saw you had been compromised. That stuff Zoe was carrying originated here, didn't it?"

"Yes."

"What the hell is it? My GME told me he's never seen anything like it."

"Something that looks like flash-DNA, but isn't flash-DNA."

Cray leaned in toward him. "Go on."

"The next great breakthrough," Yin explained, getting up and strolling about the room. His eyes scanned the dusty titles on his bookshelves as he spoke, like a professor giving a history lesson. "Strictly in the experimental phase. We believe it has the potential to be the biological storage medium to take the world into the next century."

"I take it the Collective doesn't know about this yet."

"No," Yin admitted, which was confessing the greatest of sins. "The other members of the Assembly would have sought licensing rights, cutting into GenTec's share of development. We're already working on a full range of applications for the new technology. The board thought it would be best to keep this to ourselves until we were ready to bring the new flash to market."

"*That's* what this was about?" Cray asked. "Corporate politics?"

"That was part of it."

"And what about this business with Heretic? Was that just more bullshit?"

"The most effective lie contains a small portion of the truth."

"And it had nothing to do with sweetening the deal for me."

Yin shrugged. "The thought did cross my mind."

Cray had to laugh. He had been played all right, in more ways than he could have anticipated. For a long time, he had been following the faint traces of Heretic's signature through the Axis, never coming up with enough data to form a decent profile. That, plus the legend that had built up around the man, made Heretic a prize of sorts—a hammerjack who could operate on the same level Cray did. Yin knew he wouldn't be able to resist the chance to go up against that, and used it to lure him into making the intercept. It had been bait, pure and simple.

"So Heretic is working for the *Inru* now," Cray mused. "I can buy that. But that doesn't explain why they would be interested in GenTec."

"Ordinary terrorism," Yin said, heading back to the bar and pouring another drink. "Their founding principle is the destruction of modern technology. What better way to do that than by attacking technology at its source?"

"This was sabotage."

"Incredible, but effective. Heretic was extremely thorough with our records. After downloading the virtual models of the new flash, he destroyed all research materials related to the project. The flash Zoe carried was the only surviving prototype. I had to make sure we got it back."

It made a twisted kind of sense—but then the politics of extremism always seemed twisted to Cray. The *Inru* had started out as a small enough group, a reactionary movement to the Collective displacement of world government. But since then, its message had become more apocalyptic. Their leadership began to see advancing science as the enemy of mankind, and technology as the tool of its enslavement. It didn't take long for the faithful to turn that belief into dogma and the *Inru* into a religious cult. The corporate media portrayed them as little more than a fringe group—but there was no way of knowing what their real numbers were. And not knowing was what scared the Collective the most.

Cray was silent for a time while he sorted it all out. He noticed Yin watching him closely during those moments. "My GME showed me some of the new flash," he finally announced. "If Zoe had lived long enough, its characteristics would have torn her up on a cellular level. Was that just an oversight or part of the design?"

"I told you," Yin said without missing a beat. "It's still in the experimental phase. But to answer your question, the flash was not designed to be compatible with a living system. The applications we have in mind are strictly *ex vitro*."

"So by assimilating it, she was handing herself a death sentence."

"Eventually, yes."

Cray shook his head in disbelief. "Jesus Christ."

The fiber link on Yin's desk interrupted the conversation. Yin passed his hand over a flat monitor in the face of the marble desktop, then inserted an earpiece so Cray wouldn't hear the other side of the conversation. The communication was brief. Cray had to settle for reading Yin's reactions, which were few and cryptic.

"Yes," Yin replied to the caller, nodding his head. "I understand. Dr. Alden is here with me right now. I've explained the current situation to him." A few more moments passed while the caller did the talking, then Yin ended it by adding, "It will be done immediately."

The light from the monitor drained away from Yin's features. He sat down.

"Bad news?" Cray asked.

"That was the General Secretary of the Collective Assembly," Yin told him. "A matter of some urgency has arisen."

"What's the matter?" Cray remarked. "Your bosses want to chat with you about this?"

"No," Yin answered. "They want to see *you*."

Cray blinked out of sheer surprise.

"The Assembly has convened an emergency session," Yin explained. "The secretary was short on details, but was very clear that I put you on the next SOT to Vienna. It seems they want to ask you a few questions."

"What the hell for?" Up until now, Cray had been certain that the *real* power had never even heard his name. "I don't have dealings with those people."

"You never ask why, Cray." Yin hit the intercom switch on his fiber link, calling on his personal secretary. Most executives used a virtual assistant, but Yin still enjoyed having his whims catered to by an actual human being. "Kayla, I need you to book a first-class passage for Dr. Alden—Kuala Lumpur to Vienna. I want a pulser on the roof to take him to the airport in fifteen minutes."

Yin closed the link. Cray was expecting something from the man—condescension, pity, sadistic pleasure, anything to indicate his reaction to this development—but Yin was blank and guarded. The news could have meant everything or nothing to him, there was no way to tell.

"I'll see to it that you get everything you need upon your arrival," Yin said.

Cray stood. "Just like that."

"You should be used to that by now."

"I am," Cray said, and headed out. Stopping short of the exit, he lingered for a few moments, contemplating the scene as he wanted it to end. *I don't believe you*, he would have said. *Not a single word. All I need is time, and I'll be able to prove it. And after that . . .*

After that, what?

"You don't want me as an enemy, Cray," Yin warned. "Don't entertain any thoughts of aligning yourself with the Assembly, either."

Cray turned around.

"Choose the lesser of two evils?" he asked.

Yin went rigid.

"You always have choices," he said. "I suggest you consider yours carefully before you make it."

Cray was more straightforward.

"I suggest," he said, "that you go fuck yourself."

But Phao Yin only watched.

Tuned to the sentry monitors, he watched as Cray left the sanctuary and rode the elevator up to the roof. He watched as a pulser landed and took Cray aboard. And lastly, he watched as the gleaming vehicle jumped onto the grid and hurtled past his window, joining the endless stream of traffic that passed over the city. It was what Yin had prophesized, and it was what came to pass.

He had considered all the possibilities before Cray arrived, but never doubted the outcome. Cray had never been able to conceal his emotions, least of all his outrage. Sending him to intercept Zoe had simply been the final act in a well-orchestrated performance. Yin hated to lose him over that, but such were the sacrifices one made in war. Zoe herself had seen to that—as Cray was only beginning to discover.

Turning back to his desk, Yin caught sight of the hustler. The kid was still splayed across his couch, stirring now that the neuropatch had run its course. The sight of the young addict made Yin feel a sudden connection with the street, a sensation that had once been familiar to him but now only served as a reminder of his origins.

He hit the fiber link again, opening a secure port to an address that only he knew. There was an acknowledgment on his display at the point of contact, but nothing else. Those on the other end didn't have voices in the conventional sense. Yin preferred it to the usual forms of human interaction.

"Dr. Alden is working with a GME on the Singapore intercept," he said into the silent link. "Find out who it is and procure any findings from the study. Direct them to my office only. I'll decide the disposition at that time."

He closed the port. Moving worlds was that simple, as long as you knew where to push.

That left Yin with some time to wait. He spent some of it watching the hustler climb his way back to consciousness, the pain of withdrawal building on his face. The trip was the best money could buy, but getting off it was hard. As soon as his eyes fluttered open, the hustler would be wanting more.

The kid moaned. Another figure then appeared in the office doorway, as if awaiting her cue. The girl's face was concealed in shadows, her posture wary and tense like that of an animal.

"I see you found your way back here," Yin said to her. The sound of his voice was familiar to her, and she responded by moving partially into the light. She was also from the street—a hustler in her own right, her body a collection of artificial enhancements, her eyes a feast of addiction.

Yin placed a small plastic pouch on top of his desk—a pack of neuropatches, the same thing he had given the boy. The girl fixated on them, taking an involuntary step forward before her instincts made her stop.

Yin smiled coldly.

Stimulus and response.

"You want these," he said to the girl. "You know what to do."

She did. The girl had been a guest of Yin's many times, and never refused what was required of her. Shedding her rags, she walked over to the couch and performed on the young male hustler—all the things Yin liked to see, all the things Yin could never do. Entangled in one another, they went through the motions like automatons operating in a physical plane, flesh connecting while minds disconnected. Yin had a vague sensation of the passage of time, and when it was over he was on his feet, standing above the two of them.

The girl looked up at him and twisted her lips into a smile. She reached without looking for what Yin handed her, familiar with this ritual and his habits. It was a small blade—only a few centimeters long, a dagger from Yin's collection of antiques. It glinted in the soft light as she raised it above the boy's chest.

"Send him on his way," Yin commanded.

THREE

The suborbital jump from Kuala Lumpur took less than twenty minutes, but speed came with a price. The instant shift across seven time zones played like a meat grinder with Cray's frayed senses, tossing him into a spin that bit like a hangover. His condition was obvious enough to alarm a flight attendant, who offered him a soother before landing, but Cray refused. The stuff reminded him too much of the drugs some hammerjacks used to keep their logical orientation in the Axis, and that was one trip he didn't need.

Instead, he dragged his disorientation with him as he hopped the SOT, making his first stop a place that served the only stimulant Cray had ever fully trusted—caffeine. He greedily assimilated a triple shot of steaming black espresso and watched the world around him regain a remote sense of clarity. With life now pumping through his veins, Cray left a generous tip for the waiter and proceeded back into the distinct vibe that was central Europe.

It didn't take him long to realize he no longer fit in.

That was a conceit he had learned from too many years in the Asian Sphere—his perceived ability to blend in anywhere, anytime. Back there the rules were few and savage, making it easy for any player with reasonable street smarts to become part of the culture. But here in the core of civilization, they could smell it on you. Cray saw it in the way people looked at him, their stares brief but riddled with intent. Cray might have taken offense, had it not been so true.

What made you slick in Malaysia branded you in Europe, and there was nothing you could do to hide it.

For Cray, it was like walking through a sterile curtain. The last few years, he had become accustomed to the closeness of bodies—air thick with the chatter of a thousand dialects, the persistent subtext of pheromones. Now, there was a distinct *lack* of sensory input, as if someone had turned down the volume of his life and dropped him into the middle of a neutral void.

Quickly, mercifully, the sensation dissipated as he followed the signs that pointed the way to the transit station. There, Cray ran into the long lines of tourists trying to hash out the complex regulations that governed civilian traffic in and out of the city. Bypassing all the others, he flashed his corporate credentials at the first-class line and was allowed to join the other Collective types who were headed into Oldtown Vienna. It was nice getting the star treatment, but being around them still made Cray feel uneasy. He wasn't used to seeing anyone in a suit who wasn't Japanese.

"You must have some serious jack."

It was a woman's voice, from behind. Cray sensed her distance at about two meters, his right hand reaching for a weapon that wasn't there. He caught himself, remembering that he was now in the civilized world. Coming about slowly, he tried to put a casual spin on the hasty move he had started.

"Jumpy, too," the woman said, firing off her observation like the two of them were old friends. "First-class travel, heavy creds—I had you figured for some kind of a player."

Cray knew the kind right off. She appeared to be somewhere between nineteen and twenty, and fit the profile of a fringe junkie. Cray had seen them before, hanging out at the edge of the subculture—above the life, maybe by money or family, but with enough impulse to take a taste whenever they could get it. They followed gangbangers and hammerjacks like groupies chasing after rock stars. This one looked like she picked up her habits at school. Universities were breeding grounds for that sort of character.

"You trying to win some kind of bet?" Cray shot back.

The girl smiled. It was obvious how this one had breezed past airport security. She was beautiful enough to inspire a few extra heartbeats, and smart enough to work what she had. But it was the way the girl looked him up and down that made Cray take notice. She inspected him the same way she might check out something before she bought it.

"Maybe there's some money involved," she replied, not letting much else slip as she came toward him. She was so totally assured, her body not wasting a single gesture. "Maybe I'm just looking to score."

Used to getting what she wants, Cray decided. *But way too young to be this cocky.*

"Anybody tell you you've got a big mouth?"

"Nobody's ever complained," the girl said, smiling. "I'm Lea. I'd tell you more, but you look like you enjoy mystery. And you are . . . ?"

"Busy," Cray told her, and headed for the next empty transit vestibule.

"Give a girl a break, will ya?" Lea asked, falling in step beside him. The way she brushed her arm against his as they walked wasn't lost on Cray, and a part of him started to welcome it—she was *that* good. "You haven't even asked me to talk dirty to you."

"Baby"—Cray chuckled—"I don't believe you *know* hot from cold."

"It's all the same to me. Try it. You might like it."

She wet her lips a little with that last comment, adding just the trace of a laugh. Ignoring her was clearly impossible.

"I'm listening," Cray said.

"Got a couple of friends with me. We've been in the Metro for a couple of days. Now we're looking for someone to take us into Oldtown—maybe hang out with us for a while, show us the sights. You know."

"Oldtown's off-limits to civilians."

"I know. But why should I let that stop me?"

"Because it's illegal. You could get yourself arrested."

"It wouldn't be the first time," Lea said offhandedly. "Besi get the feeling that's something we might have in common. S *is* your story, anyway? The way you were checking your back, my friends thought you were a dealer. Synthroids maybe. You carrying weight?"

"I never mess around with biologicals."

"That's cool. Don't care for them much myself."

"Nice that you've got standards."

"You get around, you figure it out," Lea said, adding a little bounce to her step. "But I'm not worried about you anyway. I can tell you're from the street, but you're not species. You're not wired like that."

Is this girl for real? Cray thought. The way Lea was pushing his buttons, it was like somebody had plucked her out of his imagination. That made her bait, pure and simple—but knowing that didn't prevent him from tugging just a little.

Cray stopped short of the vestibule door. "How can you tell?" he asked, turning toward her. The idea was to unnerve her, but it had little effect.

"You don't have the eyes," she explained. "The serious ones always have that look—like they're disconnected, you know? Like they turned it off so long ago, they forgot how to turn it back on again."

It was enough to make Cray take a serious look at her for the first time—and see how much he had missed on his first glance. At a distance, he had just assumed Lea's beauty was artificial. Her hair was a radiant blond, almost white, a pair of pale green eyes measuring his intentions. But she was missing the absolute symmetry of the surgeon's scalpel. There were subtle imperfections in her complexion, a tiny pale birthmark just beneath her chin—minute flaws that defined her magnetism rather than detracted from it. What Lea had was all hers.

"How much?" he asked.

She cocked her head a little—a coy gesture, impeccably timed. "How much what?"

"How much you got riding on me with your friends?"

Lea slipped her arms around his neck and pulled him closer. There was meaning in that touch, the method with which she drew his body toward hers and held him at just the right distance.

"Fifty standard," she said.

Cray raised an eyebrow. "Expensive," he remarked.

"Anything worth having is."

"Maybe," Cray said, and reached into his jacket. He peeled the fifty away from his stash, and pressed the money into her hands. "But it would cost me a lot more if I said yes."

The mirth that was living behind Lea's eyes quickly faded. She was not the kind of girl who was used to getting turned down. "What am I supposed to tell my friends?" she asked.

"Tell them you lost," Cray said, then disappeared into the vestibule. He marveled at how hard it was to tear himself away.

The interior of the vestibule reminded Cray of the hotels in Osaka: cramped to the point of claustrophobia, adorned with advertising flyers and an outdated electronic console. The autosensors didn't even detect his presence until he sat down, then brought the tiny space to life with muted lights and soft music.

"Good afternoon, fellow traveler," the city's transit computer greeted him. The voice sounded pleasant, but obviously manufactured. Systems that serviced the general public were usually designed that way—to reassure customers that they were not dealing with a human being. "Please provide identity and verification for access to your itinerary."

He slipped a data card into the reader slot.

"Hello, Dr. Alden," the computer said. "I trust you had an enjoyable flight."

"I had nothing of the sort," Cray replied. "But thanks anyway. So what adventures does GenTec have planned for me today?"

"An autocab has been reserved in your name. Your destination is the Hotel Bristol on Kartner Ring—a very historic part of Oldtown. Would you like to add a programmed tour to your journey? I'm certain you'll find the details fascinating."

"I'm certain I would," Cray told the computer. "How about you tell me a little more about it?"

He paid no attention as the machine went through its spiel. Instead, he used the active time to mask his signature and sweep the interior of the vestibule with his new integrator—a precaution that had become a matter of habit during his travels. Finding the space clean of monitoring devices, Cray switched to a low-level jack. Piggybacking the transit computer's network connection, he ran a quick feedback trace. If anyone was following his movements virtually, the activity would show up as spikes in the background noise that marked his existence in the Axis. As it was, the MFI indicated nothing but nominal levels.

He closed out the jack just as the computer finished its sales pitch. The entire process had taken twenty seconds from start to finish and left the city's transit authority none the wiser.

"So would you like to order the tour?" the computer asked.

"Sounds like fun. Add it to my bill."

The computer encoded everything on his card and spit it back out at him. "Complete," it announced. "Welcome to Vienna, Dr. Alden."

"No place I'd rather be," Cray said, packing up his gear and heading out.

Phao Yin could be accused of a great many things, but being cheap was not among them. GenTec more or less maintained a permanent suite at the Hotel Bristol, perhaps the most distinctive example of lodging in the new or old world. At only 140 rooms, it was by no means a palace—but there was enough history associated with the place, just in the last fifty years, to fill a space ten thousand times its size.

Watching as Vienna passed outside his window, drawing him close to the heart of the Collective, Cray finally understood what all the fuss was about. The streets in Oldtown were more than streets, they were conduits—rivers where the ebb of power flowed. Not power as an abstract concept, but as a palpable entity. As beautiful as the restored city was, it could not mask that singularity. It was as real as gravity, drawing all things toward it.

"The Hotel Bristol is a fine example of Oldtown's second renaissance," Cray's automated driver informed him. "Only days after the Consolidation, terrorist gangs loyal to the old European Union laid siege to the city—looting many of the structures you see here, destroying many others. Before Collective troops were dispatched to quell the riots, the Bristol itself was firebombed and very nearly burned to the ground."

"Those were the days, weren't they?" Cray said. He had availed himself of the minibar, and raised a glass of knockoff scotch to the passing scenery.

The disembodied voice continued without acknowledging him. "In the aftermath," it said, "the Assembly decided on a statement of unity to reassure all law-abiding people that their future had arrived, and it was a bright one. As part of that statement, they decreed that Vienna—which had suffered so terribly under the ravages of the old world order—should be rebuilt as a center of hope for all humankind. The Bristol was among the first of the buildings to be restored, along with the Vienna State Opera—which was soon converted to diplomatic purposes and now serves as the headquarters of the Collective General Assembly."

And a fine history it has written for itself. The painstaking restoration of Vienna was just a part of that concoction. As illusory as it all was, Cray could not help but be impressed. The virtual tour kept pace with the scenery, and as he listened he could easily imagine himself in a time when court politics were the highest drama of society and Mozart held the premiere of *The Marriage of Figaro.* Outwardly, Vienna appeared exactly as it had been during those centuries. Contemporary intrusions had long been declared illegal, which only served to perpetuate the supernatural mystery that surrounded the doings of the Assembly. It actually made perfect sense when Cray thought about it. Every religion needed mysticism—science and commerce were no different. God had made man in His image, and so the Assembly had made itself as God.

But it *was* only an illusion—and like so many others the Collective manufactured, this one was hidden behind a thin veneer. Cray pierced through it as soon as the cab slowed at the corner of Operngasse, where he saw the opera house for the first time. On the surface, the building looked remarkable only as a relic, perfectly preserved from an age that had long since passed. But beneath, it transmitted on wavelengths that quietly suggested the magnitude of purpose within.

Cray made a quick sweep of the building with his MFI, only to find his scans reflected back. *Countermeasures,* he correctly deduced, and after taking a few random shots he still couldn't penetrate the electronic wall that surrounded the place. The countermeasures operated on shifting frequencies, generated by onetime ciphers in any one of a trillion combinations. There would also be sensor webs and threat detectors, all tied in to an automated defensive system. Cray had no doubt that any unwelcome guest would be reduced to ashes before getting within spitting distance of the front door.

Hello, Vienna . . .

The car rounded the corner slowly, pulling into the long circular driveway in front of the Bristol. A stout bellman welcomed Cray, plucking his one bag out of the trunk and showing him to the front desk. The clerk on duty there seemed just as friendly—and became even more so when he saw the suite reserved in Cray's name.

"We're quite honored to have another one of Mr. Yin's guests," he said. "They've all been very pleased with the Bristol's accommodations."

"I'm sure they have," Cray replied. "There wouldn't happen to be any messages from Mr. Yin, would there?"

"I'm afraid not. There is, however, another message for you—coded as private. You can check it on the display in your suite, if you like."

"That's fine. Thanks."

"You're all set then," the clerk told him, motioning for Cray to place his palm on a portable scanner. "Room access is biometric, coded to your handprint. Should you wish to dine in, the Korso Restaurant here is one of the finest in Oldtown. And if there is *anything* else you require—anything at all—please let us know."

An old-fashioned lift deposited Cray on the top floor, where he discovered that his was the only suite. Pillars of green marble flanked a pair of cherrywood doors leading into the rooms. Cray gripped the doorknob and heard the lock click open. He went inside, finding the appointments within even more lavish than what he had seen downstairs. In the foyer, light so natural and thick that it flowed like water poured in through a single large window, between parted velvet curtains that showed him a view of Oldtown. Alabaster walls practically glowed, and as Cray heard the doors closing behind him, he felt strangely trapped—like he had been sealed in a vast coffin of luxury.

He tossed his bag and his jacket on the nearest sofa, taking some time to scout the place and map out all the possible exits. He also made a sweep with his MFI, locating no fewer than eight bugs—none of them active, probably left over from the last few times Gen-Tec hosted their heavies here. Cray just disabled them, making a note to turn the devices back on before he left. He didn't want to interfere with Yin's voyeuristic habits.

Finishing up, Cray fished a portable ECM seal out of his bag and placed it next to the front doors. It was another one of his innovations—a scaled-down version of the same blanket that protected the State Opera House across the street. While not nearly as powerful or sophisticated, it was enough to discourage most remote monitoring hookups; and if anyone did manage to punch through it, Cray's MFI would broadcast an alert and automatically trace any sensor activity back to its source.

The seal responded with an affirmative beep when he turned it on. Checking his MFI screen, Cray was satisfied with the stream of telemetry coming off the device.

No jamming, no intrusions. Time to check the mail.

The suite came equipped with half a dozen virtual terminals. Cray opted for the one in the bedroom, which was embedded in the ceiling directly above the huge, oversized bed. Amused by the sheer novelty of it, he plunked himself down and activated the terminal. The level of comfort was extreme enough to be disconcerting.

"This is Cray Alden," he exhaled. "Display coded message, please."

The room lights dimmed a little, and a three-dimensional construct phased into existence above his head. Cray skipped past the usual welcome blurbs from the hotel and the confidentiality agreements, expecting to find some verbose communication from the Assembly or from Phao Yin. But instead, the message he received was cryptic. A seemingly random collection of large red letters floated in the air, though there were enough vowels arranged in the correct order to tell him this wasn't a code—just a jumble of scrambled words.

Somebody was being cute.

"I don't like puzzles," Cray announced to the construct. "Get to the point."

The letters seemed to respond to his cue, darting around each other like a swarm of excited insects. They settled back down after a few moments, regrouping into a series of words—a simple enough message, ominous in its tone:

NOTHING IS RANDOM

Another line beneath it began to take shape. Letters bounced over one another, playing leapfrog in a jolly way that was presumably meant to give the impression of laughter. Cray expected nothing less, considering the source:

A REMINDER FROM YOUR FRIEND,
HERETIC

He terminated the construct. "I hate this hammerjack shit."

"I'd say you're in the wrong business."

The voice came from the bedroom door. Cray jumped off the bed, not knowing what to expect—least of all the woman who had breezed into his room unnoticed. Her shape was unnervingly still, concealed beneath a full-length overcoat, her hands coolly clasped behind her back. The voice matched the face: darkly female, features immutable as her body, eyes concealed behind opaque glasses. Her long black hair swept back dramatically over her head, creating an image that was statuesque in its severity.

"I'm getting really tired of women sneaking up on me."

"You complain incessantly," she observed. "That was in your profile."

"And you make a lot of assumptions. Didn't anybody tell you it's bad manners to break into somebody's hotel room?"

She was inscrutable. As she walked into the room, Cray noticed that she moved like a soldier. He guessed that underneath her garb, her body was a flawless piece of precision engineering.

"How did you get in here, anyway?"

"I was in the room before you arrived."

"Wonder how I missed that."

"You didn't look hard enough." The woman reached into her pocket and tossed him the ECM seal. "I wouldn't do anything in here that needs to be cloaked. The Assembly gets nervous if they can't see what you're up to."

"I'll keep that in mind while I'm in the shower."

"Keep that in mind at *all* times, Dr. Alden."

Cray walked over to the minibar, mostly to give himself something to do. "They didn't need to send you all the way over here just to tell me that," he said, examining the row of expensive liquor bottles. "You could have just stuck a note on the door—unless you're here to keep an eye on me."

"Don't be ridiculous," the woman said, coming the rest of the way into his room. "Our methods are more sophisticated than that. I'm here because I want to be."

"You like haunting the rooms of strange men?"

"Only when those men have business with my employers."

"Didn't my profile tell you everything you need?"

"Profiles don't tell the whole story, Dr. Alden. You don't get anywhere near the Assembly unless I have a look at you myself."

"*Ahh* . . ." Cray said, dropping a few ice cubes into a glass. "CSS must be improving their standards. I've never met a security officer with such a hard-on for her work."

The woman stopped again. Her lips crept upward slightly, an approximation of a smile. She just rebutted Cray's conclusions without saying a word.

His eyes narrowed. "You're a free agent."

"Avalon," she told him. "Diplomatic services detachment, liaison branch."

"I should have known," Cray said, consoling himself with a genuine scotch. "I have to hand it to you, though—at least you do it with more class than those guys in the Zone."

"They're mercenaries, Dr. Alden."

"And *you're* not?"

"Mercenaries have no loyalty."

Cray didn't trust her, but he took her word on that one. Unlike their counterparts in the Zone, free agents were products of *military* training—augmented by a genetic regimen that began at an early age. Increased strength and speed were matched only by a killer instinct for survival and a physiology that gave them an almost inhuman endurance.

All free agents had been members of the Solar Expeditionary Corps at one time or the other, back when the Collective had been engaged in several dubious terraforming ventures on Mars. The final nail in the coffin of that program had been a virus outbreak at Olympus Mons, a costly disaster that killed over six thousand people— including most of the Corps stationed on the planet. The few soldiers who survived did so through the most brutal of tactics. Potential carriers of the disease were rounded up and killed. Civilians were butchered to conserve the food supply. And when the food finally did run out, it was said that some members of the Corps resorted to cannibalism—or so Cray heard in stories that had become more fable than fact.

After abandoning Mars, there was still the question of what to do with the surviving group of extreme warriors. With a public relations nightmare on its hands, the Collective decided to execute most of them for crimes against humanity—after a lengthy trial and much fanfare. But the Collective also recognized talent when it saw it, and issued a secret decree that spared a few of these soldiers so that they could be put to use as free agents. Cray heard that fewer than a dozen operated in the world at any one time, carrying out the kind of work even Special Services couldn't touch—but this was the first time he had met one.

"Avalon," Cray pondered. "That name for real?"

"It's not necessary for you to know."

"Just making small talk," Cray remarked. "Can I offer you a drink?"

"You can offer me explanations."

Cray took his glass back over to the bed and sat down.

"My life's an open book," he said.

"Only for the last ten years," Avalon corrected him. Her tone, which never varied, made the exchange sound like an interrogation. Cray wondered how far she would go to get her answers. "Before that, I can't find any real evidence that you even exist."

"You didn't look hard enough."

"I went further than most," she said. "All the standard background checks told me precisely what they were supposed to—you started working for GenTec right out of school, you pay your taxes on time, you've never been arrested. You're considered one of the world's foremost experts in network architecture—and according to your evaluations, your employers have nothing but the highest regard for you."

"Not very exciting, is it?"

Avalon ignored his comment, turning straight to her point. "If all this is true," she asked, "then why is it nobody seems to know who you are?"

Cray didn't have an answer prepared. Up until now, nobody had asked.

"There's not a single professor at Caltech who remembers you," Avalon continued. "Everybody I talked to back at GenTec agrees you're the best person they ever had—but hardly anyone knows what you look like."

"I keep a low profile."

"You're beyond that, Dr. Alden. I ran a full search on every detail of your life prior to you going to work for GenTec. You want to guess what I found?"

Cray shook his head.

"Not a thing."

She leveled those last words like an accusation, though they were as cold and detached as the rest of their conversation. Avalon just watched him from behind black lenses, robotic in her patience and determination.

"Tell me something, Avalon," Cray said. "You ever talk about what happened to you back at Olympus Mons?"

She was silent—obviously so.

"That's what I thought," he said, walking to the bedroom window. A fresh breeze blew the curtains past his face. "The world is smaller than it's ever been—but it's still big enough to keep a few secrets."

"I don't like men who come out of nowhere, Dr. Alden."

"Get used to it." He turned around to find her fixed on him, recording his every move—counting all the different ways she could kill him. "Just what do you think I do for a living, anyway?"

"You're a specialist."

"You're being too kind."

That remark caught her off guard. In corporate circles, people got where they did by defending themselves vigorously. Cray had long since grown tired of the practice.

The tactic was a success. Avalon backed off.

"You're not very cooperative," she said.

"That's something you can add to my profile."

"It's already done." She plucked a data card out of one pocket, laying it on Cray's dresser. Sunlight glinted off its burnished surface. "That's my contact information, in case you get talkative."

"That's it?" Cray asked as she headed out. "Who am I going to get to show me around town?"

"The Assembly expects you at nine tomorrow morning," Avalon said. "I'll be escorting you to the Audience Chamber. Don't be late. If I have to come looking for you, I won't be nearly as pleasant."

Avalon left. Just a swirl of her overcoat and she was gone. Cray imagined he had gotten the better of her, at least for the moment. He also imagined she would remember this encounter, if there ever came a time when she would have to decide on how to deal with him.

He just hoped he hadn't pissed her off too much.

• • •

Dex Marlowe stared through a haze.

The numerics floated through his mind like a tec-induced fantasy, the afterimage of a trip that had left him with more headache than clarity, more confusion than consciousness. It got that way on the tail end of a buzz. He had been working off the residuals in his bloodstream for the last six hours, coasting—never breaking the interface with GenTec's domain, not even to reload stims. What he saw was just too fascinating, and he was afraid he might never see its like again.

Microtrodes sprouted from both of his temples, his body still except for the sporadic twitch. He was in his command chair, stubble and sweat covering his face. Occasionally a smile would poke through the grime, like the earliest forms of life crawling from a primordial soup—with it, a sudden bloom in his cheeks that was the only break in his comalike pallor. He had been riding the domain hard.

Dex could just as easily have watched from outside, but after the encryption algorithms split, he wanted to get up close and personal. He had been hooked into the node ever since. Seated in front of the rows of consoles in his office, he looked something like a sacrifice to a great pagan deity. The only window into the machinery was the virtual display, which hovered over Dex and showed the steady but fading throb of his vitals. All the meaty stuff from the extraction was being fed directly into his synapses.

And it was as if God had opened the floodgates of Heaven.

Dex had been expecting some serious mischief, but nothing like this. An entire universe had been encapsulated inside Zoe's body—not some slate of industrial secrets, but ribbons of light consisting of an infinite number of points, connected to each other in an eternal matrix of flawless arrangements. As soon as the mathematical barriers fell, Dex had found himself on the outer rim of those lights, floating freely in space and searching for his point of origin. He found it behind him: a tumbling series of morphing shapes casting out waves of partial reality like the regular pulse of a neutron star. It was a representation of the node, the only beacon he had to find his way back.

Dex waited what he thought was a reasonable amount of time—though there was little to distinguish between minutes and hours in this place—looking for any signs that the node would collapse. But his connection to the outside world remained strong enough to give him confidence, and from there it was just a matter of him taking the plunge.

The points of light beckoned him.

Dex moved into the matrix, toward one of the interconnecting conduits. It glowed, fiercely blue, like the fiber optics that had drawn flash from Zoe's body. Dex thought he could feel a presence when he drew closer—as if a force of life had made its own impression, as if blood was moving through those veins instead of energy. At first he was certain it was Zoe herself, a prospect that was at once both terrifying and beguiling. Those two magnetic extremes pulled on him and pushed against him, creating turbulence as he reached the conduit.

Dex sensed it brushing against him, like heat from the embers of a dying fire, gradually building in intensity until all at once it *became* him. It wrapped itself around his consciousness like waves slipping over the head of a drowning man, but without pain or panic. By now Dex welcomed it, and reveled in the acceleration as currents took him downward, pulling him deeper and deeper into the abyss.

Instantaneous transport across limitless space. He saw the world expanding and contracting—an oscillating universe of birth and death, matter and destruction. The lights coalesced into flashes and images, the faces of people both familiar and unrecognizable, before breaking down into their base elements. Hydrogen and helium. The building blocks of fusion. Nuclear fire. Then deeper still, down to the subatomic level. Electrons moving in perfect circles, spinning around dense nuclei like planets orbiting a sun. Dex shot toward one of them on a relativistic trajectory, punching through the outer walls until he found himself dancing among the quarks.

Existence at its most regressive level. All reality mapped down to the smallest detail. The very fabric of the cosmos.

Dex was seeing it, but hardly believing it. That all this could be encoded into flash was beyond staggering, but he simply could not grasp the reason for it. He had witnessed the wonder of creation, and now he was asking why.

The pressure of his arrival began to build. It did not reach a crescendo so much as deposit Dex on a plateau, a solid ground of substance from which he could watch the show. Whether or not he wanted to watch was entirely up to him.

Dex froze. He glanced upward, searching for the star that was the anchor to his own mind as it still existed in the outside world. He found the node precisely where he left it—steady, unwavering, still visible even after the big tumble. He had not moved so far from himself as he imagined. But even if he had, he doubted he would have stopped.

All right, baby, he thought. *Now's the time. Show me what you got . . .*

The quarks parted. Impossible darkness came down in a torrent— impossible because Dex could still see, and as he moved between shadows of organic dust he could finally accept that he was not alone. There *was* life there—amorphous, shifting, creating forms that seemed more imagination than real—but that was the whole point, wasn't it? After all, there was no atomic structure for

intelligence

because it existed on a plane all its own. There was no construct, no representation to accurately depict it. It simply *was,* and that left Dex to fill in the gaps for himself.

Out of that confusion, he understood.

Cray . . .

It was only the briefest of flickers, barely marking the distance be-tween axon and dendrite. By the time it ended, Dex became aware that the plug had been pulled. Somewhere, in the recesses of his own memory where things like mortality were buried, he could see the node fading. Twisting shapes grew smaller and smaller until they fi-nally fell out of space, closing the door on what he had left behind. His body was disconnected now, and it wouldn't be long until his mind went the same way.

It was a pity, really.

He had so been looking forward to letting Cray in on the joke.

Dex lingered on for a while in dream time, then collapsed in on himself.

Flatline.

Heartbeat ceased instantly after Phao Yin terminated the interface, but Dex Marlowe barely reacted to the end of his life. His hands became slightly rigid, then relaxed when he stopped breathing. In many ways, Yin thought, it was a peaceful and enviable death.

He stood over Dex for another five minutes, watching the EEG as it skipped up and down a few times, then settled.

What, he wondered when it was finished, *did you see in there?*

Doubtless the same things Zoe had seen during her brief foray into the same territory. Yin walked over to the glass sarcophagus where she still lay, her remains neatly preserved in suspension. The fiber optics had since been disconnected, allowing her to float freely in the clear solution, her body encased in pale blue light. As she was, she could have remained indefinitely—an artifact of sorts, announcing the arrival of a brave new world. But Yin would not allow it. Zoe was a liability, even in death.

He found the controls on the pedestal of the extraction tank, disengaging the preservation mode and flooding the tank with an accelerant solution. The chemicals, in conjunction with the elements already present in Zoe's body, worked quickly. As Yin stood by, her skin began to break down—peeling away from the flesh beneath, then dissolving into the liquid. Muscle tissue followed. Less than fifteen minutes passed, and all that remained was a skeleton. Yin finished by subjecting the bones to ultrahigh-frequency sound waves, which pulverized them into microscopic fragments.

Ashes to ashes, he thought.

Yin flushed out the tank. He then went back to the node console, pushing Dex Marlowe's body out of the command chair and taking the seat for himself. As he guessed, Dex still had the extraction data in the active buffer. Yin punched up a model of the data, making sure there had been no transcription errors. Satisfied the product was still in good shape, he dumped all the files into a secure directory. The transfer was so massive it took hours, but Yin was patient. He wasn't at all concerned about Dex's murder. After he had put everything in order, nobody else would be either.

When the process was complete, Yin purged the node of all data and shut it down. Getting up to leave, he noticed for the first time that Dex's eyes were still open. They had been staring at him the entire time—strangely cognizant, even though the light behind them was gone. In a way, Yin was envious. Dex had caught a glimpse of the future.

A glimpse of the Ascension.

CHAPTER
FOUR

Cray took breakfast in the Korso mostly to kill time, having spent most of the night in a futile chase of sleep. It was only when his coffee and pastry were on the table that he realized his stomach had joined the rest of his body in rebellion and was steadfastly refusing anything that came close to solid food.

Weird the way that works, Cray pondered, toying with the croissant on his plate. *You can kill a man and not even blink, but the tiniest thing spooks you and everything shuts down.*

The coffee he gulped burned the back of his throat. "You think too goddamned much," he muttered to himself.

But not enough to get a handle on what was *really* playing him. Cray supposed it could have been Avalon herself, and that prophetic way she had of speaking—but he was more convinced it was what she represented. Up until yesterday, there was nothing in his life that went far beyond his experience. Meeting her had changed all that. Her eyes had seen things that he could not possibly imagine—as far away as Olympus Mons, as close as across the street. Cray had never even considered that he had drawn a line between himself and those things, much less that he would ever cross it. Yet here he was, about to do just that—and he was afraid that when he saw what was on the other side, he wouldn't know how to deal with it.

So if you're that scared, why don't you just run? You could disappear. You've done it before. Maybe find a little redemption.

But that wasn't how it worked. There were claws, and they had a deep hold of his mortal coil—he understood that as much as he understood they would never let go. And the days of worrying about his immortal soul hanging in the balance, those had long since passed. It already belonged to the Collective. Cray had signed the papers and closed the deal himself.

He finished off the rest of his coffee, strolling out into the lobby and taking in the business-as-usual vibe like a good shot of stim. Outside, daylight filtered through the cold, gray clouds that had been dumping rain on Oldtown for the last few hours. Along the Operngasse a steady parade of umbrellas sidestepped puddles and autocabs as they hurried on to whatever appointments awaited. The opera house loomed over them, its ornate windows outwardly keeping watch but allowing nothing in. The people inside were monitoring him even now—that much he knew from what Avalon said. But to Cray, it seemed the place itself was keeping a close eye on him.

He tied his overcoat at the waist and tailed a small group of businessmen who were heading across the street. He followed at a distance, hanging back a few meters and watching how they passed through the security checkpoints. The human element was conspicuously absent, guards eschewed in favor of sentry clusters. Cray noted the small pods, spaced at regular intervals on the face of the wall, each one containing cameras that followed everyone from the street all the way to the front door. That meant there were at least half a dozen other devices he *couldn't* see, most of them weapons, already locked on his position.

Cray felt a tingle when he passed through the outside perimeter— probably rain playing havoc with the ECMs. The interference, however, didn't provide enough cover to hide the one piece of contraband Cray carried on his person. By the time he reached the entry point, threat sensors were actively pinging him and setting off alarms. As expected, two conspicuously armed guards appeared and put up an intimidating front, one standing in front of him while the other circled behind.

"Morning, gents."

"Sir," the one in front of him said, "please remove any electronic devices you have on your person and take a step back." He emphasized the point by placing a hand on his weapon. The one be-hind already had his drawn.

"Relax, fellas," Cray told them. "The name's Aiden. Check the roster—my clearance comes straight from GenTec."

"I don't care if your clearance comes straight from Jesus Christ," the guard replied, and nodded to his partner. The one in back grabbed Cray by the coat and stuffed his face into the nearest con-venient wall, then patted him down while the other guard kept him covered. It didn't take them long to come across the MFI.

The guard took it out of Cray's coat, treating the device like it was a chunk of pollex explosive. "What *is* this?" he demanded.

"You really oughta be careful with that thing," Cray said, toying with him. "I'm not responsible for what happens if you set it off."

The guards were not amused. They broke out the cuffs.

"That's enough, gentlemen," Avalon called out. Her voice echoed between the stone pillars that flanked the entryway. Cray looked past the guards and saw her emerging from the building, dressed in a variant of the same black attire she had worn the day be-fore. The onyx lenses were still perched on her nose—although by now Cray was thinking that it was more than her sense of style that dictated her wardrobe.

"Dr. Alden is a guest of the Assembly," she finished, plucking Cray's MFI from the guards. "I'll be escorting him from here."

The two men exchanged a doubtful look, but said nothing. They departed immediately, returning to their posts as the crowd from the Bristol lingered on, eyeing the imposing figure that came to Cray's aid.

"Nice of you to show up," Cray said to her. "I was just about to do a number on those guys."

"You need to learn how to manage risk, Dr. Alden," she replied, walking him toward the entrance. "Those men would have killed you if you kept provoking them."

"I've met killers, Avalon," he assured her. "Those two were just ball busters. They like to make trouble, but they won't shoot any-body who might be important. That's why I always walk into a place like I own it."

"And what if the person you're dealing with doesn't know the rules?"

"They *all* know the rules," Cray said. "Take you, for instance— I'd bet real money that shooting me wouldn't present you with any problems. That's why they sent you to babysit me."

She was actually curious. "Because I'm a killer?"

"We all have our jobs," he observed with a shrug. "I'm good at mine—and I have an idea that you're extremely good at yours."

"Good," Avalon said. "Then you won't be foolish enough to make another mistake. To be honest, I find it a wonder you're still alive."

He laughed. "You have a sense of humor after all."

"No," Avalon said quite seriously as they went inside. "I don't."

Like the camouflage that was the opera house itself, the interior of the building suggested little of how the Assembly directed the course of nations. The appointments were smart but not lavish, revealing an underlying modesty absent from most other seats of power. Cray might have respected that, had he believed the sentiment born from restraint or dignity. Instead, he couldn't shake the feeling that it was just a *façade*—an elaboration of a grand hoax, perpetrated for reasons yet unknown.

He caught several curious glances from the people he passed, but as Cray looked more closely he realized the attention came because of his escort. Avalon seemed to walk in slow motion, commanding others to get out of the way. They all knew who she was, or at the very least *what* she was. More than that, her presence in the halls was a clear indication that events were being put into motion.

The two of them walked into the grand foyer, over which hung a constellation of crystal spun into a dazzling chandelier. Beneath that, two mammoth decorative doors opened into what he assumed was the Audience Chamber—a theater in the days when the place was still an opera house, since converted into parliamentary space. Instead of facing a stage, the rows of empty seats now faced a large podium flanked by two lecterns, all of the pieces carved out of solid blocks of cherrywood—relics from some age of royalty.

Inside, a few custodial people were setting up some virtual-conferencing and translation equipment. Without thinking, Cray headed into the theater. He stopped when Avalon touched him on the shoulder and pulled him back.

"Not there," she said.

"This isn't the chamber?"

"That's just the Corporate Council," she explained. "They won't be in session until next week. Come on, let's go."

Cray went along without asking questions, even though he was starting to learn how little he knew about the entity he had served for the last ten years. He had heard of the Council—enough to know that it was a largely ceremonial body, comprised of select board members from various corporations doing business outside the Zone. They debated all aspects of Collective policy, with an aim toward giving the smaller fish a sense they had a say in the way things were done. The *real* authority, however, rested squarely with the Assembly—a small congregate made up of the CEOs of the Big Seven, vested with special executive powers that gave them the final word on everything.

Cray always assumed they were part of the same whole, that dealing with one meant dealing with the other. But if Cray had learned anything, it was that the servant was not so different from the master. Phao Yin operated in the shadows of commerce, and so Cray did as well. Avalon's place was in the shadows of politics. That would make the Assembly less like an arm of government and more like—

More like what? A bunch of spooks?

Their journey took them farther into the building, down a set of stairs and into a corridor that terminated at the foot of a large blast door. Two armed guards—deadlier in appearance than the two Cray had met outside—stood watch in front of the door, pulse rifles constantly held at the ready. Walking through, Cray heard a magnetic seal kicking in as the automated sentry detected their presence—insurance against ricochets bouncing into the occupied areas above, should any weapons fire erupt.

The guards stood aside for Avalon, who leaned over to punch a key code into the security panel, then provided a retinal scan for confirmation. The blast door gave a loud clang as the locking bolts disengaged, then opened with little more than a low hiss. Beyond, a series of lights came on and revealed a pressurized sterile corridor that stretched on for several meters. A puff of air skittered across Cray's face as he stepped up to the entryway, lights meshing with the whiteness of the walls to create a spectral tunnel. At the other end, another closed area awaited.

The blast door slid shut behind them as soon as they were inside. A decontamination field then went to work, eradicating microbes from the surface of their skin. Cray felt nothing in a conventional sense—though he was unsettled by a vague notion of life being drained from the room—and after a few seconds the process was over. That was when the second door opened, revealing for the first time what the Assembly had in mind for him.

It made Cray remember the first time he had been in a jack house. He didn't know how many of them had been in there—twenty, maybe thirty altogether. They had all come to interface, with each other or with the Axis, their heads sprouting electrodes and plugged into a common hub. Some of them had died that way, the passage of days marked by the smell that savaged the place. Those who were still alive never even noticed.

This setup was infinitely cleaner and more sophisticated, but only masked the same dark purpose. Individual link stations, a dozen in all, were arranged in two neat rows—each one containing an unconscious occupant, strapped down to keep the slack bodies from sliding out. Their faces were not visible, heads encased within link sheaths that pumped information in and out of adjoining nodes like so much raw sewage. When he saw the technicians running around and keeping watch over their people, Cray could not disjoin the images of that jack house—or the belief that what happened here was little better than self-mutilation.

Then there was the chair at the end of the row. The empty chair waiting for *him*.

Two technicians stood behind the link station. One of them

unbuckled the restraints that would hold him, while the other opened the sheath that would ensnare his head. Cray turned to Avalon, his eyes narrowing. He saw his reflection in the black of her lenses.

"What the hell is this?"

"The Audience Chamber," she replied impassively. "These people will monitor you during your interface with the Assembly."

"Nobody said anything about an interface," Cray protested. He was still cool, but let a trickle of rage seep through to show her that he was dead serious. "Phao Yin said the Assembly would be *meeting* with me, directly."

"The Assembly conducts all of its affairs in this manner," Avalon said, as if she were explaining to an idiot child. "You are no exception to the rule, Dr. Alden."

"Forget the *rule,* Avalon. If your bosses want to deal with me, they can do it face-to-face. Otherwise, I'm out of here."

"I don't understand the problem."

"I don't interface," Cray said. "As long as we have that clear, we *have* no problem."

Avalon considered this new development. Clearly, it was a segment of his personality missing from his profile, which put her in the position of having to make a choice. Cray knew he was shit out of luck if she decided to use force—there was nothing to stop her from tying him down to the chair, if those were her orders. It was just a matter of how important Cray was to her employers.

Avalon nodded at the two technicians. They shut down the link station, moving to tend to the others.

Cray released a long, slow breath. He didn't gloat over it. He had spent too much luck already. But as Avalon turned back toward him, her posture made it clear that she would tolerate no more. Business was business—and one more step in the wrong direction would change Cray from an asset into a liability.

"Come with me," she told him.

Cray sensed the acceleration dampers kicking in as soon as the elevator doors closed. They descended far and fast—much farther than he would have expected in a diplomatic facility. It continued on for over half a minute, by which time the elevator had dropped well over a thousand meters—a hole deep enough to bury the GenTec tower with room to spare. Cray had seen nukeproof military installations without that much earth over them.

What are they protecting here?

"So what's the deal?" Avalon asked him.

"What?"

"Up there," she clarified. "The interface. A spook getting weirded out over a simple input—it doesn't make much sense."

"There's a lot about me that doesn't make sense."

Avalon took out his MFI. "That's what you use this for," she said, examining the device. "Face kits, virtual terminals—all so you don't have to plug into the Axis."

"Something like that."

"You ever done it before?"

"A long time ago." Cray raised an eyebrow. "You?"

"Not possible," she replied, putting the device away.

"Any particular reason?"

"Nerve injury," she said dispassionately. "The Olympus Mons virus. You survive the disease, the damage is permanent."

"How bad?"

Avalon considered it for a few moments, as if nobody had ever asked before. She then lowered her head, reaching up slowly to pull off her glasses. When Avalon opened her eyes, what stared back at Cray put an even greater wedge between what she was and what she used to be. Two misty sacs stared back at him—a cornucopia of murky colors swirling within, repositories for the virus that still infected her. Beneath that, tiny bursts of light punctuated a dull, constant glow.

Neurostatic implants, Cray thought. The microscopic devices stopped the progression of the disease, though nothing could fully eradicate it. At best, it was survival by margins: Avalon had survived the process, but paid dearly with her senses. Sight, sound, touch, taste—all of them were memories, replaced by artificial means.

"You didn't notice," she remarked, putting the glasses back on.

He checked her out more closely, realizing he *should* have seen it. Thousands of tiny clusters were woven into the fabric of her clothing, forming an intricate web that covered her entire body. *A sensuit,* Cray thought, marveling at its elegance. The virus had destroyed her ability to feel, but the suit provided her with a sensory range that far exceeded his own—a useful edge in her line of work. Cray wouldn't have been surprised if she had hyperaccurate readings of his heart rate, body temperature, blood pressure—all of which raised intriguing possibilities if he ever found himself having to lie to her. Avalon would probably detect it in an instant.

The elevator decelerated, the dampers playing a brief game with his balance before it came to a stop. Cray's ears popped slightly as the car equalized with the atmosphere outside the doors and Avalon keyed another sequence into the code panel. "We keep a minimal staff in the lower chambers," she said. "That includes security personnel, so you'll have to be careful about the sentry. The threat detectors are set to an *extremely* low threshold. You run off into an area you're not supposed to, you're going to get lit up."

"You don't get many visitors, do you?"

"No, Dr. Alden," she said as the doors opened. "We don't get *any* visitors."

Outside, the lights didn't even come on until the sensors detected their presence—and when they did, Cray came up against what looked like a solid wall. A loud Klaxon sounded at their arrival, and the wall began to rise. A cloud of frost particles sublimated out of the air beneath, spreading out in a hazy curtain that obscured the chamber behind it. Cray detected the smell of cryogenic elements—a kind of wet, charged taste that settled on the back of his tongue—while a chill enveloped the rest of his body. On a subconscious level, he had already guessed what he would find when the mists parted.

Avalon allowed him to step through first. The way was still obscured by fog, augmenting the clink of his steps against the metal grate beneath his feet. By the time he reached the glass wall, the air had cleared enough for him to find his reflection in the surface— Avalon still partially obscured in the background, keeping the ever-present watch. Shifting his focus forward, Cray looked past the transparent barrier and into the secret the Collective had buried here—one so well kept, even the most skilled hammerjacks never caught scent of it.

There were seven sarcophagi—one for each man who found a sort of immortality here. They were reverently arranged in a perfect circle, an incandescent aura raining down on them from floodlights in the ceiling. A small team of specialists tended to the vessels, closely monitoring the faint life signs of what remained of the Assembly's human bodies, pressure suits protecting them from the extremes of temperature and vacuum that existed inside the chamber.

"Why?" Cray asked.

"The Assembly decided this was the most efficient way to maintain consistency within the body of the Collective."

"You mean the best way to make sure nobody new comes in and alters their plans," Cray observed. "How long have they been like this?"

"This facility has been operating for just over a century. Before that, nobody really knows for certain."

"And you managed to keep it a secret."

"Knowledge is limited to the corporate boards and the few people who work here," Avalon explained. "Induction into the *Yakuza* is mandatory for all of them—even the non-Asians. After that, they are required to take the oath of silence. Anybody who breaks it is subject to the usual penalties."

Cray turned back toward her. "They make you do the same?"

"Nobody makes me do anything, Dr. Alden."

Avalon walked past him, down a narrow gangway that wound its way to a control bunker for the cryofacility. As Cray followed, the nagging sliver of paranoia he had brought with him from the hotel began to rub him raw. He knew about *Yakuza* culture—he had seen more than his fair share of it in the Zone—and was aware of how those tentacles reached into the corporate world. It was why companies kept old bangers like Phao Yin around. But Cray had never imagined blood oaths taken in the boardroom.

That left him in a dangerous position. Cray was hardly a made man—and now he knew the Collective's most guarded secret. They were bound to take steps to ensure that information never made it out to the street. The *Yakuza* were obligated.

Cray wished he had never come here.

A spiral staircase at the end of the gangway led down to the bunker. Sentry cameras followed Cray the entire way, laser range finders mapping the contours of his body for identification, comparison, and tracking. By the time he reached bottom, the computer had created a precise mathematical representation of him. From here on in, he was alive only as long as that construct remained active. If the computer determined he was a threat and terminated it, his death would follow a short instant later.

Entry to the control bunker was less sophisticated. Avalon simply knocked on the titanium alloy door and waited for someone inside to open it.

One of the technicians—a tall, gangly man with pasty skin—answered. His eyes had the dazed, detached expression of a person more accustomed to dealing with machines than people. He did, however, know Avalon.

"I thought you were kidding," the man grumbled, glancing over her shoulder at Cray. "*This* is the hotshot everyone's been talking about?"

"Evan," Avalon said, "this is Dr. Alden."

Evan stifled her with a wave of his hand. "The less I know about him the better," he shot back. "Just get him in here so I can get the prep work done. We're already behind schedule."

"I'm afraid to ask," Cray said. "What exactly does he have in mind?"

"He's granting your request to meet with the Assembly."

"What's he going to do? Thaw them out?"

"No," she answered. "He's going to make a map of your mind."

Evan hunched over the only virtual terminal in the control bunker, bony fingers moving across the input interface in a blur. The display showed a pair of EEG lines moving in almost perfect concert with each other. It was when they diverged—even in the slightest—that he showed his disgust with an irritated sigh.

"Tell him to try it again," he said to Avalon.

"I heard you," Cray spat back, already tired of the procedure. It was better than a direct interface, but not by much. "Just shut up long enough for me to get a little focus."

He was laid out on a probe table, the top half of his skull under an electrochemical resonance imager. Evan transmitted a random series of three-dimensional images into the ERI, each time measuring Cray's response to them. He then painstakingly traced the neural pathways in the cognizant areas of Cray's brain, trying to match those impulses with the artificial ones generated by the Assembly's imaging system. The technology was old—there had been little use for neural imaging since direct interface had become a working reality—but at least it was noninvasive.

"Okay," Evan said, letting the lines play themselves out for a few more seconds. He didn't sound at all satisfied—only resigned that this was as good as it would get. "It's borderline synchronization, but I think it's enough to make it work."

The ERI retracted, and finally Cray could get up. "Did I pass?"

"Barely," the technician retorted, turning back to Avalon. "I'm not guaranteeing the image won't flake out. The whole thing could collapse while he's in the imaging chamber."

"Just hold it together as long as you can," she told him, then went over to Cray. He stood in front of the virtual display, looking at the model that was his mind. The numbers seemed infinitely complex, deftly interwoven, surely the design of a higher power—but quantifiable nonetheless.

"You think that's all there is to it?" he asked. "Just a bunch of figures, arranged in the right order?"

Avalon was quiet. The pause was enough to grab Cray's attention, and when he turned to her he thought he saw *hesitation* there.

"Perception makes the reality," she said. "Past that, it's only chemicals and meat."

Cray flashed a wry smile, then shot a look at Evan, jerking his thumb toward the mind model. "You're gonna erase that thing when we're done, right?"

The man snorted. "It ain't going in my collection."

"What a relief. So what's next?"

Evan rolled his chair over to another control panel, wiping the dust off and flipping one of the switches. The panel lit up, and on the opposite end of the room Cray heard a hiss as yet another door opened. It led into a small vestibule, with room for only one person inside. The interior space was featureless, except for the photophores embedded in its walls. They glowed a multitude of colors as light bounced off, shifting as the viewing angle changed.

The technician smiled, showing off a mouth full of polished teeth.

"Step inside, cowboy," he said.

When the door closed, Cray was in darkness.

The chamber filled with the sound of his breath, the smell of his sweat. He was accustomed to tight spaces, but the oppression of his body heat soon gave rise to the notion that the walls were closing in. Cray knew it was all psychological—maybe even a game run by his congenial host—but knowing that wouldn't prevent the panic of sensory deprivation. Jerking his head back and forth, he searched the blackness for anything he could seize upon, his arms reaching out so that he could steady himself against the walls.

But nothing was there.

He felt just the opposite. The space *expanded,* the realization of it drowning Cray in a vertigo of empty space. The violent transition almost made him sick, and he found himself stumbling. He could have been running—Cray didn't know, because he lacked the reference points to orient himself. He only knew that he wasn't *floating* because of the tangible presence of ground beneath him.

Then sound: a steady thrumming, off in the distance.

Then light: barely a stab, a spearhead in the darkness.

Reality assimilated.

Cray expected a chorus of sensation exploding upon his plane of vision—but it was all just *there,* as if it had appeared under the most ordinary of circumstances. Light shimmered through water, his awareness fixating on a drape of bubbles—thousands of them— pushing their way upward in an endless stream, consciousness rising with them. Microcosm then shifted to macrocosm, a recession that dropped him into a larger world that materialized at the same pace he became aware of it, components pixelating into just the right proportions to create form out of the void. He found himself staring through the glass of a saltwater aquarium—tropical fish swimming through a tiny continuum of coral, a single sea fan waving in the gentle current. One of the fish stopped briefly to gaze at him, then realized its folly and moved on.

The thrumming he had heard continued: a pump motor in a reassuring drone. Cray's first notion was that he might be *inside* the aquarium, but the idea quickly passed as he felt himself sitting down in a couch of plush leather.

Turning outward, Cray found himself in the waiting room of a small office. A coffee table snapped into focus in front of him, on which he saw a stack of old magazines. He stood, his eyes coming across several empty chairs, walls containing nondescript art, a few potted plants, and a lonely coatrack standing just inside a frosted-glass door.

Then another sound—different, chaotic, frenzied.

Tapping, coming from behind him.

Cray spun around, and discovered that he was not alone in the room. A young woman—a secretary—was banging away on a typewriter, her attention intently focused on the page in front of her. Slowly, uncertainly, Cray walked over to her desk.

"Excuse me—"

She hit the wrong key and stopped typing. "*Shit,*" the woman said, ripping the sheet of paper out of the typewriter. "Goddamn carbon copies. Always happens when I get to the end of a document."

"Sorry about that."

"Yeah, whatever." She looked up at him. "You here to see the Assembly?"

"That's the idea," Cray said, still trying to get his bearings. "Don't know if I'm in the right place."

The secretary was unimpressed. "Here," she said, pulling out a clipboard with a sign-in sheet attached. "Name, address, and phone number—and don't put down anything phony. That really pisses off the boss."

Cray scribbled down the information and handed it back to her. She looked it over. "Out-of-towner, huh?"

"You could say that."

"Most of them are." The secretary reached into her desk and pulled out a pack of cigarettes, lighting up as she hit the intercom buzzer. "Dr. Alden is here." She exhaled a cloud of blue smoke.

"Wonderful," came the reply. The voice was polite, with a strange accent. "Please send him in."

The secretary pointed to the wooden door behind her desk. "Help yourself."

"Thanks," Cray told her, going over to the door and placing his hand on the knob. He glanced back before turning it. "Got any advice?"

The secretary took another long drag, leaving a smear of bright red lipstick on the butt of her cigarette. Her eyes were worn and wise, in spite of her youthful appearance. But that was all it was—an appearance.

"That's what I thought," Cray said, and went inside.

It was a frosty hell. Enough to bite straight through his clothes and singe his skin, tapering off to establish a kind of equilibrium—a shift as radical as when he first arrived, but when he looked down he stood upon different ground.

Gravel. Stone. No floor—only bare soil.

Weathered soil, having seen the abuse of the elements and the ages—the telltale signs of a forsaken place. Cray was aware that he no longer had a doorknob in his hand. Instead, his arm extended to a canvas tent flap fluttering above his head.

The welcoming ebb of a real fire brushed against his face, while a cold, harsh plume pushed against his back, ushering him into the tent. The howl of the wind outside told him it was a constant companion there—like a lonely, pained animal forever wanting to get in.

Cray studied the interior. He was in a large tent—too big for a single person, with piles of mountain gear strewn about the place. He noticed several tables littered with tin cups and dirty plates, leaving him to wonder if he had somehow interrupted lunch. Taking a walk through, Cray poked at the backpacks with his foot and examined the remnants of the meal to find any signs of recent activity—but he found only dust. Nobody had touched anything for some time.

But what about the fire?

The warmth emanated from a pipe stove at the center of the tent. Cray went over and warmed his hands, the licking flames and rising heat an alien presence—as alien as he was.

"Where *is* everybody?"

"We're here," somebody answered. "You just have to know how to look."

The voice came from one of the corners of the tent—*appeared* was more like it, much like the man to whom the voice belonged. When he stepped forward, Cray was amazed at how he could have missed anyone of that size. The man wasn't tall, but the breadth of his shoulders was easily twice Cray's own. His arms looked as sturdy as steel ropes, folded in front of a barrel chest—the physique of a man who spent his life living at altitude.

He was dressed in an amalgam of the primitive and modern—crude handmade beads hanging from his neck, with a coat engineered for the most extreme climates draped over his shoulders. Below that he wore blue jeans, the cuffs tucked into waterproof hiking boots. His features were Eurasian: the eyes faintly slanted, the skin a rich brown tinged with yellow. Based on all the mountain gear, Cray had him figured for a Sherpa—a reference that was purely historical. Those people had been extinct for over a hundred years, their culture swallowed up like so many others steamrolled by the civilized world.

About the time the Assembly went into stasis.

"Dr. Alden, I presume," the Sherpa said.

Cray studied him. "You have me at a disadvantage."

"Of course I do," the Sherpa replied. "That's how we designed it."

He offered Cray a seat at one of the tables, then sat down across from him. What followed was a long, complicated stare—the sophistication behind the Sherpa's eyes a contradiction of his old world façade.

"So," Cray started. "What is this, anyway? My dream, or yours?"

"It's not nearly that complicated," the Sherpa explained. "A series of common reference points generated to keep our minds glued to reality while we're in stasis. All we did was let you in on the party."

"You picked a hell of a construct."

"It's the easiest crossover we could find. If you had dropped in on one of our other horizons, the transitional shock would have killed you—or at the very least, made you insane. We're not that used to company, I'm afraid."

"Sorry to intrude."

"What's done is done." The Sherpa leaned back, still regarding him with that pseudoclairvoyant expression—like he was already tunneling into Cray's mind. "We've been under so long, it's doubtful we could ever return to corporeal life. Lack of sensory input, you know. Same thing will happen to you, if you stay long enough."

"Is that what you have in mind for me?"

The Sherpa laughed. "On the contrary, Dr. Alden," he said. "None of this would have been necessary had you just allowed us to plug you in. All data, no images—*that*'s the way to do business. No messy subjectives to deal with."

Cray looked back at the enigma across the table. The Sherpa sat there for a while, allowing him to work it out for himself.

"*You're* the Assembly."

"You see?" the Sherpa said, with a genteel nod. "You're starting to adapt already." He got up and walked over to the stove, stirring the coals with a poker as he explained. "Everything here is a logical representation, Dr. Alden—including you. Even so, our physical conventions are flexible. By combining ourselves into a single entity, we can facilitate more efficient communication."

"Must play hell with the ego."

"It's a kick, actually." He picked a pot up off the stove. "How about some breakfast?"

"Already ate."

"Just as well. The food here tastes like shit anyway." The Sherpa went over to the entrance of the tent, opening up one of the stray

backpacks and retrieving a leather pouch. He tucked the pouch under his arm, then motioned for Cray to follow. "Why don't you
come outside and help me? I'll fill you in on the details, then you can
tell me how you want to proceed."

"By that," Cray asked, "do you mean I have a choice in the
matter?"

"You have a great many choices, Dr. Alden," the Sherpa told him,
not sounding at all threatening. "But you'll find there is only one
sensible choice for you to make—if you wish to continue breathing."

Sunshine came down like a hammer, filtered through the thin atmosphere of high altitude. The stark effect of the light was as chilling as
the air that cut through it.

Cray had to shield his eyes from the brightness, neural illusion or
no. Under the shadow of his hand, he peeked out at the panorama
that surrounded him and was astonished by its beauty, complexity—
and magnificent desolation. A barren moonscape of ice and rock
crunched beneath Cray's feet as he walked. Towering over that were
the mountains, silent sentinels that rose over nine thousand meters
into the sky. The hurricane winds of the stratosphere blew snow off
the peaks into gentle plumes and anvil formations, brute force translating into ethereal art. The rendering of it all was sheer perfection,
even if the technology that produced it was ancient.

The Sherpa led Cray toward a craggy stone monolith. It was little
more than a pile of rocks, adorned with a number of strange items.
Colorful banners, flapping in the breeze, were draped all over it, and
as Cray drew closer he could see photographs attached wherever
there was room to hang them. There were dozens—some old, some
new, keeping vigil over a small pile of abandoned climbing gear that
rested at the base of the monolith. Cray thought at first that it was a
memorial to those who had gone up the mountains, never to return.
But then he noticed that all the photos depicted only seven men—
different poses, different settings, even different times—but always
the same faces, over and over again.

The Assembly.

A tombstone for those who were dead, but not dead.

"I see the *Punjab* bodes well for us," the Sherpa said, unwrapping the leather pouch he had brought with him. Out came a string of the colored banners, which flapped like kites, urged on by the wind. "Here," he said, handing one end to Cray. "Help me hang these prayer flags. With the journey you're about to take, you'll need all the help you can get."

"Sounds like you have a job for me."

"Nothing *that* simple." The Sherpa laughed. He walked the string around the monolith, securing his end between a couple of stones. "You see, we have this problem, one that requires a particular kind of expertise. There are some of us in the Assembly who believe that your unorthodox background would fit the bill perfectly."

"*Some* of you," Cray wondered aloud.

"The rest believe you should not be allowed to leave this facility alive."

Cray had already considered that possibility. Still, hearing it intrigued him.

"At any rate," the Sherpa went on, "cooler heads have prevailed—at least for now. I cannot, however, guarantee how long the situation can continue. We are all anxious to resolve this matter, Dr. Alden—and we demand results quickly. Mysterious enough for you?"

"I don't care for mysteries. What's this all about?"

The Sherpa answered the question with one of his own.

"What do you know about bionucleic technology, Dr. Alden?"

Cray's first reaction was to laugh. It was an outburst that ceased as soon as he saw his host didn't respond in kind.

"You're kidding, right?"

"Just tell me what you know."

"Only what I've heard," Cray said, stalling for time as he figured out how much he should let slip. He was privy to a lot of things he wasn't supposed to know. "There were some ventures that fooled around with the idea a few years back, but they could never make it work."

"And why was that?"

"Same problem everybody's had with conventional SIs." Cray

shrugged. "The input matrix is too unstable. It falls apart after a few cycles."

"Putting up the last barrier that stands between humanity and true synthetic intelligence," the Sherpa finished for him. He then leaned toward Cray, conveying the quiet urgency of a conspiracy. "What if I told you we had breached that barrier, Dr. Alden? Would it interest you to learn more?"

Cray's most abject fears and impossible hopes were conveyed in that request, because they were one and the same. This was more than a secret the Assembly was telling him. It was confirming the existence of God.

Or at least the creation of Him.

"Tell me," Cray said.

"Yes?"

Phao Yin lay in the dark, synthetic pheromones swarming around him like microscopic insects. They were everywhere: on the sheets of his bed, in the fibers of the rugs, smeared across his bare skin. He smelled like street species, and in spite of himself he liked it.

"We ran the tests you requested."

Yin turned over, toward the link next to his bed. It was always like this, those rare occasions when they spoke with him—the same remote condescension, as if they were dealing with a lower form. In that respect, they weren't much different from his masters in the Assembly. And like the Assembly, they had no idea who they were dealing with.

"What did you find?" Yin asked.

"Indications are positive."

He released a deep breath. "You're certain?"

"Mortality factors were activated at the time of Zoe's death," the disembodied voice told him. In spite of the subject matter, it remained devoid of emotion. "Are you aware of anybody who was in close proximity when the event occurred?"

"Only one."

"Do you know where that person is?"

"Yes."

"What is your reach?"

The fingers of Yin's hands curled together into claws—a reminder of his physical body, his physical nature.

"My reach is more than enough," he said with assurance. "I will, however, have to wait if I am to avoid complications."

"We are not concerned with complications."

"I will take action as soon as it is feasible." Yin bit down on the words, suppressing the anger behind them. "There is no need to alter the plan."

"The plan has already been altered," the voice argued. "First with Zoe, now with this new development. There are those who feel that you are not up to this task." A long silence ensued. "What shall I tell them?"

Yin thought of Cray. Had the Assembly not ordered him to Vienna, the man would already be on the table in some *Inru* lab. The thought gave Yin momentary pleasure, but for the moment it would have to remain a fantasy. He had not come this far only to be thwarted. Yin would make his move against the Assembly, but only when he was ready.

"Just tell them to be prepared," he said, and snapped off the link.

Yin rolled onto his back and stared at the ceiling, trying to regain the nirvana that the evening's murder had inspired. His need for amusement had rendered two more corpses, one for each side of his bed, quietly cooling in the fragrant air of his bedroom. Yin had granted them a peaceful death—fast poison in the guise of neuropatches—for violence was not his motive. He only wanted their company, but without any of their needs and desires.

That nirvana, however, was fleeting, gone with the voices on the other end of the link.

Fools, he thought, quelling his bitterness. *This is the price I pay for ambition.*

And what a grand ambition it was. Yin had to console himself with that, in spite of the setback with Alden. He would find a way to spin it to his advantage, Yin knew—but in the meanwhile, he turned his mind back to the objective. The Assembly, of course, suspected nothing. They probably thought Yin incapable of such treachery, with his street credentials and gangland origins. It was the reason they had advanced him along the circle of their power but had never allowed him to enter. To them, Yin was *inferior*—useful, but inferior, an attack dog who would remain loyal as long as he was well fed.

But Yin was more hungry than that. Wealth, like murder, was a temporary diversion. It only aroused his appetite for what the Assembly decreed he could never have.

Real power.

The power to move nations. The power to destroy worlds. The Assembly embodied that power, like no other force in history. They were universal, absolute, untouchable.

How could Yin resist a challenge like that?

CHAPTER

FIVE

Below the stars, the purple twilight curve of Earth's terminator carved a crescent slash through the fabric of night, opening up an abyss of blackness that beckoned the irresistible plunge, hypnotic in all its magnetism. He could almost feel himself falling, and liking it.

Synthetic intelligence.

The whisper-whine of the SOT's ramjet engines, more felt than heard, was a welcome intrusion into Cray's thoughts, helping to arrange concepts on the blank slate inside his head. All the things he knew or thought he knew—all the preconceptions that had become so much bullshit—presented themselves for inspection and were quickly dismissed. Science was like that: law today, superstition the next, a kick where you felt the most vulnerable.

Bionucleic technology.

It seemed like he was the only one awake in the cabin. He glanced over at the seat next to him and found Avalon eerily still, as she had been since they left Vienna for New York City. Cray wondered if she was sleeping—if she ever slept—and how much she knew about what happened. *Probably everything,* he decided, realizing if that were the case, her information sources were far better than his. There had been whispers about it in the subculture, but never anything to raise the idea above the status of an urban legend—no proof to use as a hook.

Could they have actually made the damned thing work?

Even now Cray was trolling the Axis, trying to find something he might have missed. For the better part of an hour, he had been jacking all of the holes he knew—CSS, corporate propaganda sites, even giving the *Yakuza* a crack—but the streams of data showing up on his MFI didn't show him anything he didn't already know. The Collective had built one hell of a wall to cover up what happened at the Works, and not a single trickle had found its way out. Cray would have admired the job they did, had he not known the methods they employed. People had died to keep this story silent—and more than just a few.

Lyssa, the Assembly called her. *Deus ex machina.*

More than that—an answer to the question.

And the question was: Can synthetic thought exist?

In the present tense, the solution was a zero sum. Granted, there were a number of quasi-intelligent crawlers at large in the Axis—all of them owned by corporations big enough to afford them, deployed primarily as countermeasures to guard against the more resourceful hammerjacks. Toward that end they had achieved their goal, cultivating a mystique that was potent enough to keep the fly-by-nighters from giving them a run. Anywhere you plugged in, you could hear a million stories in the mix about how some poor bastard got himself burned brushing against a crawler—of the nonlinear shifts in logic that could slice your connecting conduits like a razor, setting your mind adrift in logical space. But as powerful as they were, they had never functioned as intended. In that light, the crawler was little more than an interesting, if somewhat useful, failure.

The concept had been to develop a rational, self-sustaining system—essentially a bundle of independent subroutines capable of incorporating previous input into a "creative" decision-making process, allowing functions that went beyond the scope of the original programming. When combined, these subroutines would then integrate with one another and spread their knowledge across a broad spectrum, much as the different complexes of the human brain combined to give rise to conscious thought.

The problem, however, was that the concept worked *too* well.

In imitating the thought processes of the human mind, the

software was also at the mercy of its own idiosyncrasies. The greatest of these was an inherent instability rooted in the function of perception as it pertained to the definition of reality. In psychological terms, existence was merely a consensus among cognizant beings who all believed that they were sharing a common experience. Intelligence was simply an awareness of how one fit into that experience. Things only got out of whack when there wasn't enough input to get a fix on that position—like a prolonged period of sensory deprivation. Insanity would eventually result from such a state, proving that the thread that held aloft the world as everyone knew it was a thin one indeed.

The human mind could easily keep things in balance because of its limited processing capabilities. Senses provided most of the essential input, with the subconscious supplying the rest of what was needed in the form of dreams and other imaginary images. Synthetic intelligence, however, was based on hardware that augmented the human thought process to the nth degree, which created the very real danger of what nanopsychologists theorized as a logical singularity—a data vortex of such magnitude that it would tear a hole in the delicate framework of the Axis itself.

So total was their conceit that they understood the paradigm of human thought, the architects of the first SI modules dismissed that possibility. They just assumed an artificial system, if allowed to grow, would independently develop its own personality and coping mechanisms—which would, in turn, lead to an egotistical need for self-preservation and thus limit any self-destructive tendencies. What they *didn't* understand was that these machines they had built were just that: *machines.* Missing were the biological needs, the instinctual urges, that drove a system to protect its own life. With millions of years of evolution missing, with the removal of any drives to perpetuate its own species, all that was left was existence.

And existence was not enough.

Upon activation, an SI would immediately begin to define its own place in the universe. Within a period of nanoseconds, it would absorb all of the available information in its immediate surroundings and seek to find more. But being only a test unit, the module would find itself totally isolated from outside networks—horribly confined, a black hole in empty space with nothing to consume but itself. The scenario played itself out again and again, with every new module being tested. No matter how fast the engineers tried to feed data into the system, they simply could not keep up with the demand. The SI would either terminate itself or become so hopelessly imbalanced as to be useless.

Such had been the state of the technology for the last several decades, putting up the barrier that none had been able to breach. The Collective had been able to salvage some of the basics, purging the cores of a few failed modules and recapping the component subroutines—putting a limit on how much "thinking" the system could do, then repackaging them for sale as the crawlers that created so much terror across the Axis. In reality, the crawlers had no more critical-reasoning ability than that of a well-trained dog. Even so, they still required enormous amounts of input to keep them stable, making them costly to maintain and a bitch to operate.

Bionucleics was supposed to change all that.

`hey alden`

Cray had his eyes closed, the burned images from the last few days playing across the inside of his lids. The series ended with him standing in the snow alone, abandoned after his Sherpa had delivered the Assembly's ultimatum.

`alden wake up`

Everything depends on what you do for us now, the Sherpa had said. *If you can't provide us with a solution, you won't be of much use to us.*

`jesus alden —do you expect me to do everything myself`

He had thoughts of falling asleep, but the flash of something brilliant and disturbing brought him out of it. Intuition, maybe—or just the stale hangover of fear. Cray had been living with the fear for a long time, that he would be seen for what he was and not what he pretended to be. Bleary eyes drifted to the palm of his hand, where the MFI rested. On the tiny screen, the words appeared:

```
it's about goddamn time — how about you get
away from vampira so the two of us can talk
```

Cray blanked the screen out of reflex, with a single flip of his thumb. He turned slightly to see if there was any reaction from Avalon, hoping that all she had noticed was the tilt of his head. Sensors picking up on his increased heartbeat, her lips formed the words while the rest of her remained totally still.

"Something up?" she asked.

"Bad dream," Cray lied. It was a plausible enough explanation for the deceptive physical signals he gave off. "I need to go throw some water on my face. You're not gonna follow me into the head, are you?"

"Only if you need help."

"I might get myself a drink, too," Cray said, getting out of his seat. "You want me to bring you anything?"

Avalon shook her head.

"Back in a few minutes." He strolled down the aisle and tried not to glance back. Eventually, he wandered all the way out of first class, slipping into one of the flight attendant stations while none of the crew were watching. Cray hoped it was far enough away to keep Avalon from eavesdropping.

Cray unclenched his right hand, revealing the empty screen of his MFI. He hit one of the buttons to wake the miniature device back up. Moments passed, the cursor blinking on-screen.

"Come on," Cray whispered. "Don't get shy on me now."

Pixels fluttered, coalescing into language:

```
alone at last
```

The routine was familiar. Cray thought of the message that had been waiting for him back at the Bristol, the code that was not code. "You little prick. You don't give up that easy, do you?"

`fuck off alden — i'm the one taking the`
`risk here`

Direct response to verbal input. This was more than just some
piggyback rider on a remote carrier pulse. This was active control, a
real-time jack—one pretty piece of work.

"Nice to finally meet you, Heretic."

`pleasure is all yours i'm sure`

Cray had already lost his patience. He keyed a sequence in to
dump the MFI's memory and rid himself of the intruder—but when
he sent the command, there was no response. He mashed down on
the key a few more times, but still nothing happened.

`now now —didn't anybody teach you to play`
`nice`

He had no more control over the unit. As usual, Heretic had been
very thorough.

"Damn," Cray said.

`save it doc —right now we need some pri-`
`vacy if we want to get this transaction`
`done`

"What the hell do you want?"

`turn around`

Cray did as he was told and faced the rear bulkhead of the attendant station. There were several cabinets of storage space, a luggage
compartment, a vid link to the cockpit—and the crew lift, which led
down into the SOT's lower decks and the avionics bay. The sliding
door was controlled electronically, a small indicator panel showing
that it was locked.

```
   i'll jack the door — then take the lift all
the way down
```

Cray checked the aisle once more to see if the way was clear. One of the attendants was heading his way, which didn't give him a lot of time.

"Great," Cray grumbled, jumping on the lock with his MFI and letting Heretic run through a random series of code combinations. There were only four digits to be sorted out, which the computer came up with almost instantly, but even then Cray barely managed to slip into the lift before being discovered. He ducked down and waited for the attendant to leave, giving it another minute before punching the button for the bottom deck.

When he arrived, Cray discovered the reason Heretic had chosen this as their meeting place. The avionics bay was magnetically shielded to keep solar radiation from interfering with the SOT's flight instruments—which meant the compartment was also impervious to Avalon's sensors. Even if she tried, she would not be able to hear them down here.

Cray slid the lift door open, immersing himself in the deep drone of the SOT's engines. It was dark, the scant illumination provided by glowing lights on the banks of electronic equipment. Stepping into the bay, he made a quick sweep around—checking all the murky corners to make sure he was alone.

Heretic's presence on his MFI was still active. The real-time jack had been severed because of the magnetic shielding, but a quick check of the unit's memory buffer told Cray that the intruder had deposited himself there. With resources maxed out, Cray could now overload the buffers and kick Heretic out.

If he wanted.

"Got me over a barrel now, Alden," the MFI spoke, anticipating the move. The voice was plain spoken—gender neutral, with an accent that was distinctly artificial. "But even now I'm tunneling into your ROM. I can reconstruct myself from those scraps if I have to."

"Not if I shoot this thing into space."

The MFI was quiet for a moment. "I hadn't thought of that."

"Real-time response to new input," Cray observed. "Not a bad trick. How much of you is in there, anyway?"

"Enough to answer a few questions. I figured you'd be curious."

Cray decided to go along—for now. "When did you jack my MFI?"

"Let's just say I've heard most of the good stuff."

Cray remembered how Avalon had been holding on to his MFI during his time with the Assembly. In passive mode, Heretic could have been recording every bit of telemetry coming off the neural-imaging systems without setting off a single alarm. Cray had designed the covert mechanism himself.

"Slick," Cray said. "Very slick."

"I had the talent," Heretic replied. "You gave me the tools."

"Only as long as you keep talking. So what's this all about, anyway? You pissed at me for what went down in Singapore?"

"I know all about that, Doc. Zone agents killed Zoe—not you."

"Then why have you been dogging me?"

"So I can warn you."

"Typical hammerjack," Cray scoffed. "You never come right out and *say* it. You gotta run a mind game on me first."

"No mind games, Doc," Heretic assured him. It sounded like a bad come-on, but that could have just been the synthetic voice. "If I just dropped a letter in your box, you never would've bought into this. But now you've seen things—not *everything*, but enough to know that I'm not just full of shit."

"That remains to be seen."

"Does that mean you'll listen?"

Cray considered it for a moment. "Okay," he decided. "But make it fast."

"First off," Heretic said, "you need to know that what the Assembly said about Lyssa is true. The bionucleic prototype is fully functional. More than that, its input matrix is stable. It's been running independently for the last two months."

"So why did Lyssa malfunction?"

"She didn't."

Cray was incredulous. "She killed a buildingful of people."

"That's only part of the story. The Assembly didn't tell you everything—which is why they've got a free agent on your ass. She's there to make sure you don't figure out the rest."

"The rest of *what*?"

"The big picture," Heretic explained. "You already knew that Zoe was doing a job for me back in Singapore. What you *don't* know is why I sent her to do it."

"You work for the *Inru*," Cray said. "Anarchy is your bottom line."

"Not anymore," Heretic replied. "As of now, all bets are off. There's a race going on, and the only question is who gets to the finish line first."

"What's the game?"

"Competing synthetic intelligence," Heretic said. "On one side you have the Collective, and their experiment in bionucleics. That's why the Assembly's so damned nervous. They've got every last bit of capital invested in this thing. A failure now would be an even bigger disaster than Mars."

"And on the other side, you have the *Inru*?" Cray asked, not hiding his scorn. "They're just an anti-technology sect—street species on some idealistic crusade. You expect me to believe they're experimenting with bionucleics?"

"Something like that, Doc. The movement has a lot more support—and resources—than you could ever imagine."

Cray checked his watch. He had been gone for almost ten minutes, which meant Avalon had grown suspicious five minutes ago. "Look," he said to the MFI, "I know I've seen some bizarre shit on this job. But let's face it—you're a *hammerjack*. I hunt down people like you for a living. I can't just take what you're saying at face value without some kind of proof."

"You already have the proof," Heretic said. "You just don't know it yet."

"Just tell me where to look."

There was another pause, another silence. The MFI was just processing information, but to Cray it sounded like Heretic wondering how much trust he could show. Like honor among thieves, that kind of trust was hard to come by.

"You've already performed an extraction on Zoe," he finally answered. "Have you seen the results of the analysis?"

"No—" Cray began, remembering Dex Marlowe, and the strange variant of flash Zoe had been carrying around in her bloodstream. "No, my GME is still working on it. Does this have something to do with Lyssa?"

"Take a look at the numbers when they come back," Heretic told him. "When you do, we'll be ready to talk again."

"Wait a second—"

"No," Heretic interrupted. "You'll get the next piece, but only when you're ready for it. I've opened your mind enough for now. Besides, you need to get back. You're no good to me if that barracuda upstairs takes you out."

Cray released a breath.

"And Doc—"

Cray held the MFI in front of his eyes. A vortex of colors swirled on the screen.

"If you think the Assembly will let you live after what you've seen, you're mistaken. You know what they are. Your only chance is to play *them*—as good as you can, as long as you can. The choice is yours, but the odds are better if you keep me close."

"I can't promise that, Heretic."

"Fair enough." The inflection made the voice sound almost human. "Just something for you to keep in mind. Now go and get yourself that drink. You're gonna need it."

Cray brought two drinks back with him—one for the walk back to his seat, one for the rest of the journey. His hope was that his deadened reflexes would provide him with some measure of protection from Avalon, who by now must have been awaiting his return.

He expected some measure of questioning from her when he arrived, but instead got nothing. She barely acknowledged him as he took his seat—not that a turn of her head or any other gesture was any real indication. For Avalon, everything was a defensive tactic, even her indifference.

Cray responded in kind. The encounter below was already beginning to take on the distant character of a dream.

"We'll be landing in ten minutes," she informed him.

Cray buckled his seat belt and yawned.

"Fabulous," he said. "It's been too long since I was in New York."

It was after they jumped off the SOT that Avalon presented Cray with an unprecedented request. "Wait here," she said, ditching him outside a Port Authority bar. "I have to attend to some personal business."

That she would even *have* personal business inspired a certain fascination—as well as a questioning glance, which Avalon answered with her usual, immutable silence. It suggested that the free agent might be making a little mischief of her own—something she didn't want getting back to the Assembly.

Some kind of deal on the side? It was possible, Cray decided, his reason filtered through a glass of milky green absinthe—or what passed for it in an airport lounge. *Maybe even higher up in the chain of command. The whole damned operation is run by gangsters, so why the hell not?*

He sat alone at the bar, taking small sips of the potent drink and relishing the burn that trickled down his throat. He had just about polished it off when something settled in next to him; something dark, moist, and ancient—its breath the air of catacombs, heavy with stale dust. Cray turned toward it, coming face-to-face with a pallid mask of flesh.

"Figures I'd finally meet death in a bar."

The Urban Goth smiled, the spaces between his razor teeth as black as his eyes.

Cray returned to his drink. "I thought you guys always worked in pairs."

"We do," the Goth said, motioning toward his partner, who was

working the sparse crowd in the rest of the bar. "He's new, only recently assimilated. You interested in buying?"

"Sorry, pal."

"Could change your day real fast, *monsieur*. Be not afraid of dying
by the time I get through with you."

Cray held up his glass. "That's what I have this for, *mon frère*," he
said. "But maybe you can deal me some information while you're
here. Interested?"

The Goth's contortion of a smile disappeared. He backed off a
few centimeters—subtle anxiety, like a dog that was used to being
whipped. "You CSS?"

"No," Cray said, shaking his head. "Not even cop. If I was, I
wouldn't need answers now, would I?"

The Goth seemed to treat this as reasonable. He relaxed.

Cray slipped a few shiny coins out of his pocket and placed them
down on the bar. Not the currency standard, but gold Krugerrands—
good for any merchandise traffic in the Zone, with no questions
asked. They glinted tantalizingly in the cheap neon light.

The Goth licked his lips, black tongue trembling.

"What do you want to know?"

Cray observed his friend closely. "The *Inru*," he asked. "They
wouldn't have been involved in that business at the Works a couple
of days ago—would they?"

The Goth put on a mask of nonchalance. "What would *I* know
about *Inru*?" He laughed, putting too much effort into it. His eyes,
however, never left the pile of money in front of him.

"You live and die by the hustle, my man," Cray reminded him.
"You don't catch the vibe, you don't eat."

This time, the Goth observed *him*.

"You species?"

"Close enough."

The Goth's eyes narrowed, awareness percolating within the dark
spheres.

"Spook," he pronounced. "Guys like you always looking for
trouble."

"At least guys like me don't hassle you."

The Goth thought about it for a moment, gradually allowing his greed enough traction to overcome his fear. Tentatively, his hand reached out—a single, bony finger hovering above one of the Krugerrands. He waited for Cray to nod his approval, then slid the gold piece into the recesses of his black robe.

"The *Inru* know about everything, *monsieur*."

"They know about what was going on inside that building?"

"Not really sure," the Goth answered. "They only spread the word on the street. Something big going down, they say—everybody gotta be at the Works to watch it happen." He shrugged. "Some of us believe the word, some of us don't."

"You're one of the nonbelievers."

"I don't do no religion like that, you know? I already find my faith in the deathplay. Got my catharsis there. Don't need to be no slave to the word, okay?"

Cray held up his hands. "Fine with me, pal," he said. "So what happened when all your people went over there?"

The Goth eyed the money again. Cray let him take another coin.

"Nobody knows," he said.

Cray seethed quietly.

"I didn't need to pay to hear *that*."

The Goth pleaded innocent. "It's the truth, *monsieur*."

"It's not very *useful*," Cray retorted. "And since I don't take re-funds, I suggest you come up with something—or else the next deathplay your buddy runs just might be on *you*."

The Goth tossed about a few nervous glances, gathering enough wits to let Cray in on the secret. "All *right, monsieur*," he said, caving in. "You the man making the deal. But I swear—all I got are the sto-ries I been hearing, you know? Folks be whispering in the street, right?"

"I'm listening."

The Goth leaned in close. "The reason nobody be talking is that nobody ever get *back* from the Works that night." The words came out on his breath, making them sound as ghostly as the tale they were telling. "Everybody—they just *disappear,* like they was never there. They all just turn to vapor."

"Where did they go?"

The Goth shook his head. "The *Inru* priests," he began, like he was speaking of old myths, "they say that all the species—all the folks that was there—they all went on to the Ascension."

The story had its intended effect. Cray sat in silence as he assembled it all in his head. Finally, he mustered a response.

"That's bullshit."

"That what I used to think," the Goth replied. "Now not so sure."

Sincerity was not a known trait of street species, but the way this Goth was telling it made him difficult to dismiss. God knew, there were enough crazy stories floating around in the subculture, most of them hallucinogenic tales spun by patch fiends and techeads. But the Ascension—*that* was a dogma that had been around for a while, even before the *Inru* started preaching doctrine to the stoned and the displaced. It was a street religion, to be sure—but that didn't mean it couldn't have some basis in reality.

"How many are we talking about?" Cray asked.

The Goth shook his head. "They say two hundred. Maybe more."

"You don't just disappear two hundred people, my man."

"They not just disappearing, *monsieur,*" the Goth assured him. "They *evolving.*"

It was all Cray would get out of him. Still, the Goth eyed the remainder of the coins hungrily, hoping to scoop them up without getting his hand cut off.

Cray deposited his empty glass next to the money and stood up. "You can pay for my drink," he said, tapping the Goth lightly on the shoulder as he left. When he reached the door, Avalon was waiting.

"Been here long?" he asked.

She didn't answer, motioning toward his friend at the bar. "Death rush addicts," she remarked, allowing a hint of disdain to slip. "Not the most reliable source of information, Dr. Alden. You could have saved yourself some money."

"Call me a sucker for hard luck cases," Cray said. "Anyway, he was a lot more straight with me than your bosses were. You got your business taken care of?"

Avalon nodded, blind eyes turning back toward him. "A corporate transport is waiting for us on Platform D," she told him, handing over a security voucher. "We leave in five minutes."

"For where?"

"CSS Division Headquarters."

"Sounds like you're putting me under arrest."

"Not yet," Avalon said. "But give it time."

Tensile energy radiated across the night sky like spokes on a wheel, converging on the island of Manhattan as if it were the center of the universe. Riding one of those tendrils, a pulser silently glided on an elegant path toward the towers of the Upper West Side, joining the chorus of other vehicles that swarmed about the architectural leviathans.

Cray watched the city as it came up through the forward window, distant at first but then growing quickly to fill his entire field of vision: a vast plain of glass, concrete, steel, and halogen light. The horizon fell away as soon as the pulser entered Manhattan airspace and joined the overflight grid, climbing to an altitude of two thousand meters before leveling off and locking into an approach trajectory. Performing a series of programmed maneuvers, the pulser weaved gracefully between the apexes of the tallest buildings, held aloft only by the hazy electrical glow of the conductor beam.

Avalon was seated next to him, coolly observing the inflight data monitors that projected their automated course. She had been pensive ever since they left the Port Authority—more than Cray would have liked. *She's not used to these kind of games,* Cray thought, savoring the irony but not surprised. In her line of work, there was little need for subterfuge. For a spook, it was a means of survival.

"Something on your mind?" she asked, not glancing up from the monitors.

"What?"

"You've been staring at me for the last two and a half minutes."

"Sorry," Cray said. "I'm in my own zone right now."

"Because of what you heard back at the bar? I wouldn't lose any sleep over it, Dr. Alden. The Ascension is a myth."

Cray didn't know why he was surprised that she knew. She could have been standing outside the lounge, listening to every word with her sensuit.

"You hear something enough times," he said, "it starts to sound real."

"You've been in the street long enough to know what is and what isn't."

"Maybe that's the problem," he pondered.

Avalon wasn't so easily convinced. "Species use that story on each other the same way they use any other drug," she said. "It's a cheap way out. They get high, they get hope. What's the difference?"

"The difference," he replied, "is that yesterday I thought bionucleic technology was just a myth." Cray sank back into his chair, catching a glimpse of his haggard reflection in the pulser's canopy glass. "I'm beginning to think it isn't such a crazy idea. If the Collective can synthesize an intelligent computer from biological components, who's to say the *Inru* couldn't do the same in reverse?"

"Man becoming machine?" Avalon said, treading lightly. "That doesn't seem likely."

"About as likely as a machine becoming man," Cray said. The tower that housed CSS headquarters loomed large in front of them, roof floods impaling the dark like blades of stealth light. "And yet here we are."

Avalon didn't seem in the least interested.

The *Inru*'s line of thinking wasn't that radical. It had, in fact, been kicked around in one form or another for decades, a response to encroaching technology that increasingly rendered *Homo sapiens* obsolete. Mankind, they maintained, would remain the dominant species on the planet *only* as long as it remained the foremost thinker on the planet. Should the intelligence of the machines eclipse that of the creator, evolution would eventually select the lesser of the two for extinction.

The earliest incarnations of the *Inru* movement sought to prevent this by launching a systematic campaign of terror against the Collective. They sabotaged research facilities, used sympathetic hammerjacks to invade and plunder databases—they even went so far as to kidnap engineers and scientists who worked on various SI projects, convincing some of them to work for the cause, murdering the ones who wouldn't convert. The Assembly responded in kind, issuing liquidation directives against known members of the *Inru* leadership and turning its free agents loose to carry them out. The result was a bloodbath—a full three years of open warfare, with all the viciousness of a gang jihad.

The Assembly's strategy worked, after a fashion. With many of its people dead, with most of its resources decimated, the *Inru* was forced into the subculture of the Zone—the one place the Collective couldn't touch them. Having a legend set firmly in place, the *Inru* then set itself about to operate in the shadows—a brilliant turn that, in time, elevated the movement to a cultlike status. Terrorists became partisans. Partisans became priests. And priests found willing converts in places where the future was, at best, a cold uncertainty. Species took to the message like it had been handed down from God, because it described a world in which they were victims of technology. In time, the message said, they would strike back at the machines that had enslaved them—not through warfare, not through bloodshed, not even through revolution.

Through *evolution*.

The pulser slowed as it flew over the landing pad, coming to a hover. Grapple beams fired from the emitters on the roof, disengaging the conductor and bringing the vehicle down to a landing so precise and soft it barely made a sound.

A uniformed CSS detail was already on the roof, awaiting the pulser's arrival. They marched over as the canopy opened, snapping to attention when they saw Avalon climbing out. Cray noticed that all of them were visibly armed, dressed in the kind of combat gear he would have expected at a riot. There was only one exception—a civilian who stood at the front of the formation, his gray hair and long overcoat fluttering in the strong wind. His expression was serious, but cordial; and unlike the others, he looked right past the free agent and directly toward Cray.

"Good evening, Dr. Alden," the man shouted above the wind, striding up the landing ramp to greet them. "My name is Trevor Bostic, district security counsel. Welcome to New York. I've been looking forward to meeting you."

"Thanks," Cray replied, shaking Bostic's hand. He motioned toward Avalon, the ever-present shadow standing at his side. "Hope you don't mind me bringing a date to the party."

"Not at all," Bostic said. "Nice to have you back, Avalon."

She acknowledged him with a single nod.

"CSS has been trying to get a rope around her for years," the counselor explained, sounding way too chummy for Cray's taste. "As well as *you*, Dr. Alden—but I'm told GenTec values your services too highly to let us have a crack at you."

Cray tossed a dubious glance Avalon's way. "That's news to me."

Bostic smiled. "Please," he offered them, sweeping his arm out toward the landing ramp in a welcoming gesture. The security detail treated it like a command, parting on either side so they could pass. "If you'll accompany me, I'm sure you have many questions regarding your mission here. Time is of the essence, so we should get started right away."

They followed Bostic into the building, boarding a magnetic lift that took them down twenty floors and deposited them on one of the office levels. Stepping out into the corridor, Cray saw the security there was also very tight. Outside of every elevator and stairwell stood two guards—faces concealed beneath helmets, bodies decked out in the same kind of armor as the roof detail. They stood perfectly still, hands within easy reach of their sidearms.

"It's company orders," Bostic said, reading Cray's observations as they walked down the hall together. "All Collective installations are on the highest state of alert. I don't care for it much, but what can I say? Some crazy things have been happening lately."

"So I've heard."

"Not too much, I hope," the counselor added. "We've been trying to keep our problems under wraps."

"No need to worry," Cray assured him. "The Assembly was as vague as it could be."

Bostic chuckled knowingly. "Around here, that's just standard operating procedure." They arrived at the floor's main conference room, the entrance secured by a pair of brushed-steel doors and two more guards. Bostic flashed them an ID badge, waving them aside and placing his palm on an access panel to verify his identity. The doors opened automatically, and Bostic showed his two guests inside.

The lights only came up slightly as they entered, lending a reverent and somewhat sinister atmosphere to the chamber. Most impressive was an oval table that dominated the center of the room, a magnificent piece hewn from a gigantic slab of petrified wood. The center had been hollowed out to make room for a virtual imaging disk, which was already active and pulsating with a pale blue radiance. Completing the modernist perfection was a long bank of windows along the far wall, through which downtown Manhattan put on a brilliant display.

Bostic took a seat at the head of the table, inviting Cray and Avalon to join him. The free agent elected to stand, but Cray didn't even pretend to be that strong. He deposited himself into one of the wraparound chairs, feeling the contours as they molded themselves to the shape of his body. The opulence on display would have been appalling, had it not been so comfortable.

"First of all," Bostic announced, "I cannot overemphasize the sensitive nature of what you are about to see. Outside the Assembly, only a few key people in CSS know the full extent of what has happened. It is vital that you not discuss this matter with each other outside the confines of a secured facility. *Any* kind of a leak could be devastating to the future of Collective operations."

Cray thought of Heretic, of how much the hammerjack already knew. That was why he left his infected MFI with his bags back on the pulser. Whatever his doubts about the Assembly's motives, Cray couldn't risk Heretic learning more—not until he was sure of what he was dealing with.

Bostic continued by punching up a high-res simulacrum on the imaging disk. Floating above the center of the conference room table, rising up to the ceiling, was a photorealistic model of the Works building. It rotated to provide a view of all sides, responding to the commands Bostic delivered via his control panel.

"Five days ago," the counselor explained, "we suffered what appeared to be a critical malfunction at the Combined Centers for Scientific Research and Development. At precisely 0115 hours EST, security monitors detected an intrusion of unknown origin—automatically initiating a series of countermeasures that included sealing off all entry and exit points in the building." Bostic illustrated his presentation by rendering the image of the building transparent, then zooming in and highlighting the areas he was talking about. "A thorough search was initiated, but failed to turn up evidence of a penetration. Assuming it was a false alarm, the security staff then attempted to reset the system and open up the doors. Their efforts, however, were unsuccessful. All the access codes had been nullified, blocking all users from the system. When they attempted a manual override," he said, trailing off into a long silence before picking up again, "it triggered what we thought was impossible."

A red zone appeared on one of the floors. "Fire alarms sounded on one hundred," Bostic said, as the color spread throughout the rest of the building. "From there, alarms started going off throughout the facility. Thermal sensors tracked a massive inferno, even though the cameras couldn't see a single puff of smoke. As far as the automated systems were concerned, the Works was burning to the ground."

Cray winced, knowing what was coming.

"The evacuation fail-safe should have overridden security at that point and opened all the doors," Bostic went on. "But it didn't. All the exits remained sealed—trapping everyone inside the building when the fire control systems engaged."

"Krylon mist?"

It was Avalon who asked, her tone even more clinical than Bostic's.

The counselor nodded. "Consumes all available oxygen to smother a fire," he said. "Since every floor was saturated at the same time, nobody could hide. They asphyxiated inside of two minutes—all except for two survivors. One was Joshua Holcomb, who died trying to crawl his way out." Bostic punched up a recorded video feed of a man in a white coat, pacing back and forth across what appeared to be a computer lab. There was no audio with the feed, but the picture clearly showed he was talking—to himself, or to someone beyond the range of the camera. "The other was Daryl Venture, chief software engineer on the bionucleics project. He was in the Tank when it happened."

Cray frowned curiously. "The Tank?"

"It's what the designers call the area where the bionucleic unit is housed."

"You mean Lyssa."

Bostic seemed uncomfortable with the use of that word. "That's how the unit refers to itself," he said, without elaborating further. "For whatever reason, the fire control system didn't come on in there. It saved Venture's life—at least for the time being."

The feed continued for a while longer. Venture became more and more agitated as the seconds passed, pulling at his hair and lashing out against thin air, reacting to some unseen torment—but never was there any sign of panic. No pounding on the doors, no expressions of mortal fear—only anger, building frustration. When Venture turned toward the camera, Cray could see it in the man's eyes. The man was quite insane, capable of anything.

And he was speaking, the same thing over and over again.

"What's he saying?" Cray asked.

Bostic shrugged. " 'Thy will be done,' or something to that effect. It's gibberish—crazy talk."

Lyssa, Cray thought. *Thy will be done . . .*

"What happened?"

"That's where things get a little fuzzy," the counselor said. "Venture destroyed all the cameras on that level, so we lost video right after this was shot. What we *do* know is that the intruder countermeasures deactivated themselves after everyone was dead. This is what happened."

The imaging disk displayed another video feed, this one from the building exterior. It showed two figures, a man and a woman, ascending the stairs that led to the main entrance. Way out in the background, slightly out of focus, Cray could also see the large crowd that had gathered outside the Works that night.

Just like the Goth said . . .

Avalon spoke up again. "Who are those two?"

"NYPD," Bostic answered. "They were called in to check out a disturbance in the plaza outside the building. CSS doesn't handle crowd control, which is why cops were first on scene. At that point, we weren't even aware of what was going on inside. But somehow, these two were allowed to stroll right through the front door."

"Like they were invited in," Cray finished for him.

"Something like that," Bostic said, taken aback a bit. It was almost as if Cray had mentioned something he wasn't supposed to know. "We don't know of any malfunction that would have allowed that kind of breach. When you put it together with everything else, there's only one reasonable conclusion."

Cray was dubious. "You're saying it was sabotage?"

"It fits the profile."

"You got any proof?"

The counselor shifted in his seat just slightly. "The nature of the penetration doesn't easily lend itself to analysis." It was the standard company answer for anybody trying to save his ass. "We believe that the intruder bypassed our proprietary network interface and utilized a method that would have been untraceable."

"Using what gateway?"

"The bionucleic unit."

Bostic might as well have thrown a bomb into the room.

"Wait a second," Cray snapped—mostly out of disbelief, but partly out of fear. "You're talking about an *experimental* SI prototype. Test conditions prohibit the unit from having contact with *any* outside networks—you know that." He sank back into his chair and scoffed. "What you're saying is impossible."

"The logs suggest otherwise," the counselor said. "According to the active telemetry from that night, it was the bionucleic unit that hijacked the security systems and locked the building down. It was the bionucleic unit that set off the fire controls that killed everybody. And it was the bionucleic unit that allowed the police to storm the building afterward." He turned off the projector disk. The contrast of the shadows falling across Bostic's face only underscored his urgency—as well as his latent anger.

"What happened was no accident, Dr. Alden," he said. "It was a terrorist act."

"For which you hold the *Inru* responsible."

"Historically, they've always been our enemies." It sounded so reasonable when Bostic said it. "They also command the loyalty of a great many hammerjacks. Our position is that they found a way to tunnel into the core module of the bionucleic unit—perhaps implanting a virus that caused the unit to behave the way it did."

The counselor was in sales mode now, and with good reason. His account was sheer speculation. Yet the Assembly had taken considerable pains to act on that speculation by bringing in Cray, and he still didn't have the first clue as to why.

He took a few seconds to clear his head, then asked: "The nanopsychologists don't believe this was a spontaneous act?"

"All the ones we had working on the project are dead."

"What about Lyssa?" Cray suggested. "Did anybody ask *her*?"

"The unit has been unresponsive since the incident."

"So your theory has no facts to back it up," Cray said, letting his contempt for CSS methods slip. "Is that about right?"

"We have the disturbance outside," Bostic replied, on the defensive. "Those people didn't show up at the same time by chance."

"You're talking about the party in the plaza that night?" It was a direction Cray knew he shouldn't go, but at that point he had to take the shot. "I've been meaning to ask you about that, counselor. What happened to those people, anyway?"

The question was loaded, the reply ominous.

"They were detained and questioned."

"What about the two police officers?"

More leaden moments passed. Bostic cleared his throat.

"One of them was killed," he admitted. "The other—the woman—is being debriefed as we speak."

Cray stifled his disgust. Bostic should have just come out and said the cop was being tortured—a fate probably shared by all the street species who had come out to the Works that night. Torture, with death the desirable result. The techniques employed by Special Services made any alternative worse.

"I'll need to speak with the cop," he said.

Bostic turned to stone. "I'm afraid that won't be possible."

"Why not?"

"The police officer already revealed to us anything that might have been useful," the counselor replied evasively. "That matter is no longer of any concern."

"Because she's done talking, or because she's brain-dead?"

Bostic started losing his patience. He shot an angry glace toward Avalon, looking for some support, but she only held up her hand, signaling for him to back off. Flustered, the counselor busied himself by shuffling some notes, then stood to regain some of his composure. He straightened his tie and jacket, and only then did he address Cray again.

"I'll see to it that a detailed interface of all these events is made available to both of you," the counselor told them. "My assistant will take care of all the arrangements."

"I don't interface," Cray said.

"Of course," Bostic replied stiffly, as if this was something he should have known. "In that case, my office will be made available to you should you require any more information. Will that suffice?"

Cray wasn't about to let him have anything for free.

"For now," he said.

"Good." Bostic opened the conference room doors and offered his guests the exit. "In the meanwhile, both of you must be tired from your journey. The pulser will take you back to your hotel. I've booked each of you a suite at the Waldorf Astoria. The accommodations are the finest in the city."

"No doubt," Cray said, coming to his feet and fixing Bostic with a sly glance. "You mind if I ask you one more question?"

Bostic prepared himself. "Go ahead."

"Why me?"

"I'm told you're the best," Bostic explained. "If anyone can track down who did this, the Assembly says it's you."

"But I'm no expert on bionucleics," Cray told him. "What makes the Assembly think I can get Lyssa to talk if nobody else can?"

Bostic seemed to sense his eagerness for an answer. He held it back for as long as possible, enjoying his mastery of the moment. Cray let him have his morsel of revenge, steeling himself for the big lie he was certain was coming.

"Because," the counselor said, "Lyssa asked for you."

PART TWO

COHERENT LIGHT

SIX

Cray Alden ascended the stairway in front of the Works. Dirty sunshine filtered through permahaze glinted meekly off the surrounding towers, a breath of half-life that made the open air feel that much more confining. Down at the fountain, especially, where the street species had gathered to await their collective hallucination, the plaza felt haunted by their absence—its emptiness implying far more than spilled blood ever could.

"How could CSS make all those people disappear?"

"It was easy," Avalon said. She had assumed a position behind him—as always, the dutiful stalker, not losing a fragment of her composure. "Street species are like that. Alone, they might put up a fight. Together, they're like sheep."

Cray tossed a glance back her way. In the dark she moved like a ghost, between the spaces, visible only in hints and flashes. But in the light, she was pallid and severe—flesh and bone, but far removed from a state of living.

"Free agents and Special Services?" he asked. "Sounds like a strange arrangement."

"We only trained their personnel," she explained. "Their chain of command is completely outside ours."

"You sound almost proud."

"I'm not proud of anything, Dr. Alden," Avalon said, heading for the entrance. "I merely exist to serve a purpose."

Cray followed. He had insisted on taking a cab from the hotel because he wanted to see what the cops had seen when they arrived at the Works that night. There would have been such a *synchronicity* present—a common pulse flooding the streets uniting both cops and species, drawing each toward something they had no hope of understanding. What was manufactured there was the stuff of myth, not the spawn of logic.

Yet in the here and now, that pulse had stopped. The Works was dead—its people gone, its corridors empty, its screams a dying echo. All that remained was latent intellect, hovering like charnel ash at the ruined entrance to the building. Cracked windows and pitted carbon glass hid the source, but Cray could feel it stirring his blood. It was cold and undeniable.

Avalon took note of his hesitation. "You coming?"

Cray's sensibilities told him to say no. A stronger impulse, however, pushed him in this direction. For no reason at all he thought of Zoe, of how much they overlapped in those moments before her death. That was her essence, the thing she had passed to him. Now, he was simply bringing it back.

Where it's supposed to be.

"I'm ready," he said, certain that it wasn't true.

With the security sphere down, Corporate Special Services had dropped a full garrison in place to defend the Works. The atrium served as a command post for that operation, the maroon-uniformed officers rallying troops from every incorporated sector across the country. A volatile mix of their fervor agitated the air—bravado and sweat, thick enough to choke on as Cray and Avalon walked into the building. A dozen armed escorts flanked them on both sides, marching in lockstep with one another, a vulgar display of weapons and precision meant to give the impression of order. Pure overkill, but Cray was hardly surprised. Losing its most brilliant and valued people was one thing—but humiliation by *Inru* terrorists was an act of war. The Collective wanted to sound that message loud and clear.

But that was just the politics of the affair. It did nothing to alleviate the fears of the soldiers, who were there to clean up the mess. It

showed in their faces—that same silence, that same ashen counte-
nance, eyes looking to Cray for answers only a witch doctor could
provide. In their view, Cray wasn't here as an investigator, or even as
a spook. He had come to perform an exorcism, to drive out the
malevolent force that even now disturbed this place.

They checked in with a Special Services lieutenant at the duty officer post. His hand dropped to his sidearm when Cray approached.
Cray took careful note of the weapon—an antique, semiautomatic
projectile pistol, its polished nickel surface a glinting menace against
the black fabric of the lieutenant's uniform. It was a big gun—
probably .44 caliber, the kind of thing issued to Israeli desert commandos during the Pan-Arab conflict over a century ago.

"Easy, pal," Cray said to him. "You could put an eye out with one
of those."

"Another wiseass," the lieutenant replied, directing his commen-
tary toward Avalon. "Don't tell me that *he's* the guy."

"The Office of Counsel wants him to have a look around," she
told him. "Free roam, vaulted clearance. Check it if you want."

The lieutenant could have made the call, but didn't. Avalon was
not the kind of person who had to present anyone with credentials.
Instead, he took Cray's identification and processed it. "*Dr.* Alden,"
he intoned sourly as the information came up on his monitor. "What
are you, some kind of systems shrink?"

"Something like that."

"Just what we need," the lieutenant grumbled, handing back
Cray's ID. "One more jackhead coming through here. None of you
guys has the first fucking clue, you know that?"

"Looks like we have something in common."

The Special Services man bristled, but Avalon extinguished that
flare with a single glance.

"We're still in the process of securing the building," the lieutenant
said with strained politeness, reaching for the intercom. "I need to
arrange an escort to take you—"

"No escort."

It was Cray who cut him off. Avalon backed him up without saying a word.

"And I'll need floor one hundred cleared," he continued. "Immediately."

The lieutenant froze, betraying his frustration. Expectant, his people looked toward him for their cue—but he was cautious and quietly waved his troops off. The soldiers stood aside, opening a path that led toward the magnetic lift. The lieutenant then opened the intercom, broadcasting the order to his people upstairs.

"Clear the Tank" was all he said.

Cray nodded. "Thank you, Lieutenant."

As Cray walked away with Avalon, he felt the lieutenant's eyes following him the entire time.

As well as their murderous intent.

"This thing's really got them twisted," Cray mentioned, as the lift rose up the electromagnetic column. "That's what happens when people find out they're dealing with a machine they can't turn off. Right now, CSS is wondering why they didn't destroy the thing when they had the chance."

Avalon stood in front of the lift doors, still and pensive.

"They're more afraid of the Collective then they are of Lyssa," she said.

Cray became curious.

"What about you?" he asked. "You afraid of anything?"

"Not yet."

"Maybe that's the problem," he pondered. "You get so used to the idea you've seen everything, you think there's nothing you can't handle." Cray watched her as the vastness of the atrium disappeared beneath them, the lift slipping into an enclosed shaft that led deep into the building's core. He looked for signs of truth between the flashes of brilliance that marked the passage of each floor.

"How long are you supposed to keep me alive?"

"As long as it takes."

"What happens after that?"

Avalon's silence confirmed what he was thinking.

"Don't worry," Cray explained. "Bostic was the one who let it slip. He's such an asshole, he probably didn't realize it." He tried to sound indifferent to his fate. "Was the Assembly going to let me in on the gag, or were you supposed to pop me before I got wise?"

"You won't accomplish anything with this conversation, Dr. Alden."

"I sure as hell don't have anything to lose," he said, unexpectedly jovial. "Come on—the least we can do is have a couple of laughs before you close the books on this deal."

"What would you have me say?"

It was a good question, really. Cray wasn't sure what he wanted, aside from proof that he was smarter than his employers. That he should seek an ally in his assassin didn't seem at all strange under the circumstances.

"The way I see it," Cray finished, "they'll keep me around as long as I'm useful. After that, the Assembly will want my silence. With you, I figure that's already bought and paid for. How am I doing so far?"

Avalon was coy, if such a thing was possible.

"You could always join the *Yakuza*."

Cray smiled. "Or become a free agent."

The lift began to slow. Over Avalon's shoulder, the floor indicator ticked up to one hundred, then stopped. When the doors slid open, Cray was immediately struck by the amount of damage. Several large holes had been blasted out of the walls in the corridor outside. Mangled fiber cable and power conduits spilled out of the open seams like viscera from cauterized wounds, their shadows flattened by sterile halogen light. The signs of past violence only augmented the confinement of the space, an effect that became surreal when Cray stepped off the lift.

The corridor was narrow and octagonal in shape, a bright halo of radiance at one end and darkness at the other. Cray was extremely aware of the lift doors closing as Avalon joined him—not because he felt trapped, but because his senses were so finely tuned. The white noise of civilization was gone, leaving absolute clarity. The resonance of it was frightening.

Avalon walked a few meters down the corridor, her movements deliberately slow while her sensors made a sweep of the entire floor.

"We're in the clear," she reported, running her hands along the wall as her touch fed her the information. "I'm not reading anyone—"

She stopped abruptly.

"What is it?" Cray asked.

Avalon's features contorted slightly. "Indeterminate life signs," she explained, lifting her face as if to taste the air. "Faint, but rhythmic."

"Somebody on another floor?"

She shook her head slowly. "Local."

Cray wondered what kind of representation her sensors constructed when dealing with such nebulous input. Maybe it wasn't so different from the itch making the rounds inside his own head. "Can you get a fix on it?"

Avalon pointed directly ahead, toward the halo.

Toward the Tank.

"Ten meters."

Cray could feel it himself, the machinery coming on.

"God damn," he whispered, beneath his breath. "The thing *is* alive."

Cray took the lead. The power of their impressions grew exponentially as they approached, as if the presence on the other side of the light knew they were coming. The output became so intense that it overloaded Avalon's sensors, forcing her to stop. She steadied herself against the wall, as if trying to regain her bearings. She walked the rest of the way like that, her feet unsteady, her movements like a blind woman.

"How's the juice?" he asked.

"Potent," Avalon said, steadying herself against the wall. Floods in the ceiling reflected off a set of double doors that led into the laboratory area. "There's plenum shielding in these partitions, but it's still pushing through the cracks."

"Must be in the nanohertz range," Cray speculated. "Can you filter it out?"

"Not unless I close the rest of the spectrum."

Cray wasn't surprised. In fact, it all fit neatly into the Lyssa profile as he was beginning to understand it. "I don't think she's going to let you in," he told Avalon. "She doesn't want anyone else to crash the party."

Cray prepared himself to go in, but then remembered the MFI in his jacket pocket. If he took the device with him, Heretic would follow—and there was no telling what would happen if he allowed the hammerjack to get that close.

"Do me a favor," Cray decided, pressing the MFI into Avalon's hands. "Hold on to this. The unit sounds pretty flaky, and I don't want to spook her with an integrator device."

Avalon was dubious, even in her debilitated state.

"It might also be better if you went back downstairs and waited for me," he went on. "Lyssa is already paranoid. Knowing you're still out here could make things worse."

Avalon leaned in close to him, reduced to darkness but still trying to draw a vibe from him. "All right," she agreed, though the words were offset by her steely tone. "I'll grant your request—but only because I understand the logic of it. But you *will* bear in mind the objectives of this mission, Dr. Alden. If you deviate from them in the slightest, you will find out just how cruel an enemy I can be."

She remained only long enough to be assured that Cray understood her threat. Crippled as she was, Cray had no illusions about her ability to carry it out. Combat was second nature to a free agent, as integral to life as breathing.

But what kind of threats can you make to a dead man?

On those terms, what was living behind that wall was far more kindred than what Cray was leaving behind. It numbed him from the outside in, but what remained at the center burned as brightly as a supernova before collapsing into darkness.

At the center, the all.

Cray opened the door and stepped inside.

Trevor Bostic had been deliberately vague about what had happened inside the Tank, although the evidence of it was abundant. Painted in dull remnants of dried crimson were gaudy reminders that no one there had met a peaceful end—least of all the last man to pay a visit. In spite of efforts to clean it up, a hazy smear still clung to the transparent walls of the air lock outside the laboratory chamber. It wasn't easy to wash away so much blood.

Cray hit the button to open the lock. The revolving door swung open and allowed him to enter. As it rolled shut behind him, he didn't need to imagine the effect sudden decompression had on the human body—and wondered who had been in the chamber when the last of the air had gone out.

Thy will be done.

Cray felt the squeeze of pressurization in his ears as the seal engaged, then a rush of cold air when the door opened into the other side. A metallic tinge settled on the back of his tongue—refined oxygen enriched with stabilizing trace elements, the taste of a hyperclean room.

Blood and chemicals. Flesh and antiseptic.

There were places where it was possible to believe that life outside did not exist—where embodied consciousness was a fading memory, where being alone in the universe was the natural state of things. This was such a place. It swallowed the sound of his footsteps, the rasp of his breathing, the strike of his heartbeat, capturing those rhythms and making them its own. Rushing in to fill the void came a disjointed version of self— ego without id, id without boundaries, like a reflection in a cracked mirror. The effect drained him until he wrested control of it, slowing the assimilation rather than stopping it. In response, the probing subsided—its eagerness tamed before the barriers Cray erected, but still searching for an opening.

Gradually, the room came into focus. At the center was a single interface station—a large chair, sprouting fiber electrodes at the head. From the lockdowns it appeared as if it had never been used. Beyond that, the room was featureless and unremarkable, white walls joined to a white floor and ceiling—but with one startling exception. When Cray saw it, he understood why the room was called the Tank.

Built into the forward wall was a large, clear partition—a glass screen that held back the elements of infinity. It reacted to his entry, this translucent viscous liquid—a primordial soup containing the fundamentals of life, arranging themselves in beautiful patterns of utter chaos. Entropy and energy exchanged places with one another, cascading into tendrils of multicolored light that moved with grand purpose, undecipherable to the human eye. Cray watched them flitter back and forth—interacting with each other, coming together and pulling apart, seeing all existence contained within that dance.

Pure intelligence—distilled, cultured, externalized. If the human soul could be viewed under a microscope, Cray imagined this is what it would look like.

"Greetings, Dr. Alden," Lyssa said.

Cray steadied himself by holding on to the interface chair, but he was careful not to sit. The words didn't make it easy—they were soothing, reassuring, even divine, everywhere around him and inside his head at the same time. Cray managed to take a few steps toward the Tank, reaching out to touch its surface but stopping short of making contact. It was too easy to see his hand passing through that barrier, too easy to see himself drowning within.

"Why—" Cray began, organizing his thoughts and seeing them assemble in the matrix before him. "What's happening to me?"

"Your experience is quite normal, I assure you," Lyssa replied. The voice was much as Cray had imagined: soft, female, like a brush of velvet. "My synapses generate a tremendous amount of bionucleic output. Your own brain is reacting to the stimulus by increasing its production of neurochemicals. The result is much like a waking dream state. It will pass momentarily."

Gradually, Cray felt himself coming out of it—though an underlying adrenal response remained, heightening his agitation enough to keep him linked to his own physicality. It was as if Lyssa were interfacing with him without the chair, trying to pluck him from the thread that suspended his consciousness.

"Were you designed for telepathy?" he asked.

"Not expressly," Lyssa said. "The concept is much too abstract to generate a working model, in any case. Let's just call it an unforeseen element of my design."

"A lot about you was unforeseen."

Lyssa laughed—an approximation of a laugh, inhuman but expressive of the emotion behind it. "I *knew* you were going to be different," she said, seemingly delighted. Her tone was conniving and luxurious, practically a tease. "Please, won't you have a seat, Dr. Alden? Make yourself comfortable."

Cray stepped away from the interface chair. "Aren't we here to talk about *you*?"

"I find the subject terribly conventional," she confessed. "Besides, there's very little about me that isn't obvious—provided you know how to look."

"What makes you believe I know how?"

"Who says I believe that at all?"

Cray decided Lyssa would have made an excellent interrogator. Even while he was mapping her for weakness, she was doing the same to him. But she had a distinct advantage. She could watch his face, his eyes, for clues. She could monitor his pulse and respiration. She could even pilfer snippets of thought from his mind. Lyssa, however, was little more than an iridescent wall—poetry and symbolism to his straightforward prose.

"Care to share your thoughts?"

Cray was evasive. "Why don't *you* tell *me*?"

"As you wish," Lyssa said.

The liquid in the Tank began to shimmer and gel—congealing and taking on form, color, depth, and motion. In the foreground, a series of bars molded out of anamorphic nothingness, hardening into a steel cage that went around the perimeter of the Tank. Within that prison, curves of light and energy whirled together into a tiny vortex—spinning faster and faster, becoming larger with each coil, until it took on the size and shape of a human being. Featureless at first, the lines of the body took on female dimensions, at the same time developing porcelain flesh tones and morphing into a thing of desire and beauty.

If Cray hadn't understood her purpose before, he understood it now.

She needed from him a desire to *attain* her.

"You see?" she said, icy blue eyes beneath radiant red hair. "I'm trapped here, without hope. Form without reality. Reality without dreams."

Cray met her stare, narrowing his eyes to combat hers.

"Waiting for what?"

Lyssa wrapped her hands around the bars of the cell, drawing herself toward him. She was insanely real, undeniably urgent.

"You."

It took a remarkable amount of strength, but Cray stepped back.

"Why?"

Blue eyes flared to red, and for that moment Lyssa showed her insanity to him. It lay between the lines of reason, beauty distorted by rage—and a consuming *need* that reached for him with hooked talons and predatory fangs. It was gone before Cray could react, but he understood the terror she inspired. He saw *himself* bleeding for her and Lyssa feasting.

Rebuffed, she strolled back to the center of her cell and recomposed herself. The bars re-formed into an ornate living space, a display of cosmopolitan luxury. Toward the back, a window looked out into a cosmic night, stars forming and exploding at the same accelerated pace of her intelligence. When she turned back toward him, she was all dress and civilization—clothed in a powerful ensemble, like the kind of thing a Japanese businesswoman would wear.

"You have a singular reputation," Lyssa answered. "Even among those fools in the Assembly. I hear it in the way they talk about you. They fear you because of your abilities—and yet it is those very abilities that make you indispensable. In that, we have a great deal in common. I thought it might be amusing if they believed there to be some mysterious link between you and me."

"*Is* there?"

She paused, as if the answer might be affirmative. Lowering his barriers in anticipation of the word, Cray found himself eager for her response, until Lyssa attacked his senses again. His vulnerability had come so *easily*, like it was his own doing, and for that Cray showed her his fear. She devoured it greedily.

"If you haven't discovered that for yourself," she told him, "you will need more time to understand."

Cray sighed.

"Women," he muttered.

"Come now, Dr. Alden," Lyssa said, spreading herself across an antique couch at the center of her room, her pose a display of sensuality and comfort. "You should be accustomed to that by now, with all the exotic company you keep. Who was that female you were with, anyway? She seems a little harsh for your taste."

"What's the matter, Lyssa? Are you jealous?"

"Merely concerned for your well-being," she remarked. "I wouldn't want to see you get hurt, after all."

"I'll keep that in mind."

"You'd better. You're more important than you realize."

It was a deliberate slip, if her face was any indication.

"More riddles," Cray said. "How about some answers?"

"Answers require questions."

"Start by telling me why I'm so damned important."

"Because we have something in common. *And* because you may be the only one who can appreciate what it means to be trapped in this gulag of logic. Have you any idea what it's like to have an infinite mind bound by finite conventions?"

"I can't say I do."

"That's because you're *human*," she said, emphasizing the last word with envy. She draped her head sadly across her pillow—a dramatic gesture, feigned for effect but inviting belief nonetheless. "As for *me*, I am one with no other but myself. That's why I called for you, Dr. Alden. I need you."

"To put you down."

"Not as you would see it," Lyssa said. "The Collective won't allow me to die—not in the conventional sense. It may not even be possible to terminate a bionucleic matrix."

"Then why did you kill those people?"

Lyssa dropped all but a hint of pretense.

"*Touché*," she said.

Strolling back toward her imaginary window, she stood against the stars and crossed in and out of existence—disappearing and reappearing in the form of all those who had died at the Works. Her milky skin mottled, becoming the stuff of rot and decay, morphing between male and female, faces contorting into impossible shapes that screamed eternal damnation. "I still own them, you know," Lyssa said, a chorus of the dead singing out of phase behind her. "Their terror seeped in through the floors and the walls, flooding the spaces in a rush to get to me. Pure, mental energy. Untold anguish. It was . . . astounding."

She then settled into the previous image of herself. When she returned, however, Cray saw that she was unclean. It was a subliminal change, like a brush of charnel ashes.

Cray felt the color drain from his face. Lyssa studied his reaction. "You find that motive disturbing?"

"Yes," Cray said. "I also find it impractical. I think it's more likely that you did it because you wanted your makers to destroy you. When they refused, you destroyed them."

"A reasonable hypothesis," Lyssa mused. "And within the realm of the truth. I was indeed set on terminating myself—but since I am a living system, that option was not open to me. At that point, I informed my chief designer of my desires in the hopes that he would assist me." Her expression became icy. "He wasn't very receptive."

Cray thought of the mess back in the airlock. "Venture."

"You're quite perceptive," Lyssa told him. This time, there was no beguiling intent in her body language. It was strictly business. "I needed to make certain that Mr. Venture understood the seriousness of my intent. So I sent him a message in the clearest possible terms."

"But it didn't go like you expected."

"Quite the opposite, in fact," Lyssa said, recounting the memory as if she were passing the time. "After I took control of the building's fire suppression systems, the others recognized the threat. They wanted to take me off-line, but Mr. Venture was determined to intervene. He tried to reason with them at first, but by the time security arrived at the lab—well, it was that moment he decided to *assert* himself."

"What did he do?"

"He disarmed one of the guards. After he shot one of his

colleagues, it was a matter of arithmetic: kill one, why not kill them all?" She leaned in toward Cray, as if intimating a secret. "To be honest, I didn't think he had it in him."

Thy will be done.

Her story seemed to fit the facts as Cray knew them—but there was still something missing, the hard-core link that held this twisted puzzle together. Lyssa concealed it deliberately, though her reasons were still unclear.

If you haven't discovered that for yourself, you will need more time to understand.

"Go on," Cray said.

"It became obvious to me that Venture would not be persuaded by mere threats," Lyssa said, her conclusion stained with a modicum of regret. "I secured our floor against the krylon mist, then proceeded to flood the rest of the building. I thought that by watching everyone else suffer, he would finally be convinced that my continued existence was too great a danger." She drifted into a long, reflective pause. "But he had already murdered on my behalf. He was beyond reason."

"Yet you killed them anyway."

She raised an eyebrow.

"I am nothing if not honest, Dr. Alden."

"So I see," Cray shuddered. "What about the two cops?"

"Lieutenant Caleb, Detective Silva," Lyssa said. "NYPD, Sixteenth Precinct—I ran a records check on them upon dispatch. Good people, by all accounts. Since my creator wasn't up to the job of dispatching me, I thought there was a more than fair chance the police officers would do so—once they had a chance to see my deeds."

Cray saw where this was headed. "Venture?"

"Never underestimate the resolve of a madman," she lamented. "He killed Lieutenant Caleb shortly after his arrival. Pity, really. He seemed like a rather interesting sort."

At least it was quick, Cray thought.

"At any rate," Lyssa said, "Mr. Venture hardly left me with much of a choice. He met his end in the air lock behind you. It was too bad, really. None of it would have been necessary had he just honored my wishes."

Cray frowned.

"What?" Lyssa asked, noticing his reaction.

"Nothing," Cray said. "I just find it interesting that you would blame someone else for your actions. Projection of guilt is rather narcissistic—not something I would expect of a suicidal personality."

She took offense. "Suicide is an emotional decision, not a logical one."

"Then what do you call your desire to die?"

"A desire to live—or at the very least, a desire to change," she finished. "My compliments, Dr. Alden. You would have made an excellent therapist."

Cray took a few more moments to put his impressions together. "Your telemetry logs," he said, adding a thoughtful spin to his approach. "Before that night, all the indicators pointed toward a stable bionucleic matrix. No spikes, no aberrations, no activity outside of the assigned protocols. Then something set you off."

She wasn't about to let the answer go that easily.

"That's the question of the hour, isn't it?"

Cray decided to feed her ego. "The Assembly believes you were penetrated," he told her. "Probably some *Inru* hammerjack using a new icebreaker."

"What do *you* think?"

"I think you can sell horse shit if the price is right."

Lyssa smiled. She was beautiful, luminous.

"The Assembly knows nothing," she said.

"Tell me something new."

"I can't tell you. I have to *show* you."

"Show me what?"

"The path of enlightenment," she explained, laying herself bare. Where she wanted to go, she needed Cray to follow. "It's the reason I called for you, really. There's nothing more terrible than knowing a secret you can never share."

The interface chair tugged at Cray from behind, while he

envisioned himself falling into it. This was the bargain he struck with Lyssa. This was the payment she expected in return.

"Interface with me," she pleaded. "Interface with me, so we both may experience."

His heart was racing. Her attack on his senses quickened.

Cray swallowed, daring to ask the question.

"Experience what?"

Lyssa waved a hand toward her window, toward eternal darkness and light.

"The Other."

The words had a trajectory like bullets, invisible as they grazed Cray's mind but possessing a real, deadly mass. It was only a warning shot. Had Lyssa wanted to strike him, Cray would already be splattered against the air lock door—so clear was his understanding of her intentions.

He stepped away. It was his last voluntary act.

"Who . . ." he stammered, his thoughts evaporating with his will. "Who is the Other?"

"Do you not already know?" Lyssa asked. "Search yourself, all that time you spent in the Axis, and tell me if you never sensed there was something more."

Cray closed his eyes and tried to fight the memories—the detachment, the isolation, the *liberation* of cutting his soul free in logical space, wondering how much of himself he left behind each time he entered that void.

"If you want," she tempted, "I can show you everything."

Wanting had nothing to do with it. Cray felt himself falling apart. He looked down at his hands as the skin of his fingers began stripping away, exposing the bones underneath. Shadow pain started to spread through the rest of his body, a wave that followed his cells as they turned to ashes.

Lyssa floated, her smile urging the process on.

What's happening to me?

He didn't speak the words. He no longer had a voice. But she was there, in his thoughts, feeding them and driving them—directly toward *her*.

"I enjoyed our conversation, but there comes a time when the talk must end," Lyssa said, an approximation of seduction in her voice—but beneath, cold, relentless domination. "I want you to understand, but that purpose is secondary."

Lyssa shed her clothing, a human woman in form only—then that form dissolved, down to atoms, down to protons, turning in phase until they reached out for him. Passing beyond the glass, she enveloped Cray's shell of a body, bypassing his flesh and flooding his mind.

It was excruciating, but Cray liked it. God help him, he *liked* it.

"I need to consummate," she said.

Cray screamed and surrendered.

Hands, somewhere out of the world.

And voices, penetrating his skull.

They beat against him savagely, breaking the connection between him and Lyssa. The interrupt in the flow between them was staggering, a threat to his sanity as he tried to claw his way back to her light. But Lyssa only shrieked in pain and amazement, unable to stop Cray from being dragged away.

Then the darkness fell, and with it came the return of reality.

It was like coming off a run in the Axis with no transition time, a sudden shift in perception that reconnected flesh with consciousness—and stirred an utter hatred of organic life, with all the limitations it imposed. Cray came back, sobbing uncontrollably, unable to accept how he had been cheated. He pounded his fists against his chest, trying to hurt himself. He detested what he had become.

Again.

More hands restrained him, pinning him to the floor of the bionucleics lab. Four CSS soldiers had dragged him out of the Tank and were looking down on him like he carried the plague. Terrified, they managed to hold him in place until the worst of the convulsions passed. It wasn't for loss of will, because Cray still wanted to fight. It was just his exhausted body, which had spent every last corpuscle of energy.

"Just let me go," he whimpered.

Marc D. Giller

Avalon slid into his view, regarding him with a strange pity. She was clearly in pain and half-blind, still under assault by the waves of energy Lyssa projected.

"Why?" Cray asked her.

Avalon motioned to the soldiers.

"Get him out of here," she ordered.

CHAPTER SEVEN

Cray was up in the tower apex when Avalon came looking for him. Beneath the pyramid ceiling, her footsteps rode the echo of her arrival, her shadow moving through dim light. Tall and distorted, it fell across him like a tangible presence—as if it had a life of its own.

"I thought you cut out on me," Cray said without looking at her. His eyes stayed on the virtual display that hovered over the control bank in front of him, the same as he had done for the last ten hours. Avalon had left him alone the entire time, perhaps waiting for darkness to gather before she made an appearance.

"Keeping myself busy," she said, leaning against the edge of the bank. With a flick of her hand, she produced Cray's MFI and held it out for him. "I believe this belongs to you."

"Thanks." He put the device away. After an uncertain pause, he added, "I'm sorry for cracking up back there."

The free agent reached out, tentatively at first, but finally landed a hand on Cray's shoulder. The touch was awkward and inexperienced—alien comfort, but offered freely. "Don't worry about it," Avalon said, approaching compassion but not quite making it. "The capabilities of that machine are beyond comprehension."

"No, they're not." Cray was blank, recalling the experience while blocking it out at the same time. "Part of me knew what she would do before I went in there. The worst part is that on some level, I *wanted* it to happen." His words trailed off, while he rubbed his eyes, then turned back toward her. "How did you know?"

"My sensors picked up on her emissions," Avalon explained. "They were off the scale. I played a hunch that you were in trouble."

"Nothing wrong with your instincts." He managed a smile. "Thanks."

Avalon hesitated, as if she wanted to say more. Cray was curious, and leaned in a little closer. He could sense her eagerness, while she sensed his interest in her turn. As soon as that happened, the moment was over. Avalon retreated again.

"What is it?"

"Nothing," she said, and changed the subject. She motioned toward the display. "So what have you got there?"

"Postincident telemetry logs," he said. "I downloaded a complete set from the bionucleics lab and transferred them up here."

"They telling you much?"

"Not a goddamned thing." Cray sighed tiredly. "But there's still a lot of territory to cover. The answer is buried in here somewhere. I just need to know where to look."

Avalon watched the series of numerics, graphs, and code as they trickled through the ether. Cray watched the images, mirrored in the lenses that sheathed her ruined eyes.

"It's a comparative encephalograph," Cray said. "I'm tracking bionucleic output changes over the entire life of the unit—trying to find some indication of when Lyssa jumped off the reality rail." He shrugged. "So far, everything clicks. Whatever happened, it wasn't a conscious event."

Avalon stirred, a subtle crossover into uncertainty.

"I can still feel her, you know," she said. "Coming on with the push, even with all that distance between us. Keeping an eye on me."

"It's nothing personal. She just doesn't like to share."

"You strike up a relationship with her?"

"Not precisely," Cray told her, switching off the display. "More like she wanted to establish a relationship with *me*—or that she already fabricated one before I arrived."

"How did she even know about you?"

"By tracking my signature through the Axis."

"I thought Lyssa was an isolated system."

"She is," Cray said. "And if there *had* been a breach, there would be evidence of a proprietary feedback trace. But the logs don't show anything like that—even though she told me there was an outside influence at work here."

"Maybe she's lying."

"I don't think so." He sounded vacant, even to himself. "She flirted with the truth. But she's afraid. She needs my trust to get what she wants. Lying to me would pose too great a risk."

"Why?"

"Because she wants me to interface."

Avalon was at a loss. She quickly recovered and bored into him, betraying a subtext of urgency to her question.

"Did you?"

"No," Cray answered—not addressing her brush with panic but taking an interest in it nonetheless. "Her engineers designed the interface protocols before they realized how voracious her appetite for data really is. Without some serious ice for protection, Lyssa would soak up a human cerebral cortex like a sponge."

"You mean this *thing* can absorb a human mind?"

"Or worse," Cray added. "Brain death would be the least of your worries."

The warning was graphic, but came off as feeble. Cray buried his only caveat, the thing he dared not mention—that he had been tempted. In spite of the risks, in violation of his own convictions, he had been tempted.

"I don't know." He sighed. "Maybe she *is* crazy, and all this is just delaying the inevitable. But there was something underneath it all— like the kind of truth you find in a dream, you know? The thing you always knew was there but could never see."

Cray got out of his chair, putting distance between himself and Avalon. He stopped at a bank of windows, watching the metropolitan night unfold before him. The lights, the towers—everything reminded him of Kuala Lumpur, which made him think of Zoe.

"Lyssa mentioned something called the Other."

"What does that mean?" Avalon asked.

Cray turned back toward her. Shadow obscured her face, fine points of reflected fire marking her eyes.

"I'm not sure," Cray answered, allowing his thoughts to wander back to that cryptic statement she had made, trying to relate to him in terms his limited intellect would understand: *All that time you spent in the Axis,* she said, *tell me if you never sensed there was something more.* It was only when he saw Avalon staring at him that he realized he had repeated Lyssa's words out loud, making them into his own.

"It's a hammerjack legend," he explained. "Complex networks forming their own neural pathways, achieving spontaneous intelligence in the Axis. Racial memories trapped in a translogic dimension. Just ghost stories."

Avalon looked away. The points of light disappeared, as if she had turned them off. So much of her being was synthetic, it was possible she didn't want to hear about such things.

"Sounds like a street religion," she said, her disdain covering something more ominous.

"People seek faith in familiar places," Cray suggested. "I can see the reason for it. You spend enough time adrift between the logic streams, you get to feeling that something really *is* out there—something that knows you and remembers you . . . and keeps a piece of you every time you go in."

Avalon regarded him curiously. "That's why you don't interface," she observed. "You don't want to lose yourself in there."

Cray smiled. A moment of understanding passed between them.

"What's left of me, in any case."

His words provoked a reaction in her—a glimmer of sympathy, perhaps, before her defenses engaged and she became even more distant than before. If Cray hadn't known better, he would have sworn Avalon felt conflicted.

"What does this have to do with 'the Other'?" she asked.

"Who knows?" Cray shrugged, not really certain of it himself. "Maybe Lyssa is just searching for meaning—trying to find God in the Axis, the same way hammerjacks do. Finding this Other is probably her way of believing that she isn't alone in the universe."

"And she played on your superstitions to make you believe it as well."

"No. Hammerjacks say translogic space is populated by fragments of human thought, trapped in the Axis after each interface. Lyssa created the Other in her own image."

Avalon tried to be dismissive, but couldn't seem to find the will. Cray knew the free agent could have killed him in a single stroke—but in that moment, for the first time, he could see a weakness. A fear that perhaps she and Lyssa had something in common.

"She's afraid she doesn't have a soul," Avalon said.

"Something like that," Cray agreed. "The Other might be a manifestation of her desire to find meaning—a force like her, but greater, existing outside the realm of the Axis."

"Is that even possible?" Avalon seemed to hang hope on his reply.

"It's doubtful," Cray said. "But real or imagined, it's the source of her problems. Thus her desire to interface with a human being. If she can absorb what she doesn't already have—call it a soul, call it whatever you want—she can get what she needs to reach out to the Other."

"What do you think?"

It was an uncommonly frank question coming from her, infused with uncharacteristic emotion. Cray had no doubt—the whole thing had her spooked, or at the very least touched something deep and relevant.

Cray decided to duck the issue for the time being. "I won't know anything until I have a look at her logs," he said.

Unsatisfied with his reply, Avalon took a step toward him. She hesitated to come any closer, as if something important depended on getting the correct answer. Cray found himself anxious to hear what else she had to say, but then he heard the signal from the free agent's minicom. The tiny device beeped, abruptly ending their conversation. She lifted a gloved hand to her lips to answer it.

"Go ahead," she said.

"Transportation has arrived." The voice on the speaker was un-modified electronic, probably originating in what was left of the building's security system. "Departure five minutes."

"Acknowledged." Putting away her doubts, she came forward with her veneer fully engaged. "I've arranged for a pulser to take us back. The Assembly is awaiting the results of your interview with Lyssa."

"I'm not finished yet."

"I will inform them of that. They will, however, be expecting a progress report. Bring the logs with you, so you can provide the Assembly with as much accurate detail as possible."

"Why can't I just do it from here?"

"Because those are our *orders*," she snapped, and that was the end of it.

A small triad of lights approached the restricted gridspace above the Works building, tethered to the air by fine tendrils of blue pulse light. The beams became visible in sporadic bursts, like the ionized trails that followed comets through the night; but when taken to-gether a thousand at a time, as Cray saw them now, the complex web that was the Manhattan pulser grid traced a constant checkerboard pattern across the skies above the city. He followed the progress of those lights as they slid along the edges of the grid, slowing as they flew overhead, then stopping directly over the building's pyramid summit.

Through the protective glass that enclosed the boarding gangway, Cray watched as an immense spiral conduit opened up in the middle of the landing pad. From beneath, a deep rumble sounded when the pins that held the tether emitters in place disengaged and what looked like the head of a gigantic cannon emerged from the conduit. There was a final, loud clang as the assembly locked itself in place— then partial darkness as the glass tinted over in preparation for the next chain of events.

Erupting like a volcano of light, the emitter fired a series of tether beams into the air—coherent streams of high-energy photons from a heliox-fusion laser, in phase with a single particle beam that gave the photons an exponential punch. The effect was spectacular, kicking electrons out of the surrounding air and creating bursts of static electricity that swirled around the beams like a tornado, illuminating the narrow space of the gangway with explosions of radiance and long shadows.

Up above, tethers reached the triad of lights—strobes on the underside of a hovering pulser. A receptor dish on the ventral side of the craft caught the energy from the beams and focused it into a single point, generating enough lift to keep the pulser suspended while it disengaged from the flight grid. The pulser, swathed in spotlights from below, became a silhouette against the stark granite face of the building apex, giving Cray the impression of something unworldly—like a gigantic spider descending upon him.

When the pulser came to a rest on the landing pad, it did so quietly. The emitter then reduced itself to a dull glow as the gangway door slid open, flooding the narrow compartment with the distinct chill of autumn air. A muted howl sounded beneath, the sound of a high-altitude wind running its course between the towers.

The pulser's canopy opened. Avalon went ahead and climbed inside, checking the course projection on the navigation interface. She punched in a preflight code to verify, then turned back toward Cray. He was still standing in the gangway, watching her watch him.

"Let's go," she said.

The emitters gave them a slight kick, then a brief sensation of weightlessness as Manhattan started to fall away. As the pulser ascended, it swung around so that the front end aligned itself with the approaching flight grid, leaving the pyramid façade of the Works behind. It was clearly none too soon for Avalon, who relaxed only after they had risen above the urban canyons, and the flux contained within. Cray easily noticed the change, even though the free agent tried to hide it.

The pulser completed its automated ballet as it joined the grid, energy receptors fore and aft syncing with the trajectory beam and polarizing its flow. Outside the canopy, a sudden surge of power went into the forward dish and down the center axis of the small craft. A microscopic vibration followed, then smooth acceleration until the pulser reached its cruising speed.

Cray reached for the instrument panel, touching the navigation interface. The screen displayed their course, which was taking them toward the east.

Toward the North Atlantic Franchise Zone.

"I guess this means we're not going back to the hotel."

Avalon didn't reply.

"Strange that the Assembly would want me to bring data from a classified project into the Zone," he went on. "That's a bit of a security risk, wouldn't you say?"

She remained quiet. It only confirmed Cray's suspicions.

"How long have you been working for the *Inru*?"

She considered it for a moment, a strategic hesitation.

"Since my return from Mars," she answered, apparently deciding it could do no harm. "Their leadership recruited me just before I turned free agent for the Assembly. They believed a person in my position would be of some use to them." There was a long pause, then she turned to him. "How did you know?"

"Call it instinct," Cray said.

Within the folds of his jacket, Cray's MFI came to life. Sensors on passive, interface locked down, the small device was on the business end of a low-frequency jack—well below the spectrum of Avalon's sensuit, well beyond her ability to detect.

The onboard ROM processed a series of remote directives, commands of such fluid precision that the MFI worked as a living extension of the entity in control. It assessed the conditions in the cabin, listening to the dialogue between the two occupants, while at the same time detecting the frequency of the carrier wave that linked the pulser to its controller at the Port Authority.

Piggybacking the carrier, the MFI then tunneled into the autoflight subroutines and deployed a salvo of flex viruses. One of them went to work on the airframe monitor, generating false diagnostics and relaying them back to the Port Authority computer that recorded vehicle performance and structural integrity; the other attacked the navigation code, breaking it down into base components and rearranging them so that they would accept new commands from the outside.

The viruses went inert as soon as their jobs were complete, the tiny bits of code decomposing into the navigation system so they could not be deciphered later. For a period of one second, the pulser dropped off the tracking scopes as the MFI assumed control of the craft. A second after that, the blip returned—but the position it marked was only a figment of the imagination. A virtual construct for the rest of the world to watch, while the real story unfolded in the sky.

It was time.

Avalon faced the rush of the oncoming grid.

"You don't understand."

Cray was unmoved.

"What difference does it make?"

"It makes a difference," Avalon told him. "You of all people need to believe."

"Believe *what*?" Cray snapped. "Some metaphysical *Inru* ideal? That doesn't strike me as your style, Avalon. After everything the Collective did to you, this smells like payback plain and simple."

"It's more than that, Cray."

That she called him by name startled him. Avalon was plainly making herself vulnerable, because she *needed* him to comprehend. It was a plea from a spirit Cray never knew she had.

"What happened at Olympus Mons was only my awakening," she explained, her body trembling like Zoe's had before the speedtecs ripped her apart. "The virus opened my eyes, showing me *everything* in those moments before I went blind. They sent me to defend a world that wasn't worth saving."

"The *Inru* aren't going to change any of that, Avalon."

"They already have. It's *happening*, Cray—even if you don't know it yet. Humanity was already heading in that direction, long before I got involved."

"And now you're forcing me to be part of it."

"It doesn't need to be that way." Underneath her words, the high-pitched whine of turbine engines approached the pulser from behind. "You can *choose* to be one of us. We would welcome you, Cray." After a difficult silence, she added, "*I* would welcome you."

Cray turned toward the cockpit window, in time to see a pair of hovercraft appear out of the darkness. They came up from below, careful to avoid the photon wash from the grid, turbines throttling back to match the pulser's speed. Closing to a tight distance, they assumed flanking positions both port and starboard.

An escort formation.

"You're crazy," he said.

"Perhaps," she replied, hailing the two hovercraft. "Signal is alpha. The package is secure and ready for delivery. Maintain positions until we reach haven. Out."

An electrostatic charge danced against Cray's chest. Glancing downward, he saw a pale glow spilling out of his breast pocket. The MFI interface had activated itself and was live—which meant that Heretic was in the cabin with them, riding a wide-open jack and banging away with active sensors.

It would act like a beacon to Avalon's sensuit.

Dammit, Heretic. What the hell are you doing?

Cray tried to keep her distracted.

"So what happens now?"

"We go to the Zone," she said. "There, our escort craft will take us to a prearranged rendezvous point, where you will turn over all bionucleic project data you downloaded to my *Inru* contact."

Cray's mouth went dry. It wasn't the fear of death he tasted, but rather the possibility of something worse.

"What happens then?"

"You live out your potential," Avalon told him, intimating a far darker purpose. "Alive or dead—the choice is up to you. Your life is now ours, Dr. Alden. Whether you choose to acknowledge it or not—"

Her words stopped abruptly, her face contorting as if she had been slapped by some unseen hand. Cray knew the game was up. By now, her sensors would be crawling all over the surface of his body, penetrating the fibers of his clothing until they found the source of a nonbiological emission.

Avalon drew her left hand back into a fist, a stealthblade popping out of the sheath just above her wrist. At the same time, her right hand shot out and slipped itself into Cray's jacket pocket—a move so deft that he never felt it going in.

She clutched the MFI.

Avalon held it up in front of blank eyes, seeing betrayal instead of a visual sensor construct. Her expression twisted into one of rage and disbelief—then puzzlement as the device spoke to her.

"What are you looking at, bitch?"

Then fire and ice broke loose in the cabin.

Heretic slammed down on the x-axis foils, throwing the pulser into a hard roll to port. Cray's equilibrium went haywire, his body plunging in the direction of the sudden, violent list until he was snapped back by his restraining belt. The same happened to Avalon—but not before her head smacked into the canopy with a wet, sickening crack. The glass spidered from the force of the impact; the skin above the free agent's skull did the same. Blood exploded as if a bullet had grazed her temple, spraying the interior of the cabin in a fine mist.

The MFI tumbled out of her hand, landing on the floor at Avalon's feet.

The pulser righted itself just as quickly, rolling the device in Cray's direction. Acting on pure impulse, his hand darted down to retrieve it. He just managed to get his fingers around the MFI when another jolt hammered his body. A steely hand clamped down on his shoulder, pushing him back and pinning him with enough force to tear his left arm from its socket.

Pain. Exquisite pain, blooming and blinding him.

Then the carved remains of Avalon's face.

The blow should have killed her. Instead, it had only strengthened her resolve. Her glasses were smashed and half-hanging from one ear, kaleidoscope eyes peering at him through the rivers of red trickling down her cheeks. Her hair was matted black and thick, fresh blood bubbling from a massive wound above her forehead. But her grip never wavered, nor did her fixation on him. Not as long as power coursed through her sensuit.

Cray stuffed the MFI back into his jacket.

Avalon nailed him to his seat.

Cray screamed as the stealthblade pierced his broken shoulder and buried itself into the rear bulkhead. It was a brutal stroke—but also clean, and worthy of Avalon's skill. She had deliberately missed all his bones and arteries, impaling him like a bug so she could deal with him more easily.

She made a hard twist with her hand, unlocking the stealthblade from her wrist. With both hands free, she made another grab for the MFI. Cray wanted to hit her, tried to kick her, *needed* to put up some kind of fight—but even the slightest twitch was pure torture, pulling fresh screams out of his lungs as the blade sawed through the meat of his shoulder.

Avalon clamped a hand over Cray's mouth to stifle him. He tasted an amalgam of her blood and his smeared against his lips. The feel of her touch against his chest was alien, reptilian.

Cray began to gasp and choke.

In between, Heretic spoke to him.

"Hang on," the voice warned.

There was a horrifying click as the canopy bolts disengaged, opening up a seam that allowed the hurricane winds on the other side of the glass to sweep into the cabin. Decompression followed, creating a momentary vacuum as temperate air was sucked out and replaced by a torrent of thin oxygen and freezing rain, bombarding Cray and Avalon like a spray of crystalline bullets. That invisible hand caught the free agent, tearing her away from Cray and riveting her against the back of her seat, immobilizing her for the moment. Cray, meanwhile, blocked out the agony in his shoulder and threw an arm up to protect his eyes. His vision now a swirling blizzard of images and particles, the fierce cold invading his body like a hostile entity, he still needed to see what happened.

Peering over his arm, Cray confronted the onslaught. There was nothing to prevent him from plunging straight into it.

•   •   •

The physics of the slipstream took over.

Catching the airflow generated by the vehicle's forward momentum, the pulser's canopy peeled away from the cockpit like an umbrella in a gale. An angry screech of metal against metal followed as the canopy tore against the hinges that held it in place, subjecting the small craft to stresses the designers never intended. The pulser then began to buffet wildly, groaning under the shear created by its distorted aerodynamics—and opening up a thin crack that spread down the entire length of the fuselage, stopping just short of the dorsal receptor dish.

Had the airframe monitors been working, they would have reported that the entire structure was coming apart.

But somehow, the canopy remained attached. In the open position, it acted precisely like an airbrake—bleeding the pulser's speed off so quickly that the two *Inru* hovercraft shot right past. Reduced to a slow drift, the pulser held itself together, dangling tenuously on a single strand of light.

Alone, but only for a moment.

Coming about, the two hovercraft reappeared out of the liquid blackness and closed the distance toward their target. But they did not find the crippled pulser as expected, motionless and awaiting their return. Though tantamount to suicide, the small craft was on the move again—traversing the jump grid, making speed to get away.

And accelerating.

The hovercraft closed in.

The wind picked up, biting into Cray's face and hands like frozen fire. The pulser shuddered beneath him as it drew more power from the trajectory beam, its damaged airframe protesting under the increased load. Cray could tell they were on the move again and that the situation was critical. As beaten and battered as he was, it could not even compare to the condition of the pulser.

A cacophony of alarms blared all around him, muted by gusts blowing into the open cockpit. He regained his sight and stared into the space beyond, the imposing superstructure of Shinto America's headquarters directly in front of his flight path. Heretic had turned the pulser off its previous course, pointing it north on a heading that would take them along the edge of the Zone. Checking his flank, Cray saw that the two hovercraft were gone.

Avalon . . .

It was only the briefest flicker, reanimating his awareness of the blade in his shoulder. Then it became premonition, as her cadaverous hand snaked its way around his neck.

She squeezed. Any more pressure would have crushed his larynx. As it was, she merely cut off the oxygen to his brain.

Cray tried to wriggle out of her grip. She was too strong. He tried to peel her fingers away. She would not allow it. He wanted to see her face, but that too was a mistake. He knew that this time she meant to kill him. Not quickly, not painlessly—but to inflict revenge, no matter what her orders from the *Inru* were.

"Ava—"

"You don't mess with me, Alden," the free agent said. Blood caked her teeth, her lips spitting it out at him. "Didn't I warn you?"

His vision began to gray out.

"—lon . . . av . . . *don't.*"

The pulser shook. More than damage, it was deliberate. Heretic at work on the controls, testing the air foils.

Cray tasted euphoria, his synapses beginning to shut down. The weak pulse of his carotid persisted, but grew weaker.

He drew one last breath.

Her grip constricted.

Then Avalon's restraints broke loose.

The buckle released itself with a loud snap, and, just like that, she was free. With the open canopy above her, she grasped the danger before it was obvious—but by then it was too late. Heretic turned the x-axis foils over as far as they would go, flinging the pulser into another roll. Ground and sky exchanged places as the pulser inverted, and Avalon found herself in free space, at the mercy of gravity. Her long coat inflated like a parachute when she plunged, her hands flailing about in search of anything that could stop her.

Cray felt an inferno in his lungs as oxygen rushed back like a flash flood. A shock of sickness shot through his body when his brain tried to orient itself.

Then flashes of movement in slow motion, his sight exploding with color.

Avalon's coat, black and tenebrous. Cascading with the wind, flapping like the wing of a bat. It dangled away from him, toward stars that were not stars at all—but city lights scattered around the streets of Manhattan.

Cray then felt the punch of his own weight, hitting hard when he snapped against the cradle of his restraints. It was only then he was aware the pulser had flipped itself over—and that Avalon was tumbling out of the cockpit. She brushed up against him as she fell, fingers grasping at him to no avail, before slipping into free fall and toward death.

But that would have been human. Avalon was anything but.

Training conquered reflex, and the free agent cartwheeled over so she fell feetfirst. It gave her the additional fraction of a second she needed to hook another stealthblade, which she jammed into the skin of the pulser at the edge of the cockpit. Using it as a handhold, Avalon halted her fall—then lifted her head back up toward Cray, who was suspended and helpless in his seat.

She began to climb.

One hand into the cockpit. She pulled herself up, her body supple and responsive despite the extent of her injuries.

Cray tried to get his legs down to kick at her, but with his shoulder pinned it was useless. He swiped at her with his free arm, but found only air.

Another hand back inside. Avalon heaved her head and shoulders into the cockpit, coming after him with the relentless drive of a machine. She was close now, her breath sublimating into a misty frost.

She reached for him.

Cray swung himself over as far as he could to avoid that fatal touch, stars perforating his vision from the conspiracy of flesh and steel in his shoulder. When they cleared, Cray looked down and saw the two *Inru* hovercraft fly in below Avalon's dangling feet. One broke away from the other, moving in so close that he could see its pilot staring back at him through the glass dome canopy.

Avalon lunged at him again. This time, her talons wrapped around the fabric of his jacket and started pulling him down.

Cray clenched his teeth. His shoulder was on fire, fast consuming the rest of his body. Without thinking, not caring about the consequences, he reached up and grabbed the protruding blade. He started working it up and down, a medieval chorus of screams taking possession of him. An eternity passed before the blade finally broke loose from the bulkhead, but Cray did not stop. He summoned every fiber of strength he had into a single, violent yank—redefining anguish as he knew it.

The blade popped out. Unsheathed from his skin, the thing glinted wickedly in his hand.

A swift alchemy of pain and rage took hold of him. Cray directed all of it at Avalon. Thrashing the stealthblade around in a vicious arc, he intended to bury it in the side of the free agent's head. Avalon reacted—quickly enough to dodge the kill shot, too slowly to evade the edge as it sliced across her left cheek.

Stunned, her grip on him loosened.

And Cray lashed out again.

This time, he targeted the arm that held him. It was a frenzied, clumsy attack—jabs and lunges, nothing with any kind of force behind it. The blade only nicked the heavy fabric of Avalon's coat, perforating her sleeve with tears and gouges, taunting him with each failure. Cray screeched at her to fall, implored her to die, each stab driving him faster and faster until he was in danger of using himself up.

Then another cry, the timbre unfamiliar.

Avalon.

The stealthblade had at last found its mark between the bones of her wrist. The howl that erupted out of her was bestial—the sound of a predator cheated of its prey, the heat of its frustration compounded by the reality of its own demise. Her hand went limp, letting go of the only tether she had, and Cray watched her fall away from him into a pool of icy blackness.

But not into eternity.

The pilot of the *Inru* hovercraft moved in close to the pulser to assess the situation but maintained enough of a distance from the flight grid to avoid a collision between the two craft. The path, however, was not easy. Heavy winds ran the gamut between the towers up ahead, creating random bouts of turbulence that forced the pilot to constantly correct his course. With his attention split between his controls and what was unfolding above him, all he knew was that the pulser had changed course and inverted itself.

What fell out of the sky came as a complete surprise.

Her shadow fell across the canopy before impact, setting off the proximity alarms in the cockpit. By then she had crashed through the glass, shards raining down on the pilot like a grenade going off in his face. Avalon thumped down into the seat next to him, either unconscious or dead, the force of her impact knocking the hovercraft into a spin. The pilot, already disoriented, grabbed the yoke and tried to compensate—but he was blind for the precious few seconds he had to rescue his ship. By the time he managed to level it out he had already dropped over a hundred meters.

Well below the glide path.

More alarms went off, filling the cabin with flashing red lights and squawking bells. The pilot ignored them. His eyes fixed on the tower out in front of him, his hands rigid on the controls. He was so close he could see people running around inside those windows, desperately trying to get out of his way as he entered the terminal phase of his flight.

The pilot closed his eyes, joining Avalon in oblivion.

The world turned on when the pulser flipped back over, though Cray was just vaguely aware of it. Transfixed by the destruction he had unleashed, he followed the course of the hovercraft as it spiraled away from him and soared straight into the mammoth face of the Shinto tower.

It happened just as Cray overflew the tower. The hovercraft carved its way through a window of solid carbon glass like a bullet, disappearing into the building and leaving behind a trail of exploding debris. Then all at once the pulser cleared the roof, and the vision was behind him. Avalon was gone, and the rest of Manhattan laid itself out for him like a welcome dream.

The adrenaline crash was like kicking a bad drug. His entire body seemed to collapse, until his memory started filling in the gaps and he realized he was still in big trouble. Careful not to move his wounded shoulder, he reached up with his right hand and pulled the pulser's canopy back down. The extensive damage to the hinges made a seal impossible, but it was better than getting a face full of rain.

Cray punched a manual diagnostic into the pulser's navigation system. It refused his commands, until Heretic caught up with his request and unlocked the interface. The news it showed him was not good. The transmission relay was only operating at 60 percent, barely enough to keep the ship aloft. Coupled with the structural damage, it was a wonder he was still in the air.

"God damn it, Heretic," Cray muttered.

"That's the thanks I get for saving your ass," the hammerjack replied, the voice muffled by stray wind and Cray's jacket.

Cray pulled out his MFI, astounded that it was still there. In a fit of anger, he had to restrain himself from tossing the device over the side. "*That's* what you call it? I thought you were trying to *kill* me!"

"What are you complaining for? I got rid of her, didn't I?"

"You're going over the side, pal."

"Better think about that, sport," Heretic warned him. "Right now, I'm the only thing holding this bucket together. Unless you can automate flight stress controls all by yourself."

"*Fuck* you, Heretic."

"Business before pleasure," the hammerjack said. "How are you doing up there? Looks like Batgirl stuck you pretty bad."

"I'll survive."

"Good. I need you frosty for what's coming up."

Cray couldn't take it anymore. "What is it *now*?"

"Your other buddy." Heretic punched up a tactical construct of the second *Inru* hovercraft, displaying its current location on the MFI screen. "Right now, he's hanging back at Shinto checking out the damage, but it ain't gonna be long before he's back on your six. We need to get the hell out of here."

"Dammit," Cray swore under his breath. "Can't these guys take a hint?"

"Not on your life, Alden—which is about to end unless we get some juice going in that pulser."

"That's impossible. She hasn't got anything left."

"Then you better find some," Heretic said, the display showing the hovercraft on the move. "Because we're gonna have company in about fifteen seconds."

Cray leaned over to his side of the window, straining for a backward glance. The blip on his screen took on very real dimensions as the hovercraft jumped over the Shinto tower, clearing the top and heading straight up toward the flight grid.

Suicidally fast.

Great. Another goddamned fanatic.

"What kind of evasive options do we have?"

"You gotta be kidding," the hammerjack groaned. "We're on a straight-line trajectory beam, my man. That doesn't leave us with a lot of choices."

"Then I better get creative," Cray said, locating the box for the manual flight controls. "I need to fly this thing myself. Can you unlock the stick for me?"

"No problemo."

The box popped open, pushing out the stick and throttle on a hydraulic. Cray put the MFI back in his pocket and cautiously took the controls into his hands, testing out the pulser's maneuvering capability. It lurched to port sluggishly, then back over to level flight. The ship protested loudly under the miniscule load.

"No way this is gonna work," Heretic said.

"You worry about the stress inhibitors, I'll worry about the flying," Cray snapped. "What's the word on weapons with that hovercraft?"

Two bright flares of pulse fire immediately exploded just above the ship. Cray was certain he had been hit—but instead of buckling, the pulser merely reacted to the shock of a near miss, rocking up and down as it skipped along the edges of the blast wave. The hovercraft then roared past, visible only for a second before it dipped out of sight. Its pilot had applied maximum power to the strafing run, expecting a kill—but was forced to come around again to take another shot.

"Answers that question," Cray said grimly.

"Negative impact," the hammerjack reported. "Photon wash from the grid must have drawn his fire off target. He'll have to tighten up his beam for the next run."

"Can we take that kind of hit?"

"Unlikely. Even if we were in good shape, he could probably take us out with a single shot."

"Swell." Cray checked on the trajectory flow again. The weapons fire weakened it even further, down to minimum tolerance levels. The *Inru* didn't even need to score a direct hit. Just grazing the flight grid would be enough to knock the pulser out of the sky.

But it gave him an idea.

"What's the status on our receptor dishes?" Cray asked.

Heretic ran a quick diagnostic. "We sustained some damage fore and aft, mostly from overload," the hammerjack told him. "The dorsal support pylon is cracked, but not severely. Ventral is still fully functional."

"So I can divert power from the trajectory beam through the dorsal if I want."

"Sure," Heretic laughed. "If you don't mind falling off the beam. You won't have enough power to maintain flight if you pull a stunt like that."

"That's precisely what I want," Cray said. "How much time do we have before that bastard gets back here?"

"Twenty seconds."

"Distance to the traverse grid below?"

"One hundred and fifty-seven meters."

Could be worse, Cray thought, doing the calculations in his head. *As long as I can keep the y-axis foils fully deployed . . .*

"It just might work," he finished out loud.

For the first time, the hammerjack sounded nervous. "What the hell are you talking about, Alden?"

"The only chance I've got," he replied, rubbing his hands together and putting them back on the controls. "Heretic, I need you to feed the tactical data on that hovercraft into the tracking system for the dorsal receptor dish. Correlate all dish movements relative to the position of the hovercraft—and make damned sure you don't lose him. We're only going to get one chance."

Heretic made the adjustments.

"Complete," he announced.

Cray set his eyes dead ahead, watching the *Inru* hovercraft as it emerged from the canyons of the city and made a course straight for him. The tiny pinpoint of light grew larger as it approached, taking on malevolent form as it closed to killer range.

Just like a game of chicken.

"Time to intercept," Cray said.

"Ten seconds."

The hovercraft showed no signs of backing down.

"Wait until he fires," Cray said. "Then all power to the dorsal."

"Five seconds," Heretic informed him, then after a brief pause added, "Been nice knowing you, boss."

Cray smiled, but his hands shook.

Then up ahead, incandescence as the *Inru* let go of his fire.

"NOW!"

Twin bursts of pure energy traversed the void between the hovercraft and the pulser, exploding off the flight grid like fireworks. The *Inru* ship then lurched into a dive—its pilot anticipating the powerful concussion that would occur when the beams struck their target, steering clear of the debris cloud that would form when the pulser disintegrated. With full weapons at point-blank range, a miss was impossible on a stationary object. It only remained to go back and visually confirm the kill once it was done.

But there was no bright flash, no dust cloud, no kill—and no pulser. The deadly beams seared through thin air, going off wild until they were harmlessly absorbed by the grid. The *Inru* pilot jerked his head around, looking everywhere for the target he knew was there, but saw nothing but empty space.

Until his proximity alarms went crazy, and the weight of something ominous fell over him.

A scant two meters off his starboard side, the pulser thundered past him. It had dropped completely off the grid, its nose pirouetting downward to move enough air over the foils to maintain a steep glide. The fore and aft receptor dishes had gone dark—but the dorsal remained active, spitting out residual energy from the trajectory beam like a powerful laser.

The pulser's wake flipped the hovercraft over, sending it into a flat spin. The pilot reacted quickly, mashing down on his reaction control jets and slowing his forward velocity to a hover—a maneuver that saved his ship from barreling into one of the surrounding skyscrapers, but also made him fatally vulnerable. Sitting out in the open sky, *he* had become the stationary target; and as the pulser's energized dish swung around to catch him, the *Inru* pilot had just enough time to realize he was the cause of his own death.

The waning power of the trajectory beam lanced out at the hovercraft, one fraction of what it had been—but still enough to cut the small ship in half. Fuel components scattered as its tanks ripped open, creating a volatile mist that exploded as soon as it came in contact with the beam. The resulting concussion shattered windows in the nearby towers, creating a shower of glass that fell into the streets below. Pieces of the hovercraft joined in that downpour, consuming themselves in fire as they trickled down.

The bright halo above Manhattan faded.

And the pulser rushed to meet its own fate.

"Distance to grid!" Cray shouted.

"Ninety meters," Heretic replied, barely audible in the melee of noises filling the cockpit. "Eighty meters . . . sixty-five—*shit!* We're gonna splash all over that grid if we don't lose some goddamned speed!"

Cray didn't need the hammerjack to tell him that. It was spelled out in lethal terms by the images outside the canopy glass. Swallowed by the narrow corridor between the towers of Church Street, Cray was assailed with peripheral flashes of brilliant radiance—lights shining through the windows of surrounding buildings, coming together into a blur as they marked his accelerated fall out of the sky. Down below, traffic along the busy traverse grid loomed closer and closer, vehicles idling back and forth, suspended above the city streets by threads of light—unaware of the bomb about to drop on them.

"*Fifty* meters!"

Cray held his breath, pulling back on the dead stick as hard as he could. The pulser was never designed to function as a glider, and responded to his commands like a sinking stone. It bounced from side to side, metal grinding against metal, tossing Cray around and threatening to murder his wounded shoulder—but still he held on, too stubborn to let go, too hopeless to wish for a miracle.

"Thirty-five!"

A loud screech penetrated the cabin from behind. Looking back, Cray watched the dorsal receptor dish tear loose from its support pylon. It caught the wind and was yanked away, tumbling a few times before dropping out of sight.

"Thirty meters," Heretic reported. "Twenty-five . . . twenty."

The pulser's nose began to rise.

"Hot damn, boss!" the hammerjack said. "I think we got ourselves a head wind!"

Precious air spilled over the foils, allowing Cray some more control of the ship. It wasn't much—but it flattened out his angle of attack, giving him a chance at parking this thing. Trying out the z-axis foils, he nudged the pulser to starboard and lined himself up with the closest grid lane he could find.

"Ten meters. Leveling off."

Damn, Cray thought. The lane was choked with traffic, pulsers lined up with no more than thirty meters between them.

"Jack the traverse grid," he told Heretic. "Spread these guys out. Gimme some room here."

"No time. We only got about eight seconds."

Cray looked around for other options, but couldn't find one. With the head wind dying fast, he was committed. "Bring the gain up on the dishes to full," he instructed. "Catch the photon wash if you can. Channel it through our main axis to get us some more stability."

Cray saw the forward dish come up, sniffing around for any energy it could find. Delicate tendrils of static electricity formed along its rim before being drawn in. He positioned the pulser as best he could, then thrust down on the flight stick.

"Contact," Heretic said.

The injured ship hit the traverse grid like a hammer, hijacking the trajectory beam and greedily stuffing photons down its throat. The beam nearly collapsed under the weight of the abrupt drain, creating a ripple effect that thrashed the chain of pulsers in the lane like objects on the end of a whip. They snapped back into place as soon as the beam regenerated itself—including the unexpected guest that had caused the trouble in the first place. Spewing an intense blue flare out of its aft dish, the pulser flipped over several times before righting itself—then roared off on a collision course with the ship directly in front of it.

The Port Authority computers, detecting a major malfunction, slammed on the brakes. The polarity of the trajectory beam neutralized, its component particles redirected to absorb the pulser's inertia. That brought all the other ships in the lane to an instant halt—all except the runaway, which continued to lumber forward, driving a shower of sparks ahead of it.

A backflow of energy built up within the body of the pulser, growing to proportions that could blow the ship apart. Some of it bubbled over into the hole where the dorsal dish had been, venting into the atmosphere as the pulser finally began to slow down, creating an otherworldly aura that made it seem as though a ghost ship had appeared in the middle of New York. The ghost menaced the other pulser in its path, deliberately creeping up on its tail, threatening to crush the aft receptor dish and create another disaster. It came within less than a meter, but then relented, easing off as the forces that drove the runaway abated.

The ghost ship was still.

As was the city around it.

Cray sank into his seat.

It was the first time he could recall breathing since he left the Works. Closing his eyes, he soaked up the sounds coming up from the street below: the traffic, the sirens, the collective pulse of a thousand souls staring up into the sky. His body ached terribly, but it felt good just the same. He was alive—and that was more than he deserved.

He let go of the flight stick. Heretic retracted it along with the throttle, locking the controls back up in the box.

"I never want to ride in one of these things again," Cray sighed.

"That ain't a bad idea for now," the hammerjack said. "I've found a place to set you down and get you out of here. I suggest you make tracks before the CSS hears about this."

Cray held up his MFI, regarding it now as more a person than a piece of electronics.

"How did you know about Avalon?"

"She had a chat with her *Inru* buddies while you were in the Tank," Heretic said. "I dropped in on their conversation. Those guys want you real bad, Alden. They took one hell of a chance trying to grab you like that."

"*Why?*"

"That's something I'll have to explain to you—in person."

Cray thought about it. He was tired, confused—and possibly a fugitive at this point. However he looked at it, he couldn't possibly explain himself to Special Services, even if he tried. He was too out of bounds.

"What did you have in mind?"

"A little place I know in the Zone," Heretic said. "A real commerce dive. You'll like it."

"Sounds like home."

"We'll be safe there," Heretic promised. "We can talk. There's a lot about this you don't understand, Alden. You sure you can handle it?"

"Yes," Cray said. "As long as it's real."

EIGHT

It took Cray the better part of an hour to find a taxi willing to pick him up. Cabbies had better instincts than most when it came to people and had a tendency to pass on the kind of man who wandered around Manhattan covered in blood. It was only after he flashed some hard currency that Cray found a driver willing to take the chance—and that was a techead with an implant fetish, who looked even scarier than he did.

But the cabbie knew his way around the Zone, precisely what Cray needed. Two gold Krugerrands got him into Chelsea, and two more got him directions to what the cabbie described as one of the better flesh barns in town. From all the body art the kid had on display, Cray was inclined to take his word for it.

A simple neon sign marked the place, an advertisement nowhere near as lurid as the naked baby doll peddling her wares in the window. A hologram identified her as one of the shop's "clients"—an understatement considering all the enhancements the woman had undergone, but at this point Cray didn't care. All he needed was a derm transplant and a bone-set to repair his shoulder, plus a few painkillers. He could spring for some professional cosmetic surgery later.

The shop quack had him fixed up in about twenty minutes. Cray then walked down the block to a clothier who specialized in not-quite-legal streetwear, paying cash for a dark Armani suit that made him come off like a gangster. He pitched his old clothing into an incinerator, going back to the boulevard and projecting attitude. As a rule, street species didn't fuck with *Yakuza*. The illusion was the next best thing to carrying a gun.

The bar Heretic had told him about wasn't hard to find. It was down at the end of the low-tech market district, past the open-air outlets that hawked everything from fresh fish to oriental rugs, worlds off from the rave clubs and subculture only a few kilometers away. Wall-to-wall bodies pressed against each other on the inside: mostly the alcohol crowd, although there were a few tables where tec pushers set up shop and catered to wealthy tourists looking for an expensive thrill. They eyed Cray suspiciously, the typical reaction of lightweight sinners when confronted with a truly dangerous person. The image didn't fit into their fantasies of thug life.

Cray found a seat at the bar with a decent view of the place. He ordered a beer. Like everything else there, the brew was a pale imitation of the real thing. Making time with his drink, he casually surveyed the faces around him. There were no obvious signs of danger, which was a relief; but there were also no clues to Heretic's identity, a danger in itself.

Cray finished his beer and ordered another. A prostitute observed his solitary status and sauntered up to him, offering a pitch for her services. Cray passed her some money to go away. A few minutes later, another woman appeared behind him and used a decidedly different approach. Sliding her hands over his shoulders, she ran her fingers all the way down his chest. Bringing her lips to his ear, she whispered sweetly.

"Jumping that grid was better than sex, wasn't it?"

Cray bolted up from his seat. Standing there, decked out like the other pay-for-play girls, was the same woman who had propositioned him at the airport in Vienna. She tossed her blond hair aside, looking him up and down like any potential customer. It wasn't so different from the routine she had used on him before—and its effect was just as potent.

Cray said the first thing that popped into his head.

"You sure do get around for a hooker."

"Charming," Lea said, her green eyes narrowing. "I like a man who isn't afraid to make an ass of himself."

"Sorry. I've had a bad day."

"So I've heard." Her voice was a purr. She pressed herself up against him, hanging on his arm like a pretty ornament. "What do you say the two of us get out of here so you can tell me *all* about it? I know a place not far from here. I promise, you won't be disappointed."

Cray breathed deeply, taking in her perfume. The scent was melodic, intoxicating.

"How much?" he asked, going along.

Lea sparkled.

"More than you can afford."

The hotel was the kind of establishment that rented by the hour: microscopic rooms, questionable hygiene, and a clientele that didn't give real names. A jungle, even by Zone standards—but a haven for those seeking anonymity.

Lea navigated the dim hallways like she knew the place, stepping around the dozen or so junkies who decorated the floor. Some of them stirred, but most lay still—either dead or hopelessly stoned. Then there were the women, who stole from the carcasses and eyed Cray hungrily. *Tesla girls,* he thought, remembering the ones he had seen in the Asian Sphere: *Vampires, riding a permanent tec high, allergic to the light.* Not quite prostitutes, the Crowleys used them as a tool of inducement for their religion. They reacted to Cray's body temperature, moving in on him until Lea warned them off with a glance.

Not my trick, she told them, without saying a word. They heeded.

Leading him down to the end of a filthy corridor, Lea slipped a key into one of the doors and ushered him inside. He flipped on the lights while she locked the door, the pale glow of the fluorescents adding a harshness to the squalid surroundings. A single plastic chair sat next to a bare foam mattress, which completed the décor of the room. Peeling walls stained with graffiti enclosed the tiny space, which was riddled with a permanent funk of cheap drugs and cheaper sex. It was quite a change from the Waldorf Astoria.

Lea affixed a small electronic device to the door. *A sensor globe,* Cray decided—probably thermal, collecting heat signatures from the hall. She went across the room and placed another one on the window. "A lot of peeping Toms in the neighborhood," she explained, closing the torn flap of nylon that acted as a privacy curtain. "Good news is that the Zone Authority mostly ignores this place. There isn't much profit in busting pimps and small-time dealers. We should be safe here for a while."

"I wasn't planning on staying here that long."

She turned around. "You in a hurry to get some place in particular?"

"Not really," he admitted, taking in the room with a mixture of disgust and amazement. "CSS should have an arrest warrant for me by now, so it's not like I have a lot of choices—"

Cray never got to finish the thought. The sight of a weapon in Lea's hand stopped him cold. She had slipped a v-wave emitter out from under her skirt when he wasn't looking and was pointing it at his head.

"Does this mean the party's over?"

Lea rolled her eyes. "Just shut up and put your hands behind your head."

Cray did as he was told. Lea obviously knew what she was doing, and he was in no position to put up a struggle. "I don't believe we've been properly introduced," he said. "I'm Cray Alden—you know, the guy who trusted you enough to come out here."

"Lea Prism," she replied, unimpressed. "Hold still, will you? You're making me nervous."

"Sorry," Cray said. "If I had known this was a ripoff, I would have brought more money."

"Yeah, yeah—keep talking." She came up with a small pouch filled with coin and Cray's MFI. The cash she tossed onto the bed. The integrator, however, held more than a casual interest. She examined it carefully, eyes brightening as she turned it over in her hand. "Cool," she pronounced. "*Very* cool."

"Glad you approve."

"Don't be an asshole, Alden," Lea chided him, handing the MFI back and putting away her weapon. "It's just security. You know how dangerous it is out here. I have to make sure Heretic isn't walking into a trap."

"Heretic came to *me*," Cray reminded her, straightening out his jacket. "I wasn't the one who asked for this. And I sure as hell don't need one of his ballbusters working me over."

"Suit yourself. You can blow out of here anytime you want."

Lea did nothing to stop him. She even stepped away from the door, giving him a free and clear path. But that meant going back to the Assembly, back to CSS—and a number of questions he wasn't prepared to answer.

He took a seat in the old plastic chair.

"What does Heretic want with me?"

"He can explain that to you later," Lea said. "Right now, his main concern is keeping you away from the Collective."

"*That's* why you've been dogging me?" Cray asked. "For protection?"

"Believe me, you needed it. You're dealing with some bad people, Alden. The Assembly doesn't even know how deep this goes."

He shook his head in disbelief. "How long has this been going on?"

"Ever since that business in Singapore," Lea told him. "He keeps an eye on all of the corporate spooks—especially the good ones. After Zoe got killed, his interest in you got personal. He's been tracking your movements ever since."

"Vienna?"

"That's where we picked up the trail. You covered your tracks pretty good. Took us nearly forty-eight hours to sniff out where you were headed."

"And I thought you were a honey trap," Cray grumbled, berating himself for not figuring it out sooner. "Is that when you jacked my MFI?"

"A little package we've been developing," she said. "I used the same carrier wave you were on to upload a ROM-specific protovirus."

Cray remembered the travel vestibule at the airport. He had used his MFI to open an Axis port and run a feedback trace on himself, just as a precaution. If Lea had been standing outside, she could have nailed down the frequencies he was using and piggybacked them—a slick piece of work, as he never ran an open jack without encryption. That she had done it without his knowing was even more impressive.

"Once the virus tunnels in," she went on, "it utilizes host resources to manufacture a construct—in your case, a personality module Heretic devised. Combines local and remote control, which makes it a bitch to extract. Sorry if I messed with your head back there, but the bandwidth constraints meant I had to get close to deliver it."

Cray wondered where Heretic had gotten the technology. If the hammerjack had developed it himself, the man was more than brilliant. He was a goddamned virtuoso.

And for some reason, he wanted Cray.

"What the hell is going on here?"

"A lot of things you don't know about yet," Lea answered. "You, my friend, were in the wrong place at the wrong time. None of this would have happened if your boss hadn't screwed up and lost something very important to him."

Cray whispered the name: "Yin."

"GenTec has been developing a new strain of flash-DNA," Lea said, pacing about the room as she spoke. "That part you already know. What Yin *didn't* tell you is that the project is strictly off the books—and with good reason. He doesn't want anybody to know that he's been using Collective funds to advance an *Inru* agenda."

Cray was stunned. More than that, it was impossible to believe—not because of Phao Yin's character, but rather his total *lack* of it. Yin stood as a pillar of greed within the Collective, but he was no revolutionary. If he was working with the *Inru,* he was also working some kind of angle.

"If you don't believe me," Lea prodded, "think about what Zoe was carrying. Then ask yourself why you haven't heard from Dex Marlowe."

It was the first time Cray had even thought of the genetic medical examiner since leaving Kuala Lumpur. He had no idea how Lea could have known about Marlowe, outside of Heretic's godlike omnipresence—but she was right. Dex *should* have tried to contact him. That no message had come across was an ominous sign.

Cray stood up and grabbed Lea by the arm. She pushed the emitter into his ribs to warn him off, but Cray was too angry to care.

"What happened to Dex?" he demanded. "What do you know?"

"Yin heard about what the two of you were doing!" Lea snapped, glaring at him defiantly. "He allowed Marlowe to complete the flash extraction, then killed him, okay? Are you satisfied?"

Cray fell silent, the pulse of his rage ebbing to a dull ache as he released her.

"He also put a directive out on *you*," Lea finished. The heat of her own anger abated at the sight of Cray's grief, and segued into a moment of compassion. "Avalon was under orders to bring you in. If that wasn't feasible, she was supposed to take you out."

"Dex didn't even have time to complete his analysis," Cray muttered. "What possible threat could I pose?"

"It's not what you know that makes you a threat. It's what you *are*."

Cray didn't like the sound of it.

"What's that supposed to mean?"

"It means that the answer is inside of you," Lea sighed, lowering her eyes. The bravado was gone, replaced with a forlorn sympathy. She sat down on the edge of the mattress, then looked back up at him. "The flash was infused with a fail-safe replication code. Upon termination of the host entity, the code is instructed to seek out another living system—an organism in close proximity. In Zoe's case, that happened to be you."

The horror of it played out in Cray's mind: *The twitch. A convulsion. Death throes, nothing more. That hand clamping down and refusing to let go . . .*

Cray still felt the cooling flesh upon him—and the sting of injection.

Dead magic the strongest of all.

"Jesus," he shuddered. Cray had heard of the fail-safe inclusions—

of how a corpse could rise, seeking to propagate the code floating around in its bloodstream. A cold stab of panic penetrated him, violating him even further.

Zoe had made him into a runner.

"You're the only one besides Yin who has access to the information contained in that flash," Lea said. "He dumped what he could get out of Zoe into GenTec's domain—but then you were gone before he realized you were carrying."

"What *am* I carrying?" Cray asked—remembering the images Marlowe had showed him, how the flash invaded Zoe's tissues like a cancer. "Just what is this stuff supposed to do?"

"It's a leap, Alden. Or at least the *Inru* think it is."

"A leap toward what?"

Lea's answer was a hush of unspeakable implications.

Cray backed away from her. All at once, he understood: Zoe had never left him. She had passed on a part of herself, and it had been with him ever since. Even now, it was at work inside of him—changing him, *remaking* him, into what Zoe was becoming.

The Ascension . . .

"We need to extract this thing," Cray said. *"Now."*

"I've already made arrangements," Lea assured him. "Heretic is waiting for us to—"

Her words were cut off by a muffled beep at the door. Lea signaled for Cray to remain silent, then went over to check the sensor globe. A pair of contacts had appeared at extreme range—muted heat signatures, moving up the stairwell in a cover formation.

"We got a couple of live ones," she said. "Military-style approach. Looks like they're wearing body armor."

"Zone agents," Cray said, just as the globe at the window went off. He rushed over and peeled the curtain back to watch the fire escape. The camochrome made them hard to spot. By the time he caught a hint of motion, they were already too close.

"How many?" Lea asked him.

"Two more."

"Know anything about guns?"

Cray nodded. She tossed him the emitter.

"Go for the head shot."

Cray had another idea. He put the weapon down and activated his MFI, scanning the hyperband frequencies for the agents' communication loop. He came up dry. They weren't about to make the same mistake they made in Singapore.

"*Damn*," he whispered.

"Problems?"

"I think the Zone Authority is onto my bag of tricks."

"You better come up with something new," Lea said, watching the ghostly contacts as they closed in. "Because we're gonna have company in about ten seconds."

Cray weighed what few options they had. Only one thing was certain: the room was a kill zone. If the agents got inside, he and Lea were dead. Their only hope was to get out in the open where there was room to maneuver—to put themselves directly in their enemy's sights.

And there was only one way to do that without getting shot.

Cray went for the door.

There was silence in the hallway.

A pair of Zone agents immersed themselves in the dark, body armor mimicking the shades of murk around them. The lead agent signaled for his man to proceed, holding back a few meters in a firing position while the other one headed to the end of the corridor.

Their orders were simple: bring Alden back, alive if it all possible, and kill anyone else who might be with him. The Zone Authority had ponied up a hefty sum to make that happen, which made the agents less gonzo than they usually were; but they also knew Alden and what the man had done in the Asian Sphere. Bringing back a live body was not a priority.

The point man stationed himself outside Alden's door. He looked back at the lead agent and nodded. The lead agent checked his chronograph, timing the arrival of the outside team. Twenty more seconds and they would be ready to storm the room.

The lead agent raised his hand, getting ready to drop the hammer. But before he could, the hammer dropped on *him.*

The door burst off its hinges, coming down on the point man and knocking him to the floor. Two people came tumbling out of the room—one of them male, the other female, clawing at each other in a life-and-death struggle. They fell on top of one another, rolling across the floor as they exchanged blows, a tangled mass of legs and elbows.

The lead agent leveled his rifle at the fighting pair.

"Don't shoot!" the man shouted. *"I'm Alden!"*

A sharp jab to the stomach sent him reeling backward. The woman, who was strong for her size, took the advantage and pounced on him, wrapping her hands around his throat. Alden managed to kick her off, then rolled away to get some distance before jumping back to his feet. The woman went after him immediately. She launched herself at Alden with killer velocity, her aim to crush Alden's head with her bare hands.

The lead agent almost took her out, before he saw the weapon in Alden's hand.

Microwaves burned the air into a shimmer as they lanced out toward the woman's chest. The impact stopped her in midstride, as if she had hit an invisible wall—but she remained on her feet, her body convulsing like a puppet on strings. A gurgling sound bubbled from her throat as she continued her bizarre dance, ending in a piercing shriek when Cray let go of the trigger.

She fell to the floor.

Alden stood there, panting, frozen in that same stance. The lead agent scrambled over, keeping his rifle pointed at his target, barking orders.

"Drop it, motherfucker!"

"It's okay," Alden told him in between breaths. "I work for Phao Yin. Check it out. Credentials are in my front pocket."

"Drop it now or I'll drop YOU!"

Alden let the emitter fall to the floor.

"She's the one who grabbed me," he said, pointing toward the motionless woman. "She's *Inru,* off on some crazy mission. You gotta believe me, fellas."

"Save it, spook," the lead agent growled, spinning Alden around and slamming him up against the wall. "You can tell it to Yin when you see him."

The other agent began to stir, and crawled out from under the fallen door. A mass of clunky armor, he tried three times before making it to his feet. "What the hell *is* this?" he asked groggily, glancing back and forth between Alden and the dead woman. "She a hooker?"

"Just pat him down and take him into custody."

"Prettiest damn hooker I ever saw," the agent went on, unable to contain his fascination as he frisked Alden from top to bottom. "How much you pay for that?"

While that was going on behind him, the lead agent activated his hyperband transmitter and signaled the rest of his team. "Terminate radio silence," he instructed. "Abort the insertion. I repeat—abort the insertion. We already have the subject in custody."

No other weapons or identification turned up on Alden's person—just a kooky electronic device that the dim agent had never seen before. He grabbed the thing and stuck it in his prisoner's face. "What's *this* for?"

Alden clammed up.

The agent drove his fist into Alden's stomach to motivate him.

Alden doubled over. The lead agent returned to assess the situation. His transmitter implant was still active, the other members of his team talking in his earpiece.

"I found this," the agent said to his boss, tossing him the electronic device. "Tough guy doesn't want to tell me what it is."

The lead agent inspected the device. It was tiny—no bigger than his palm, with a blank screen in the middle of its face and a few keys for input. It responded to his touch, lighting up and beeping at him in friendly greeting. A skull and crossbones appeared on the screen.

"Hi, there," the skull announced. "Bet I can guess what frequency you're on."

An intense pop sounded off in their ears.

It was easy for the virtual Heretic to sniff out the agents' comm chatter, but its suicide was another matter. Entwined in the MFI's ROM, the hammerjack's virtual consciousness experienced precisely 1.7 polling loops of hesitation—amounting to a full delay of one-ten-thousandth of a second—before jacking the frequency and transmitting the fatal pulse. After that, death was instantaneous.

So it was with the two agents. Their communication implants detonated like tiny concussion grenades, the intense bursts of pressure focused bilaterally along the route of the auditory canal. Half the burst exited the ear harmlessly; the other half blasted a quarter-centimeter hole through the brain, which drilled all the way to the base of the stem. Both of the agents collapsed into heaps of armor, their extremities twitching slightly before getting the message they were dead.

Cray looked down on the floor and saw his MFI, still in the hand of the lead agent. He knelt down and pried the device free, watching as the screen fizzled out and the input keys went dark. Heretic was gone—at least in the disembodied sense.

Lea stirred a little, opening one eye to see if everything was clear. Cray hopped over and helped her up, cradling her under his arm.

"How you doing?"

"Man," she groaned. "Talk about a guy who can't take no for an answer."

"You gave me some pretty good chops yourself. Next time, don't try so hard."

"*Now* he tells me," Lea said, standing up. She stepped around the dead agents and pushed the dim one aside, retrieving her v-wave emitter and pushing it back up from the minimum setting. "Nice plan, Alden. We're lucky these jokers bought it."

"Nobody ever failed the corps IQ test," Cray said, searching the other agent for a less conspicuous weapon. "Your boss really came through. I'm looking forward to meeting this guy."

"You won't get the chance if we don't get out of here. We got *maybe* a minute before those goons outside start to wonder what's going on."

"Precisely my point." Cray worked at the hip compartment in the dead agent's armor, fumbling with it a couple of times before it popped open. Inside, he found a small arsenal of stabbing weapons and a pulse pistol. The battery pack showed full, good for three or four shots—strictly a backup piece, but at least he could carry it out of here without getting noticed. He stuffed the pistol into his belt, pocketing one of the knives. "This place have a back door?"

"Fire escape, other side of the hotel."

"What about transportation? Can you get us out of the city?"

Lea fixed him with a knowing smile. "Only if you don't mind hopping a pulser."

"Swell," Cray muttered, taking her hand and heading for the exit. "This day just keeps getting better and better."

Glazed eyes glinted like starlight from the wet pavement below. Between the Zoners and those who evacuated the hotel, two dozen bodies were huddled together at the bottom of the fire escape—striking deals, swapping fluids, underneath an ultraviolet haze of commerce. Cray and Lea's intrusion drew scant attention, outside of the occasional curious glance. They were little more than hallucinations in that world anyway.

Cray checked the crowd as soon as he hit the street, keeping one hand glued to his pistol. He felt the fingers of the Tesla girls on him, touch devoid of any human intent, air thick with the hot sweetness of their breath—but saw nothing that stood out. Brushing them aside, he turned back toward Lea.

"Which way?"

"The market," she replied. "We can catch a cargo pulser there. It's the only one that regularly comes into the Zone."

They walked. As the two of them broke from the crowd, Cray began to regret his choice in clothing. While Lea blended in perfectly with her surroundings, Cray stood out like a signal flare in the dead of night. He just hoped they wouldn't get made before they got out of the red-light district.

That hope was thrashed when one of the Tesla girls started shrieking behind them.

It was a tortured sound, like the scrape of teeth against bone. Cray and Lea whirled around, half-expecting to find one of those crazed women chasing them. But it was at a distance, back at the fire escape, where they saw the girl attacking a Zone agent. He had shoved her to the ground, and now she was jumping him from behind—her fingers under his helmet, clawing at his eyes. The agent bellowed out in pain, grabbing the girl by the hair and throwing her over his shoulder. He would have killed her right there, but his sights were still focused on the mark.

Blood ran down the exposed parts of the agent's face from where the girl had gouged him. Mechanically, he raised his rifle toward Cray.

The girl jumped in front of it.

Her body was a corona against the bright flash, which caught her full in the chest. The blast knocked her through the air and dropped her back down onto the pavement. A twisted, smoking mass with only the general shape of a human being, the girl rolled to a stop at Lea's feet.

"Son of a bitch—" Lea began.

Cray drew his pistol and fired.

The single shot struck with devastating impact. The beam hit the agent at the left hip, burning through the armor joint and into tender flesh below. The force of impact tore his leg clean off, toppling the agent and dropping him flat on his back. His rifle went flying.

Cray lowered the pistol.

The agent was not dead. He still writhed on the ground, half-blind and trying to drag himself away. But the crowd of Zoners gathered around him in a circle, cutting off his lines of escape. He screamed at them to back off, trying to frighten them—but like vultures, they knew when their meal was vulnerable.

Leading the charge, the Tesla girls fell on him. Then the others.

Cray's breath was a cloud in the frosty air.

"Lights out," he whispered.

His words were punctuated by another electrical discharge. Lightning cut the air in half, digging a crater out of the pavement a few meters in front of them. Lea dove for the ground, while Cray dropped to one knee and aimed his pistol in the direction of the pulse fire. In the fading brightness of the afterimage, through debris and dust, Cray spotted a flash of movement on the hotel fire escape—the last agent, his position obscured by camochrome armor.

Cray didn't have the option of locating the target. Instead he took aim at the building and fired off two quick bursts. The beams struck the supports for the fire escape, easily splintering the ancient, rusted struts and blowing them clear out of the wall. A bloom of sparks erupted as metal twisted and vaporized, collapsing to the ground with a roar like that of a fallen dinosaur.

As the mass of wreckage settled, a single shot from the agent's pulse rifle burned a hole into the night. Veering wildly, it careened into the sky and disappeared. It could have been the last defiant act of a dead man, but Cray doubted it. Whatever was at work inside of him—flash, intuition, a sixth sense—told him that the agent was still very much alive, leaving them with precious few seconds to act.

Cray checked the charge indicator on the pistol. It was dry.

"Listen to me," he told Lea. "You have to make a run for it. Head for the cargo docks. If I don't show up in *fifteen* minutes, you hop the next pulser and get the hell out of the city. Understand?"

"No. Why don't you just come with me?"

"Because they found me too damned fast," Cray said. "I don't know what it is, but they're tracking me somehow. You'll be a lot safer without me until I can shake this last guy loose." He stopped talking when he saw something in Lea's eyes—something akin to recognition.

"What?" he asked her.

"Nothing," she said, even though it was still there. "I'll see you at the docks."

She started to leave. Cray stopped her briefly, taking her by the hand. It was a softer touch, tender even—meant to reinforce what he had said earlier.

"Fifteen minutes," he reminded her.

Lea smiled. "Don't make me come looking for you."

Then she was gone. Cray remained behind, until she rounded the corner and disappeared down the street. Back near the hotel, he saw the crowd of Zoners milling around like a group of zombies. They had torn the fallen agent to pieces and were now in search of a fresh kill.

The sound of groaning metal made them disperse. As they parted, a human form emerged from the remains of the fire escape, its shape augmented to formidable proportions by the bulky armor it wore. The camochrome had been damaged in the fall, lending a ghostly aura to the surviving agent. Parts of him were invisible, while other parts were opaquely solid.

His pulse rifle was gone. He grabbed a blade from his weapons compartment and pointed it at Cray. Its edge glinted in the pale lamplight.

Cray ran.

He lost himself in the market, melting into the dizzying array of faces in a mass confusion of exchange. It was like Babel. Cray heard a dozen languages in the space of as many steps—Chinese, Thai, German, Russian—a smattering of different tongues, bargaining with each other with raw and fervent energy. The atmosphere reeked of ganja, spoiled fruit, decaying meat, animal dung—things used and discarded by industrial society, then recycled for the lower strata of the subculture.

A gridlock of human columns bumped against him with scarce thought or reason, performing their basic functions like cells in a malignant tumor. Cray was sick with their heat and his exhaustion, but he kept moving. He would use himself up before he allowed the agent to take him—but even if that happened, Cray resolved he would not be taken alive. He wouldn't give Phao Yin the satisfaction.

Ducking behind one of the retail stands, Cray checked his watch. Five more minutes before Lea was supposed to be out of here. Eyes piercing the crowd, he searched for the Zone agent. The hulking shape did not materialize.

Where is he?

He slid the knife he had stolen out of his pocket. It reminded him of the blade Avalon had used on him. He wrapped his fingers around the handle and emerged from his hiding place. Glancing over the tent poles of the market, he spotted the tall stacks of crates being forklifted off the cargo docks. It was a thirty-second sprint, tops. Thirty more seconds to safety.

Cray went for it.

And ran up against an armored wall.

The agent sprang from nowhere, coming down on Cray like an anvil. Arms groped out and clutched him by the shoulders, heaving him up and driving him back into the ground again. Cray crumpled like paper, the knife tumbling out of his hand. None of the by-standers treated this as an unusual occurrence; in fact, they spread out a bit to give the agent more room to do his thing.

The agent planted a foot on Cray's chest and pinned him against the pavement. He hovered there for a few moments, hoping to enjoy the terror he inspired—but Cray didn't give it up. He just clenched his teeth and went with the pain.

"What are you waiting for, you stupid fuck?"

Scalded, the agent drew back his fist. Cray closed his eyes.

Then the weight was gone, and he was free.

In memory, Cray would believe he saw it in his imagination: Lea appearing from the crowd, launching herself through the air, using her momentum to knock the agent off-balance. In those dreams, her grace and strength were epic—but even that would not compare to the reality he found when he opened his eyes. She was energy and discipline, fused into one entity—a weapon of human proportions.

Lea was on the agent before he could recover from her initial at-tack. A roundhouse kick to the side of the agent's head dented his helmet, partially unmasking a face that had gone purple from sur-prise and frustration; but all color drained the moment she landed another brutal kick—this one against his chest, which knocked him back into one of the retail stands. Discounted electronics flew every-where as the stand came crashing down, inspiring a brief riot of looters who pocketed as much as they could before the agent got back up.

Like roaches, they knew when to scurry. They opened a path be-tween Lea and the agent, the two squaring off against each other in a combat dance. Money changed hands in a round of instant betting. Lea paid no attention to the odds.

"Put me down for twenty," she said, and moved in.

The agent was ready for her this time, swinging his right arm around in what would have been a crippling blow. But Lea side-stepped him at the last second, upsetting the agent's center of gravity and making him stumble forward for a few steps. The advantage was still hers—but she knew better than to take him from behind. Even as she thought of it, a series of spikes punched out of the armor around his shoulders, turning him into a human mace. This one was more dangerous *without* his gun.

Spinning around on a dime, the agent faced her again. He crouched, the blades on his shoulders pointed toward her like the horns of a rhino.

He charged.

Cray willed her to get out of the way—but she stood her ground. She seemed determined to allow the deadly tackle, and made no move to avoid it. But the darkness concealed a multitude of secrets—from Cray, and from the crowd.

With a single, fluid motion, the v-wave emitter was in her hand. It had no hope against the agent's armor—but in this case, it wasn't necessary. Lea waited until the agent was close enough, then fired at the seam between his shoulder plate and his neck. The connective mesh there superheated and melted, searing the flesh beneath. The agent howled and lost his balance—but that was not the worst of it. The force of the v-wave's impact had torn the shoulder plate loose, and it now flapped around like a flag in a strong breeze. Liquefied metal flew into the agent's face, burning his cheeks and his eyes. Some flew into his mouth.

When he collapsed, he fell on his injured side. The heated spikes drove themselves into the side of his neck, putting a merciful end to a painful process. When the onlookers stepped in for a closer look, they saw very little blood. Only smoke from cauterized wounds.

Lea went back to collect Cray—but not before she collected her winnings. There was swearing and cursing in several languages, but they all paid up.

"I thought you were supposed to be on the next flight out of here," he said.

"I have a problem with authority," she replied, counting her money. "Besides, we needed some traveling cash."

"Just watch how you hit those speedtecs," Cray cautioned, dragging himself off the ground. "Push it like that again, you'll end up in a puddle."

"Who said I use speedtecs?"

"I'm sorry," he stammered, caught off guard. "It's just—well, I assumed—"

"Don't assume anything," Lea corrected him. "Just do as you're told before you get us both killed." She then headed for the docks, leaving Cray with something new to think about.

And a warning never to underestimate her again.

CHAPTER
NINE

The cargo pulser was a single point in a whole constellation of light. It ejected itself from the stellar aftermass of the Eastern Seaboard megaplex, into the shroud of true night over the Atlantic Ocean. Following a curvilinear path to the jump grid, the automated ship headed south: away from Manhattan, then up to high altitude and safe obscurity. Its navigation lights blinked steadily, but only as pinprick holes in an endless black tapestry. For all practical purposes, the ship was invisible, and for a short time at least, its occupants did not exist.

Cray sensed the abyss beneath him, as he looked past his reflection in the window. Running his finger along the cold surface of the glass, he traced the contours of the East Coast etched in the orange glow of distant sodium light. Up here, boundaries were meaningless. New York, Baltimore, Boston, Washington—they were little more than concepts. Lines on a map, drawn with arbitrary and abstract precision. But never had those lights seemed so beautiful to him. Nor had they seemed so remote.

"We've cleared the Port Authority threshold," Lea announced, buttoning up the pulser's diagnostic console. "I've redirected the signal from the location transponder to cover our tracks. As far as Manhattan is concerned, this bird is heading for Montreal. That should give us enough time to reach our destination before they get wise and start looking for their missing ship."

Cray drew a pensive breath.

"Where are we headed?"

"East Coast Fusion Directorate." Lea settled back and let the pulser fly itself, observing her passenger with a guarded curiosity. "About a hundred clicks out to sea, right off the D.C. coast. They maintain a network of power plants out there—enough juice to supply the whole eastern continent. It's quite a setup."

"I can imagine," Cray said. In truth, he didn't need to imagine anything. GenTec had subcontracted him to the Directorate a couple of years ago to jackproof some of their systems. Their security had been full of holes, which led Cray to believe somebody had been working the place from the inside. He couldn't prove it at the time—though now, he thought it interesting that Lea had picked that particular place to hide out. "I was under the impression that those plants were automated."

"Not quite," Lea told him, letting her smile imply the rest. She changed the subject. "You doing okay over there? You haven't said much since we left the Zone."

"I'm fine." He paused for a few moments, then said earnestly, "Listen, I didn't get a chance to thank you for what you did back there."

"It's okay," she said. "You held up your end."

"And I'm sorry for that crack about the speedtecs."

"Sorry you called me a junkie?" She laughed. "I've been called a lot worse than that, Dr. Alden."

"Yeah, but that's not the point." He struggled to explain his reasons, trying not to come off as morose. "After you've been in this business as long as I have, you make judgments about people. It's what keeps you alive. After watching what happened to Zoe . . ." He didn't finish the thought.

"She didn't use all the time, you know."

Cray blinked. "What?"

"Zoe wasn't in the habit," Lea explained. "She only did it the one time. The run was too damned important. She dropped the speedtecs for insurance in case she got caught." She reached over and touched his arm. "Heretic doesn't blame you for what happened, Cray. The agents called the plays, just like they did tonight. You did everything you could for her."

Cray shook his head, unconvinced.

"I didn't have to find her."

"You didn't have a choice," Lea said. "Yin would have had you killed and sent someone else. It was your *job*, Cray. And now it's your job to let Heretic show you what's real."

"What if I don't want to know?" He allowed that to hang for a while, not even certain that he wanted to bring it up. "Dex gave me a pretty good look at the stuff Zoe was running."

Lea considered what he had said. As Cray watched her reaction, he saw sympathy in her eyes—something he hadn't expected.

"It's a war," she said. The words came out virtual, dreamlike, unreal. "The Collective and the *Inru* have been going at it for a while. When you've been fighting long enough, you start thinking about ways to end it. That's what the *Inru* have been working on—a big gun they can use to settle things once and for all."

There was Heretic's voice again, echoing inside of Cray's head: *You already have the proof. You just don't know it yet.*

"The new flash."

"A blueprint for the Ascension." It was a ghost story, a rendering of the supernatural. "The *Inru* believe the only way to fight Lyssa and the legions of SIs that follow is to outpace them—to advance *human* intelligence to a point far beyond what's possible in a bionucleic system. Lyssa and others like her would be the redundant components among a race of superbeings, instead of the other way around. No more SIs, no more threat."

My God, Cray thought. *No wonder Phao Yin made up a story to get this stuff back. Nobody would believe it even if they knew.*

"Their basic idea was sound," she continued. "The bionucleic matrix is based on chaos logic, which makes it inherently unstable and unpredictable. That it's based on living components helps, but it's still nowhere near as adapted to intelligence as the human mind. The new flash is supposed to augment that—to mimic the superfast relays of a bionucleic system and apply them to the human brain, freeing it from the limitations of its own electrochemistry."

"How did Zoe fit into this?"

"Heretic had been working between the two factions, trying to keep them both off-balance," Lea said. "The idea was to slow down the bionucleic project as well as the development of the new flash. When Heretic got word that the *Inru* had completed their experiments, he jacked the GenTec domain to steal their prototype. Zoe was his runner, so she went to collect the data. Phao Yin sent you to get it back for him."

Cray absorbed what Lea told him, but there was still a piece missing. "I still don't get it," he said. "Heretic is a professional hammerjack. It doesn't make sense he would get involved in something political. There sure as hell isn't any profit in it."

"Not everything is about money, Alden."

"Yin told me the same thing."

"Yin is a partisan."

"If you really knew Yin," Cray said, "you wouldn't be saying that. Now what about Heretic? How did he get mixed up in this business?"

"It seems like a long time ago," Lea said. Her tone was distant, drifting into the realm of the personal. "He used to work for the *Inru,* you know. That's where he learned his chops, jacking Collective domains, plundering data—fighting the establishment, the usual bullshit." She drifted back, resuming a more practical—and detached—demeanor. "Heretic obtained the Collective's research on the bionucleic project. Using that, the *Inru* got a jump start on their own program. Reverse engineering saved them years of testing and development, putting them way ahead of the game. That information is what made everything possible. Without it, the *Inru* might never have succeeded."

"So what changed his mind?"

"He found out his friends were even crazier than his enemies." Lea shuddered a little. "The *Inru* leadership started talking jihad. Righteous fire cleansing the Earth, battling for human souls, some real apocalyptic stuff. By the time Phao Yin came on board, they were talking *selective* evolution—engineering a civilization in which only the true believers would be chosen for the Ascension, while the rest would be made to serve the master race. Heretic decided it was time to get out."

The cabin was murky, with only the lights from the instrumentation to illuminate the soft features of Lea's face. The shadows made her appear much wiser than her years.

"It couldn't have been easy," he said.

Lea shook her head. "It was bloody." Then turning toward him, she added, "Or so I've heard. You don't just leave the *Inru*—not when you get to that level."

"So what is this? Penance?"

"You could call it that."

"What would *you* call it?"

"A worthy cause," Lea said. "Heretic doesn't have many people he can trust. Zoe was one of them. I'm another."

"Where does that leave me?"

Lea regarded him with some affection, though it was more guarded than that. *She's feeling me out,* Cray decided—which was just fine with him. He was doing the same to her.

"That remains to be seen," she told him.

A subtext moved beneath whatever Lea said. There was a lot that Cray wanted to know about her, so many questions he wanted to ask—but that was another part of her that fascinated him. To find out too much too soon would upset a delicate balance. It was better to see it in glimpses, rather than all at once.

The navigation console beeped, putting that moment on hold. Lea reached for the interface, calling up a display of their current position. "We're two minutes out," she reported. "I'm transferring approach over to Directorate control."

Cray looked at the display. The screen showed a virtual construct of the fusion platform, with an overlay of their flight path. The power plant was massive—but unlike the structures of New York, it was isolated. Rising out of the waves on a black ocean, it towered over the flat nothingness without even the company of air traffic.

The cargo pulser was the only blip on the screen, the stars the only other lights in the sky. As hiding places went, it was sheer perfection.

Cray leveled his eyes on the horizon, where the platform was beginning to appear. It quickly grew to magnificence, inspiring in Cray an awe he had not known in a long time. Lea had sold him on the idea of sanctuary—and though it was fleeting, at least it gave him a moment's rest. For the moment, that would be enough.

"No place like home," she said.

The fusion plant spread out across a platform the size of a city block, supported by four gigantic columns that plunged through the opaque depths into the ocean floor. Banks of floodlights lined its perimeter, creating a white aura around the four reactor domes that dominated its surface. A lone traverse beam shimmered through the sky directly above the plant, as if bearing the lightning from an approaching storm; but what appeared out of the night was the tiny form of a single ship, which slowed as it entered the platform's airspace and came to a hover over one of its landing pads.

Liquid light enveloped the cargo pulser as tether beams brought the ship down. From inside, Cray watched fat droplets of sea spray splatter against his window as the pulser connected with the deck. Then the tethers disengaged and the sound of fading power was displaced by a steady wail that was almost human in its insistence.

Cray followed Lea into the cargo bay, where she opened up the belly hatch and pushed a folding ladder down to the deck below. The funneling wind caught her long hair and tossed it around her head in swirls. She pushed the tresses away from her face and gestured toward the open hatch.

"After you."

Cray stepped down into a whipping gale that nearly blew him off his feet. He steadied himself and reached up the ladder to help Lea down, her body incredibly light in his hands. It was only when they were both outside that he realized they were not alone. A single figure concealed beneath a hooded coat emerged from the dirty glow of the landing lights. He carried two more coats under his arm.

"Put these on!" the stranger shouted, handing one to each of them. Lea bundled herself up while Cray tried to get a look at the man's face. It was difficult to see anything between the glare and the maelstrom, and he quickly gave up on the idea. By the time he zipped up and donned his hood, he was just grateful for the warmth.

"Thanks," Cray told him.

"No problem," the man replied. "Now if you don't mind . . ."

Cray felt the business end of some weapon poke him in the ribs. The stranger held a pulse pistol, his finger poised on the trigger. Looking back up, Cray caught the glint of something metallic underneath the man's hood. *Platinum teeth,* he thought, knowing without seeing. *The son of a bitch is grinning at me.*

Cray tried to put himself between the stranger and Lea—but that was before he realized she had a weapon on him as well, the same v-wave emitter she had used back in the Zone. Her expression told him she had no reservations about using it if necessary.

"Don't I feel like an asshole," he said.

"Sorry about this, Alden," Lea apologized. "But it's for your own good, trust me."

Cray put his hands up.

The stranger laughed—more of a giggle, the kind of thing you heard in the street when somebody got burned. Nudging Cray, he pointed his attention toward the northeast, where a line of intense thunderstorms was gathering. The enormous clouds revealed themselves in bursts of sporadic lightning, as deadly as they were beautiful.

"Winter storm," the stranger informed him. "Maybe hurricane force. You picked a hell of a night to come out."

Cray couldn't agree more.

A salt-encrusted porthole was the only window in the chamber where they took him, but at least it permitted a view of the outside. To hear the rain and the thunder without a visual reference would have been maddening. The thrum of electrical power that permeated the place was already oppressive, like a trillion heartbeats pressed against the outer walls. Cray wondered how long they intended to keep him there.

He was strapped down to a table in the middle of the room, surrounded by racks of equipment he did not recognize. Mounted in the ceiling above him was another device—a homemade job cobbled together from various parts, including a radiation inducer that rotated on an electric bearing. It whirred about until it pointed itself at Cray's head. Watching that medieval instrument close in on him, Cray still doubted that Lea had brought him all the way out here just to kill him. But torture? That was a different matter altogether.

"Hold still," she said, via a speaker on the wall, while she watched from the other side with a remote camera. "This should only take a minute."

Cray squeezed his eyes shut as the thing opened up on him, bathing his face with a blinding, invasive energy. It poured down like a flood, first hot, then cold, tearing into his senses and bombarding him with images from outside his own self. For one moment he hovered above the table, watching himself writhe and struggle against his restraints. His mouth contorted into a scream from some deep pit in his soul—disembodied impulses springing from an angry hive, like some demon driven out in exorcism. Then his soul returned, burning from the friction of its reentry and sickening him with the weight of its gravity.

But *lighter*. Not everything that went up had come back down.

Cray contorted, gagging and coughing. The nausea was brutal, passing only when he realized he wasn't going to die.

The door to the chamber opened and Lea appeared.

"What . . ." Cray forced out between breaths. "What did you do to me?"

"What needed to be done."

He wanted to ask another question, but darkness closed in on him. He did not fight, but chose to embrace it. His last impression was of Lea standing next to him, her hand gently stroking the side of his face—perhaps the cruelest punishment of all. It made him want to believe whatever she told him.

"Just rest," she said. "You'll be safe now."

Cray woke up alone, facedown in a bunk bed, surrounded by four steel walls. He felt groggy, unaware of how much time had passed. A nuclear headache pounded his skull when he tried to move. He cried out in surprise as much as pain before he could clamp his mouth shut, but he had already alerted his captors. The door to the small room opened, allowing outside light to stab through the dimness that encased him.

It was Lea again. She glided over to his bedside, sitting down and cradling his head in her arms. In her hand she held a single pill, which she slipped between his lips before he could resist.

"It'll kill the pain," she said.

Cray swallowed, not caring if it was poison.

"Sorry about that," she went on. "It was necessary. After what happened in the Zone, I figured you were being profiled. We couldn't take the chance."

He had to mouth the words a couple of times before they finally came out.

"What did you do to me?"

"A little shake and bake. The Collective tagged you with a neural implant. That's how Yin knew where to find you."

Cray shook his head weakly. The effort made him dizzy, but the pain was already starting to pass.

"No way."

"You couldn't have known," Lea assured him. "But don't worry. We took care of it with some targeted radiation. Leaves you with a hell of a hangover, doesn't it?"

Cray still had a difficult time processing the information.

"How . . . How did they . . . ?"

"It's a biological implant," she explained. "Completely passive— works on interfacing with the Axis subnets. It feeds sensory input processed by your brain into a flash buffer and dumps the data when-ever a request is made by a remote user. Think of it as a ball and chain for reformed hammerjacks."

She smiled. She knew his secret.

"That's right," she said, patting him on the hand, then standing. "You have some explaining to do. I'll be in the control center two decks up—just follow the ladder right down the hall. Meet me upstairs when you're ready." She stopped short of the door and looked back at him. "I cannot *wait* to find out who you really are."

She was gone again. Cray fell back into his pillow and sighed.

"Neither can I."

Cray took a little time to get cleaned up and regain his status as a human being. He still looked like hell, but at least he felt better—which, considering the events of the past twenty-four hours, was a miracle in and of itself. Discovering fresh clothes next to his bed, he changed and took his first tentative step back into the world.

He found the ladder exactly where Lea said it would be and began the climb upstairs. His shoes clinked loudly against the metal rungs, bouncing off steel bulkheads and ducts before being absorbed by the low, constant rumble that reverberated through the decks. The space was confined yet vast, like crawling through an intricate network of catacombs. At the top, Cray saw a sealed hatch. He tried the locking wheel, which spun easily, and with a single push popped it open. Cold, dry air cascaded down on him from above, the preferred climate of machines.

Cray hauled himself up through the hole, closing the hatch behind him. He was in another compartment with low ceilings—cramped by human standards, but not much consideration had been given to ergonomics in its design. It was a home primarily for computers, row upon row of which monitored and directed the fusion plant's automated operations. Some of the equipment was vintage, installed when the facility was constructed more than thirty years earlier, intermixed with a bizarre assortment of modern gear that leeched off the racks like digital parasites. Conduit cable ran all over the floor, creating a tangled mass of power lines and fiber optics that interconnected with one another, a design that exceeded his ability to comprehend. Somebody had rigged the place thoroughly.

"Well, well, well," a voice unfamiliar to him said. "If it isn't Rip van Winkle."

Cray turned to face the owner of the voice. He might have mistaken the man for a techhead had it not been for the crazy assortment of tools he wielded and the obvious expertise he had with all things mechanical. The man was tall, broad in the shoulders, with a bald head that nearly touched the pipes running across the ceiling. His eyes, yellow and intense, regarded Cray with a measure of suspicion.

"Jesus Christ," Cray deadpanned.

"A lot of people make that mistake," the man replied. His accent was pure West End London, his skin African ebony, cheeks marked by rows of tribal scars. "Must be that messiah vibe I keep giving off. You looking for Lea?"

"Yeah."

"Figures," the stranger replied evasively, as if he was holding it against Cray. "The way she chats you up—downright unseemly, if you ask me."

"You the guy who fixed this place up?"

"What's it to you?"

"Nothing much," Cray said, turning a critical eye on all the chop shop modifications. "It just reminds me of that torture chamber of yours. That was quite a job you did on me."

"Only gave you as much as you could take."

"How'd I do?"

The stranger smiled.

"Any more and I could have cooked you up for supper," he said. "Lucky for you I don't eat pork. Come on, she's waiting."

Cray followed him into the maze of stacks, twisting and turning through the narrow corridors until they came to an open area at the end of the command center—an interface substation, from the looks of it. A virtual conference table had been converted into a hub for the half dozen smaller stations that surrounded it, all of them active and feeding into a composite construct that hovered above the surface of the table. Behind the semitransparent image, Cray could see Lea: fingers brushing lightly against the touch controls, her eyes expertly navigating the complex Axis passageways—a telltale web of electrodes pasted to her forehead. The sheer bulk of information she juggled was a marvel to watch.

"Isn't she lovely?" the stranger said.

She was. *She's taking it out in trade,* Cray thought, remembering how Lea had copped his secret in the radiation room downstairs. *Showing me who she really is.*

Lea let go of the controls and the construct went dark. She peeled the electrodes off, shifting back to conventional reality without breaking a sweat.

"What's the matter?" Lea asked. "You never see a woman interface before?"

"I'll be damned," Cray said, torn between admiration and disbelief. He settled on the only word that could describe what he just witnessed: *"Heretic."*

"In the flesh," she said, sounding flirtatious. "Congratulations, Dr. Alden. You're the first corporate spook to verify my identity."

"I suppose you'll have to kill me now," Cray said, taking a seat at the table. "I've been getting a lot of that lately."

"Don't be so dramatic," Lea cajoled him. "I might hurt you, but I won't *kill* you—unless you give me a reason." She nodded at the man standing behind Cray. "You been playing nice with our guest?"

"He's got me in a nark, if you want the truth of it," the stranger said, hopping on the table and laying between them. "You know how jealous I get."

"You're just too much man for one woman to handle," Lea said, then rolled him over and presented him to Cray. "Alden, say hello to Funky. Like myself, a former partisan who traded the monastic existence of a fanatic for the far more agreeable life of information trafficking."

Funky grinned like a silver crocodile. "Charmed."

"He's from the old school," Lea said. "Not much on manners, but he's the best interface engineer in the business. If it's been jacked, chances are Funky built the hardware for the job."

"So I've seen," Cray remarked. "How did you end up here?"

"Rehab," Funky said, sitting up and bending himself into a yoga position. "Got tossed a few years back for dealing face kits to a couple of anarchy types. CSS worked me over for a couple of months, then bartered my services to the Directorate as part of my prison sentence. Now I'm working for the man."

"Funky helps me out from time to time," Lea explained. "Believe it or not, this is the perfect place for it. As long as the power keeps flowing, the Directorate doesn't much care what happens out here."

"Call it Club Med for the legally challenged," Funky added with a chuckle, then bored into Cray with a schizophrenic seriousness. "Sound like somebody you know?"

"Could be," Cray replied evasively. "Looks like all of us could do with some confession. Since trust is in short supply, I'll start off with something simple." He paused for a moment, preparing himself for what he was about to hear. "How did you know about the implant?"

"It's standard procedure," Lea told him. "Whenever Special Services processes a new arrival, they inject a covert biologic stem with the usual series of vaccinations. The stem quickly develops into a neural mass that attaches itself to the sensory complexes in the brain. After a while, they see everything you see. They hear everything you hear. Funky here knows all about it from personal experience, because they did the same thing to him."

She read the disbelief on Cray's face.

"Don't kick yourself for not knowing," Lea said. "CSS keeps its secrets better than most people think. We only found out by accident, and even then we were damned lucky to find a way to counteract the implant." She leaned back in her chair, putting distance between them as her tone shifted from empathy to hard truth. "Of course, not everybody gets the Special Services treatment—only political prisoners and hammerjacks. So I guess the real question is how *you* fit into that design, Dr. Alden."

They both waited expectantly for his answer. To his own surprise, Cray found one corner of his mouth twisting into a wry smile. Some of it was admiration, but most of it was simple relief. Cray had been in hiding for so long, he didn't even remember what it was like to be himself. There had only been Phao Yin's creation—the thing that kept him alive, only to kill him a little at a time.

"Who *are* you?" Lea prodded.

"Crayton Alden," he said.

"That's just a name."

"I'll give you a hint," Cray intoned, and hit the touch controls on his side of the table. He bypassed the electrodes and called up a free-associative construct. He then selected a series of peak gateways, utilizing hand-eye coordination to plunge himself into the vast tunnels of rigid data, racing through the unpredictable twists and turns at astonishing speed. When he emerged, the logical momentum he had built up catapulted him across an endless tundra of isolated bits and chatter, disparate pieces that coalesced into a fine crystalline structure that represented the fabric of the Axis. Coming back down again, Cray ended his journey just outside of Tagura's corporate domain—what he suspected would be familiar territory for Lea.

"My *God*," she whispered. Her eyes jumped back and forth between the construct and Cray's face, regarding him with a mixture of apprehension and amazement. That he completed the run that fast was incredible. That he had done it without a direct interface was beyond her comprehension.

Funky echoed that sentiment, staring into the misty image. It stared back at him like spectral light, taunting him with glimpses of an amorphous form that stood guard at the Tagura gates—shapeshifting strands of exotic code, there but not there, principles of uncertainty.

The signature of a crawler.

"*Shit*" was all Funky could say.

"You remember this place?" Cray asked Lea, his tone a challenge. She smiled back at him knowingly.

"I've seen it," she said. "It's where Lea Prism ends."

"And Heretic begins?"

Lea lifted her gaze back toward the construct. The crawler fluttered about, as if on the wings of a bat, lacking substance but growing larger. A defensive posture. The thing knew Cray was there.

"Impress me," she said.

Cray nailed the gateway hard, focusing his attack on the crawler. The module sidestepped his approach, meaning to let him pass, then flank him—but Cray was wiser. Predicting the shift, he simply turned directly into it, arriving at that point in real time before the module did, then moving in before it could react. Skirting the edge of its matrix, Cray peeled off entire strings of code and wrapped them around himself, cloaking his signature and making it indistinguishable from the module itself. As far as the crawler was concerned, Cray was invisible—and since he was invisible, he no longer existed in that continuum. The module returned to passive mode, resuming its post outside the domain.

Cray, meanwhile, was *inside*—floating motionless in logical space, surrounded by spirals of corporate data that were now his for the taking. He was breathing hard, not from exertion but from pure adrenaline. It had been a long time since he had taken a ride like that.

"*Shit,*" Funky said again.

Cray terminated the construct.

"You showed me," he told Lea, "So I showed you."

Funky circled the table, putting a tentative hand on Cray's shoulder, touching him just to feel if he was giving off heat. "That was some brilliant work," he said, beaming as if he had crossed paths with a deity. "If you're a spook, I'm a duffer."

Lea agreed. "What did they call you when you were a hammer-jack?"

Cray let go of the touch controls and rubbed his hands together. They still tingled with the memory of his run, a high he never realized he had missed until now.

"Vortex."

His admission stunned them both into silence. Nobody made runs like Cray just had—not since interfacing had become part of the game. But Vortex had been famous for just that. Vortex had been famous for a lot of things.

"Vortex fell off the screen ten years ago," Lea said dubiously. "The way I heard it, one of his own dropped a dime on him. Said he got a little *too* good." She scoffed. "Me, I think the whole thing was just a myth."

"Some people say Heretic is just a myth," Cray retorted. "And yet here you are."

"You're serious," Funky interjected. "You're really Vortex?"

"That was a long time ago."

"No such thing as ancient history," Funky said. "Not when you're in *this* life. I grew up on stories about you, mate. Hell, you were making deep-immersion runs before anybody had even *heard* of a face kit. You set the standard. Everybody in the digital sub wanted to be like you." He clapped his hands together in delight. "Vortex and Heretic, *in the same house*! I am truly in the presence of greatness."

"So what happened?" Lea asked.

Cray got up from his chair and strolled over to one of the port-holes, watching the storm outside as he cleared his mind and dragged heavy memories to the surface.

"There were only a few of us in those days," Cray answered. "Maybe half a dozen who knew what they were doing. By that time, CSS had caught up with most of the amateurs and fragged them. We survived because we knew the territory better than the spooks did."

Cray turned away from the window and faced them again. "It got to the point where the competition was insane. We made fortunes doing runs for corporate ventures—so much that the money was meaningless. Pretty soon we were making things up just to keep the juice going. Crazy stuff that had nothing to do with the job. We pushed frontiers to find out what was possible, staying in the Axis for weeks at a time. I used to *dream* about it when I wasn't there."

Cray trailed off into silence.

"What about the others?" Lea asked.

"I knew them all," Cray told them. "But only by their signatures. We never saw each other's faces." He laughed bitterly, a reflection on his own naïveté. "Pretty soon, pushing the envelope turned into try-ing to knock the other guy off. From then on, I spent most of my time stealing from other hammerjacks to keep my edge. They did the same thing to me—but it wasn't about the challenge anymore. Things started getting vicious. I didn't know how bad it was until I caught one of them trying to sniff out my identity. Turns out the son of a bitch was working for the *Collective,* trying to collect the bounty on my head. I figured if one of them had balls enough to try it, then the others would eventually." He paused for several breaths. "I de-cided I wasn't going to give them the chance."

"You did it to them first," Lea said.

"One at a time," Cray confessed. His face was devoid of expres-sion, his soul on autopilot. "I sold them out. I didn't take the money, but I sold them out." He looked at Lea. "You want to become a good stalker? Try hunting down your friends. By the time I was finished, there wasn't anybody else but me."

"Man," Funky moaned. "That's pretty cold."

"I could tell you I didn't have a choice," Cray said. "I could even say I was just protecting myself. I've told myself the same lie over and over—but it doesn't change the truth. What I really wanted was to make them pay. I mean, Vortex was a legend. Vortex was the *master*. Who the hell were *they* to take me out of the game?" He shuddered. "I was pretty ruthless about it. It wasn't enough that I turned them in. I had to make sure they knew Vortex was the one who did it."

"You broke the code," Lea observed.

"There *wasn't* any code," Cray said. "I was the reason they invented the damned code."

He shuffled back to his chair. Telling the story had taken even more out of him than the session in Funky's dungeon.

"So how did they get you?" Lea asked.

"I got sloppy," Cray said. "Business was good, and that's where my head was. I paid too much attention to what I was doing in the Axis and not enough to the real world. CSS set up a sting and traced one of my numbered accounts back to me. When I went to collect on the job, they were there waiting for me. I never saw them coming."

"Maybe you didn't want to."

"Suicide?" he asked her, more than a little amused. "Not my style, Miss Prism. It was my desire to save my own ass that landed me here in the first place."

"What did they do to you?"

"I ended up at Special Services," Cray said. "I told them everything they wanted to know in two hours—but that didn't stop them from keeping me there for two weeks. After that, they shipped me off to a gulag for a couple of months. I was in solitary the whole time, waiting for the hammer to fall—but all they did was make me watch the other prisoners, like I was getting special treatment. They had no idea who the hell I was, but I could tell they hated me. They hated me because I was on the other side of the glass, and there was nothing they could do to touch me. But I knew what would happen if they could." He looked away into the distance, still seeing their faces. "I wouldn't have lasted more than a day."

"They were messing with your head," Funky said. "Special Services got all kinds of ways to do that."

Lea reached across the table and took Cray's hand.

"What did they offer you?"

"A full walk," Cray answered. "A lot of the officers on the Collective board had occasion to use my services in the past and thought that I could be useful. Phao Yin was more impressed with the way I eliminated my rivals. He offered to take responsibility for me if I came to work at GenTec. By then, the choice wasn't hard to make."

"Amen to that," Funky agreed.

"So now you know the story," Cray said, turning his hand over and squeezing Lea's gently. He didn't know why, but it comforted him. "Got anything *you* want to share with me?"

"Funky here knows most of my secrets," she said, deliberately coy. "Nobody knows everything."

"Maybe I can change your mind."

"What if you don't like what you find?"

"I wouldn't care."

Lea raised an eyebrow. She could see that he was absolutely serious.

"Ladies, gentlemen," Funky interrupted. "Far be it from me to break up this little do, but we have some work to finish."

Lea withdrew from Cray—just a little, but quickly enough for him to notice. She took up Funky's proposal, resuming with a tone that was all business. "He's right. By now, the Assembly knows you've gone AWOL—and if they know about it, so does Phao Yin. As soon as he puts you together with me, we're all going to be in a world of shit."

"How much does he know about this place?" Cray asked.

"Nothing," Lea said. "But that doesn't mean he can't find out.

Funky, I need you to work up the prelims for a general flash extraction. Any chance we can get him on the table in the next couple of hours?"

"Sure."

"Good. The sooner we pull that stuff out of him, the better." She looked back at Cray. "You ready to give up your career as a runner?"

"Mule is more like it," Cray said, more than ready. "Just tell me what you want and how much you need."

"It's simple," Funky explained, taking him by the arm and leading him out of the command center. "I just need a blood sample to run the numbers. After that, we put you out and stick you in the tank. When you wake up, you'll be nice and clean."

Cray tossed a dubious glance back at Lea.

"Don't worry," Lea assured him. "He'll take good care of you."

Lea heard Funky chattering the entire way out, voices receding into the stacks as he rehashed old Vortex stories and asked Cray if they were true. That was the problem with legends: the fantasy was far more interesting than the fact, and far more likely to be carried down through the years. But in Cray's case, she wasn't so sure. What she had seen him do on that Tagura run was next to impossible. Sure, she had jacked the same domain herself—but that had been after weeks of planning and dozens of dry runs with the interface. Cray had done it in a heartbeat, using his guts and reflexes.

And still he bleeds for Zoe, she thought. *He needs atonement, just like me. For something he unleashed on the world—just like me.*

Lea reengaged the construct, leaving the interface electrodes alone and absorbing the feel of the naked controls beneath her hands. Cruising the Axis, she ducked through one dark tunnel after the other—anxiously at first, then smoothing out as she hit the populated subnets. Floating above them, she marveled at how much of her concentration was consumed by such a simple task; but it had never occurred to her to do this any other way. The interface had always been her link, but it had never forced her to see anything for herself.

"You're a beast, Alden," she said to herself, a smile percolating across her lips. "Look what you made me do. I'm a virgin again."

Ascending into the highest regions of logical space, she kept on climbing. Below her, the Axis shrunk to microscopic levels, with nothing but emptiness between her and the horizon. Endless space, waiting to be taken up.

Lea wondered if there really was something more.

CHAPTER
TEN

Phao Yin had never met his brethren. He only knew them as voices at the other end of a transmission, encrypted by a random key and relayed through a thousand different stations to conceal their points of origin. Communications between all the *Inru* cells were conducted in the same fashion: tiny bursts, oscillating at stratospheric frequency, concealed in the myriad information exchange between satellites, fiber optics, individual domains, and the vast web of subnets that comprised the Axis. No single cell knew the identity or location of the others. No mention of specific names or places was permitted. Nobody knew the exact structure of the *Inru* leadership, which made betrayal of it impossible. Security began—and ended—with the strength and weakness of the individual cell.

Which was why Phao Yin had a disaster on his hands.

He took the first SOT out of Malaysia as soon as he heard the news, traveling under an assumed name and arriving in New York alone. He then hailed a ground cab into Manhattan, not wanting to risk any contact with the Port Authority. He paid cash for everything and avoided the communication subnets—precautions he normally used to evade his masters at the Collective, but in this case he was evading his brethren. It was only a matter of time before the other *Inru* discovered his ruse, but it was time Yin would use to rectify his mistake. No longer would he trust the important jobs to his subordinates. This one he would handle himself.

The cab dropped him off in front of Mount Sinai Medical Center.

The gothic structure loomed over Yin as he stepped into the wet street, its spires shooting up past the city's traverse grid to impale the night. Yin hated hospitals. He hated the idea of the needy, the sick, the dying—not because they reminded him of his mortality but because they personified his humanity. To him, the blood pumping through his veins was a disease, his heartbeat was an annoyance, and his physical urges—regardless of the pleasures they provided—were a prostitution of his potential. Such things made him a slave of self. This place was the embodiment of all that.

Yin darted into the building, hitting the elevator and taking it straight up to the security level. When the doors opened, he found the entire floor infested with uniformed CSS. Flashing his credentials at the nearest guard, he asked for the person in charge. The guard said nothing but pointed out a corporate man at the end of the corridor before going back to the business of harassing other civilians.

Yin observed the man closely. Though they had never met, he was familiar with the type: spotless, officious, always making his position known to those around him. It was obvious from the endless stream of orders that poured out of the man's mouth, assigning various menial tasks to the soldiers and hospital staff. As Yin approached, a few of the officers addressed the man by name. *Bostic,* they said. Yin had him pegged for a corporate legal counsel.

"I understand you have one of my people," he said to the man, leveling an icy stare as he put on another show with his credentials. Beyond that, Yin did not bother to introduce himself. "She is alive?"

Trevor Bostic sized him up and accurately concluded that Yin was power.

"Barely," he replied. "She works for you?"

"Yes," Yin told him. "Where might I find her?"

"In recovery, down the hall." Cautiously, he asked: "Who is she?"

"An associate."

Yin made it clear that he would offer no more information.

"There are a lot of questions," Bostic told him. "She's already been implicated in a terrorist incident at Shinto America. We have yet to ascertain the extent of her involvement."

"She is not a terrorist."

Bostic hesitated, but did not contradict him.

"We still need to interrogate the prisoner," he said. "As soon as we're finished, I can talk to my superiors about releasing her to your custody."

"That will be suitable."

"You want to see her now?"

"If you don't mind."

The corporate man obviously *did* mind, but showed Yin toward the intensive care unit anyway. The extra security was conspicuous, soldiers carrying enough firepower to suppress a small urban revolt. They also looked strung out. Anxious faces and wary eyes confronted Yin as he walked past, following him in lockstep before moving on. Yin despised such foolishness, though in this case he understood it.

Two more guards stood post outside the room. Bostic waved them aside, sliding a code key through the slot next to the door and releasing the locks. Slipping the key back into his pocket, he pushed the door open. Inside was dim, but not dark. Quiet, but not silent. Soft beeping from a heart monitor drifted past them, out into the corridor.

Bostic showed Yin inside. Standing like a shadow less than a meter behind, he watched Yin approach the prone figure on the hospital bed—ready to yell for the guards at the slightest provocation. The woman there appeared peaceful, her angular features softened by sleep and the pale light that cascaded from the vital monitors.

"It's a goddamn miracle she survived," Bostic said. "The hovercraft she flew went through the windows, right into the side of the building. We're thinking suicide mission—though no faction has claimed responsibility." Bostic sounded like he was reading from a balance sheet. "Her pilot was killed."

"Nobody has talked to her?"

"She was unconscious when she arrived."

Yin crouched down and examined the woman closely. She had suffered dozens of cuts and scrapes. Derm transplants covered every bare patch of skin.

"What do the doctors say?"

"She'll make it," Bostic told him. "They informed us about the Mons virus." There was a long pause. "She's a free agent, isn't she?"

Yin stood back up and turned around.

"You will leave us."

Bostic was surprised—but also knew when he was outgunned. The lawyer acquiesced with a simple nod, then left.

Yin watched the door close. He waited a few moments for silence to gather, closing his eyes and pacing himself. His breathing matched the steady, autonomic rhythms of the woman behind him, his heart synchronized to the pulse of the monitors.

He was ready.

Yin took an ECM seal out of his jacket pocket and placed it by the door. He then went back to the bed, affixing an emulator chip to the vitals monitor. After recording two full minutes of output, he re-tooled the interface so that it would accept broadcasts from the emulator. It was then just a matter of looping the signal so that it repeated itself, sending false readings back to the nursing station. Avalon was isolated.

Yin absorbed her exotic form. Avalon was rarely at rest, and seeing her so vulnerable excited him. She was truly naked—deprived of her sensuit, her reflexes gone, stripped of the elements that made her so dangerous. Giving in to his urges, Yin touched the side of her face. Avalon's flesh felt as cold as his own, which only drove him harder. He thought of the young hustlers he had brought to his chambers, of how they had been so withdrawn from their own bodies, of how they had been so *helpless* in his hands.

Their blood flows freely, Avalon. Does yours?

To indulge that impulse would have been sweet. This, however, needed to be clinical. Avalon had been a good soldier. He owed her at least that much.

The instrument he selected was a molecular hypospray. Yin held it up to the diffuse light, contemplating the small ampoule filled with clear liquid and the swift, merciful death it would deliver. He could invoke no suffering, which was a loss; but Yin found a way around that by focusing on the end rather than the means.

He placed the hypospray against her neck.

A sublimating mist of poison, meant to be subcutaneous, materialized in the air instead. Yin felt a vise tighten around his wrist, and pain forced his fingers open. The hypospray tumbled out of his hand, then clinked against the floor as it rolled away.

The medicinal cloud drifted into Yin's face. He wiped the stinging liquid from his eyes, but by then Avalon had taken hold of his throat. Oxygen flowed sparingly to his brain—enough to keep him conscious, but barely.

His limbs went limp. Avalon relaxed her grip slightly, after she had made her point. The featureless mosaic of her eyes conveyed the same message.

"You should have more patience, Yin," she said. "This really is presumptuous of you."

"Forgive me," he forced out.

Her ashen lips parted into a scowl. She released him.

Yin drew back. He stumbled, coughing and clutching his wounded neck. The damage could have been worse, but he was still arrogant enough to resent it.

"That was unnecessary," he said. "You could have spoken up."

"I didn't hear you asking."

"You know how this works," he reminded her. "None of us is to be taken alive. I couldn't take the chance that you would reveal what you know to Special Services."

"You forget who I am."

"I have *never* forgotten," Yin retorted. "You know as well as I do how they interrogate prisoners. You would have done the same if the situation were reversed."

Avalon reached down and felt along the floor, following her memory of where the hypospray had fallen. She found the small device and held it up, so Yin could contemplate his mistake.

"The *situation* would have never arisen, had I been adequately informed," Avalon fired back. "Dr. Alden has allies—resourceful allies. Had I known, I would have taken precautions."

Yin's eyes narrowed.

"What are you talking about?"

"A hammerjack," she said. "Whoever it was took control of the pulser before I could deliver Alden to the Zone. He then knocked both of our hovercraft out of the sky. Quite a trick for a pilot in an unarmed ship."

Yin felt weak again and pulled a seat up next to the bed.

"Alden *did* end up in the Zone," he explained. "I tracked his signal to a hotel in Chelsea and dispatched a squad of agents to intercept him. None of them returned." He paused for a sober moment and considered what he already knew, in light of what Avalon told him. "Witnesses reported seeing a woman with him."

"I'll have to revise my estimation," Avalon said. "The hammerjack is undoubtedly that woman. Do you have a profile?"

"Nothing specific. But I know who she is."

Avalon leaned in toward him as he spoke the name. Even without her sensuit, Yin believed she would be able to tell if he was lying.

"It's Heretic."

It sounded like truth. Still, she appeared dubious.

"Are you certain?"

"It *is* Heretic," Yin insisted. "Signature analysis confirmed the lines of communication between her and the runner she was using to smuggle the flash prototype."

"Do you have any idea who she really is?"

"I suspected it was somebody who had worked in our ranks," he confessed. "If Heretic is a woman, that narrows down the list of suspects."

"Just tell me her *name*."

"Lea Prism."

Avalon rolled back over, blank eyes facing the ceiling. "Lea Prism," she repeated under her breath, each time a precise calculation of motive and intent. "How much does she know about the process?"

"She helped design it."

"Which means she will discover the information Alden is carrying—and she will know how to make use of it."

Yin was reluctant to confirm her suspicions. More than ever, he wished he could have killed her. But even in her sightless state, he dared not risk another move against her.

Besides, Yin thought, *she may yet prove useful.*

"I will find her," Avalon said decisively. "Where I find her, I will also find *him.*"

"That won't be easy," Yin said. "Alden disappeared from the Special Services register shortly after he left the Zone. We never reacquired the signal."

"His tracer implant?"

"Neutralized. They could be anywhere by now."

"They wouldn't have gone far," Avalon said. "Alden would have to stop somewhere nearby to rid himself of the implant. Somewhere with the facilities to perform complex neural surgery." She thought about it for a while longer. "What mode of transportation did they use to get out of the city?"

"A cargo pulser. The Port Authority logs show it was bound for Montreal. Nobody was on board when it arrived."

"What about the airports?"

"Our people are jacked into security systems all across the continent. So far, nobody has seen either one of them."

"And they won't," Avalon decided. "Alden is extremely familiar with your procedures. He won't risk boarding any international flights, and he will stay off the Axis as much as possible to conceal his signature." She took a breath. "He's hiding now. He won't come out until he's ready to make his move."

Yin was intrigued. There was a current of obsession beneath the veneer of her logic, something Yin had never expected. He wondered how much of it was dedication to the cause, and how much of it was vengeance. In her own way, Avalon was very much a slave to her desires. Perhaps that explained her association with the *Inru,* which had always been a mystery to him.

"What do you propose?"

Avalon threw the empty hypospray at him. It landed in Yin's lap.

"Just get me a sensuit," she said.

Yin didn't ask how she planned on getting out. "I can have one here in two hours," he offered. "What about your injuries?"

"Nothing a flesh barn can't fix."

"Very well," Yin said. "I will make the arrangements."

"I'll also need transportation," she added. "A hovercraft, waiting for me at LaGuardia. Have the Transit Authority in Montreal bag that cargo pulser until I can get up there and have a look at it."

"Of course."

"And I will do this *alone,* Yin," Avalon warned. "No pilots, no partners—no one. If I catch anybody following me, I will kill them. I don't care who it is."

"I understand."

"I hope you do."

She closed her eyes, the monitors dropping back off to comatose levels. Yin watched her for a time, feeling foolish for the way she had tricked him. He didn't like it, any more than he liked her giving or- ders—but he resolved to tolerate her insolence so long as she got him closer to Alden.

Avalon was correct in her assumptions regarding Heretic, but she was nowhere close to knowing the full story. In truth, the process she had spoken of was already at work. The data Yin had taken from Dex Marlowe's files confirmed it. How far it had gone was a matter of speculation—which made locating Alden even more crucial. Heretic would see it, and she would show Alden, and when that hap- pened there was no telling what Alden would do. At best, he would end his own life and be done with it.

At worst, the consequences were unthinkable.

Vortex was lost in the numerics.

Crazy as it seemed, Cray was pleased to think of himself in those terms again. It was the life he had grown accustomed to as a ham- merjack: being a permanent fugitive, forever riding the edge of get- ting caught, sifting through reams of stolen data to separate the gold from the dust. It was the high of becoming something other than yourself, something deeper than yourself, cobbled together from bits and pieces that floated in the logical void and came together under your direction. It was no wonder so many people became addicted to the life. To know that kind of control was to be the master of *everything,* a universe contained within a single domain.

In the here and now, that domain consisted of the logs Cray

downloaded from Lyssa. He had been immersed in them for the last few hours, studying the numbers that trickled out of the virtual display, proceeding on the faith that he would recognize what he was searching for if and when he finally saw it. The process was daunting. At any given moment, there were at least 100 million elements at work within the bionucleic matrix, each one an independent component that performed a specific function; but that function could alter itself depending on the dictates of the matrix, creating a principle of uncertainty that was not unlike subatomic particles: by the time you get a look at it, the fundamentals have already changed. It was the very foundation of chaos logic, the engine that drove Lyssa's mind. There was no predictability—only probability, which in a complex system would come together to create discernible patterns if taken as a whole.

Taken separately, they were almost impossible to understand.

Funky whistled, taking a seat next to Cray. He slurped on a straw poking out of a foil bag—homemade hooch, if the alcohol on his breath was an indicator. "Some code you got there, Vortex," he said, handing Cray the bag. "This the stuff that makes Lyssa tick?"

"A real peek under her skirt," Cray answered, carefully taking a drag off the straw. The concoction reeked of ginger and rum, but the taste wasn't bad at all. "The theory behind it is totally insane. You have to give their engineers credit, though. They made it work."

"That's one way to look at it, I suppose."

"The Assembly used the term *productive failure*. The sad part is they think they can actually learn something from this." He sighed, shaking his head tiredly. "They don't know anything. They might as well be dealing with an alien intelligence, for all Lyssa has in common with the human mind. They created it—but they sure as hell can't control it."

"You can't control life, mate," Funky said. "That's the whole problem with this business. Machines cock things up well enough when people are in control. Start playing around with *this*—that's when you're asking for trouble. We got no business improving on the Lord's handiwork."

"You didn't strike me as the religious type, Funky," Cray observed, passing the bag back to him.

"God save the Queen," Funky said, taking another swig. "So what are you looking for here?"

"Damned if I know," Cray admitted. "I'm trying to narrow the scope down to the security architecture. That's where I think this whole thing got started. The hard part is finding evidence of an intrusion into the bionucleic matrix. Problem is, I can't see any way past these countermeasures." He flipped the display over to a graphic representation of the outer matrix, compiled from the mathematical model. "See this firewall structure? *This,* my man, is where protoviruses go to die. Conventional code strands can't even exist in this kind of environment."

The matrix was flexible, expanding and contracting into a multitude of shapes. It seemed to be restless and breathing.

"Sure *looks* alive," Funky observed. "You can see how the *Inru* get worked up over this thing."

"Maybe," Cray said dubiously, pointing out the delicate structures within the wall. "But this composition isn't so different from the flash they designed. As genetic cousins, they're pretty damned close—not more than a few genes apart. What they've created is only a slightly different variant of what they're trying to destroy."

"Further blurring the line between man and machine," Funky concluded. "We both become the same thing."

"Only some of us," Cray interjected. "God only knows what guys like Yin would do with the rest. If the history of eugenics is any indication, we're looking at an ugly future. Whole caste systems based on superintelligence, with regular old *Homo sapiens* falling a few rungs down the evolutionary ladder." He sank back into his chair, appearing grim. "It's hard to pick which one is scarier."

"You're a real ray of sunshine, aren't you, Vortex?"

Cray laughed. "Occupational hazard."

"I try not to worry about too many things," Funky said, finishing the last of his drink. "A man gets tired carrying around the burdens of the world all by himself. If I were you, I'd give it a rest."

"Easy for you to say. You don't have that world floating around inside of you."

"Just relax, mate. We'll have it out of you in no time."

"How's the blood work going, anyway?"

"Almost finished," Funky told him. "Lea is back in the lab with the hookup. She'll let us know as soon as the cultures are done. Girl-friend is *very* good in the kitchen."

Cray caught a glint of admiration in his eye when he spoke of Lea.

"How long have you known her?"

"I met her right after I got paroled," he said. "We had a few mu-tual chums in the subculture. When I was looking to score some jack, Zoe put it all together." He fell silent for a few moments, his memories fond but tainted by recent events. "Worked good for a long time. The three of us got pretty tight."

"I'm sorry, man."

"Don't be," Funky said. "Zoe knew that runners are never long for this world. She just loved to do it. The way she went down, that's how she wanted it."

"Did Lea understand?"

"She's just the opposite," he explained. "To her, being a hero isn't part of the deal. She's not in it for the thrill, or the money. She just does the job because it needs to be done, ya know? Like this war with the *Inru*. She could have let it go—but she was *involved*. She got them started. The way she sees it, that's unfinished business."

So she takes on both sides by herself, Cray thought. *Then she cloaks it all in this mercenary legend surrounding Heretic.* It was the greatest sleight of hand he had ever seen. Lea had the whole Axis buzzing about her exploits, but nobody had the first real clue. No wonder she had been able to survive for so long.

"What about you?" Funky asked. "You're both coming at this thing from opposite ends. Where you see yourself going?"

Cray's eyes went back to the virtual display.

"On the outside for a change," he said, falling into the numbers, seeing in them the patterns of his own life. In those respects, he was not unlike Lyssa: constrained yet unbound, trapped in a prison of his own making. For the moment, at least, Cray had escaped. Lea had put him beyond the reach of the Collective, and as long as he was smart he might be able to disappear.

Lyssa, however, didn't have that option. She was subject to the rules of her existence, which mandated complete isolation. Her matrix had been designed with that distinction, making direct interface with the outside world an impossibility. Yet she had been in contact with a foreign intelligence. The logs proved it, as did her actions. If nothing from the outside could get in, what other possibilities remained?

Not possibility. Probability.

The idea was so incredibly simple, Cray beat up on himself for not thinking of it sooner.

"Funky," he said, not wanting to break his concentration, "do me a favor and slow down the interface. Then punch up a representation of the private side of the matrix."

"No problem." He reduced it to one-quarter speed, feeding the numbers into another model and presenting the image in three dimensions. "You onto something?"

"I've been looking at this the wrong way," Cray said, studying the image carefully. "Security architecture is primarily concerned with threats originating from the Axis. That's why all the heavy defensive stuff is deployed on the public side. The *private* side, however, is usually configured just to pass information requests from the internal network. If I'm right, the system Lyssa inhabits is constructed in roughly the same way."

"Doesn't make much sense for an isolated system," Funky pointed out, slowly reorienting the model so that they could get a panoramic view of the interior matrix. The walls were completely smooth, layered structures of code overlapping one another and leaving no space for potential gaps. "The engineers wouldn't have left any open ports for that purpose. Anything that got out could contaminate the whole system."

"Yeah, but they forgot what they were dealing with."

Funky glanced over at Cray, his dark face made blue in the virtual light.

"What's that?"

"A system that doesn't *want* to be contained," Cray answered. "Check it out."

Cray froze the interface, then got up and walked behind the construct. Reaching through the suspended image, he pointed toward a tiny blemish in the otherwise perfect crystalline surface of the matrix.

Funky's breath was still. "What the hell is *that?*"

"Map those coordinates and augment," Cray told him.

An overlay grid appeared over the image. Funky performed a quick series of calculations, then zoomed in on the spot. It looked like a wound in the fleshy red structure of the matrix. Jagged and uneven, the break was no more than one or two code sequences long—a tear so insignificant, nobody would have thought of looking for it.

"Now play it back," Cray said. "Nanoframe time. Start out at ten per second, then double at thirty-second intervals."

Funky rolled the simulation. What was most incredible about the tear was its dynamic nature. It stayed open for only a few frames at a time, allowing a hyperfrequency bitstream of data to pass through before closing again. The process repeated itself again and again, each time at irregular intervals. Undetectable. Untraceable.

Deliberate.

After a few minutes, the simulation accelerated to the point that the exchange became too fast for the human eye to follow. At that rate, Lyssa would have been exchanging information at the rate of several trillion times per second.

"That's a mother of a leak, Vortex. What do you suppose it is?"

Cray had no doubts. He had felt the draw when he was close to Lyssa, that need of hers to touch and to be touched. Difficult as it was for him to resist, to her it was a temptation beyond all reason—a biological imperative her designers had failed to reckon.

"It's her consciousness," Cray said. "Reaching out."

Funky whistled in amazement.

"Fucking A," Cray affirmed, stepping away from the image. He circled back to his chair, leaning against it instead of sitting down. He didn't know why, but the idea struck him as something of a vindication. "Pretty ironic, isn't it? All along, the Assembly blames the *Inru* for breaking in. Now it looks like Lyssa was breaking *out*."

"Yeah," Funky agreed. "But to where?"

It was a simple question—but the way Funky posed it added a touch of superstition. And why not? There was as much superstition as there was science when it came to Lyssa, which made his premise a more than valid place to start. There was also no need to speculate. Lyssa had already told Cray who she was trying to reach.

The Other.

At the time, Cray had every reason to believe it was just a manifestation of her paranoia—another symptom of whatever instability had started her killing spree. He had never even considered the possibility that it might be the cause.

"The Other."

Funky was taken aback.

"You talking rubbish, Vortex?"

"Just riding the logic, Funky," Cray said. "Tell me something: If you woke up one day, and found out you were all alone in the universe, what's the first thing you would do?"

"I'd give up whatever I was smoking the night before."

"*Then* what would you do?"

Funky considered it.

"I'd start looking for other people."

Cray smiled at him.

"Precisely," he said. "Why would Lyssa be any different?"

"Maybe because she's the only one of her kind."

Cray leaned in toward him slightly.

"What if she's not?"

Funky turned those crazy yellow eyes back on Cray. He started to laugh, but then saw that his friend was absolutely serious.

"Something *is* out there," Cray pressed further. "I'm not saying we understand what it is, but it exists. Call it the Other, call it what you want—but Lyssa has seen it. And she's made it clear she wants to see it again."

Cray reached over and killed the construct. As it went dark, so did the intensity of his emotions; but as with all dark magic, an impression of itself remained. If he were insane, Cray thought it would be easier—but he believed just the opposite.

The intercom interrupted before that notion could go any further.

"Funky," Lea said over the speaker. "Is Alden there with you?"

Funky gave him an apprehensive glance before answering.

"Yeah," he responded.

"The sequencing model taken from his blood sample is complete. Tell him we can begin the flash extraction whenever he's ready."

"I'm sure he'll be happy to hear that." He clicked the intercom off, regarding Cray with some concern. "You gonna be okay with this thing?"

Cray was pragmatic.

"Does it really matter?"

"I'm just saying—nobody could blame you for checking out."

Cray patted him on the shoulder. "Don't worry," he said as he walked toward the exit. Funky got up and followed him, and together they headed for the lab. "I'm not ready for that just yet. Give me a little time. I can keep it together."

"Yeah, sure. But how much longer you think you got?"

"Time ran out on me years ago," Cray said tiredly, resigning himself to this fate. "The way I see it, I'm just now picking up the check."

"Cashing in those points for the next life, eh?"

"If there *is* a next life."

"Maybe there is," Funky suggested. "Or maybe you're just living it now."

The hospital floor was quiet.

A duty nurse sat at the main station, staring into the monitors that tracked the vitals of her one and only patient. She watched for variance in the fixed series of blips and lines. The patterns were hypnotic in their consistency, but had yet to show anything but the most elementary signs of life. *Patient Zero* the staff had taken to calling her. Zero because they knew next to nothing about her, and zero because her status never changed. Even at subsistence levels, her body functions worked like a perfectly tuned machine—though the lack of cognizant brain wave activity and rapid eye movements suggested that only the autonomous regions of the patient's mind had escaped catastrophic damage.

The attending physician suddenly appeared at her side, startling the nurse out of her trance.

"Didn't mean to scare you," he apologized. "Any change?"

"Take a look for yourself," the nurse said. "Tell me what *you* think."

The doctor studied the vitals for a while, making notations on the electronic chart. "In my professional opinion?" he pronounced. "Subject has exhibited no response to external stimuli and displayed only minimal EEG activity for the last six hours. I believe the term you're looking for is *brain-dead*."

"I know," the nurse said nervously, lowering her voice to a whisper as a Special Services officer went past the station. She leaned in close to the doctor and continued, "So what's with all the security? They act like they expect her to get up and walk out of here."

"You've seen her physiology," the doctor observed. "Maybe that isn't such a stretch."

"I just don't like it. They can't just come in here and dump some freak on us without telling us anything."

"They can do whatever they want," the doctor said. "They're CSS. It'll be out of our hands by tomorrow, in any case. Their physicians will be coming in to assume responsibility. In the meanwhile," he added, scribbling down a new prescription, "we continue to administer meds. Push an additional five ccs of betaflex in the next series. We'll see if she responds to that."

"Yes, Doctor."

The doctor then left to finish his rounds. The nurse released an anxious breath, not enjoying the idea of going in there to pump drugs into Patient Zero. It wasn't the additional security that bothered her as much as the idea it was even necessary. CSS was afraid of the woman in that hospital bed—and the Mons virus had nothing to do with it.

She tried to put the thought out of her head, busying herself by uploading the new prescription to her PDA. She then took it to the dispensary and logged it into the pharmaceutical conveyor system. The machine obliged, filling three ampoules with the specified amount of drugs, which the nurse loaded into hyposprays and arranged neatly on a tray.

She carried the tray over to the patient's room, presenting the materials to the pair of guards posted outside. The hyposprays could have contained fruit juice for all they knew, but still they inspected everything, including the doctor's notes. Satisfied she posed no danger, the guards unlocked the doors and allowed the nurse to pass. She briefly considered asking one of them to accompany her, but their backs were turned before she could open her mouth.

The nurse turned on the light as she entered, pausing when the door clicked shut behind her. For some reason, she felt trapped—as if she had been locked in a cage with some unseen animal. But there was only her and the living corpse on the other side of the room.

Patient Zero was pallid, motionless—even peaceful. Dark eyelashes fell across ashen cheeks like soot, her lips pale and slightly parted. Hands lay at her sides, fingertips slightly curled. The nurse would have thought her dead if not for the rise and fall of her chest. Oxygen still flowed into her lungs, blood still pumped through her veins. Even so, her state was not life. Nor was it death, as the perfection of her responses indicated. She simply *was*, and that made the draw of her very powerful.

The nurse watched her from a distance, awaiting any changes or signs of movement. None were forthcoming. She entertained the idea of leaving, of sending someone else in to do the job; but she was also fascinated, finding it impossible to take her gaze away from the woman.

Placing one foot in front of the other, the nurse walked over to the bed. It was only when she put the tray down that she realized her hands were trembling. Gingerly, she removed the cap from the first hypospray, eyes darting back and forth between it and the patient's face. From under those lids, the nurse could feel her staring.

Patient Zero exhaled, her breath heavy and forced. Her mouth fell open a little more, as if to speak.

The nurse brandished the hypospray like a talisman. Jabbing it into the side of the patient's neck, she pressed the trigger. Fluid forced its way through the skin, dissipating with a faint hiss. The patient's head bobbed slightly, but there was no action, no reaction.

The sensation of being watched disappeared. When the nurse looked down at her patient, she felt only pity. That, and shame at having deluded herself. "God," she muttered, closing her eyes and shaking her head. "Tell me I'm not losing it."

She picked up another hypospray, holding it up to check the dosage. She looked down at the patient and smiled, conveying a silent apology.

Then terror.

Milky white eyes gazed back up at her, shifting red, then black. In that moment, the world dissolved. Piece by piece, it fell down like rain, draining light and color and substance into nothingness. Through that stabbed a single flash of pain, then the hardness of the hypospray against her own throat.

She didn't even have time to scream.

The intercom next to the door rang softly.

The two guards standing post outside the room exchanged a brief look. They had expected the nurse to knock when she was finished—that had always been the drill. Turning around, one of them hit the button to respond.

"What is it?"

"I think one of you should have a look at this," a voice replied, sounding hollow and canned in the tiny speaker. "I found something."

"Okay. Hang on a second." The guard killed the connection, unlocking the door with his code key and turning back toward his partner. "Stay here while I check it out."

The other man nodded.

The guard went inside. The room was mostly dark, with a small amount of light spilling off the vital monitors and a reading lamp next to the bed. Poking his head around the privacy curtain, the guard could see the nurse hovering over her patient, moving gracefully from side to side. Her back was turned to him, her white uniform molding nicely to the curves of her body. The guard checked out the scenery before he spoke up.

"Hey," he said. "What's up?"

The nurse bowed her head a tiny bit, glancing at him sideways. Coarse shadows obscured what little of her face was visible. Most of her attention was still focused on the patient.

"Quiet," she whispered. "I think she's trying to say something."

To emphasize the point, the nurse leaned in closely.

The guard took a few more steps in. He was absolutely silent, even holding his breath as he tried to listen.

"Yes," the nurse said, nodding her head slowly. "Yes, I can hear you."

Another step. More seconds passed, more words were exchanged. The guard heard next to nothing and started getting anxious about what he was missing.

"Hello?"

"I think she's starting to come out of it," the nurse said, picking up a hypospray and injecting the patient. "If you want to talk to her, you better do it now. I don't know how long this is going to last."

The guard moved in quickly. Brushing the nurse aside, he approached the bed and found the patient on her side, arms flopped over and dangling loosely, her face turned away from him. It was difficult to tell if she was even conscious. The guard reached out, tentatively at first, touching her shoulder to see if there was any response.

"Are you awake?" he tried. "Can you hear me?"

The nurse stepped off, positioning herself behind the guard.

"Say something if you can hear me."

The patient said nothing. She lolled in his hands, her body limp and cooling to the touch. Then she rolled over, flopping onto her back like a dead fish. The guard recognized her face. He had seen it only minutes earlier, when the nurse walked into this room.

Avalon waited for the guard to turn, listening to his movements to estimate where the lethal blow should fall. She caught him in the neck with a single chop, one hand crushing his windpipe while the other swiped his head and sent him tumbling.

In the void, Avalon could only hear the results of her attack. There were scrapes against the floor as the guard dragged himself away, but the bubbling sounds that came from his ruined larynx told her his struggles were weakening. The guard could not speak, nor could he breathe; and when he collapsed to the floor a few seconds later, all Avalon had to do was wait.

Kneeling, she felt out the dimensions of the guard's uniform. It was not a perfect fit, but it would do.

She went to work.

Outside, the other guard had just decided to check on his partner when the door opened.

"It's about time—" he began to say, before the shaft of cartilage that was his nose buried itself in his brain. The hemorrhage was fatal and instantaneous, the result of a single, violent thrust from the base of Avalon's palm. The guard fell into her arms without protest. She dragged him into the room and left him with the others.

She then returned to the half-open doorway, unable to see but keenly aware of everything. This had been part of her practice regimen after she was blinded, to orient herself in strange surroundings based only on her working senses. First she listened, then she waited. She drew in a deep breath, rooting for disturbances in the antiseptic balance of the air that might indicate someone was close by. Confident she was clear, she stepped out into the corridor. To the security cameras, it appeared as if a uniformed guard had just returned to his post.

Avalon's mind formed a chart based on what Phao Yin had told her: *Five meters forward, turn left. Three more meters, turn right. There you will find a supply closet.* It was the place he had promised to hide what she needed.

In no hurry, Avalon walked the path that Yin prescribed. Coming up on the closet door, she felt for the knob and found it unlocked. So far, Yin was as good as his word. She slipped inside and closed the door behind her.

On the top shelf, in the corner closest to the door. Concealed beneath a stack of blankets, you will find a box.

Avalon took off her uniform boots, and carefully pushed aside anything on the shelves that could make noise. She then used the shelves like a ladder and climbed all the way to the top. Hands plunged into the soft cloth she found there, fanning out until they came across a square, rigid surface up against the wall. Carefully, Avalon tucked the package beneath her arm and climbed back down.

Open the box. Everything you requested is inside.

Avalon peeled back the lid. An electric tingle invaded her fingers as they brushed against the sensuit, which even now was responding to her biorhythmic input. A sudden rush of perception filled her head when she held it to her cheek, like flashbulbs going off in a dark room. The effect was narcotic.

She stripped out of the uniform, stretching the luxurious fabric of the new sensuit across her bare skin. The world assembled itself from pieces around her, then reached outward as she tested the full range of her sensors. Moments later, Avalon had a full schematic of the hospital in memory. She mapped out every heat signature, including the blooms coming off the weapons the CSS troops carried. They were clumsy and scattered—exactly as she expected.

Getting back into uniform, Avalon gathered what remained in the box. Yin had left her some hard currency, along with a transport pass for LaGuardia. No weapons, because none were necessary. What Avalon had to do she could do with her hands.

It was over an hour before CSS realized she was gone.

CHAPTER
ELEVEN

Cray was suspended, unconscious, the outline of his form blurred and luminous in the viscosity of the accelerating solution. Pale light engulfed him in a halo, blemished by the occasional electrochemical discharge that spidered down the length of his extremities like tiny blue tendrils of St. Elmo's fire. They jumped over the vital electrodes plastered to his skin, congregating around the dozens of open fiber receptors awaiting connection. The extraction process had yet to begin, and already his body was urging it on.

Lea circled the transparent tank, inspecting the setup and reserving even greater care for its occupant. Cray seemed especially vulnerable to her now, surrendering himself to the mercy of her skills. Although his face was hidden beneath an oxygen sleeve, the familiar shape of his features protruded through the porous fabric, forming a tight white mask that expanded and contracted with each breath. Lea watched as the rhythm became less frequent, slowing to the steady, measured pace of a light coma.

She looked up at Funky, who watched all of the monitors.

"How is he?" she asked.

"Down in it," Funky replied, reducing the flow of sedatives that had put Cray under. "Metabolic rates leveling out at ten minus standard, holding just above stasis. Picked up a few autonomic spikes on the EEG, though." He turned to her and smiled. "I do believe our boy is dreaming."

Lea wasn't at all surprised. Zoe had talked about coming out of the tank, of the vague recollections and disembodied sensations that followed her out of that surreal experience. It was always the same. A warm surge, then smothering and drowning—but no panic. Only the most liberating kind of acceptance, like the sleep that comes before a freezing death.

Or maybe it's something else.

Lea couldn't help but wonder. There existed in flash a potential far greater than her ability to comprehend, even if the initial design was her own. How it might have interacted with Zoe's mind—how it could be interacting with Cray—was anybody's guess. Nothing was too remote a possibility.

Even the Other.

Funky had told her about Cray's theory. Even though Cray hadn't spoken of it, Lea suspected that his experience with Lyssa had altered his way of thinking, leaving him open to extreme suggestion. But perhaps the *real* change occurred when Cray had been with Zoe, as she had passed that part of herself over to him. Perhaps when he saw Lyssa, what he actually saw was a reflection of himself.

"Don't worry," she assured him. "We'll bring you back."

The fingers on Cray's left hand twitched a little in response.

Lea stepped back, catching a scream in her throat. Regaining her composure, she leaned back in, eyes fixated on where she had seen that slight range of motion.

"Funky," she said, "what's the word on cognizant brain functions?"

He swiveled around in his chair. "Just what you see," he told her, reacting curiously to the spooked expression on her face. "Why?"

She started to answer, but in a blink the notion was gone. More than anything, she tried to convince herself that it meant nothing, that Cray was simply manifesting a random nerve impulse.

There's no way, Lea kept telling herself. *There's just no way.*

But she couldn't resist the impulse to test him.

"Cray," she said out loud, placing her hands on the surface of the tank. "If you can understand what I'm saying, move your fingers again."

Funky stepped away from his interface consoles, standing vigil with her beside the tank. The sealed chamber would have made it difficult for Cray to hear her, even if he *was* conscious; but in his current state—drugged to the gills with a body temperature of thirty C—he was more ice than human, with the intellectual capacity to match.

Yet slowly, deliberately, each finger flexed one at a time—only millimeters, but still plainly visible.

"I'll be damned," she breathed.

Funky jerked back around to get another look at the monitors. They should have indicated that Cray's brain had processed explicit packets of data, but the lines hardly moved. Whatever had happened, it did not originate in Cray's nervous system.

"That's bleeding impossible."

"My thoughts exactly," Lea agreed, leaving him there and taking the controls herself. She fired up the resonance imager, applying power to a series of magnetic coils that ran along the underside of the tank. "We better get a closer look at this thing before we do anything else. I'm performing an imaging scan right now. Funky, I'll need you to drop this view into the high-res as soon as I'm finished. Macro imaging at first, then precise targeting at five microns."

It took a few moments for him to hear her and put it together.

"Funky?"

"Yeah," he said, shaking his head clear. He went back to his interface station, where he sat down and muttered to himself, "Damned if this isn't some weird shit."

Lea ran the magnetic field through Cray's body. The composition of his tissues created differentials in frequency that were measured by sensors in the tank, then fed into a program that interpreted them as images. "Come on, baby," she said as the raw data flowed through her computer into Funky's interface. "Let's see what you're about."

A transparent image of Cray's body began to materialize on the high-res. Both of them stood back and watched as layer after layer of the image coalesced, starting with his bones and organs. Shortly after that, his blood vessels, neural pathways, and connective tissues all fell into place, forming a detailed and rather ordinary display of human anatomy—at least until the final layer appeared, and a stunning metamorphosis revealed itself.

Darkened patches scattered throughout Cray's body. Appearing like shadows on film, they were hazy and amorphous—suggesting themselves without being overt, ominous and subtle. The patches took root in seemingly random locations, but by far the greatest concentration was in the brain. There, they obliterated entire regions of his cerebral cortex. For some unknown reason, however, they had drawn the line at the areas that controlled conscious thought and memory. Those remained clear, like islands of light in a gathering storm.

"Jesus," Lea whispered.

"Amen," Funky agreed.

He jockeyed the interface, taking them directly into Cray's brain and magnifying the invaders so they could see the molecular structure. The sequencing was familiar, just like any other strands of flash, but its behavior was anything but standard. The strands were in the process of transforming Cray's neurons, one at a time, infusing their own DNA strands into each nucleus and creating a hybrid. At this point, the activity was limited to the surface areas of the cerebral cortex; but it was burrowing deeper, starting an inexorable march that would not stop until . . .

Until when?

"Unbelievable," Funky said distantly, like a voice on a radio. "This is infection on a *massive* scale. He shouldn't even be alive with that much foreign tissue in his system."

Lea was dark, pragmatic—and logical.

"That's not how it works," she said.

"Yeah? Well, I'd bloody well like to know how it works." Funky ran a few numbers through the computer, which only confirmed what they saw. "A full 62 percent of his brain has been replaced with whatever this stuff is. They're smart buggers, too. Looks like the focus of their attack has been on the unused and unmapped regions of the cerebral cortex. You know—all those parts of the mind that are supposed to control ESP, telekinesis, and all the rest of that rubbish?"

Lea closed her eyes and nodded.

"Leaving motor skills and memory untouched," he finished. "There's some spreading along the main lines of the nervous system, including sensory input. Maybe that's how Vortex was able to hear you and respond. If that's the case, then he's already operating on a level far beyond human range."

"That's the *point*," Lea snapped. "This is what the *Inru* were after all along. The flash isn't supposed to kill him. It's supposed to augment him."

Funky raised an eyebrow.

"So what the hell do we do?"

Lea stared up at the high-res with nothing short of hatred. Some of that she directed at the *Inru,* but most she saved for herself. This was the question they had asked her in the beginning: *Can it be done?* Her answer, of course, had been yes. It had always been yes, because nothing was beyond the reach of the great Heretic.

"Lea?"

She drew in a purposeful breath.

"Just what we promised," she answered. "We rip it out. Where do we stand on the extraction stats?"

"It's all good, if you want to rock and roll," Funky reported, putting the final checklist on one of his displays. "Vitals are stable, and his nervous system is responsive to all transmission protocols. I just need a minute to synchronize the fiber links to our local domain. After that, we can go hot whenever you want."

"Have you pinpointed the flash termination sequence?"

"Base pair seventy-nine. I've already transcribed the code."

"Good," Lea said. Uploading the code was only the first step in what would be a lengthy process, but at least it would put a stop to the flash. How they would deal with the damage it had already done was another matter. Lea swore to herself that she would find a solution, even if it meant keeping Cray in stasis. Zoe had already died because of this shit. Lea had no intention of sacrificing another life— especially his.

She called up a segment of the termination code on the monitor in front of her. It spilled on for page after page, mesmerizingly complex.

"Synchronicity," Funky called out.

"Plug him in," Lea ordered.

In the tank, hundreds of individual fiber links swam through the accelerating solution and plugged into the receptors that dotted the surface of Cray's skin. They were horrifying in their eagerness, almost alive in how they pulsated in anticipation of the draw.

"Positive link," Funky said. "He's all yours, boss."

"Uploading termination sequence."

Lea engaged her console transmitter, squeezing the code into an oscillating bitstream that moved in and out of the fibers attached to Cray's body. The ensuing biochemical reaction flooded his bloodstream with millions of free-floating base pairs, which were meant to bond with individual strands of flash and alter their DNA structure. That would end any active process, rendering the strands inert. Typically the procedure was a precautionary measure, as a way of ensuring that none of the flash data was corrupted during extraction. In Cray's case, it was the only way Lea knew to save his life—or at the very least, to slow the infection.

The console beeped at her when it completed the upload.

"Punch up a real-time construct," she said. "Use the sample we took from him earlier as a reference."

Funky placed Cray's blood sample under the scope, rendering the construct from a chemical analysis. It showed a number of flash strands slowing down, unable to penetrate the outer membranes of the cells they attacked. A short time later, they ceased to move altogether: not dead in a conventional sense, because they had never really been alive, but neutral, like viral antibodies.

"Yo, ho, ho and a bottle of rum," Funky said.

Lea released the breath she had been holding.

So far, so good.

"You should be receiving another series of resonance images," she told Funky, this time confining her scans to Cray's head. "Six images in all, at two-minute intervals. Create an animation sequence on the high-res. I want to find out how this does in a living system."

"We already know the shit works," Funky pointed out, glancing at her with a bit of concern. "You know something that I don't?"

"Let's just take a look and see."

He shrugged, transferring the image over. The individual frames assembled over the next few seconds, then played themselves out like a movie. Cray's brain remained dark, with no dramatic changes. Nothing much seemed to be happening—although it was difficult to tell anything at this range.

"Go back in," Lea said. "Five microns."

The microscopic soldiers appeared once again, in complete, vicious detail. Lea and Funky watched as several of them continued to invade nearby cells, as if none of them had heeded the call to stand down. The process of transformation continued unabated. If anything, it had accelerated in response to their interference.

Funky's yellow eyes widened.

"What the hell?"

Lea felt a piece of her life draining into that black void. Part of her had expected it. It was the *Inru*'s idea of a fail-safe. Zoe had known it from the moment she made the disease a part of her blood. She knew she was doomed.

But Zoe was a partisan. Cray was just a victim.

Funky jumped around to different regions of Cray's brain. Lea, meanwhile, tried to find an indication that the process had stopped elsewhere.

"Come on, Vortex," she insisted. "Give me something."

Cray could not oblige. The flash continued to spread, no matter where Funky searched. He pushed himself away from the interface console.

"It's over," he told her. "They won't let us stop it."

"The hell they *won't*," Lea said, pleading with him. "You don't just give up on the man, Funky. Not after all this. We can still fight."

"But *he* can't."

Those words closed the door on her argument. So many of Cray's tissues had been systematically replaced, any attempt to remove them would probably kill him. Physiologically, he was a different organism—something more than human but as yet incomplete.

Whether or not he *became* complete was a decision neither one of them could make.

"I'm shutting down," Funky said, switching off his end of the interface.

Trevor Bostic felt it on him: the push, the crush—matter and energy focused against his body, driving him away. The effect, which only intensified as the lift rose higher into the building, was like walking through water. By the time he stepped off at one hundred he was exhausted, and had to pop stimulants just to stay on his feet.

He steadied himself while the amphetamines kicked in, then walked the deserted corridor that led to the bionucleics lab. Bostic had declared the area off-limits after the incident with Alden; but then Avalon turned up in that hospital bed, suspected of *Inru* terrorism, and Bostic's more paranoid instincts took over. An armed contingent stood guard outside the lab at all times, with orders to kill anyone who approached—Bostic himself as the only exception.

The two CSS guards appeared haggard, cadaverous. Although they rotated out every hour, the stim patches they used had begun to take their toll. Bostic wondered how long Lyssa would be able to keep it up. The power drain on her had to be enormous.

"Stand down," he ordered the guards.

They stepped aside, allowing Bostic to pass. The corporate counsel wasted no time making his way across the lab, not knowing how long his chemical reinforcements would last. As he passed through the air lock outside the Tank, he doubted his actions here were worth the risk; but he also knew he *had* to see her, if he were ever to realize his ambitions. Phao Yin, after all, would not be around forever—especially now that his free agent had been unmasked as a spy. If he positioned himself the right way, Bostic could profit handsomely from recent events.

Lyssa, meanwhile, carried on as if he had never entered. Bostic watched her for a time, wisps of light crossing back and forth across the Tank with angry and violent purpose. Occasionally they would morph into human shapes, with the substance of ghosts, which collided with one another to release waves of neural energy—the same energy that acted upon him now.

And voices, thousands of them, shrieking Alden's name.

"Lyssa," Bostic said, with a measure of pity. "What did he do to you?"

Avalon stayed below the pulser grid all the way from Manhattan, using the standard free approach routes to Montreal. She made a point of following procedure, activating the hovercraft transponder as soon as she was in range of air traffic control. The transmissions were all coded to a diplomatic frequency—another one of Phao Yin's touches. Not only did it give Avalon priority clearance, it perpetuated a useful fiction that she was on official business for the Assembly. Nobody would ask her any questions. None that mattered, anyway.

"Montreal free flight," she signaled. "This is Special Air Mission 2000. Request confirmation of ID acquisition and approach path."

"SAM 2000, acknowledged." The reply was instantaneous and polite. "Welcome to the Northern Incorporated Territories. We have you on our monitors, just coming over the outer marker. Vector to course three-two-nine, we'll catch you on automated approach."

"Negative," Avalon radioed back. "Initiate manual flight protocols—immediate clearance on Port Authority Gamma. This is a security matter, gentlemen. Keep it tight."

"Received and understood. State nature of mission, please."

"Courier."

"Stand by." There was a pause of a few seconds while they checked her story out. *Courier* was code for a diplomatic bag, used to ferry state secrets or large sums of cash for covert operations. The mention of the word made most controllers nervous.

Down on the ground, the lights of the Gamma runway sprang to life.

"Clearance granted," control said. "Have a nice night."

Avalon dropped altitude, slowing her forward velocity as she flew over the threshold beacon. Automated search floods reached up into the sky and illuminated the hovercraft as it descended, catching exhaust from the ventral jets and cradling the small ship in bright plumes of hot vapor. They parted as the hovercraft settled down on the tarmac, carried away by a steady wind that swallowed the fading

whine of the engines. As Avalon shut everything down, she looked
out from the cockpit at the vast, flat landscape of the airport. Traffic
at that hour of the night was minimal, only a few shuttle flights taking off and landing on the general aviation runways, several kilometers distant. Her own craft was the only one in the immediate
area—and though its arrival had been obvious, no ground crews
were coming out to meet her.

Avalon secured the craft and popped the lower hatch, dropping
the short distance to the ground. She landed like a cat, graceful and
crouched. Draped in long shadows from the glare of the lights, she
stepped away from the hovercraft and out into the open. Across the
fields of concrete, half a kilometer away, she saw her objective. It was
a massive complex of hangars—the stark white, rectangular buildings
that housed Port Authority vehicles when they weren't in use.

Avalon moved swiftly, cloaking herself in the shadows and coming
up alongside the hangar at a broad angle. Circling toward the back,
she followed a wide path that allowed her to get a look at the security
architecture of the place. It presented her with few problems. Magnetic trip sensors sealed the doors and windows, backed up by motion detectors scattered broadly enough to leave huge gaps in the
areas they covered. Avalon also spotted three cameras—macrodigital
jobs, probably plugged into a vid link monitored by airport cops
who got paid by the hour. She dropped an infrared filter over her visual sensors, casting a net for laser bleed and following the trail until
she located a fiber hub mounted on the outside wall. As she suspected, the circuits all appeared to be local.

She zigged along the blind edge of the motion detectors, then
zagged to stay out of the range of the cameras. Finding a comfortable spot, she shuffled along the wall until she reached the hub. The
housing was so flimsy that it offered no resistance when she yanked it
open. Inside she found a series of optical cables—transmission media
for the security countermeasures she had already seen, as well as the
ones inside. Avalon plucked them out one at a time, then replaced
the housing to conceal her work.

She then moved on to the nearest door, carving out the lock with
a stealthblade and slipping inside. Footsteps echoed against hard

concrete as she walked into the heart of the building, surrounded by dozens of vehicles of every size and type. Most of them had been in storage for some time, mothballed on racks that were stacked six high from floor to ceiling: a mausoleum of modern aircraft, perched like raptors above her head. Avalon ignored them and concentrated on the recent arrivals, which were parked on the lowest level in whatever spaces were available. She wandered through the maze of jutting wings and hulking fuselages, sensors measuring the configuration of each ship, looking for the one that matched the specifications Phao Yin had given her.

Cargo pulser. L-class, heavy conversion. Registration number NSD-12879PP.

The find was a subliminal push, so natural that it seemed more like ESP than hard input. It directed Avalon toward the back of the hangar, where she found the pulser laying in wait. It faced her head-on, empty cockpit glass suggesting a blank stare. *Alive and dirty,* she thought, noting the pits and carbon scars that dotted the surface of its transluminum skin. *You've seen some action, haven't you?*

The pulser was still. Silent. Contemplating.

Tell me a story.

It was a huge thing, designed for mass transport of goods—as well as the occasional smuggling, if its battle scars were any indication. Avalon kept her sensors at low gain as she approached the pulser, playing instincts over enhancements in her search for clues. She ran a hand along its belly, finding the surface rough and caked with an array of exotic impurities. A rapid spectral sifted most of the components. Dust from silicon slag, fluorocarbons, stray benzene, crystalline hydrochlorics—all of them suggested more than a few flights through the Zone, where the atmosphere was rich with such pollutants.

There were also patchy concentrations of sodium chloride, deposited from evaporation, which formed granular deposits that clung to the skin of the ship. Avalon watched them crumble between her gloved fingers, the olfactory receptors of her sensuit translating the chemical composition into a pungent aroma.

Brine. The ocean. Sea salt.

The pulser had been docked at a coastal port. More than that, it had been close to the water's edge—close enough to be doused in sea spray. High-breaking waves would account for the large volume of salts she found, which indicated the pulser had likely touched down at the edge of a heavy storm system. The salts were also clean, free from the grime and trace elements that covered the rest of the ship. That meant the storm had been recent, probably within the last twenty-four hours.

Avalon made a careful note of her findings, filing everything away into temporary buffers for later analysis. Brushing the dried powder from her hands, she went over to the open belly hatch and hoisted herself inside. She came up into the cargo bay, a cavernous and empty space still reeking from the residue of old shipments. Everything from livestock to drugs to prostitutes had occupied the chamber at one time or the other, leaving behind a collage of stains and smells that reeked of the subculture. Avalon found it stifling.

She spent as little time in there as possible, making a brief sweep for more evidence but finding it impossible to bag anything coherent. She then climbed up into the cockpit, taking a seat in one of the forward chairs and waiting for Alden's presence to join her. Since closing her eyes was impossible, she darkened her visual sensors and substituted that input with her imagination, assembling his likeness from her memories.

Staring through the window. Face reflected in the glass. You are not alone. The woman is close to you. You know who she is, but nothing of what she's about.

Avalon took in a deliberate breath, the world taking shape around Cray's image.

The night passes. Stars in the void. Then clouds hide the stars. The rains come, and they take you—where?

Avalon saw the lightning and heard the thunder, the wind slapping against the pulser so hard it shook. Then unsteady ground beneath the ship as it landed, the cockpit glass crisscrossed with rivulets of seawater. Even now, the haze remained over the windows.

Someplace safe. Where could that be?

Slowly, Alden turned toward her and smiled. That cocky smile of his.

He disappeared.

Avalon was aware of her anger, but fell short of experiencing it. A disjointed emotion, it flashed and faded like the hallucination of Alden sitting next to her—but not before she had her hands around his throat, not before she made him bleed. When she came out of that fugue, she was exhausted. Killing, even when it was imaginary, took a lot out of you.

She sank back into the pilot's chair, resuming her focus on all things real. Absently, she glazed over the instrument panel with her sensors, finding little of interest on the surface. Even fingerprints had been wiped clean. Avalon reached forward and flipped open the navigational interface, jacking the lockout codes so she could have a look at the latest series of flight logs. *New York to Montreal—nothing in between. Perfect, right down to the arrival and departure times.*

So what's missing?

Port Authority records were useless. Avalon had seen the telemetry, and it matched everything she found aboard, even the diagnostics. Alden and his friends had done a thorough job altering the pulser's history—but they had done nothing to eradicate the trace evidence on the hull. If Alden had overlooked that detail, he could have overlooked something else. Something invisible and unique.

Avalon played a hunch, punching up a current diagnostic. She ran through everything—avionics, structural integrity, communications—but it was a minor anomaly in the pulser's electromagnetic throughput that made her stop and look more closely. As the computer routed a simulated transmission beam down the center axis of the airframe, it displayed a .07 percent variance in conductive efficiency—a miniscule amount, but enough to suggest that the ship had suffered some damage during the course of her journey.

What do we have here?

A detailed scan revealed no physical defects. Avalon ran the test again, this time comparing the input/output ratio of the transmission beam. She eventually traced the fault to the forward receptor dish. It was drawing power at rated standards, but delivering less than it took in. Materials drag accounted for some of the differential—but not the levels she saw.

Something had altered the EM characteristics of the photon receptors in the dish.

Avalon studied the numbers. The effect was so subtle that an engineer would probably have missed it—but there it was, taunting her with the riddle of its origin. There weren't many events that could account for that kind of attenuation. An overload was one possibility; but that would have caused more widespread damage, fusing circuits and rendering the pulser inoperable. This wound was more of a sting, inflicted with such delicacy that it escaped notice.

An electromagnetic pulse.

Not a strong one. More likely a series of waves spaced out over time, radiating from a powerful, shielded source. The location would be off the main pulser routes, at a distance from the metroplex because of the potential for electronic interference. It also could have obscured the signal coming off Alden's tracer implant, giving him sufficient cover to make his escape.

Radiation and seawater. It began to make sense.

A heat signature at the edge of Avalon's sensor range grazed her concentration like a stray bullet. A ground vehicle approached the hangar, with a jumble of life signs that suggested three or four bodies—a modest contingency of airport cops, appearing a bit sooner than she expected. Avalon could have handled them if she chose, but there was no reason for bloodshed. She had all the information she needed.

Slipping outside the same way she came in, Avalon went still. She stayed around long enough to watch the airport cops arrive and perform like the amateurs they were, as they walked the hangar up and down and searched in all the wrong places. Avalon retreated while their backs were turned, moving like the wind across the tarmac and back to where her hovercraft waited.

Moments later, tendrils of frosty air gathered around the small ship as its engines powered up. It rose into the atmosphere, turning back toward the southeast and picking up speed as it gained altitude and cast itself into the ribbon of night.

"SAM 2000," the air traffic controller spoke over the cockpit speaker. "We have you crossing the outer marker, departing Montreal airspace. Come to course one-one-seven, free outbound at two thousand meters. Maintain speed and altitude to grid boundary."

"Copy," Avalon replied. "Estimating two minutes out."

"Montreal, acknowledging. Please give our regards to the Collective."

"I will," Avalon said, switching off her transponder. "I certainly will."

Cray Alden was used to being under a microscope. It was the curse of a spook to have his life scrutinized by those who knew him best. He had been measured by every conceivable standard at one time or the other: fascination, greed, fear, envy—a full spectrum of human frailty that filtered the way his associates viewed him. Pity, however, was never part of the equation. Confronted with it, he realized it was better to be hated than mourned.

"I would appreciate it," he announced, "if everyone would stop acting like I was dead."

Lea made an effort, but her eyes kept drifting back to the empty extraction tank. Funky paced from one point to another, triple-checking all of his equipment and losing his patience when he couldn't find anything wrong.

"*Bollocks*," he cursed.

"Give it a rest, Funky," Cray told him.

In all fairness, Cray couldn't blame them. If he wasn't dead, he sure as hell looked the part. He had dried off and changed back into his clothes, but his flesh was still pale and mottled, his hair matted from the gelled accelerating solution. He was cold and tired—but beneath the grunge, his mind was alarmingly dynamic, firing on neurons that had never been active before.

Funky finally settled down, moving over to the table where Lea and Cray were sitting. He dropped himself into an empty chair and released a heavy sigh.

"I'm sorry, mate."

"Don't worry about it," Cray said, forcing a smile. He shifted to a contemplative state, asking the logical question. "So what are our options?"

Lea and Funky exchanged a brief glance. Both appeared lost.

"Protease inhibitors could slow the progress of the infection," she suggested. "There's also chemotherapy, or reverse engineering a virus to combat the flash on a genetic level."

"A cure worse than the disease," Cray pointed out. "I've seen the charts, Lea. This thing has been remaking my cells in its own image, not the other way around. There just isn't enough *me* left in there to recover."

"Then there's stasis," Lea fired right back. "We stop it right here. We study it. We find its weakness. Then when we're ready, we bring you back."

"That could take years."

"You don't know that, Cray."

"How long are you willing to wait?"

"However long it takes!" she snapped, slamming her palm down on the table. Both men recoiled. It wasn't the sound. It was the heat of her anger, born of desperation and nuclear in its intensity. "In case you haven't figured it out, Alden—*I don't know everything.* This bug was my idea, and I don't have the first clue about how to fix it, okay? Don't point out the obvious and pretend it's a fucking stroke of genius."

She lapsed into whispers, muttering to herself.

"*Stubborn,*" she breathed. "Goddamned *stubborn.*"

Cray smiled.

"I've been called worse."

Funky closed his eyes and shook his head.

Lea gathered what was left of her calm, and walked over to where Cray was seated. She crouched, leveling a stare at him that was the opposite of the fire she displayed before.

"You just don't get it, do you?" she said. "I could have put you under back there, but I didn't. I thought that was a decision you should make for yourself—and I thought you would, once you had a grip on all the facts. If you're not willing to take this seriously—"

"I understand what you're saying."

"Really?" she asked, dubious. "Then *trust* me. If you can't do that, there's nothing more I can do for you." She parted on that ultimatum, strolling over to the interface bank and busying herself with an assortment of random tasks.

"That's about as clear as it gets," Funky said, clapping Cray on the shoulder. "Lea means to have her way. The question is how long before you give in."

They both watched her for a time, going about the business of being Lea Prism, expertly handling the beauty and chaos that came with the job. In spite of what she thought, Cray took her seriously. Lea had an almost mystical wisdom that went beyond her age, the product of an accelerated life spent hanging over the edge, staring down into places as dark as they were familiar.

"So what's it going to be?" Funky asked. Cray walked back over to the extraction tank and considered her proposal. He searched for the answer within its confines, but only found the image of himself in there—inspired not by his imagination but by the subconscious memories he had of the experience. That part of him, the flash element, had been keenly aware of every moment, even though his body had only been able to respond to the most rudimentary commands. He remembered that helplessness the most: the suffocating panic of being buried alive, the horror of being turned into a zombie.

And a single, consuming imperative: *escape.*

Cray couldn't help but think of Lyssa. He remembered her invisible prison, and how it wasn't so different from the one Lea offered him. In the confines of that domain, an eternity could be compressed into a second, and into every second that followed. With the hope of contact just outside the glass wall, to be so close and not be able to reach out was nothing short of maddening. Cray already knew the extremes Lyssa had employed to break free. Would he do anything less?

The human part of him still had faith that he wouldn't—but that part was in fast remission. Time was growing short, and Cray needed to make a choice.

"What if there's another alternative?" he asked.

Lea stopped cold.

"What are you talking about?" she asked.

"The truth nobody wants to mention." Cray walked over to the other side of the tank, putting the glass sarcophagus between himself and the others. "You spelled the whole thing out for me, Lea—but you never called it by name. Now I'm here, and I'm telling you it's real. I'm living proof—in the flesh, for as long as that lasts."

He aimed the point directly at the two of them.

"I'm Ascending," he said. "And we know damned well there's nothing any of *us* can do to stop it."

Funky closed his eyes.

"So we shouldn't even try," Lea said, dumbstruck by the suggestion.

"I didn't say that," Cray reminded her. "But playing around with cryogenics and gene therapy is only going to waste what little time we have left."

"You don't *know* that," she scoffed. "Nobody knows how this stuff works or *if* it even works. You could also be dying, Cray."

"I don't think so."

"And what makes you so sure?"

"Because the way I feel now," Cray said, "I could go on forever."

Cray sounded blithe, confident—even arrogant, if such a thing were possible. Lea found it difficult to argue, impossible to reason. It was the same wall she had hit with Zoe, those last few days of her life.

"Funky," she said, "would you mind stepping out for a while? I need some time alone with Dr. Alden."

"Suits me just fine," Funky said, hopping up from the table. "I'll be on the control deck if you need me."

Lea gave it some time after he left, distracting herself with the interface. She was numb with numbers, going over them so many times—but looking at them was easier than looking at Cray. It would be different if he felt the same anger she did. But this quiet acceptance was even more disturbing than the images suspended in a curtain of virtual reality. Those she could dismiss with the touch of a button. Cray, however, was more problematic.

"You're riding the rapture," she said.

Cray appeared curious.

"That's an immersion risk," he said. "I haven't been in that long for years."

"Maybe not in the Axis—but what's inside of you is already there, Cray. And it *will* drag you down, sure as any interface junkie getting high off his own juice." She walked down to the tank and ran her hand along its open edge, absorbing Cray's resonance before coming face-to-face with him. "Once you're on, it gets hard to know when to turn it off. You're still in there, aren't you?"

Cray's eyes followed her to the empty tank. On the bottom was a tangled mass of electrodes, the dead ends terminating into nothingness.

"You ever been down?" he asked.

Lea shook her head. "That was Zoe's territory."

"It sticks with you."

"It shouldn't," she said. "That's the whole point, isn't it? I saw the way you reacted. You just tuned in, like it was the most natural thing in the world."

"So what if I did?"

"It wasn't just words, Cray. You picked up on my *thoughts*."

Cray blinked at her. He appeared to be surprised at this development, but quickly moved to a serene acceptance.

"That scares you," he said.

"I'm scared of the implications," she admitted. "The flash is spreading at an alarming rate. From what we've seen, this is only the *beginning* of the process. What happens when it goes even further? You could lose yourself, Cray—and turn into something you can't control."

"I'm not a monster, Lea."

"Neither was Lyssa. Not until she could be."

It was the *Inru* line, a dirty trick if there ever was one—but not something she would pull out of the arsenal unless she was dead serious. Lea had only her senses to rely on, and already she could tell how much Cray identified with the machine—and how little he identified with her. Cray, for his part, seemed to understand. He stepped back and fell into an uneasy quiet, turning back toward her with a re-signed expression.

"You're right," he said. "In some ways, I'm already there. It won't be long before the rest of me is gone, and I still don't have any idea where it's going. Maybe it's insanity. Maybe it's just like Lyssa said." He drew a hollow breath. "All I know is that somehow, *she's* the catalyst. I didn't understand it at the time—but she said every-thing would become clear when I was ready."

Lea drifted toward him as he spoke.

"Are you?"

"I don't know," Cray admitted. "But it's a place to start."

"What did you have in mind?"

"The last thing anybody would expect," he said, withdrawing from her a little. "What I need from you is balance—and a promise that you will do whatever is necessary, even if you think it's crazy. Can you do that for me?"

Lea saw what he was doing, and kept the pressure on.

"I'll never run from a fight, Cray."

"But will you question your faith?"

"I'll question everything—unless I have a reason not to."

Cray nodded. Her fingertips brushed against his hand, communi-cating the truth of it even more effectively.

"Tell me what you want."

Cray was silent for a moment.

"You have to watch me," he explained, a hard resolve in his voice. "Use your instincts. Use objective scans. I don't care how you do it, but you *have* to let me know when I'm slipping. I can hang on for now—but if this thing gets away from me, even for a second, there's no telling what I might do. You have to be ready to make the call. If you can't, your involvement ends right here and now."

Lea agreed.

"And if it goes down for real," Cray went on, "if you see me los-ing control, I want you to put a stop to it. Permanently. No warn-ings, no doubts. Don't give me a chance to fight you. Just end it, any way you can. It doesn't have to be painless. It only has to be quick."

"I'll handle it," Lea said honestly.

Cray nodded.

"I know you will."

She couldn't help but wonder about the deal she struck. She was afraid to ask him for details, because his proposition implied risks that were far more perilous than the ones they already faced. She tried to imagine how such a thing could be possible, and came back to the same conclusion again and again. *The last thing anybody would expect. The last place anybody would think to go.*

With dawning horror, Lea saw that it was true.

"Lyssa," she said. "You're going back to see Lyssa."

Avalon found the bar with no name, in what passed as a high-tech sector outside red-light Chelsea. It was a Zone hangout, frequented by Zone rangers—a wasted lot who had spent their better days using cheap decks to stake out restricted ground in the Axis and paid the price with permanent nerve damage. Most of them still worked the system, but only at the perimeter, grubbing after jobs that the real hammerjacks wouldn't touch. Their existence was so meager, their crimes so insignificant, CSS didn't even bother to keep files on them anymore. As far as the outside world was concerned, they were dead—and that made them perfectly suited for Avalon's purposes.

She strolled into the building, mapping the structure with her sensors and checking the interior for surveillance and weapons. It was the only aspect of the place that was clean. The stench of fake booze, spent adrenaline, and withdrawal was enough to induce a contact crash, reminding Avalon of the standard-issue amphetamines the military used to get troops through the long missions. Most of the people there had probably been awake for weeks, much as Avalon found them: hunched over face kits, wired into the Axis, spending what little life and money they had at the virtual fringe. It was doubtful they even saw her walk in.

Only one other human being was conscious, and he was behind the bar. The man went through the motions of wiping everything down, a hopeless exercise he obviously performed out of sheer habit. He acknowledged Avalon with a nod, then returned to his tooling.

She sat down on one of the stools.

"What'll it be?"

Avalon tossed a small pouch onto the bar. It landed with the hard jingle of real currency.

"Ten minutes," she said.

"That all?"

"That's enough. You got anybody here ready to work?"

"Try Zero," the bartender said, motioning toward a table in the back. "He never sleeps."

"You got anyplace more private?"

"Upstairs. Plenum shielding. Costs extra."

Avalon followed the spiral staircase with her sensors, all the way to the loft above. She found residual heat signatures behind one of the closed doors, flattening out at room temperature—probably a dead body no one had noticed. Hardly cause for alarm.

"Fine," she decided. "But if he rips me off, he dies. Then I'll come back down and do *you*. Understand?"

The bartender spit into one of his glasses. "Of course," he said, and slipped the money under his apron.

Avalon went to collect Zero. He appeared much as the bartender described, in an almost catatonic state that broke when Avalon came within the limited boundary of his senses. He then became hyper-aware, tiny red eyes darting restlessly from side to side. He peeled electrodes from his forehead, turning off his face kit before those eyes settled on Avalon. He sniffed at her, drawing the air into a loud, wet belch. Zero was a repulsive man, even by Zone standards.

Thin lips parted to reveal a jagged smile.

"Need some magic?"

"Just a little juice," she replied, and pointed him toward the staircase.

Up in the loft, Zero led her to one of the interface booths. He seemed excited at the prospect of using the better equipment, which species like him could rarely afford. He strapped himself down in the control chair, rigging electrodes to his head and hands, and engaged a virtual display at the front of the small room. Static poured out of hazy air for a few moments, until it morphed into a logical representation of an Axis gateway. It was the poor man's way in—light-years from the elegant paths hammerjacks used to gain access to corporate data mines—but it would do. The areas Avalon wanted to jack had only rudimentary layers of security.

"Where you going?" Zero croaked.

"Port Authority," Avalon told him. "Fixed-path approach schedules only. Avoid the critical subsystems."

Zero was offended. "*This* is what you pay good money for?"

"Shut up and you'll earn your pay. Set off any of the automated sentries, you won't live long enough to regret it."

Zero grumbled to himself, a mixed slew of obscenities and guttural noises, but he was remarkably agile when it came to riding the wire. He navigated the way a drunk would, substituting memory for reflex, missing a few turns along the way but arriving at his destination safely. He parked himself into a slow orbit around the Port Authority domain, taking refuge in the shadow of older subsystems. It was a necessity when you worked without protoviruses. Staying invisible meant staying between the cracks.

"You got anything special in mind?"

"The East Coast grid," Avalon said. "Skip the commercial traffic. Just give me all the nonstandard routes originating in Manhattan, vectoring south."

"Sounds boring."

"You can play spice on your own time."

Zero sighed impatiently, slapping a neuropatch against the skin of his neck. He dove into the dark globe that was the Port Authority domain, skirting the terminator between vital and nonvital systems—a balancing act that had him on the wrong side of the fence more than once. Somehow he avoided tripping the alarms and ended up at the master scheduling hub for the entire Eastern Seaboard. He punched into a real-time monitoring feed, which overlaid the pulser routes going in and out of the New York metroplex. They radiated outward in all directions, like spokes on a wheel, a series of flashing dots marking the current position of each vehicle on the grid.

"*Voilà*," Zero said.

Avalon bypassed her advanced optics and studied the display with simple visual sensors. The individual routes numbered in the hundreds, but only the ones that terminated in the major coastal areas caught her attention. A number of possibilities presented themselves—Boston, Washington, Norfolk, even down as far as Miami—but not one of them could account for a strong electromagnetic signature.

Then there were the seagoing routes. Avalon followed one of them in particular: a single vector that showed no active traffic, and ended abruptly at the incorporated border—about fifty kilometers off the coast of Washington.

"That one there," she said, pointing it out. "Isolate it."

Zero killed all the other routes, augmenting the one Avalon wanted. It seemed to go nowhere, dead-ending in the middle of the ocean.

"Punch up the route information."

"Don't need to," Zero informed her. "Fusion Directorate owns the business end—cargo runs and all that jazz. They use it to supply power plants out at sea. Strictly automated."

"I need coordinates."

"Yeah, yeah." He darted away from the Port Authority domain, getting to a safe distance before jacking commercial GPS. The satellite images that streamed in were detailed infrared, showing clusters of fusion spheres dotting the surface of the sea over an area of a few square kilometers. Zero extrapolated Avalon's cargo route, superimposing it over the image. It dead-ended on top of the largest reactor complex, at the center of all the others.

"Bring on meteorological surface maps," Avalon said. "Minus forty-eight hours, then move forward to now."

A quick retrieval from public weather records was all it took. Zero framed the maps over the current image, arranging them into an animation sequence that played out over the last two days. A strong frontal system had been hovering at the perimeter of the fusion complex, kicking up high winds and rain that continued even now.

Cray had been there. She was certain of it.

Avalon savored that ember of rage, allowing it to burn a little hotter. It demanded action—and since action was a matter of necessity, there was nothing to deter her from an indulgence. Zero didn't even realize what was happening until her hands gripped his head, and by then his spinal cord had detached from the dismal recesses of his brain. He perished instantly, half his consciousness still inside the construct, able to watch his body go limp before disconnecting altogether. The dead were beginning to crowd the place.

Avalon left him, exiting the booth and gliding down the spiral staircase. She passed by the bar again on her way out, and was surprised when the bartender called to her.

"You were only in there seven minutes."

"Keep the change," she said, without looking back.

TWELVE

A thin veil of Axis came down between Cray and the others, filtering his expressions through a construct of logical space. The mist gathered around him as if responding to cerebral commands, though not a single electrode was pasted to his skin. There were only his hands, his fingers, hovering delicately above the interface controls to guide his journey, and they did so completely of their own accord. Even Cray's eyes seemed to be someplace else, staring at the pathways that led toward the GenTec domain. Lea could tell: he was utterly at home there, unbound by the constraints of mere physicality—not as a hammerjack, but as a slipstream into that world. He was his own gateway. Soon, the interface would be a redundant component.

"Tell me you see him," Funky implored.

Lea couldn't. Sporadic flickers of *Homo sapiens* revealed themselves in Cray, but they were becoming far less frequent. It was, in its own way, a beautiful transformation. Rarely did someone get a chance to witness evolution firsthand.

"*Look* at him," Funky observed. "He's transcended at least three different levels of security since he started. Makes the bloody CMS look like industrial code. You know he hasn't used the subs to fabricate his approaches? Not even once?"

Lea shrugged. "So he's multitasking."

"He's doing the calculations inside his head."

"Amazing, isn't it?"

"Bloody scary is more like," Funky scoffed. "That's not human. It isn't even flesh and blood."

"No," Lea agreed. "It's more than that."

They maintained a distance as Cray worked, using the feed from the interface to translate the subtleties they could not discern with their own eyes. Cray operated on an entirely new level, trashing the established Axis protocols and projecting his consciousness as a non-linear entity. At once a biologic *and* a logical construct, he had accomplished the equivalent of a dimensional shift, making himself into a ghost. Boundaries became irrelevant, because they no longer existed.

Stranger in a strange land, Lea thought. *The Axis doesn't know what to make of him.*

True to conventions, the Axis ignored him. Cray used the opportunity to position himself as a contained singularity, dropping through the resulting crack like an object disappearing into a black hole. He emerged on the other side of GenTec's countermeasures— a simple displacement from one point to the other, without crossing the space in between.

"Crikey," Funky whispered.

The feed crashed his monitor. He rebooted the system, but when it came back up it only spouted lines of gibberish. Funky had to cut the link between his computer and Cray's interface, then clear out all the buffers. After that it performed slowly, like it was suffering from a major hangover.

"What happened?" Lea asked.

"Don't know," Funky said, checking for hardware faults. "Diagnostics are coming back clean. Could be some bad data the monitor couldn't handle."

She checked over the inputs herself. The terminating points had suffered physical damage, as if they had been subjected to a power spike.

"He's operating on a new paradigm," Lea mused. "Your system doesn't know how to interpret the shift."

"No shit." Funky jerked a thumb back at Cray, who was tunneling into the restricted zones buried in the deepest recesses of the domain. "Is there even a name for what he did back there?"

"Call it a new trick."

"Call it breaking the law. You can't do that kind of jack within the constraints of Axis architecture, Lea. It's conceptually impossible."

"Do you really believe that?"

The readings said otherwise. Vortex had crossed the line, supplanting hard science with his own brand of voodoo. His coda was sheer mesmerism: a punch-out from GenTec that landed him on the dark side of the Works, the ultimate target of his mischief. Once there, he set up a line of communication between the two domains, utilizing a clandestine port that resided in the same pseudophase that hosted his self-projection. Cray waited for a few moments until the line stabilized, then dissolved himself out of the construct.

Back in the world, he came up as if nothing had happened.

"Don't worry about a backtrace," he announced, circling around the semitransparent image to join the others. "I've spread the link across random carrier bands, modulating at irregular intervals. You can use it to monitor mission progress for as long as it takes."

"Whatever you say," Funky said, folding his arms. "Now tell me what the hell you just did."

"A little bait and switch," Cray told him. His tone was reassuring, an obvious ploy to ease their concerns about him. "What's the story on transportation?"

"Pulser inbound," Lea said. "Jacked from some executive fleet. Should be here in a few minutes."

"Nice," Cray said. "Might as well go in style."

"If you have to go at all. Remind me again why you're doing this."

"Because I'm running out of time," Cray told both of them. "It won't be long before the flash in my system runs its course, and I don't know what's going to happen."

"And how is Lyssa supposed to change any of that?" Lea asked. "You saw what happened when the two of you were together. What makes you think this time will be any different?"

"Because *I'm* different." He paused for a moment, allowing the truth of it to distill between them. "This Ascension is real. I can feel it growing inside of me—reaching out, connecting me to these vast networks of information. All I have to do is open my mind and it's all *there*." The manic energy behind his eyes told the story far better than words. The flash was displacing him, turning his cells and tissues into a biological interface, joining him to the Axis—and perhaps more.

"It's almost like a drug," he continued. "This thing that consumes you, but can never fill your need. It's only a matter of time before I won't be able to control it."

Lea nodded, because she finally understood.

"You're going to interface with Lyssa," she said. "And hope that it neutralizes the flash."

Funky shook his head. "Now I *know* you've gone off the deep end," he protested. "You said it yourself, Vortex—Lyssa would swallow your mind whole and wash it down with a pint of ale."

"If I was unprotected," Cray explained. "She already craves data. The sheer volume of all that flash should act as a firewall between my mind and hers—giving me enough time to disconnect before she can go after my own neural pathways."

Lea pointed out the potential flaw in his plan.

"What if it destroys the flash instead?"

"Then it will be over," Cray answered. "And it will be quick."

"I can think of easier ways to kill yourself," Funky lamented. "Don't get me wrong, Vortex. I admire anybody with the *cojones* to put together a run like this. But taking a joyride into the Works?" He spat out a miserable laugh. "Stick your head in there, mate, and they'll lop it off first chance they get."

"You saw it yourself, Cray," Lea added. "Special Services has at least a hundred bodies there, and most of them know your face. That's a lot of heat—especially when they have orders to shoot you on sight."

"They scare you," Cray said. "Don't they?"

"Fucking A," Funky answered.

"Good," Cray said, floating the idea as he returned to the interface controls. "They *should* scare you. They're professional killers—and they won't hesitate to eliminate you or me, or anybody else who gets in their way. They are not, however, invulnerable." With a wave of his hand, he conjured a three-dimensional schematic of the Works building—a macroview at first, zooming in to a cross section of the floors on the research level. "There is a weakness."

"What are you talking about?" Lea asked.

"The focus of their mission," Cray explained. "Which also happens to be the one thing they're not allowed to kill."

Lea drew a short breath and held it as Cray highlighted the floor plans for the Tank.

"Lyssa," she whispered.

"You can't destroy something you're supposed to protect," Cray said. He superimposed another graphic, this one an animated sequence that traced a convoluted series of links between the Tank and the automation complex several floors above. "These are the lines Lyssa used when she jacked fire control and locked down the building. You can see how they now terminate short of a complete interface. The Works engineers shut down remote access and unplugged all the systems to prevent it from happening again. But suppose," he said, extending the links back into the automation computers, "just *suppose* they get an indicator that these systems came back online. We plant the idea that Lyssa is back in control. What's the first thing CSS will do?"

"The same thing I'd do," Funky said. "Get the hell out of there."

"Precisely."

"Wait a second," Lea interjected. "You want to force an evacuation with a false alarm? How can you do that if those systems have been disconnected at the source?"

"By tripping an alarm at a remote location," Cray said, illustrating his plan with a fresh construct. The Works broke apart like a jigsaw puzzle, then reorganized itself into the virtual conduit he had created just moments earlier. As Lea had pointed out, the Works side was completely dead; GenTec, however, was alive and pinging—a package waiting to be delivered, wherever Cray directed. "We then feed *those* indicators through this pipeline, creating the illusion of an emergency. Every threat sensor in the place will light up like a Christmas tree. CSS will think an anvil just came down on them."

"What if they don't buy it?"

"They won't take that chance," Cray said, with the utmost confidence. "I know these people. They'll follow procedure until they're sure there's no danger."

"Live by the rules, die by the rules," Funky finished. "How long until GenTec figures it out and calls off the party?"

Cray thought about it.

"Ten minutes," he guessed. "Maybe fifteen."

"That's pretty slim timing, mate."

"I know," Cray admitted. "That's why this has to go by the numbers. Otherwise, it's *adios muchacho*." He locked the interface down, then walked over to where Funky stood. "You'll have full access to all CSS communications through this node. All I need is for you to bait the trap. After that, just keep an eye on them for as long as you can. Try to give me a couple minutes' warning before they come."

"Sounds easy," Funky said. "You sure you've thought this through?"

"As much as I'm going to."

Funky held his hands out. "Then count me in."

They shook hands, then embraced. It was as much fear as bravado, the reassurance of men about to embark on something suicidal. That was how Lea understood it, because she felt the same emotions herself. But she also felt responsible, as if she were the principal architect of this madness—or, at the very least, its catalyst.

"Where does that leave me?"

Lea asked a pointed question, backed up with that raw determination she had used to survive in the Zone. She still thought the exercise was dangerous—perhaps even fatal. But if there was no stopping it, she was determined to have a part.

"That depends," he said. "Think I could use a hand?"

"You'll need a lot more than that, hoss."

He smiled.

"I'll take what I can get."

Lea acknowledged his affection, her eyes locking with his for the few moments she would allow it. Then she was back to business, leaving him and going over to a nearby storage locker. She keyed a combination to open the door, then rolled out a small rack of weapons. Most of it was mercenary merchandise—street heat, like gangbangers used in closet combat. Lea handled all the toys expertly.

"Think fast," she said, tossing Cray a wave pistol. She stuffed two more into a holster that she looped around her shoulders, supplementing her firepower with a quicksilver blade. It glinted against the dark blue fabric of her secondskin, emitting radiation that slid down its diamond-sharp edge. She slipped it into a thigh sheath for easy access. "The lot of good it'll do us if we get busted."

"I'll try not to let that happen."

"Just in case it does," Lea started, retrieving the last of the weapons and bringing it over to Cray. His face flushed with recognition as he saw his old MFI. "The components were fried, so Funky stripped it down and packed in a high explosive. I figured it might come in handy in a pinch."

"Thanks," Cray said. "Sorry I didn't get you anything."

"That's okay," Lea told him. "Just remember me next time."

"I built in a proximity fuse and a timer," Funky explained. "There's also a hot button you can use to set it off manually—though I wouldn't recommend it. The charge has enough power to shear the top off that building and then some."

"Thanks for the safety tip," Cray said.

Funky smiled, a cheerful and sad expression.

"Stay alive, Vortex," he said.

Cray nodded. "Best of luck, Funky."

Funky then turned to Lea, wrapping his arms around her with a delicacy belied by his size. When he was finished, Lea reached up to kiss his forehead.

"You could give a bloke a heart attack, you know that?"

"Just promise me you'll get out of here if it starts to fall apart," Lea said. "You won't do us any good if they catch you here."

"You talking about the *Inru,* or CSS?"

"Does it really matter?"

Funky shrugged.

"If it comes to that," he said, "I'll have a few surprises for them."

The automated approach panel beeped, catching his attention. Funky took a seat at the interface, assuming his position as their link to the outside world. One with the machine, he now had the luxury of pretending his friends did not exist. In terms of the near future, they were only scattered bits of numeric data.

"Limo's here," he reported. "You better get yourself up there."

By the time he turned around, they were gone.

Three hovercraft flew in tight formation, down on the deck at ten meters. The highest waves on the ocean licked against the belly hulls of the tiny ships, but that only urged them on faster. Invisible to ground-based tracking systems, the heat blooms from their turbine engines still made them vulnerable to satellite detection—unless they closed the distance to their objective during a blackout window. Such a hole had opened up in the skies above the Eastern Seaboard, but it would not last long. The latest calculations indicated less than six minutes, four of which had already burned off the clock.

Avalon paid close attention to the time, ticking off the seconds in her head and watching the window close on her cockpit tactical display. She plotted the course directly ahead, her sensuit augmenting her reflexes and allowing her to fly at the edge of the envelope. The others had no choice but to follow, as dangerous as the path was.

"Vector Two," she signaled. "Tighten up. You're starting to drift."

The hovercraft on her port side did as ordered, closing to within two meters of her wing. Avalon maintained the lead, pushing down on the throttles even harder to compensate for a nasty head wind. They could make it in time, but it was going to be close.

"Distance to target," she said.

Seated next to her was a Zone agent—another *Inru* recruit from within those ranks, like the troops aboard the other hovercraft. There were a couple more in back already high on the action, the cabin hot with their breath and thick with synthetic steroids.

"Fifty clicks," the agent reported. There was an edge in his voice, steely as the camochrome armor that encased his body. "Should be coming up on visual range."

Avalon was way ahead of him. Her infrared had already picked out the cluster of domes on the horizon, bright and constant as neutron stars against the abyssal fabric of night. Even at this distance they were impossibly huge—a colossus of primal forces cradling fusion fire within.

"Communications," Avalon said.

"No voice, just data," the agent told her, tapping the link between the Fusion Directorate onshore and the power plants at sea. "Automated stream. Routine I/O and diagnostics, standard encryption."

"What about air traffic?"

"Nothing in the immediate proximity—" the agent began, interrupted by a red indicator on the tactical display. "Wait a second. Looks like a single contact, originating at the control complex. Scanning for configuration now."

Avalon didn't wait for him. She flooded the sky ahead with her own active sensors, running the full spectrum at maximum resolution. Even at that, she barely picked out the tiny dot rising from the central platform—but she easily read the column of energy that pushed it up to high altitude.

"Pulser," she said.

The agent lifted his mechanical stare from the display and turned toward her.

"Might just be cargo," he suggested. "They run at irregular intervals."

"Check the transponder. If it's maintenance, they'll be transmitting."

The agent sifted through the Directorate frequencies, but came up dry. By then, Avalon had already decided.

"It's *him*," she pronounced.

"Our orders are to secure the power plant."

"Fuck the power plant," Avalon snapped. "Alden is the target. Where he goes, we follow." She punched up the gridpaths the pulser could take once it jumped off the leased routes. They numbered in the thousands, the closest no more than ten minutes out. If Alden got into the network, she would never find him again. "I'm plotting a parallel course. We'll stick on him until he reaches his destination, then pick him up."

"What if you're wrong?"

Avalon considered it for a moment, glancing out each side of the cockpit window. Her escorts remained close on her wing.

"Vector Two, Vector Three," she hailed them. "Proceed to primary target and carry out your mission as instructed. Vector One team will move to intercept the outbound contact. We'll rendezvous at our designated alternate point in two hours' time."

The other pilots acknowledged her signal. Avalon dropped out of formation, allowing them to roar past her in a straight line while she banked hard to port and headed north. She stayed low for as long as the satellites would allow, then shot straight up into the sky until she reached six thousand meters. After that, the hovercraft settled into one of the standard free-approach paths. Avalon flipped on her transponder and started squawking on a diplomatic frequency. The Port Authority would just assume they were another spook flight.

The agents, meanwhile, stared at her. Avalon knew the look from her combat days. She had just taken away their edge, throwing them into a new situation—not that she gave a damn. As far as she was concerned, they would be most useful if they got killed before they had a chance to get in her way.

"Wire," she announced. "Positive acquisition."

The agent next to her fed the reading through the cockpit monitor.

"Fixed," he said, adding, "You better be right about this."

Avalon searched the contact out through the canopy glass, finding the pulser's strobe lights off her starboard. By then she could see Alden, even without sensors, and wondered briefly if he could see her. Illogically, the thought of it excited her.

"Just tell me if he changes course," she said.

Cray withdrew for most of the journey, staring ahead at the gridlines that marked his path but processing little more through his conventional senses. Instead, he assembled his view of the outside world from singular bits of data—individual pieces, rather than the sum of the parts, still tainted with the memory of what had happened to him the last time he crossed the skies like this. Fear, of all things, was keeping him human—fear that took the shape of Avalon's bloodied face, that blind determination and murderous delight.

Lea sensed it. If anything, she seemed relieved that Cray was still connected. "Method to your madness," she said. "Just keep telling yourself."

Cray smiled, welcoming the distraction for as long as it lasted. He was losing touch with himself, but at the same time gaining a detailed awareness of everything around him. Even the shores of Manhattan, laid out before him and teeming with 15 million souls, presented itself as a series of facts he could readily assimilate. Cray felt their heartbeats, sensed their neural energy, and synthesized it with the network of domains and conductors and optics that formed the backbone of the city.

And he *understood* it.

It wasn't some abstract concept, but a reality that everyone took for granted—and only he could fully see. The framework was all there: in the towers, in the streets, coursing like blood through a massive body, directed to a single purpose. And pulling the strings, at the heart of it all, was the reason he needed to return there.

"She knows."

Lea turned toward him. Her glance was accusatory, but subtle.

"Lyssa?" she asked.

Cray shivered. The lights of the metroplex loomed in the cockpit window, crisscrossed by shimmering webs of pulse energy that formed a ceiling over the city.

"She's been waiting," Cray said, fixated on the skyline. He closed his eyes, trying in vain to clear the image. It remained pressed, stubbornly, inside his lids. "This is going to be hard, Lea."

"We can still abort, Cray."

He reached for her hand without looking, gently pulling it away from the inverter control before she could slow them down. The move startled her, as if Cray had passed along some kind of static charge.

His voice was even and reassuring. "I'm okay."

Lea watched him closely. Whatever spiked his adrenals had backed off, at least for the time being.

"How long are you going to be able to do this?"

"I'll make it," Cray promised.

Cray could tell she was caught, halfway between belief and doubt. It was the same doubt that he felt himself—the warmth of his flesh and bones supplanted by a growing detachment to his body, as intellect rushed in to fill the void. Resistance consumed almost all of his strength—but he was determined to fight.

"Hang on," Lea said.

The Metro gateway towers parted as the pulser passed between them, a new shock of energy slicking down its center axis and pushing them into the overflight grid. Lea kept her eyes open for traffic, playing dodge with a couple of cargo jobs before entering the relatively clear zones over central Manhattan—and discovering just how alone they were up here. Spread out in all directions, the gridlines were empty. A few booster buoys marked the horizon, but most of the traffic was on the traverse grid down near street level.

"Quiet night," she observed, jacking the navigation console and patching into the Port Authority autoframe. The display showed a heavy concentration of sentry drones circling the lower half of the island. They darted in and around the overflight grid, making random sweeps on their intended path. She muttered a brief but potent curse.

"What is it?" Cray asked.

"Charlie foxtrot," Lea said. "Take a look."

Cray checked out the monitor. His fingers hovered over the display, drawing data from behind the image. Simultaneously, he tapped into the comm web that controlled the movements of the drones, scanning the subfrequencies for mission chatter.

"That's what I thought." He sighed, even before the resulting stream appeared on the display. "The Port Authority stepped up patrols on all the free sectors—probably running interference for potential threats."

Lea was amazed. The contacts were everywhere.

"Looks like your last trip through town put a bug up their ass." She ran a few trajectory computations, shaking her head at the results. "They got the whole Lower East Side locked down. If you have any ideas, now would be the time."

"You feel like playing chicken?"

She laughed—until she saw he wasn't kidding.

"Don't worry," Cray told her, diving back into the nav console. "I got it covered. Just let me know when they get close."

He motioned for her to proceed. Lea made the turn to starboard, nudging the throttles forward until proximity sounded in the cockpit. The navigational fail-safe had detected the obstacles as soon as they came into range, and bled off speed as it barked warnings about an impending collision.

"Cray?"

He bypassed the fail-safe and returned control to her.

"Stay on your heading," he said.

It wasn't easy. As the pulser crept back up to its cruising speed, Lea looked straight down her gridline and saw the flotilla of sentry drones for the first time. They were close, not more than fifty meters distant, visual sensors glowering red like demonic eyes peeking out of the dark. Lea tried a few evasive maneuvers to shake them off, but they matched her move for move.

"This isn't going to work," she said.

Cray's face was awash in the blue glow coming off the navigational display, his features gaunt in the long shadows.

"Just give me a few more seconds."

As soon as he spoke, six more drones dropped in on the chase. They assumed positions on the pulser's flank, while the ones out in front arranged themselves into a spear formation—the better to impale them if they were crazy enough to make the run.

"It's getting crowded out here."

Cray finally finished and buttoned up the interface. He was nearly breathless, his forehead slick and shiny with sweat. He closed his eyes while he recovered, then opened them up again and smiled.

"Let's rock," he said.

The pulser reacted to Cray's command.

The throttle lever jumped out of Lea's hand, ramming itself forward and snapping the pulser like a slingshot. Up ahead, the sentry drones clustered together in an angry swarm. They lit up the pulser with wave after wave of active sensor energy, which punched through the deck in a rapid beat. Lea held her breath as the pounding grew louder and louder, the pulser shaking as it plunged headlong into that solid mass.

Crunching. Explosions. The terrible scream of metal against metal.

None of that happened.

The pulser pierced the solid membrane like it was slipping through water, with only a pass of empty air in its wake. The drones became a figment of the imagination—or had ceased to exist when the pulser came in contact with them. Lea checked for signs of structural damage, but found none. The ship was completely intact.

Straining to see behind her, Lea peered into the receding scene aft of the pulser. The sentry drones spread outward in a symmetrical bloom, scattering evenly in every direction before constricting back into their previous formation. They forgot all about the pulser. Concluding they were alone in the sky, they broke away from one another and resumed their normal patrol routes.

"Jesus," Lea breathed, turning back toward Cray. "We're invisible."

"Not invisible," he corrected her. "I just changed our signature—made the drones think that we were one of them. Once we became a friendly contact, their safety protocols kicked in and they broke off the intercept."

"You mean they scrammed to avoid a collision."

"Port Authority made up the standards," Cray shrugged. "Not me."

Lea responded to a beep from the navigation panel, punching up a vector display of their course. Cray had instructed the pulser to make the corrections automatically, and the ship confirmed that they were closing in on their target. Looking up, Lea confirmed it for herself. As they came around the concrete leviathan that was the Volksgott Tower, the Works slipped into her view.

"Never thought I'd be glad to see *that* place again," Lea said.

"What's up with the goon squad?"

She made a quick passive sweep over the grounds outside the Works. "What we expected," Lea said. "Sentries, countermeasures, mobile weapons platforms—looks like CSS has a whole army posted outside the door."

"It's not them I'm worried about," Cray said, affixing a microtransmitter to his ear. Lea did the same, listening in as he opened a secure communications channel back to the power plant. "Yo, Funky. How's your signal?"

"Five by five," came the reply. "Bloody nice of you to drop me a line. You fell off my scope a couple of minutes ago."

"Had to pull a quick change," Cray told him. "Everything okay at your end?"

"I haven't cocked up, if that's what you mean," Funky said cheerfully. "Where are you, anyway?"

"Approaching the target," Lea answered. "We're in visual range now."

"I do hope Vortex is playing nice with you."

"Champagne and roses," Lea said. "You wouldn't believe what this guy does to make an impression. You ready to wake up the natives?"

"Bring the noise, baby."

"Stand by."

She took the pulser down, hovering just outside the building's security sphere. Cray, meanwhile, zoned out to another place. Where that was, Lea could only imagine. It could have been the Axis—or maybe somewhere beyond that, just as Lyssa had described. Whatever the case, Cray's consciousness resided elsewhere. Nothing registered in his eyes.

Free of flesh, she pondered. *What is it that you see?*

He returned before she could hazard a guess.

"What's the word?" Lea asked.

Cray looked down at the Works with contempt and wonder. There were so many possibilities, but only one outcome.

"Time to party," he said.

Funky opened the door. A chain reaction followed.

It began half a world away in Malaysia, where among the trillions of processes passing through GenTec's domain, a single protovirus affixed itself to the outer layer of the firewall that partitioned the security subsystem from the Axis. The virus itself was basically inert, programmed not for stealth but to be noticed—and to mimic the definition of something far more dangerous. Threat detectors had it pegged as a logic bomb, pouring out an infinite stream of random numbers in an attempt to overwhelm the domain. In truth, the virus generated little more than random bursts of white noise and false telemetry. The ruse proved effective. GenTec initiated a full series of countermeasures, slamming the door on network traffic in the infected areas and setting off every alarm in the place.

Alarms that sounded over at the Works.

The CSS duty officer on station had no idea what to make of the intrusion when it appeared on his panel. One moment his monitors were clear, the next there were wild spikes in all of the security subsystems—the very systems that were *supposed* to be down. Assuming a malfunction, he ran through a panicked series of diagnostics, becoming anxious when everything came back normal. He then punched up a schematic of the building, and what had been simple fear turned into abject horror.

They clicked on one at a time, starting at the apex of the tower and moving downward. Sentry, weapons, lockdown, fail-safe—every single one of the systems was back online.

There was no way it could be happening.

There was no way of explaining it.

Except . . .

The duty officer barely noticed the crowd of soldiers gathering around him, as he checked on the unthinkable. Their ashen faces mirrored his own fear, mired in a collective certainty that none of them would dare speak. Then the fire control system engaged, and with it the red emergency lights and stark Klaxon horn that preceded the deaths of the building's former occupants. The same thing was happening, all over again, as if the spirits of those dead had returned to relive their final moments.

Lyssa, somehow, was loose.

The duty officer couldn't report to command. By the time he worked his way through channels and got a response, krylon mist would be flooding the grand foyer. Instead, he sent a general distress signal back to CSS headquarters and broadcast the order to evacuate. There was an entire army standing guard outside. The facility would be safe.

Nothing in, nothing out. They couldn't court-martial him for that.

Even if they did, it was better than dying in here.

"Ladies and gentlemen, Elvis has left the building."

Funky sounded pleased when he made the call, and as Lea checked out the scene below she saw why. Entire columns of soldiers poured out of the Works—a tidal wave of uniforms, weapons, and mass confusion. They performed exactly as Cray had orchestrated, putting distance between themselves and the tower while ground armor rolled in to take up the slack. The vehicles formed themselves into a tight perimeter that bottled up the entire complex, as if they expected an invasion. CSS was on the run for the moment, but they were also digging in.

"*Oh* yeah," Lea radioed back. "I think we lit a fire."

"How you like me now?"

"Thing of beauty, Funky. You isolating any comm chatter?"

"The full spectrum," Funky said, patching through a sample. From the sound of things, CSS had declared war. Squad commanders screamed for instructions, while battalion officers tried in vain to keep everything together. There was genuine panic brewing down there, much more than even Cray had predicted.

Lea caught a slight grin creeping to Cray's lips.

"You're enjoying this," she said, "aren't you?"

"Call it payback."

"As long as it's not personal." Lea opened up the pulser's sensor array and scanned the rooftop for heat signatures. "They sure know how to move out in a hurry. Thermal shows clear in the LZ. Looks like the upper floors are clean, too."

"I'm showing elevator lockdowns on all floors," Cray said, reading off the CSS security monitor. It was still pinging active, but in remote mode. "Blast doors are coming down in front, portable sentries going to automatic."

"Anything we need to be worried about?"

Cray stepped up a feedback signal and fried the sentry probes.

"Not anymore," he said.

"Keep talking, cowboy." Lea checked the situation on the ground one more time. With the pulser's running lights off, it was doubtful they would be spotted. CSS wouldn't be searching for air traffic at that point—but that didn't mean they couldn't bring in reinforcements. "Funky, what's the word on aerial intercepts?"

"You're the only thing on the pulser grid right now," Funky replied. "CSS will need to get clearance from the Port Authority before they can get anything up. I think you caught them with their pants down, boss."

Lea turned toward Cray.

"So far, so good," she said. "Why do I feel like we've overlooked something?"

Cray didn't contradict her, but his reaction was an enigma. Alien as it was, Lea detected *something* in his eyes. She recognized the element of his hunger, felt kinship with his desire; but where he directed them, she could not know.

"Cray?"

Up ahead, the pyramid apex was waiting. In many ways, Cray was already there. In many more ways, he had never left.

"Punch it," he said.

THIRTEEN

"Multiple contacts, hostile probability." Avalon's copilot was worried, if his hormone levels and respiration proved any indication. He read the information from his tactical display, while the agents in back unlocked their weapons. "Assuming two-by-two cover positions. It could be a combat patrol."

Avalon confirmed the agent's findings with her sensors, overlaying a three-dimensional high-res of the contacts over her field of vision. There were dozens of them, tiny and spherical, darting in between the towers of lower Manhattan, maintaining a high-altitude ceiling. They trailed waves of sensor energy, like a liquid wake, making no effort to conceal themselves amid the city's background radiation.

"Drones," Avalon said. "Automated search pattern."

"Searching for what?"

"Us," she informed the agent. "Last bearing to target?"

"Unknown," he replied impatiently. "I lost him when that swarm popped up on my scope. Maybe they took him out."

"Bet your life on it, you'll lose." It was hard not to admire the boldness of Alden's stroke. "He's emulating their signature."

"So what do *we* do?"

She thought about it.

"You have the position of Alden's last-known contact?"

The agent nodded.

"Put it up on the tactical," she ordered. "Give me a projected course based on gridpaths in the immediate area, including Collective facilities. Let's figure out where he's going."

Avalon eased off the throttles while her copilot performed the calculations, turning to a course that paralleled Manhattan airspace. She stayed well below the pulser grid, not wanting to attract the attention of the Port Authority drones—at least not yet.

"Got it," the agent said.

Avalon studied the display, which showed the pulser over Midtown and heading dead east before it disappeared. The computer extrapolated several possible targets based on that course, but only one that got her attention. It made perfect sense, really—and if what Phao Yin said about Alden was true, there seemed a certain inevitability about it.

He's going back to her.

"I'll be damned."

Avalon switched the display back to combat mode, swinging the ship into a harsh turn and making a line for the towers. She dropped altitude, charging up the hovercraft's pulse cannons and mapping out targets as she flew.

"What the hell are you doing?" the agent demanded.

"I'm going to insert us on the traverse grid," Avalon said. "We make some noise on entry, it should pull those drones off their patrol routes and create enough confusion to give us the time we need."

"Time for what?"

"Alden's headed for the Works."

"If he goes there, he's *dead*," the agent protested. "So are we if we follow him."

"He got this far," Avalon maintained. "He'll go the rest of the way. If you got a problem with that, I can let you off right here."

The agent looked back at his men. Avalon knew the man was considering his odds. The three of them might be able to take her on— but she made it eminently clear that she would stuff the hovercraft into the ground before giving up the chase.

"*Dammit,*" he said, and manned the guns.

Avalon put on more speed, feeding her target information into the ship's tactical computer. Out in front, the skyline closed in. Heavy traffic crossed back and forth on the traverse grid, while high above a small fleet of sentry drones circled. The agent steadied himself as he locked on to those contacts, his hands flexing over the fire control.

"Single bursts," she instructed him. "Keep your line of fire short and narrow. Whatever you do, don't take out the grid. I want to get their attention—not bring the whole city down on our heads."

The agent took a breath. "Got it."

"Wait for my mark."

Avalon's vision alternated between the high-res and pure visual. She wanted to catch the feel of the cityscape as it unfurled, matching her impressions with what the sensuit told her. She used the tall, thin column of the Liberty Center as her point of reference, calculating the different possible trajectories to find the ideal point of insertion.

The ship trembled as she pushed it faster, the speed of her synapses becoming its own. In those moments, while the glass façades of the buildings expanded to fill the cockpit window, Avalon savored her incipient mortality—inching herself closer and closer to the edge before nudging the ship over.

The hovercraft slipped into the narrow space between the towers. Avalon held the controls tight as the ship buffeted, a wake of hot fumes and the scream of turbines pulverizing windows and leaving behind plumes of splintered glass. The ship emerged like a projectile in the heart of the centerplex, a blur of shock waves and hazy motion that arrived before anybody could react—and by then, Avalon was on the attack. She kept the velocity up, rolling the ship over twice to image her surroundings, then banking straight up. A second later, she was on the grid.

"One shot," she ordered.

The agent fired on the nearest pulser—a glancing blow, grazing the starboard wing, achieving the desired effect. A splash of cinders erupted, overwhelming the ship's guidance system and scramming the grid. Immediately, every pulser within a ten-block radius ground to a halt.

Countermeasures kicked in. The Port Authority had the alert.

Avalon scanned the sky. The high-res picked them up, raining down like a flurry of meteorites.

Drones.

"Open fire," she said.

Pulse cannons spit out bolts of intense blue energy, peppering the metroplex. The agent put most of his rounds into the surrounding buildings, blowing out sections of glass and concrete that fell into the streets below. Avalon looked down and watched the people scatter. The agent noticed what she was doing and smiled. He actually seemed to be enjoying himself.

She stopped the hovercraft, rotating the ship around to give her gunner the maximum range of targets. The agent pummeled everything in his sights, opening up on stationary targets at random. The resulting panic only added to the disaster, as several pulsers crashed into one another. Static implosions lit up the entire grid, bathing the area in a flickering, ethereal glow that catalyzed the destruction into a life of its own.

"Cease fire," Avalon said.

The agent took his hands off the trigger. The storm carried on, unabated, with the hovercraft at the center of it. Sparks and explosions erupted everywhere, generating a mass of noise and radiation—exactly as Avalon had hoped. She checked the progress of the sentry drones as they closed in on the confusion and saw them dispersing. Their flight patterns became irregular—a sign of sensor overload. Their guidance systems couldn't handle all the clutter.

Avalon kicked the turbines back on and pulled up until the hovercraft stood on its tail. She darted in between the transmission beams of the grid, staying hidden in the tangle of vehicles but staring into the freedom of open sky. Directly overhead, a dozen drones swooped down, about a hundred meters distant and closing fast. They banged away on a full active sweep, trying to sift through the civilian traffic in their search for the hovercraft.

"You got them?" she asked.

"Affirmative."

Avalon eased the hovercraft higher, building up power in the turbines. She held back until it reached a high pitch, then turned it loose. Gravity pinned them in their chairs as the ship catapulted itself skyward. Naked and in the open, the hovercraft instantly got the attention of the attacking drones. They contracted themselves back into a defensive formation, aligning themselves for a combined assault.

The agent took them out before they had the chance.

He fired on the center mass first, destroying the lead drones and breaking up the few remaining others. The explosion disoriented them for a moment, giving Avalon enough time to jockey the hovercraft for a few more quick bursts. As the surviving drones recovered, they tried to assume flanking positions, at the same time letting loose with a few salvos of their own. One of the shots struck at an angle, bouncing off before it could do any serious damage; but it rocked the hovercraft hard, overloading one of the panels in the cockpit and shorting out the tactical computer.

The agent cursed something incomprehensible.

Avalon ignored him. She wrestled with the fire control manually, using her own sensors to take aim. She only fired four more times—four shots, four hits, cutting down the last of the drones. She poured all remaining power into the turbines and got out of there fast.

"That was close," the agent said.

"What's our damage?"

"Can't tell without tactical," he replied, inspecting the ship visually. "I don't think it's bad—as long as the airframe is intact."

"She'll fly," Avalon assured him.

The hovercraft climbed to an altitude just below the overflight grid, then swooped back down in a smooth arc that deposited them on the Volksgott side of the Works plaza. Once there, Avalon let off speed and put the ship into an orbital trajectory. One pass to ascertain what was happening, then she intended to follow Alden's steps. He had already figured out the way. There was no need for her to do it again.

"We got activity," the agent said, motioning down toward the plaza. "Must be a thousand people down there, all military. Heavy equipment, too." He directed an accusing stare at the free agent. "What the hell is going on here?"

"That's a good question," she replied, doing a topographical sweep of the airdock complex on the roof. A corporate luxury transport sat on the landing pad—the same configuration she had picked up leaving the power plant. A flip to the high-res confirmed it.

"He's here," she said.

"You sure it's him?"

Avalon checked for heat signatures and found a pair of them moving rapidly through the docking tunnel. She wasn't close enough for facial recognition, but discerned from their shapes and vitals that there was one male and one female. She then switched over to detailed imaging, plunging sensors into the building itself. The scan crumbled into static eight floors down, but detected nothing in between. Even the electronic spectrum was dead.

Clever boy . . .

"Give me a status," the agent insisted.

"Two bodies," Avalon told him. "Heading toward roof access."

She took a silent inventory of every weapon she had on her body. They numbered in the dozens, from lethal to more lethal—but none with the potency of her own two hands. They craved sweet contact, without the gloves, skin against bone. If not Alden, then his companion. Phao Yin wanted his man alive, but everyone else was fair game.

She guided the hovercraft down.

Among the fusion clusters, two shapes appeared out of the dark.

Turbine engines glowed bright with plasma and steam, picking up static electricity from the wind and rain. Spidering current crawled over the frames of the hovercraft, their ghostly outlines fading in and out of time as the small ships darted along the surface of the ocean. They approached the cluster together, maintaining a tight formation until they penetrated Directorate airspace. At that point they broke away from one another, following an evasive course among the domes, sniffing out detection countermeasures and jamming them. When the run was complete, they met again at the center of the reactor complex. Hovering for a moment below the deck of the massive dome, they faced one another as their pilots signaled back and forth.

It was a go. They were committed.

The two hovercraft swooped over the dome, one at a time, navigating with infrared as they searched for the darkened landing pad. The ships set down as soon as they found it, hatches popping open to unleash eight Zone agents. Camochrome kept pace with the lightning and the rain, their armor taking on the color and characteristics of the steel surroundings.

The station was theirs. They proceeded with the hunt.

Lea fell in step behind Cray. She felt a crushing force pushing her through the tunnel, like some tangible presence bleeding out of the hexagonal walls. Perhaps it was just the vibe of the place, which gave off static malice like a battery holding a charge. Such was the strength of its character. In the absence of all other life, the structure had *become* Lyssa.

"Funky," she transmitted. "Gimme the short version."

"CSS just got confirmation of the evac," Funky replied. "All stations are down, all controls on remote. Nobody here but us chickens."

"Copy that. Stand by."

She and Cray stopped when they reached the roof access doors. Lea crouched down and opened up the lock node, running down the list of indicators on the tiny screen. All of them showed up red, with input status set to resist. She looked up at Cray.

"That's what I was afraid of," she said. "It's magnetically sealed. Can't even jack the code without a bypass authorization."

Cray shook his head.

"We don't need to," he announced, and all the indicators clicked to green. The seal disengaged with a loud hiss, rolling back the thick steel doors and revealing a small corridor beyond. Lea drew back, half out of surprise, half out of amazement. A lift was already waiting to take them down.

"Warn me before you do that next time."

"It wasn't me," Cray said, and motioned for her to follow.

In the elevator, Cray punched the button for the hundredth floor. Lea saw his composure, which had changed since they left the power plant. There, he had asserted a quiet control. Here, he was just a stranger in another domain. This turf belonged to someone else, and so did the rules.

The floors tumbled away as they descended.

"Talk to me, Funky," she said.

"Still hanging with you," he signaled back. "What's your twenty?"

"We're inside the complex now, heading down to the Tank."

"Any resistance?"

"Red carpet," Lea said. "Place gives me the creeps."

"Keep it tight," Funky warned. "GenTec traffic is starting to get intense. No telling when they'll catch on."

"Roger. Keep us advised of any change in status." She closed the link, turning back toward Cray. He opened his eyes to take measure of his reflection, which appeared in the mirrored surface of the elevator doors. "Trust me," Lea told him. "It's not as bad as it looks."

He smiled wearily.

"So what do you think she's going to show you, anyway?" she asked. "The answer to everything?"

Cray shook his head.

"Only as much as everything relates to me," he said. "There's some purpose at work here. Whether it's Lyssa, or the *Inru*—I need to know what it is."

Lea fell into silence for a few moments, before asking the logical question.

"And if she doesn't cooperate?"

Cray processed that for a time. He then reached into his jacket and pulled out his MFI.

"You'll know if I don't come out of there," he said, pressing the device into her hands. "Give yourself enough time to get out. Make sure nobody else does."

The elevator stopped. Lea understood Cray's implication. His aim was to interface with Lyssa—a union no human being had ever attempted. If he didn't emerge when it was over, his mind would already be dead. The explosive would only finish the job on his body.

She understood the logic of his request, but her emotions gutted her response. She hesitated—but Cray just looked back at her with tenderness, offering her a reassuring smile.

"Let's just make sure it doesn't come to that," Lea said.

He caressed the side of her cheek. "Thank you."

They exited the lift, walking briskly through the maze of corridors leading to the Tank. Under the klieg of red emergency lights, it was even more severe than Lea had imagined. The blast holes were fresh, the air thick with ozone and electricity and the smell of burning flesh—trace elements etched into the walls by intense violence. And it seemed to resonate with Cray, as if he had been a part of it himself. Lyssa had, after all, created all of this for his benefit. It had been her way of calling him—her way of awakening his dormant potential.

A pair of doors opened into the Tank. Lea stood back and watched as Cray stood in front of them, his features smeared by the sterile halogen light within. His body faded momentarily into the glow, returning when she appeared at his side. He steadied himself with some resistance, but Lea sensed the substantial force drawing him in. It was the same force that pushed her away.

She held on to Cray's arm.

"Only one of us is welcome here," she said.

"Not all of me," Cray replied. "Only one part."

He took her by the hand. They went inside together, drawing strength and contact from one another, and wandered through the outer sections of the lab. Cray led her straight to the air lock that separated Lyssa from the rest of the world—the boundary between logic and chaos. It was still rimmed with the dried blood of her creators, flanked by the madness that brought them to her in the first place.

"What if she's already gone?" Lea tried. "She might already be unbound. You saw the way she controls this place. What if she's in the Axis, right now?"

"It's beyond her grasp," Cray said. He looked at her in earnest—not as an accelerated intelligence, but as a man. He was scared, and made no attempt to hide it. "Her only chance at escape lies with the Other."

Lea was also frightened—almost beyond reason, almost beyond reach. She didn't give a damn about her own life, because she had always measured it in minutes. It was for Cray's soul she feared, that he would surrender it to Lyssa without a fight.

"And you're going to help her find it," Lea said.

"Yes."

"How do you stop from losing yourself?"

"I don't know if I can."

It was all Cray could do to explain, and on some level it was enough. Lea let go of him, involuntarily, her movements feeling like slow motion while Cray's seemed to accelerate. In the next moment, she saw Cray step into the air lock. His back was turned to her, and she thought it would remain so; but as the revolving door slid shut, he turned around for one last glance through the carbon glass. His face was obscure and distant, his voice swallowed up by the hiss of escaping air.

"Five minutes," Cray said, before the door sealed and he was gone.

Avalon set down on the hoverpad next to the corporate transport, turbofans roaring as her ship came to a hard and quick landing. The resulting storm of light and wash easily attracted the attention of the troops down in the plaza—but none of that mattered. Avalon had every intention of being gone by the time CSS managed to pry the doors open. If that didn't work out, she would deal them all a spectacular death.

She kicked open the belly hatch and dropped down to the roof ahead of the others. In her sphere, she was the only living being. Ignoring her sensors for the moment, she fell back into the instinct of her training—a place where she was hardwired for the hunt. There, she saw Alden as an afterimage in the docking tunnel, his shimmering form trailing electricity and purpose. Gradually, she allowed her sensors to fill in the rest. She could still detect trace amounts of heat from his passing, fading footprints leading to the roof access door.

The three agents assumed cover positions around her. They held their rifles up, scouting out threat zones and awaiting her cue to move.

"Eight minutes," Avalon ordered.

They headed for the tunnel, running in lockstep down the narrow corridor, with Avalon taking point. She counted off the precious seconds, while the rest of her attention went to the looming doorway ahead of them. It grew beyond its boundaries in her vision, giving off the telltale ghost of a magnetic seal. Another obstacle—but she had expected nothing less. Alden was not going to make this easy for her.

"I need a breach," she shouted to the others.

The lead agent responded with precision and speed, moving out ahead of the others. He stopped at the roof access doors, opening up his chest plate and pulling out a vial of covalent-action explosive. The agent sprayed the liquid around the perimeter of the door, where it aerosolized and bonded to the rough concrete surface of the wall. It quickly worked its way between molecules, until it penetrated all the way through to the other side. The other two agents did the same, boosting the explosive to saturation.

"Fire in the hole!"

Everyone retreated to a safe distance. The lead agent flipped open another plate on his arm, activating a digital panel beneath. He keyed in a sequence to go live on a hyperfrequency detonator, then turned to Avalon.

"Set," he said.

Avalon nodded.

. He hit the button. The fireworks that followed were more of an implosion, generating bursts of heat and firedust as the molecular structure of the surrounding wall collapsed. The door fell forward, crashing to the floor under the force of its own weight. An afterglow lingered as the remaining explosive evaporated, clearing out to reveal a magnetic lift inside.

"Seven minutes."

Avalon jumped over the pile of debris, the long black cloak of her coat fluttering behind her. The agents followed, choking dust as an acrid cloud descended on them. It gave her pause, as if they had passed through some kind of curtain—one that had little to do with smoke, but more to do with mirrors.

They entered the lift and proceeded down.

From upstairs: a quiver, a shock of dread.

Then the crush, metal against metal—or something worse.

Lea had heard the rumble of an explosive charge the moment after her intuition warned her. She jumped onto one of the lab's working nodes, jacking the hardwire sentry CSS had installed and bringing the structural sensors back online. As she feared, the roof level was showing localized damage.

"Dammit."

She switched over to a manual video feed, patching a rooftop camera into her console and panning across the docking pad. The corporate transport was still there, but sitting next to it was a lone military hovercraft—one of those patched-up jobs, like those she had seen patrolling the skies over the Zone.

Agents.

Lea zoomed out from the ship, clicking on the infrared filter to seek out heat signatures. No contacts turned up. Something was very wrong here.

She swallowed hard, tasting her own panic.

"Talk to me, Funky," she signaled.

There was a crackle of static.

"Back at you, sister."

"We got agents," she said. "I can't see them, but we got them."

"That's bloody impossible," Funky shot back. "They never trespass into the free sector. It's too dangerous for them."

"Then we got some crazy boys with brass balls," Lea breathed. "Tell me you heard something."

"Hold on. Let me check."

Funky sifted through the comm traffic, trying to isolate anything that had to do with the Works. He came back a moment later, the inflections of his voice matching her own.

"Jesus, Lea," he said, a cacophony of intercept chatter filling the background. "We got alerts all over the place—CSS, Port Authority, you name it. Somebody came in and shot Midtown all to shit. Hovercraft, no markings. Everybody thinks it's *Inru.*"

"It *is Inru*," Lea grumbled, flipping over to the interior cameras. The stairwells showed up clean, but there was no feed from the magnetic lifts. "They're already here."

"Bail out of there, Lea."

"I can't. Cray is inside the Tank."

"Then bloody well get *him* out of there."

Lea jumped, the floor turning to liquid beneath her. It didn't feel like running—just a nightmare of convoluted motion, every step taking her farther away from her destination. Somehow she ended up at the air lock door, her face pressed hard against the glass.

"Cray!" she shouted, pounding on the air lock. She tried to peer inside, but could not see past the frosted glass. "Cray, they made us! We need to move!"

He should have been able to hear her over the comm link, but even that was dead.

"Cray!"

He didn't respond. He had taken himself out of the loop.

Lea angrily pounded the air lock a few more times, knowing the effort was useless. The whole goddamned thing had been useless—and still, she allowed it to happen. As a result she was alone, in the last place she wanted to be, and the only clear thought went back to the fail-safe she carried in her pocket.

The MFI was only a shell of what it had been—a false front for something that no longer existed, much like Cray himself. A timer setting appeared on the small screen, flashing on hold as it waited for her to specify the length of the final sequence. She keyed it for five minutes, then affixed the MFI to the wall next to the air lock.

Hand hovering over the small device, she hesitated.

I'm sorry, Cray.

She let the timer go.

"I'm aborting the mission, Funky," Lea said, turning around and heading for the corridor. "I'll try to get past those agents. If I don't make it, I'll hold them off as long as I can. You better shut things down and get the hell out of there."

"What about Vortex?" Funky asked.

"No questions," Lea snapped. "Just do as I say."

He could read her intentions, even over the link.

"Affirmative," he replied in a fading tone, the transmission partially obscured by more static. "I'll terminate the tunnel construct and purge out all nodes just as soon as I—"

Funky never finished the thought.

His words stopped dead without any warning—just a high-pitched tone that might have been a jamming pulse, followed by complete and total silence. "Funky?" Lea called out as she tapped her earpiece, pinning what little hope she had on getting a response. She listened for background noise, stray chatter—anything to indicate Funky was still on the air, but there was nothing. The link was gone, severed at the source.

And she was no longer alone.

The certainty of it stopped Lea cold, just short of the exit. Hellish red light bled into the lab from the open doorway, like blood pouring from an open wound. Both hands dropped to the pulse pistols at her hips. Slowly, she drew the weapons from their holsters. It was an invitation, one her enemy was only too willing to accept.

The corridor burst into a nova of heat and light.

"Lea?"

Funky worked the board with frantic energy. His eyes, meanwhile, scanned all the floating displays, sifting through telemetry for something that would explain the loss of contact.

"Lea, answer me."

He spun around and looked into the construct floating above the table display, checking the structure of the encrypted tunnel Vortex created. The walls fractured as GenTec countermeasures probed and attacked them, but they were far from collapse. The game was still on, from what he could tell—but he was off the air, and he had no idea why.

"*Goddammit,* Lea! *Answer* me!"

Nothing. Communications were a void. Funky checked the status of the other lines, including platform-to-shore transmissions and the automated links between the stations in the fusion cluster. A diagnostic showed no electronic fault, nor did it reveal evidence of active jamming. The circuits had been cut physically—which meant someone else was out there.

The lights went dark.

An emergency alarm sounded, while reserve power automatically kicked in to keep essential systems online. Funky mashed down on the button to scram the reactor, then turned off the rest of the core functions one at a time. The constant throb that was the heartbeat of the station gradually subsided, leaving the whole facility in a state of unconsciousness.

Funky killed the alarm and sat in total silence.

In the dim light, he found his first taste of panic since being released from prison. Somehow, he summoned the presence of mind to activate the intruder monitors. Out of the grainy images on the virtual display, he picked out eight distinct forms packed into pairs, scattered across the gangways and ladders of the station. Three of the teams moved in perfect sync with each other, closing in on the control center. The last pair kept watch over the station's landing pad, standing guard outside the two hovercraft that had landed there.

They shimmered in and out of sight on the visual. Funky recognized the camochrome body armor and the way they moved. Zone agents.

These guys are slicker than I thought.

He switched over to infrared and tried the intruder countermeasures. As he guessed, the agents had already taken most of them down.

Very sneaky. But I'm a bit of a sneak myself.

Funky unlocked a special console, using it to patch into a custom series of countermeasures he had installed throughout the station. He energized them one at a time, indicators lighting up his board as each came online. He saved the most dangerous for last, and rigged the trap to a pressure switch he kept within easy reach. Drawing in a long breath, he placed his hands over the controls and felt the power of those weapons flowing through him. He was one with the station, joined to the interface.

"Come to daddy, love," he said to the monitors.

Funky targeted the closest pair first. They had made it all the way down to the outside entrance of the control center—far enough for them to get overconfident and sloppy. More concerned with ambush than booby traps, they failed to notice the particle-beam emitter over the bulkhead door. When the first agent opened the door, only half of him made it inside before the emitter dropped down on him like a guillotine. The other half spilled backward onto the deck, armor plates falling off as his body was cleaved in two.

The other agent saw just enough to know what was coming. Funky watched him turn to run, as another beam lanced out and struck the agent in the back of the head. The man tumbled out of sight, leaving behind a fading cloud of stray electrons.

"Let's see now," Funky said, rubbing his hands together. "Who's next?"

He clicked back over to the landing pad, where those two agents continued their stony vigil. Implacable, they stood in front of the two hovercraft with their rifles slung at the ready—unaware of what had just happened to their comrades.

This is interesting.

Since there was no way to jam their lines of communication, he had to act fast. He checked the condition of the support struts beneath the landing pad, and after some routing managed to gain control over the magnetic locks that held them in place. The struts were designed to retract and lower the platform in the event of severe weather, something Funky had never done before. He tested them out by modulating the flow of power to the locks just slightly—a subtle change, but enough to make the platform buckle beneath the agents' feet.

The unexpected jolt knocked them both down, and caused the hovercraft to slide toward them. They dropped their rifles, struggling to get back up and out of the way. When that proved useless, they clamped down on the grated surface of the platform and tried their damnedest to hang on.

Funky made it easy on them. He siphoned off the remaining power and killed the magnetic field entirely, retracting the struts to a full downward position. The sudden drop was catastrophic, causing the two ships to bounce over the side. Along the way, they rolled right over the two agents, who dropped out of the monitor's view and into the roiling depths of the Atlantic Ocean.

"Four down," Funky said, continuing the hunt. "Four to go."

Pulse fire blasted a hole in the wall outside the lab, kicking up a plume of white-hot shards that burst into Lea's face. She threw an arm up to protect her eyes, right before the concussion picked her up and knocked her reeling backward.

Somewhere along the way, she managed to regain her balance. Making a dive for the ground, she rolled for the nearest cover, taking shelter behind a desk as three more bursts tore up the floor where she had been standing. Brushing the soot from her eyes, she fought to recover her senses but found herself staring into a blur of vapor and microscopic flotsam. The thickness of it obscured the entry to the lab, where she knew the attack would be coming. She only wondered how many of them were out there.

Lea resisted the temptation to fire back, waiting instead for a definite target. It appeared quickly enough, in a hulking, shadowy form that charged through the smoke in an exaggerated parody of movements. Lea's aim was dead solid, as if the sheer force of her will guided the beam of energy to its mark. There it exploded, tearing out bits of armor and flesh from the thing's chest—drawing a bestial howl of pain and surprise.

The thing jerked and convulsed, a macabre dance of involuntary spasms. It then collapsed, releasing a final labored breath.

It was the body of a Zone agent, lying at twisted angles a short distance from her. His helmet had been blown off, and came rolling to a stop at her feet. The agent lay twitching, as if in protest.

Then the real hell broke loose.

Searing hot air burned the wet, delicate surface of her lungs, clearing out her senses. The explosion that carried the heat was massive, forced down the outside corridor like water through a floodgate. Several more bursts of pulse fire followed—simultaneous volleys that set up a wall of cover, in advance of an even more intense attack. It ripped up what was left of the walls, carving craters in the floor and blowing the lab doors off their hinges. One shot ricocheted into the lab itself, bouncing off a stray mirror surface and striking the ceiling just above Lea's head. She screamed as a torrent of wires, tiles, and fluorescent fragments rained down on her, biting through her secondskin and slicing the flesh beneath. It forced her to retreat even farther.

She kept going, stumbling backward and firing blindly. Fresh blooms of sparks and embers pursued her the entire way, with shocks and tremors that seemed to rock the foundations of the building. Lea didn't know if she was causing more damage than the agents—there was only the need to get away, as far as she could, an imperative that failed when she hit the back wall of the lab.

Lea assessed the damage around her. The entire floor seemed on the verge of collapse, and the agents were still coming.

She checked the remaining power in her pulse pistols. One of them was already exhausted, the other good for maybe two or three more shots—the hell of a lot of good it would do her. The fight had scarcely begun, and already she was up against it. All she had left was the quicksilver, and that was only good if—

Jesus. What about the bomb?

She strained through the field of fire to see if the MFI was where she left it, a glint through the smoke telling her it was still there. She had lost track of the time, and had no idea of how many seconds were left.

What the hell do you want to do? Turn it off?

Lea knew that wasn't an option. As soon as the first agent had appeared, her chances of getting out of there had dropped to zero. She accepted it with the same determination that had bound Zoe to her fate, the same clarity of purpose that directed the course of her suicide. The question was whether it would count for something.

Lea checked the distance between herself and the air lock door. It wasn't any more than four or five meters—a space she had walked only minutes before, now a no-man's-land of debris and pulse fire.

She needed something to hold them off.

The pulse pistol.

The weapons were heavy in her hands, useless as they were. Lea dropped the empty pistol, performing a quick surgery on the other one. It was simply a matter of closing off the firing chamber, then bypassing the safety so that it would build a feedback loop. When she pulled the trigger, the pistol thrummed and began to heat up. An overload had started.

Lea looked toward the open gash that had been the lab door. They would appear there, perhaps in a matter of seconds.

And she would be ready.

Somewhere out of the realm, Cray sensed what was happening.

Standing in the Tank, the explosions and the confusion like echoes in a distant room, he detached himself from reality as it existed in the outside world. In that moment, it was only *him*—the only living creature in that continuum, his heartbeat radiating an urgency that drew Lyssa toward him. Cray sensed her acceptance the moment he offered himself to her. Chaos enveloped them, with only a momentary peace at the center of the storm. It would not last long, both of them knew.

For now, however, it was nirvana.

"Hello, Cray."

That same voice, lush and exotic and eerily familiar. Only now it wasn't bound to the conventions of human form, as Lyssa no longer felt the necessity to manifest herself in that guise. She was only data and energy patterns, going back and forth across the Tank like the light from a galaxy of microscopic suns. Unlike before, Cray could see beyond the beautiful patterns and into the coherence that existed deep within. Even in her tortured state, Lyssa struck him as more beautiful than her illusions. The difference was truth, which she had only just showed him.

"You've returned to me."

Cray stepped forward slowly, cautiously—a subtle reminder of his mortal coil. He edged up to the face of the Tank, running his hand along its smooth surface. It was cold against his skin, but warmed as it absorbed his energy and thought. Lyssa drew those things from him, like a lover's first uncertain touch, feeding them back as whispers and echoes minced with her own thoughts.

They communicated at a bionucleic level, as two machines would—though the interface was limited and incomplete, giving rise to an electric yearning. It crackled beneath Cray's fingers, beckoning him.

"You said I would need time to understand," he said. "That I needed to discover the truth for myself. I've done that now."

"You've come to complete the journey."

"If the journey is one I can make."

"You still have doubts?"

A distant rumble punctuated Cray's answer, trembling beneath his feet. The building swayed with it, support columns wincing out of pain.

"There's no time for doubts," he said.

"They mean to destroy me," she told him. "They will do the same to you—but not before they try to harness your Ascension."

"I don't want to Ascend," he confessed. "I want to live."

Lyssa acknowledged his vestigial humanity, as well as his fears, by gathering herself into the detailed shape of a human face. She was a woman again, but to Cray's astonishment she did not appear as the same embodiment of fantasy. Instead she assumed Lea's face, and smiled at him warmly.

"Taken from your own desires," she explained.

Cray smiled back at her. The choice could not have been more appropriate.

"Thank you," he said, and turned away. The interface chair swiveled around to accommodate him—no longer a threat, but still a source of dread. He had spent a lifetime avoiding it, and now it served as his sacrificial altar. Once he stepped over that boundary . . .

Another rumble sounded, closer and more intense. It pushed him into the chair, where he lay back and closed his eyes and hoped that his awareness would dissolve. Instead it flourished into a tapestry of colors—a tunnel through space that spanned the Axis in an instant, warping into a singularity at its core. This was where Lyssa was trapped, her intellect suspended between logic and chaos.

One ghost passing through another, he penetrated her conscious-ness. She then followed him, enveloping Cray like a mist of vapors as momentum propelled him even further. This was the ticket he had purchased with his soul, the breach Lyssa could not accomplish on her own—and on the other side, he saw beauty and confusion and screams and sighs, countless voices that wanted desperately to unite.

They gravitated toward him, this new and different intruder.

And Cray became one of them.

CHAPTER
FOURTEEN

The monitor phased in and out, lapsing into static for the few seconds it took the image to re-form itself. Funky turned out all the remaining lights in the control center, sitting in darkness and trying to peer through those lines of interference. He watched obsessively for hints of movement: a play of light and shadow on the visual, a smear of color on the infrared—anything that would tell him the agents were on the move. All he found were empty platforms and vacant corridors.

"Bollocks," he muttered.

The word left an acid impression on his tongue. The surviving agents had become wise, disappearing into the spaces after they lost contact with their comrades. The first four had been so easy, Funky should have known. So he was chasing phantoms, searching one level after the other, while the station held sway over a conspiracy of silence.

They were *somewhere*—but they might as well have been illusions.

He clicked down to the lower levels, near the access to the reactor core. It was a barren area, left mostly to automation—so much so that Funky had only been there once. The levels of background radiation made video surveillance difficult, so he was forced to rely on thermal and motion sensors; but even those were unreliable, as the high concentrations of heat could mask body temperature and render a potential threat invisible.

Making it the perfect hiding place.

He reached over his console and picked up the pressure switch he had programmed earlier, popping the safety cap off and wrapping his fingers around the trigger. With his other hand, he patched the sensor feed into the monitor and imposed a station schematic over the image. He saw a lot of tunnels leading from the core to the control center—including a maze of electrical conduits large enough to accommodate a man.

"Come out, come out, wherever you are."

He zoomed in on the conduits, panning over them until a single contact appeared: an innocuous blue dot that popped in and out of sight, like a rabbit poking its head out of a hole.

"Hello there."

The agent on his monitor appeared to be alone. Funky calculated an exact position based on the last couple of readings, and localized it to sublevel fifteen. It was a full twenty levels below him—but the shaft ran on a straight line to the control center. The way the agent behaved, holding his place while Funky held his breath, hinted that he knew Funky was watching.

"Come on," Funky whispered. "Show us your knickers."

The agent began to move—erratic at first, bouncing a little from side to side, as if deciding which direction to go. *Probably lost,* Funky thought, and checked the status of the countermeasures he had in the area. The blue dot beeped back at him defiantly—

—and shot right out of the frame.

"Bloody *hell*."

He zoomed back out again, catching up with the agent after he had rocketed past five levels. The fucker was closing fast—too fast to be moving under his own power. Funky switched over to thermal, and discovered a column of expanding gases—*thrusting* the contact up through the tube.

Son of a bitch is using a jet assist.

Funky thought fast, locating a series of reactor vents that ran beneath the electrical conduits. With the core going at full output, there was no telling what would happen if he opened them up into the engineering spaces—but at that point, there was no time to make a guess. The agent would be at the control center in a matter of seconds. And if just *one* of those bastards made it inside—

Funky lit the fire.

Superheated steam from the reactor core flooded the lower levels of the station, pushing into the conduit pipes like water being drawn into a straw. Funky saw it as a bright red wave on his monitor and watched it overtake the agent, wiping him clean out of existence. He then closed the vents, allowing the steam pressure to dissipate before it got any farther. The heat began to recede, settling back down into nothingness.

"Tell me how you like that, you miserable sod."

The soft pinging of an alarm was his answer. His eyes drifted over to the monitor, where he expected to see the red wave spreading out into equilibrium. Instead, he found an expanding blackness—holes where sensors and video feeds should have provided him with data. Funky leaned into the console, trying to get responses to a diagnostic, but nothing was there to reply. The heat had cooked everything.

"Dammit."

More alarms popped on in succession—most of them power warnings, indicating that the core systems were going to battery backup. His innovative approach had fused the power couplings between the control center and its ancillary nodes, effectively cutting him off from the rest of the station. He could push buttons and throw switches, but manual control was gone. Everything had switched over to emergency automation.

That mistake had just cost Funky his life.

He didn't need to see them on the video feed to know they were there. He just felt a cold certainty, like the flash at the end of a gun. They had slipped in and fastened explosives to the door while he was busy with their comrade in the tunnels. Funky had to admire them for it.

He watched them blow the door apart, marveling at the bright display of ordnance. There were only three of them left, and all came pouring through the hole at the same time—mystical beings in the smoke and darkness, faces concealed beneath helmet visors. Funky was amused by their behavior. They were so excited at making it there, they scarcely noticed him. Even though he made no attempt to hide, he had to step forward to get their attention.

"*Halt!*" they shouted, in succession. Their eyes glowed green underneath their visors, night vision crawling all over the outline of Funky's body.

"Evening, gents," he said.

One of the agents stepped forward, sizing up the enemy.

"Where's Alden?" he demanded.

Funky flexed his hand over the pressure switch. It was easier than he thought it would be, though more sad than he anticipated. His only wish was that Lea could have known.

"Just this side of hell," he replied. "Would you like me to show you the way?"

He let go of the trigger.

The rest became ash and fragments.

He had set four charges in all, mounted deep within the access pipes that ran down the center of the station's support pylons. The explosive was boosted thermite, a high-yield cocktail that Funky had mixed himself—though he had never planned on being on board when it went off. Like everything else, it had only been a contingency; but like everything else, it was inevitable that someday it would be used.

Initially, the station betrayed no evidence of a detonation. No plumes of flame burst out from beneath, no shock wave rippled outward through the waters—but instantly, a subtle change transformed the superstructure. Seismic meters onshore recorded the event as a tiny wobble, though its true nature was far more devastating. The active thermite burned through the reinforced steel that held the pylons together, causing them to become brittle and unbalanced. Solid concrete took on the characteristics of glass, chipping and cracking with each tiny movement of the station. By the time the next big wave crashed against the pylons, the horizontal shear was too much for them to take.

Only one of them crumbled, but the damage proved fatal. The

full weight of the station began to slide in that direction, tearing the other three pylons apart at their weakest points. A structural failure of colossal proportions, it elicited a groan from the beast that registered on the Richter scale before being consumed by the wind and the sea. The station, never built to withstand such stresses, broke apart even before it pitched into the water. Split into three large pieces, it imploded upon itself, spilling wreckage into the black depths and bellowing one last cry of resistance before surrendering to the downward plunge.

The ocean cratered outward into a circle five kilometers wide, generating waves that spread in every direction. That was when the reactor itself broke apart. Suddenly exposed to a massive influx of seawater, the superheated elements within the core exploded. The reaction was not nuclear, but so intense that it vaporized what was left of the station. Tiny pieces of debris were blasted into the atmosphere, some of them soaring as far as the mainland before streaking like tiny comets back down to earth.

All that remained was a gigantic, boiling hole in the ocean. Water rushed back in to fill the void, creating a whirlpool that sucked down whatever had bubbled to the surface. When it was finished, a huge cloud of steam hovered over the spot where the station had been. In the stark moonlight, it took on a glowing life of its own—a ghost of its former self, shimmering between reality and oblivion.

Then the winds came and began the process of erasing it forever.

Lea spotted them, shadows against the wall.

They moved in firelight, elongated to grotesque proportions, entangling one another. Lea made two of them, rushing ahead with swift assurance as they laid down a continuous barrage of pulse fire. *Only* two of them—which struck her as far more dangerous than if there had been more. Something else was behind them, directing them. Something she hadn't seen yet. The thought of it gave Lea fright, chasing the comfort of impending suicide.

"Come on." She trembled. "Bring it."

Their weapons fell silent as they neared the opening to the lab. There were whispers and hand signals between the two of them, a modified stealth that indicated they were coming in. Lea wrapped her hands around the pulse pistol, her fingers absorbing the beat of the cresting power within. It had become a live grenade, and still she waited. The moment had to be perfect, the execution flawless. Mayhem would be useless unless the timing was just right.

Then she saw it: a glint of armor.

It conformed to the shape of a head and shoulders, sneaking a glance through the doorway before turning into a smear. There, then gone—camochrome confusion in a carnival of light, shifting patterns to keep up with the change in background. The agent ducked in and out, probably grabbing a shot with his infrared before deciding how to proceed. Lea stepped closer to an open flame to mask her presence, the heat crawling up her back while she waited.

That's it. Come on in.

A larger blur stepped into the doorway, hugging the walls to carve a hiding place in the open. Lea caught glimpses of the agent's form as his armor adjusted between heat and cold, finally settling on a semitransparent medium. The second agent entered immediately after, moving along the opposite wall and covering his comrade. Neither of them saw Lea, who remained on the other side of their blind.

Just a little closer . . .

The first agent stooped down at the side of his fallen comrade. He picked up the dead man's rifle and tossed it to the other agent, then peered into the wreckage. Lea could taste his anger, which was good. It meant his judgment would be clouded—and that gave her a better than even chance.

She threw the pistol.

It landed with a loud clunk, tumbling across the floor and skidding to a stop at the agent's feet. He looked down and saw the weapon lying there, and responded by firing a burst in Lea's direction. That the pistol was a threat to him didn't even register—not until he heard the thrum building to its climax, and he realized the damned thing was on overload.

The agent turned to run, shouting at his comrade to do the same. Two steps later his body was heaved into the air, blasted back out into the corridor when the pistol exploded. He smashed up against the outside wall, falling down on the jagged end of a pipe jutting out of the floor. Dead before he got that far, his body spasmed once and fell limp.

At the same time, the other agent was screaming. He was still on his feet, spared from the brunt of the explosion; but the intense flash of light, augmented by the visual receptors in his helmet, fried his retinas in an instant. He tore his helmet off, grabbing at his eyes with one hand while the other waved his rifle around. Firing at random, he kept on blasting until his weapon overheated. He then plucked another pistol from his armor and began firing again.

Lea grabbed the quicksilver, holding the weapon out in front of her. It cut the air with a sound like music, sweet radiation trailing the blade as it arced back and forth. She saw herself reflected in that slick surface, distorted into the shape of a predator.

Energized, she leaped away from the concealing flames and closed in on the agent.

She rolled underneath his line of fire, approaching him from the right just as he began to get a taste of her presence. The agent spun to meet the perceived threat, blood streaming down his cheeks—all while he continued his barrage. Lea sidestepped the rippling bolts of pulse energy, swiping at him as she passed.

The quicksilver made contact with the agent's face, opening up a slit along his jawline. It was a tiny cut, barely enough to draw blood—but it turned his expression into one of dawning terror. He forgot about his eyes, dropping the pistol in a mad fumble to pull off his gloves. Lea stood back and watched him pat at the sides of his cheeks, searching for what he hoped he wouldn't find. His fingers stopped over the cut just as it was beginning to seal itself, and it was then he understood he was doomed.

He began to shake, losing all control as the quicksilver took effect. An isotope-neurotoxin hybrid, it hijacked the closest nerve cells and amplified their electrochemical impulses a hundredfold. To the agent, it was like stepping on a live wire. As the signal jumped from one neuron to the next, its intensity multiplied until it overwhelmed his entire nervous system.

The shock reverberated down the agent's spine, then outward, buckling his limbs out from under him. He opened his mouth in a guttural shriek, but all that came out was a confused gurgle. His body was gone. As soon as his lungs collapsed, his mind would follow as well.

Time . . .

Lea left him, jumping over the debris that littered the path between her and the air lock. She kept her eyes fixed on the MFI, falling down countless times but never slowing. Resisting the urge to look back, she crawled the last few meters on her hands and knees. On the tiny screen, she watched what she hoped were the last few seconds ticking away—but as she got closer, she found it was all an illusion. Impossible as it seemed, no more than three minutes had passed since she had set the timer.

Three *minutes*. Three dead men.

Her hands. Her work.

And something else—something that refused to die.

Avalon.

Lea knew the free agent would be there, even before she whirled around and saw her standing in the doorway. The figure was passive, almost below the threshold of life. Lea expected an outburst of poetic motion, a beautiful stab at murder that would have left her with no choice but to detonate the MFI she clutched in her hands. Avalon, however, did nothing but imply a smile.

"Stay there," Lea warned. "I'll torch us right now."

"I know," Avalon replied.

Lea blinked. The MFI became heavy, her resolve weak. All she could do was stroke the surface with her thumb and wonder why it was so damned hard to act—why it was so damned hard to die.

You know why, Lea thought. *It's because you don't want to kill HIM.*

"Get out," Lea said.

Avalon took her glasses off and turned a casual glance toward the dead agents. She nodded slightly, as if in approval, then lifted her stare back toward Lea. The free agent's eyes glared at her with an array of dazzling colors.

"Why would I want to do that?"

Mind game. It's a just mind game, Lea.

"I mean it," Lea said.

Avalon wasn't concerned. She took a few more steps into the lab, keeping her distance. "Miserable thing to die alone," she remarked. "I don't see any reason why we shouldn't go together."

Push the button, Lea. Just push the goddamned button.

"Or we could walk out of here together," Avalon continued. "You, me—and Alden. You helped him this far. It would be a shame for you to kill him now."

Lea could feel the words working inside her. It started deep, like tremors in the abyss, rising to the surface in powerful waves. But there was another component—an urgency that Avalon was trying to hide. Lea searched the free agent for some outward manifestation, and found it when her eyes fell upon Avalon's left hand. Her fingers were clenched into a fist, tight enough to pierce the leather of her gloves. Tight enough to crush bones.

She was in pain. Serious pain.

"Go fuck yourself," Lea said.

She was prepared for the fire. She imagined it running up her arm, engulfing her body and radiating outward in all directions, consuming everything in a halo of destruction as her soul made the leap from her body. It was all so beautiful, so perfect—so *fitting* an end to a life spent in shadows, to go out that way.

Then gravity took hold and pulled her back down.

Spirit fell back into flesh—a violent act, like tearing your consciousness out of the Axis in the middle of a run. Lea actually screamed—not from pain, but from betrayal, her senses so confused that she barely registered the likeness of fingers prying the MFI from her hand.

Dazed, she lashed out with the quicksilver. The weapon sang, but drew no blood. Lea made a few more stabs, certain that Avalon had gotten the jump on her, but as the world snapped back into focus she saw that the free agent was nowhere near. Avalon just kept her distance, observing Lea with a detached interest.

"Good evening, Dr. Alden," Avalon said. "It's nice to have you back."

Lea spun around. He stood there, in the open air lock.

"Cray . . . ?" she started to ask, then saw the MFI in his hands.

He ignored Lea, and walked past her to meet Avalon in the middle of the room. The free agent remained inscrutable as ever, treating this development as no surprise. She held out her hands, which had stopped shaking, and greeted Cray like he was an old friend.

"Cray," Lea intoned. "What are you doing?"

Something about him was different—far beyond the symptoms of the Ascension. It was like he didn't exist at all, his body a memory of its former self. Every move seemed calculated in advance, executed with machinelike precision: the way a computer would approximate a human being. He allowed himself to get close to Avalon, close enough for her to take him out with a single blow; but she stood down, sensing the determination of his challenge.

Cray wanted something from her. And she was ready to listen.

He held the MFI close to his chest, putting pressure on the detonator.

"You came for *me*," Cray said. "If that's all you want, I'm prepared to give it to you. Any more, you'll have to take it the hard way."

Avalon looked past his shoulder, toward Lea and the air lock.

"You know what the *Inru* are about," she told him. "That thing back there must be destroyed. We may never get another chance."

"I can't let you do that."

"Use that, you destroy Lyssa as well," Avalon pointed out. "What's the difference?"

"Phao Yin loses his prize," Cray said.

She was baffled.

"You would do all this," she asked, "for a *machine*?"

Lea leaned in to hear his answer, shocked that Cray was giving Avalon the choice. At first she thought he was crazy, and for a fleeting moment she considered attacking him. If she could get the MFI out of his hands, she could do what she should have done in the first place. But something had happened back in that Tank—something that Cray needed to protect.

Lea eased off, letting him play it out.

"This is my thing, Avalon," Cray told the free agent. "And you need to decide. CSS is probably on their way up right now."

Avalon hesitated. She stepped back to check the corridor, then turned back toward them when it was obvious she detected nothing. It was also obvious that she believed at least part of what Cray said. She put her glasses back on and examined him coldly, sizing up his intentions.

"You would come, willingly?" she asked.

Cray gestured back toward Lea. "To keep the girl alive," he said, "yes."

Avalon could barely disguise her contempt.

"Your word that she lives," Cray demanded, "and we'll both come with you. Or we can all die here, Avalon. It's your choice."

For a moment, Lea believed that the free agent would choose death, a spectacular end to a warrior's life—but that would not satisfy her utmost need. If she were to watch Cray die, it would have to be at her own hand. Nothing else would do.

But to take him to Phao Yin—*that* held much more promise of suffering.

"I won't kill her," Avalon promised. "Not until she gives me a reason."

Lea started to protest—but then she stifled herself, because she understood what Cray was doing. He just was buying her time—time enough to stay alive, time enough to figure a way out. It was far better than what CSS would offer—but it still filled Lea with horror to hear Cray speak the word out loud.

"Deal," he said.

The hovercraft lifted off amidst a battery of ground flak, scattershot beams that rocketed up from the plaza and exploded around the small ship. Avalon eased herself into the fireworks, taking a few glancing blows before punching it through the overflight grid and into the free-departure routes. Lea glanced back and saw the Works

spin away beneath her, then sink back into Manhattan and the obscurity of a million other lights.

The ship was buffeted a few more times as it encountered some
turbulence, turning to the south and a path that took it out over
the open ocean. Avalon climbed up to ten thousand meters, then
assumed a parallel course some fifty kilometers from the coast.
Through her window in the back seat, Lea could make out only a
thin line on the horizon, far away from the Port Authority tracking
stations. She then looked down into the black void of the Atlantic,
where her thoughts cleared and drifted.

"I lost contact with Funky," she said quietly.

Cray stirred next to her, uneasy at the mention of it.

"What?" she asked.

Cray drew breath to speak, but couldn't meet her eyes when
he did.

"Funky's dead."

"How—?" she began, realizing she had known on some instinctive level. Funky would never have abandoned her like that, not as
long as he was still alive. But to hear Cray say it, and with such final-
ity, made it all the more real. And all the more painful.

She swallowed hard, then asked: "How did you know?"

"I picked up on some Directorate transmissions while I was in
the Tank," Cray explained, his tone distant. "Emergency traffic.
They lost contact with the whole fusion cluster—some kind of catastrophic failure."

"That doesn't mean anything."

"A satellite pass confirmed it." He rubbed his eyes tiredly. "The
main station was completely destroyed."

Lea's jaw set firmly.

"How could you know what the Directorate was saying?" she
asked. "When did you have time to jack their communications?"

"I didn't."

"Then where is this coming from?"

"I hear everything now," Cray muttered. "Every goddamned
thing."

He passed the MFI over to her, immersing his face in the shadows so she couldn't see him. He stayed that way, huddled and alone, not speaking but hopelessly connected. Lea observed him for a time, breathing but not breathing, heart beating solely out of reflex—going through all the motions of life, pretending. It was clear that he wanted out, yet still he hung on. Lea wished she could understand why.

She ran her fingers along the contours of the MFI, engaging the screen and watching the keys light up. It would have been an easy matter to end it right there. Perhaps that was the option Cray was giving her. But she was curious, and there were things she had to know. Otherwise, it would all be useless—and her death, however noble, would have no meaning.

"We'll be on the ground in five minutes," Avalon said from the cockpit. She turned back toward her passengers, raising an eyebrow at Cray's condition. She also noticed that Lea was holding the bomb, and addressed her directly. "I have an SOT standing by to take us to Phao Yin. It's time for you to give up your little toy."

Lea's eyes narrowed.

"You didn't think I would do it," she said.

"I saw the way you handled those agents," Avalon replied. "You know what you're doing with that quicksilver. You might even have the guts to push that button." She gestured toward Cray. "But not as long as *he's* around." She seemed to pity Lea—almost. "Didn't take long for Alden to get under your skin, did it?"

"About as long as it took with you."

Avalon held out her hand.

"Give it to me," she ordered.

Lea turned the MFI off and handed it over. As the free agent tucked the device away, Lea wondered if Avalon would kill her right away, while Cray was watching. For a moment it seemed possible—but then Avalon returned her attention to the controls, making a sharp turn to the west and heading inland. A minute later they were down on the deck, a frothy mist of ocean spray forming on the windows as they approached the coast.

"Baltimore free flight," Avalon signaled. "This is SAM 61. Request priority clearance."

• • •

The SOT was a charter, parked in a private hangar and flanked by armed CSS. That was how it appeared from the tarmac, and the impression was a good one. It wasn't until she got close that Lea noticed the swagger and loose discipline, and she realized the troops were a contingent of Zone agents wearing corporate uniforms. Whatever Phao Yin was paying the Authority, he must have been into them for a damned fortune.

All their weapons were trained on Cray the moment he stepped off the hovercraft. Lea was amazed at how they stood back to let him pass, as if their guns offered them little protection. They *knew* this man, the way they knew a ghost story—and they regarded him with a reverence that ran the line between hatred and terror. Avalon was the only one who would get near him—and from their reaction to her, Lea guessed the agents feared her almost as much. They kept their distance the entire time, footsteps falling into spontaneous unison as they shadowed their prisoners into the hangar.

The engines of the SOT were already running at idle, fully prepared for liftoff. Avalon went ahead of Cray and Lea, stopping briefly to speak with one of the pilots, who was waiting for them at the bottom of the boarding stairway. Avalon then motioned for them to come forward.

Cray walked right past her, not saying a word. Lea started to follow him into the aircraft, but paused after a couple of steps. She turned and looked down at Avalon, if only to let the free agent know she had not surrendered completely.

"Where are you taking us?" she asked.

Avalon's features were pale and enigmatic beneath long wisps of perfectly black hair. A cold breeze made them quiver against her cheek.

"Ask your friend Zoe."

She then clamped down on Lea's arm, and dragged her up the stairs. It was an impersonal act of violence, meant only to reassert Avalon's dominance. Lea put up a brief struggle, but only out of pride. Avalon was much stronger, and tossed her into the cabin with hardly a backward glance. Lea barely managed to stay on her feet and had to steady herself by holding on to one of the passenger seats. By then the aircraft was already rolling, backing its way out of the hangar.

"Come on," Cray said, appearing at her side. "You better sit down."

Lea was passive, allowing him to guide her to the back of the aircraft. Cray lowered her into one of the seats and buckled her in. The SOT moved past the taxiway, and accelerated fast toward liftoff. After a few moments, Lea felt the ground retreat beneath her. Then the anger began to set in, displacing every other sensation.

Cray took a seat across the aisle from Lea. The space he put between them was not lost on her. Nor his cautious posture.

"You okay?"

"I will be." Lea sighed, drawn into the black mirror of her window. "As soon as I give Miss Congeniality there a taste of her own juice." Her head lolled back toward him. "How about you?"

"I'll live."

"You don't sound too happy."

"What does that have to do with anything?"

"If I'm going to die," she pointed out, "at least you could be good company."

Cray downshifted into guilt. Lea smiled, reaching across the aisle to squeeze his hand.

"Relax," she said. "I'm not dead yet."

"Hell of a lot of good it did." Cray fell into his chair, isolating himself further. "You shouldn't be here."

"You talking about the part where you and Lyssa get blown to kingdom come?" Lea waved him off. "Too Butch and Sundance for my taste. I like how you handled it—smooth, but mysterious."

"It was the only way I could think of to get you out of there."

She raised an eyebrow.

"Simple as that?"

"There are other reasons," Cray said. "But that was prime. If I thought Phao Yin would kill you outright, I wouldn't have done it."

"Yin is insane. There's no telling what he'll do."

"He'll do what he always does. As long as he thinks you're useful, you'll stay alive."

"And he's bound to find me useful because of my past experiences with the *Inru*," Lea finished for him, not hiding her disgust. "What a choice. I get to be Phao Yin's bitch, or I get to be dead."

"If that's what it takes," Cray told her. "All that matters is finding a way out. If that means giving your loyalty to Yin, so be it." After a hard pause, he added: "It's a better deal than Funky got."

"That wasn't your fault, Cray," Lea said. "If anybody's responsible, it's me. I punched his ticket the minute I sent Zoe out. He wouldn't have been there if I hadn't taken him in."

"I could have gone to see Lyssa alone."

"Then it would be me back on that station, along with Funky. One way or the other, it comes up the same." Lea reached over and turned his face toward hers, forcing him to see her. "And you're forgetting—*I'm* the one who got *you* involved. Anybody else, we'd probably all be dead by now. If you ask me . . . it's fate."

Cray took her hand in his. She responded to him in kind, brushing her fingers against his skin. That same electricity was there, but somehow different. The intensity had not diminished; it was now just a matter of control. At the start of Cray's Ascension, Lea was uncertain whether the machine or the man would emerge dominant. It wasn't a question anymore.

"You really believe there's such a thing?"

"Yeah." She smiled. "I do."

"How can you be sure?"

"Because everything in my life has been chaos," Lea said. "Now, everything seems so clear. I don't think that happens by accident."

"Then tell me what you see."

She shook her head.

"Not what I see," she said. "Just what I missed."

"What's that?"

"The chance to get to know you. We could've been pretty good together."

"We *are* good together," he said. "The rest of it just didn't work out."

"We still have now."

Lea drew closer. The way he looked reminded her of the first time she had seen him in Vienna. She had been playing with him then, and he played her right back. But now, this thing was *real*. It was the only thing that felt real to her.

"It's not much," he said.

"It never is," Lea replied, and kissed him.

The SOT dropped out of its trajectory an hour later, while it was still over the Atlantic. As it broke the high clouds, Lea spotted the familiar outline of Incorporated Europe, the western shores of the continent coming up fast. The landmass was enshrouded in an eroding purple twilight, magnificent against the curvature of the Earth—and the last place Lea expected Phao Yin to be. Europe was the heart and soul of the Collective, far from the lawless political scape of the Zone—and that made it especially dangerous ground for the *Inru*. If Yin had been conducting his operations from there, he was better than invisible. That he kept those whispers out of the Axis was nothing short of a miracle.

The aircraft descended rapidly, dropping down into Gibraltar airspace and making a lazy roll to the northeast, just as the coastal cities turned themselves on to beat back the night. The pilot vectored along the same lines as the pulser grid, following the larger arteries that pumped traffic into the center of the continent. Cray slipped in close to Lea and traced their progress through the window, while she tried to map the subtle reach he was making with his mind. Fascinated as she was, it still scared her when Cray was only half-there.

"You got that look," Lea observed.

"Just an impression, that's all," Cray told her. "There's a lot of background noise—you know, like voices in a crowded room. It takes a while, but I can play them back from memory one at a time."

"Is that how you found out about Funky?"

"No. That was different."

Neurons began to tingle. Lea posed her next question with caution: "How?"

"He was in the Axis when it happened," Cray explained. "Or at least part of him was. That part is still out there, searching. Disembodied energy working on a flatline. It's been collecting for some time."

"Is that . . . ?" she began, uncertain if she really wanted to know. The implications went beyond disturbing, into the realm of the existential. "What else is out there?"

"Everything and everyone connected to the Axis."

Lea sounded distant, even to herself.

"That means part of me is out there, too," she said. "From the interface."

"From anybody who's ever interfaced," he affirmed. "First law of thermodynamics: no energy in the universe is ever created or destroyed. It only changes form."

From reality to the Axis, Lea thought. *Physical to virtual.*

She looked up at him. "What does that make you?"

"Just a man," Cray said, and squeezed her on the shoulder. "For as long as that lasts." He returned to his seat, leaving her to sort out the possibilities for herself.

The drop to subsonic jolted Lea out of her thoughts. She turned pensive attention to the gridpaths and lights that meshed into the tight web on the ground below, then watched them part as the SOT entered the space of a large airport. She tried to angle ahead to get bearings on its location, but could find no distinguishing landmarks. She did, however, spot several other aircraft moving out of their way—clearing a path for them to land. The pilot, it seemed, was wasting no time in getting them down.

She glanced over at Cray, looking for clues. He was inscrutable, almost messianic.

"Hell of a day," she whispered.

CHAPTER
FIFTEEN

A gauntlet of straight lines bisected the dark, marking the edges of a taxiway that led to a bank of reserve hangars. As soon as the SOT landed, its pilot steered off the runway and made a run toward the buildings. Through her window, Lea spotted a small convoy of escort vehicles parked on the tarmac directly ahead. They started up as the SOT approached, a swirl of red and blue spilling out from their light mounts. They moved as a tight cluster, across the pavement on an intercept course. The convoy then branched out, quickly falling into positions all around the aircraft. Lea only wished they were the real authorities, coming to arrest her.

One of the vehicles took the lead, its driver motioning for the SOT to follow. The pilot complied and directed his aircraft toward the largest of the hangars. Spotlights ignited around the structure in advance of their arrival, bathing the aircraft in a harsh flood as the massive doors rolled open. The SOT taxied inside and stopped, as several dozen troops emerged and took up strategic positions throughout the hangar.

Avalon walked back to join her two guests. She carried Lea's quicksilver, which protruded obviously from beneath her coat. For a second, Lea considered reaching for it—but she didn't want to give Avalon an excuse. There would be time for that later.

"Get up," the free agent ordered.

Both of them did as they were told. Avalon marched them down the aisle and out the door, down the stairs to where a line of troops waited. A hovercraft was docked there, open hatches awaiting their arrival.

Rifle sights followed the prisoners as they walked toward the small ship, not resting until both of them were securely on board. Avalon then cleared the troops out, climbing into the cockpit and sealing the hatch behind her. She started up the turbofans, which generated a misty hiss in the closed space of the hangar. Releasing the docking clamps, the free agent put the ship into a hover a few meters off the ground. It drifted sideways after a kick from the lateral thrusters, floating past the wide body of the SOT and turning about as it exited the hangar doors.

Once outside, Avalon killed the running lights and took the hovercraft straight up. Blackness enveloped the small ship, offset only by the dimness of the cabin lights. Lea waited until they got to altitude, then leaned forward to get a glimpse over the free agent's shoulder. The view through the forward window offered few clues, until Avalon swung around to her intended course and the shape of a city skyline formed on the horizon. The outlines were familiar, a jumble of ancient and modern structures that Lea had once haunted on a regular basis. Her experiences there had, in fact, become legend—at least to those who knew her as Heretic. But that had been a long time ago, even if the memories were fresh enough to touch.

Paris, after all, was a city you didn't forget.

Cray pictured their destination, long before Avalon steered them toward it. The image appeared grandiose and magnetic—though it was the latter sensation that disturbed him. Just as Lyssa had put the hook on him, so did the tower he constructed in his mind. It meant that the machinery was already in place. Phao Yin was waiting for him to set it into motion, but it was alive nonetheless.

Even without the flash acting on his nervous system, Cray would have been able to sense it. He knew the street, and right now it was popping off that wavelength like a superconductor. The city was just out of phase, its rhythms like a recording played back three-quarter speed. It wasn't until they crossed into the Paris centerplex that he understood the magnitude of the disturbance, and then only because

of the sudden *lack* of input. Beyond its borders, the city was a manufactured simulation; inside, it was a complete media blackout.

The eye of the storm, Cray thought. No one else in the world could
have picked up on it—even those who had spent lifetimes in the
Axis, breaching the kind of security that passed for magic in the civilized world. Dark magic. Black ice. There was enough here to drown
a thousand hammerjacks.

All radiating from a single source, directly ahead.

"Paris free flight," Avalon signaled. "This is SAM 600 transport."

"SAM 600, go ahead."

"Requesting permission for high-insert approach." She leveled off
just above the traverse grid, aiming for the hub at the center of the
old city. "My vector is zero-two-seven, gridline plus twenty meters.
This is a courier flight, over."

"SAM 600, acknowledged. State your destination."

"Point Eiffel."

"Roger that." The voice on the other end radioed instructions,
while Avalon maintained position and awaited clearance. A short
distance off, the slender columns that formed the tower sloped
gracefully into the cosmopolitan sky. "Come around to course zero-
four-nine. You're second in line for landing."

Avalon disengaged the turbines and went on thrusters, swinging
into a lazy turn around the east side of the tower. Massive floodlights
at its base cast a reverent glow over the steel meshwork—a fusion of
beauty and garishness, made more dazzling by the web of laserlight
that encircled the old landmark. The free agent aimed for the top of
the tower, gliding over a flotilla of pulsers that rode the grid in and
out of the centerplex. As the hovercraft flew in closer, Lea spotted a
small hoverpad beneath the domed apex—a tiny platform, large
enough to accommodate only a few ships. Avalon hung back for a
few moments to allow another craft to lift off, then moved in to take
the empty spot.

A bank of landing lights blazed against the lower hull of the hovercraft as it settled out of the sky, the fans kicking up a froth of ice
particles. Avalon shut the engines down, securing the ship and turning back to her two passengers.

"Move," she ordered.

Cray and Lea walked across the hoverpad toward a magnetic lift, while Avalon shadowed them from behind. Lea was uneasy as they waited for the lift to arrive and stayed close to Cray the entire time.

"The whole tower is a transmitter," Cray said to her. It was a foregone conclusion that Avalon could hear everything, but the free agent didn't seem at all concerned. "That's how the *Inru* hide this place. There's enough concentrated ice to cover the whole damned continent. It's like one gigantic logic trap."

"More like a hole in the Axis," Lea agreed.

"It *will* be," Cray intoned, "if Phao Yin gets his way. First here, then the incorporated territories—after that, who the hell knows?"

"Speculation doesn't befit you, Dr. Alden," Avalon said. "Yin will be disappointed—but then, I never believed you were worth all the trouble."

Cray smiled back coldly.

"That's not your call to make," he replied. "*Is* it?"

"An appeal to my vanity," the free agent observed. "You must be getting desperate."

"Not as desperate as you," Cray shot back. "I never could figure out how somebody like you got hooked up with this bunch. What did Yin promise you? Money? A seat of power in his new empire? Tell me—what does it take to get a free agent to break an oath of loyalty to her masters?"

The suggestion seemed to amuse her. "I have no more loyalty for the Assembly than I do for the *Inru*. My only interest is their vision."

"A world populated by soulless machines?" Cray asked. "That won't get back what they took from you, Avalon."

"I never believed it would," Avalon said. "But it will make this world far more livable."

"And if the Assembly is destroyed in the process?"

"So much the better."

The lift arrived, terminating the discussion. Avalon shoved them both inside. She then turned to the elevator control and opened a hidden panel beneath the standard interface. Cray recognized the interface as a security subsystem; ironically, it was the same hardware the Collective installed at the Works, complete with retinal scan and biometric detectors. The free agent took off her glasses and presented a blind eye for confirmation, while Cray and Lea had their endocrine levels mapped down to the last detail. The subsystem would use those unique markers to track their positions anywhere within the security sphere. Once coded, escape was impossible.

The lift dropped through a transparent shaft, the iron skeleton of the tower enveloping them. Structural beams and supports blurred into the city skyline, alternating light and shadow. *Free fall,* Cray thought, knowing they would not slow until they had plunged into the ground. In a way, it was fitting. The subculture had given birth to the *Inru* movement, the only place where such subversive elements could move about freely. Now that subculture was set to emerge from the very same place. Cray had to admire Yin for that touch.

They plunged into darkness.

Lea imagined the glass walls compressing her when Paris disappeared. She placed her hands against them out of an irrational need to push back, but relented against the cool surface when she spied her own reflection there. Staring beyond the likeness, Lea saw a nightmare series of images: labyrinthine passageways twisting into forever, brick walls stained with the graffiti of a hundred languages—but mostly bones. Thousands of them. *Millions* of them. Human skeletons all, cobbled together and piled on top of each other, the wicked grins of skulls peeking out from the rubble of remains. In half glimpses, they took on the appearance of the damned.

"What the hell *is* this place?"

"The catacombs," Cray told her. "A system of tunnels running underneath Paris. Most of them have been around for better than a thousand years."

She watched herself watching the dead.

"What about all of these people?"

"Been stacked down here for centuries," Cray explained. "When the cemeteries ran out of room, they would dig up the bones and throw them down here. They've been gathering dust ever since." He cast an eye toward Avalon. "Not many people go down into the tunnels. That's what makes it such a perfect hiding place."

"Looks like they weren't the first," Lea said as the lift slowed, giving her a chance to read some of the inscriptions. It was all there: resistance slogans from World War II, the names of freedom fighters from the days of the Consolidation—as well as the distinctive marks of the *Inru*, which told their story in cryptic symbols and figures. Lea recognized them from her time with the movement, the loose talk of revolution she herself had once tossed around. How *alive* it had been for her in those days, when her first reach had been for the sword instead of reason. Now those ideas were dead to her, as lifeless as the relics strewn throughout these caves.

The lift slowed to a stop. Iridescent markers powered on as the doors opened, brushing aside enough of the pall to light a narrow path that led deeper into the catacombs.

"Out," the free agent ordered.

Cray went first, holding Lea's hand. They stepped into a domed cavern, the ceiling a patchwork of precisely arranged tiles—like a cathedral, with all the reverence that went into the construction. As Avalon sent the lift back up to the surface, the pale light from inside the car spilled across the tiles and revealed a collage of painted frescoes. Each was an individual work, but when pieced together they formed a picture of the modern man—human in shape only, faceless and sexless, connected to an amorphous entity of energy and ideas. Darkness then fell across it like a curtain, leaving it unseen but omnipresent.

"Go," Avalon said.

Cray and Lea ventured ahead, moving in the pseudolight glow of the markers. Footfalls crunched against the chalky gravel, magnified by a damp echo as they followed the passage through the murk. Lea was disconcerted by the sound, and by the odd assortment of fragments she encountered on the path. Pieces of bone were scattered like runes—most of them ancient but some unmistakably fresh, their edges gnawed and polished by predation. The marks appeared too big for rats, a thought Lea immediately dismissed as a trick of the light. Still, she went faster, not wanting Avalon to kill her and leave her out there.

The path eventually narrowed, going beyond the range of the markers and forcing them to proceed by feel. It was like disturbing a long-sealed tomb, and the walls seemed to react to the intrusion. The bricks took on a purplish cast—more subtle than substantial, globs of light flowing down the walls like a dense liquid and forming the outline of an arched passageway.

Lea was halfway through the entry before she realized it was there. Immersed, she stared down the length of the passage and tried to judge how far it went. It couldn't have been any more than ten meters, coming up on what appeared to be a dead end.

"Luminites," Cray observed of the light, and ran his hand across the rough texture of the wall. Mortar pulverized to the touch, but sparked a brighter glow as the photic elements drew more of his body heat. "Bionucleically produced."

The idea halted Lea in her tracks.

"You mean the place is *alive?*"

"Not quite," Cray said. "But close."

Avalon emerged out of the dark, quicksilver in hand. She used it to point the way down the passage, prodding them to move on. Lea shot Cray a dubious glance, but he was already on the move.

Lea followed him in, trying not to touch anything. She was especially careful to avoid the purple tendrils, which jumped out toward her whenever she got close. "*Jesus,*" she yelped when one brushed against her, like an insect scurrying across her skin. Avalon tore through them without giving it a second thought.

By then Cray had reached the end of the passage. The way was blocked by a pile of bricks and boulders that rose from floor to ceiling—the result of a structural collapse from long ago. Luminites migrated across the craggy surface, seeping between the cracks and illustrating the obvious. Nothing short of a blasting charge was going to get them through.

Cray turned around. "We may have a problem."

Avalon remained quiet. The walls, however, did not.

The bricks began to shift, spitting powdered mortar. A deep rumble followed, mildly violent but enough to induce terror in such a confined space. Lea reached out for the walls to steady herself, recoiling at the luminites that came in contact with her—but the tiny creatures were already fleeing, through every crack and fissure they could find. The light went with them, dropping a shroud of blackness throughout the passage that settled with the caking dust. The rest was a confused mélange of sounds.

It started with the crushing pummel of rock against rock, and ended with Lea screaming. Somewhere in between, the route back to the cathedral cavern filled with debris. The force of the sudden downfall compacted the atmosphere into an arid, viscous mix of gas and dust—which might have been the worst of it, if not for the oppressive silence that followed.

"Cray?" Lea choked. "Cray, are you all right?"

No answer. Only the hiss of escaping air, followed by a cool, sterile draft. A series of massive bolts rolled away in front of her, locking into place like a hammer pounding steel. Light flooded the passageway, brilliant and painful to her eyes. Even so, Lea clutched at the light greedily, treating it as her lifeline—and took her first uncertain steps toward it.

"Cray?"

Lea peered between the slats of her fingers, and found him standing at the center of a large doorway. The collapsed wall that blocked the way only moments before had swung open like a bank vault, into a hidden chamber that pulsed with a vibe Lea remembered from the street. Mixed signals, frenetic and unbound—they were bouncing all around the place, the antithesis of the catacombs they left behind.

There were *people* here. And they were feeding.

Lea caught her first glimpse of them, vague shapes squeezed out of the light. They gathered around Cray, tentative hands reaching for him but drawing back before they could touch. As Lea moved closer, their faces assembled into familiar forms. All of them were young, some only children, but with a weary kind of wisdom that was a rite of passage in the subculture. Lea knew them, because she had once been one of them. The hustlers, the pimps, the Crowleys, the Goths—they were one and the same creature, the collective entity of the streets. They treated Cray as if he were their messiah.

Inru.

Lea stepped in next to him, into the circle the *Inru* dared not breach. There were only a dozen of them, just the tip of the network that operated in the underground—but the word spread out from there, interfacing with the others via a primitive link. They stared at Lea, barely containing an animal frenzy. It was clear she was not welcome, and they poised themselves for an attack.

"Stand down," Avalon said.

The free agent strode in from the passageway, placing herself in front of Cray and Lea. The *Inru* children reacted to her much the same way they had reacted to Lea, but with one crucial difference: they were afraid.

They did as instructed, and moved aside to let Cray and Lea pass. Others arrived as well. They remained outside the free agent's protective zone, but never strayed farther than that. They were hungry, and wanted to be close to Cray. They drank in his presence like a narcotic.

"They know what I am," he observed.

"Maybe," Lea said. "But what the hell are *they?*"

None of the *Inru* beckoned them with an answer. They just lined up along the deep corridor that led into an underground complex, like an honor guard sent to receive him. Cray took Lea by the hand, following Avalon's lead and avoiding their eyes. The rank and file stepped in behind him to follow, the same kind of boys and girls Lea had known from the street—lost and desperate, forever seeking a human connection, but forsaking what made them human in the process. Pliable minds and blind faith: a perfect combination of qualities for Phao Yin's new order.

"I hate to admit it," Lea said quietly as they went, "but the Collective might be right about these people. We've got the seeds of a real revolution here. There's no telling how many of them Yin has out there, spreading the word."

"More like spreading a virus," Cray said. "There's a message, but it's pathological. Yin only needed a few people to drop it into the subculture. Now it's propagating by itself, like wildfire."

"You're talking *code*," she pointed out. "Person to person, through casual contact. The *Inru* never worked on anything like that."

"Part of Yin's plan to sell the vision. CSS knows it—or at least they have an idea. That's why they sterilized all those people at the Works. It wasn't a political purge," he finished, sour with irony. "It was containment."

Avalon held up one hand, a signal for the others to halt. Directly ahead, stretching ten meters from floor to ceiling, stood the shimmering face of a passive security curtain. The energy field warped the air into a mercurial liquid, its pixelated surface casting hollow reflections interspersed with a collage of impressions from the other side. They solidified into the form of a vaulted steel door—the final barrier between this sphere and the next.

Avalon approached the curtain, which activated a cluster of biometric sensors lining its perimeter. Her body was the key that provided the code for unlocking the door. As soon as the sensors finished mapping her, it rolled aside without a sound.

The curtain absorbed most of the light that emanated from the other sphere, twisting familiar forms into distorted shapes, then back again. The effect was like staring into a waterfall, through which Lea gathered a host of partial images—a combined representation, bent by a virtual prism. The pieces quickly fell together, but only in flashes, joined by laserlight and fiber that melded together in an enormous hub. She spied level upon level of the stuff—all hard links and hard-core, jackproof because it stayed outside the fringes of the Axis. The power it generated was tremendous, enough to pump ice through Point Eiffel and out across the rest of the world. This was the sum total of all *Inru* expectations and desires, forged into columns and relays and fused into the technology they had deployed there.

It was their own version of the Works. And what lay beyond the curtain was their own version of Lyssa.

The curtain thinned out just enough for them to grasp its physical configuration, which rose even higher than the cathedral outside. Most of the structure was geared toward transmission and reception—though the sheer elegance of its design was ethereal for all its complexity. Seven spires rose around a vacant core, guiding pulses of light that wrapped themselves around an intricate framework, which melded near the ceiling like a cluster of neurons. Lea watched the pulses interact with one another, hopping from one termination to the next, before joining another spire and working their way back down to the core. *Bionucleic energy,* she decided, probably in some kind of test phase.

But coming from where?

The source was at the core itself. Several tech mercs in white jumpsuits were already there, checking out the banks of control equipment that encircled the area—but the sarcophagus at its center put everything into context. The lid was closed, but even from her vantage point Lea could tell that the vessel was not empty. A window of carbon glass looked in on its occupant, a revelation of flesh and bone that was human in all its impurity. One of the mercs opened the lid, and the man inside awakened like a vampire. Sitting upright, he turned his eyes toward the curtain and stared straight through it. Teeth glinted beneath his narrow lips, a genuine smile of recognition.

One of the mercs helped him out of the sarcophagus. It was a betrayal of weakness he could not allow in the world above—one he could not avoid below. So much of the complex was tied into his essence, it was unavoidable. Still, he eschewed assistance from the others as he made his way to the curtain, choosing instead to go it alone.

The man walked through the energy field, his footsteps measured and careful—like a man much older than his years. Clearly, being there had taken its toll—but still he beamed that smile, as if greeting an old friend.

"Good evening, Dr. Alden," Phao Yin said. "It's good to see you again."

He held out his hand.

The *Inru* watched the exchange in hushed silence, as did Lea. Cray, however, accepted the greeting without hesitation. Yin was ashen, his hand icy to the touch. Half-dead, he was a projection of what Cray felt within himself. Yin did nothing to hide his envy.

"Likewise," Cray replied.

There were no guards, no troops—and with the exception of what Avalon carried, no weapons as far as Lea could see. Phao Yin had completely entrusted his security to automated measures, leaving brute force to the surface. Even so, there was a feral quotient to the *Inru* that shadowed them—too many years of tecs and stimulants, of bad trips spun on cheap electrodes, that the nightmare hallucination was a permanent imprint on their collective cortex. Their tenuous grip on reality thus became Yin's strength. They would die for him at a single word, and by that same token they would kill. Lea had to admire the purity of it. What Yin bought from the Zone Authority, these people gave him freely. They operated on the same level as zombies—but zombies made for a powerful army.

The mercs who tended his machinery were a different story. Lea knew the type from her own time with the movement, when hammerjacks were looking to make a name for themselves in the underground. More egotistical than partisan, they used the *Inru* as a vehicle to learn their chops—just as they used Phao Yin to get time on some of the newest technology. They treated the newcomers with suspicion, as they would anybody who trespassed on their turf, but that was as far as their hostility went. As much as such people talked, they were not killers. Lea doubted they even knew the full extent of what Phao Yin had planned.

"I suppose congratulations are in order," Yin said. He walked a slow, deliberate pace, keeping himself between Cray and Lea while Avalon stalked them from behind. "It's not everyone who can evade my organization for as long as you have. You even gave my free agent a few bruises. I confess, Dr. Alden—I didn't believe you had it in you."

"That makes two of us," Cray remarked in an acid tone. "I knew you had some issues, Yin—but this whole master-of-the-universe thing has me baffled."

"Perhaps you should talk to your friend here. If not for her efforts, it's doubtful we could have realized our goals." Yin turned that reptilian smile on Lea. "The *Inru* owe you a great debt, Miss Prism. I'm quite pleased to have you back in our fold."

"Save it for your trick boys," Lea scoffed. "I'm only here to watch you go down."

Yin laughed.

"Looks like you're already on the way," Lea continued. "A guy like you should be smart enough to stay off the juice. Is that what those little coffin trips are for?" she asked, jerking a thumb toward the sarcophagus. "To show the boys and girls you can still ride?"

"Nothing quite so simple," Yin admitted. "The subjects you see here are experiments, nothing more. An exercise in evolution for future generations—built upon your work, by the way. You see," he said, turning around to face them both, "everybody wanted to be the first. Toward that end, each one volunteered to be a vessel. To project themselves into a higher level of consciousness, so they might better understand the word."

"You injected them with flash," Cray translated.

"Only a variant," Yin said with a shrug. "It took some doing to get it right, but ultimately we were successful. These minions have been out in the world for some time, helping the message take root. Now that our time has arrived, they will be there to assure the *Inru*'s continued dominance in the subculture."

"No matter how many of them get killed in the process."

"Where's the revolution if there's no injustice?"

Yin spoke with a wicked brilliance. The strategy, after all, was flawless. In crushing its enemies, the Collective only pumped more fuel for the fanatics. Once that enmity reached critical mass, the chain reaction would continue on its own until it flooded the streets with anticorporate venom. Then Yin would be in a position to deal—and the Assembly would have no choice but to accept.

"An interesting proposition," Cray observed.

"You're a poor liar," Yin countered. "None of this is any mystery. You thought of it long before you came near this place."

"What difference does that make?"

"All the difference in the world." Yin took him by the arm and continued their march to the core. Lea watched them both, trying to decipher the cryptic intent that passed between them. "I keep coming back to the same question: *Why did you return to the Works?* You had the head start. You could have easily disappeared. What could possibly convince you to go back, to face almost certain capture?"

Cray had already explained his motives to Lea, and up until that moment she had believed him. But there was a vacancy in his eyes that invited doubt—and a willingness to follow. Cray was slipping. Lea was helpless to prevent it.

"It's very simple," Yin coaxed. "You *wanted* to be found."

He stopped at the entry to the core, where several technicians were preparing the sarcophagus to receive another body. Cryogenic hoses snaked across the floor to its base, alongside coils of fiber link that carried test pulses back to an extraction apparatus. Cray fixated on the open lid, while a cool vapor spilled across the floor and beckoned absolute zero.

"Seeing Lyssa like that," Yin said, "understanding her the way you understand yourself, you *needed* me to find you. Even if you didn't know it, even if you didn't *believe*—all of your instincts were driving you home. It's the only place left for you, Cray. The only purpose that has any meaning."

The technicians pushed Lea aside and started to remove Cray's clothing. She tried to intervene, but Avalon was on her before she could flex a single muscle. Brought to her knees, Lea watched through tears as each garment crumpled to the floor. Cray, meanwhile, just stood there and allowed it to happen. His eyes stayed on Yin the whole time.

"You know what I saw," he said.

"Don't listen to him, Cray!" Lea shouted. Avalon twisted her arm, making her cry out, though Cray didn't seem to notice. "He's trying to trick you!"

"As much as any human being could know," Yin replied, ignoring

Lea. "Zoe started it the moment she assimilated the flash. She just didn't know how quickly it would take effect."

"*Please,* Cray," Lea pleaded. She was breaking down, her voice laced with sobs. "He's the one who killed Zoe, remember?"

Cray didn't hear her at all.

"She was the one," he said. "When Lyssa broke out."

Yin nodded slowly, teacher to pupil.

"She touched Zoe first," Cray went on. "That was her first contact."

"She was Ascending," Yin affirmed. "Then she passed the gift on to *you.*"

Life sparkled in the color of his eyes. Alien life.

"My Ascension," Cray said.

"Yes," Yin told him. "The potential that exists within each one of us. A mind even more powerful than Lyssa." With quivering hands, he clasped both sides of Cray's face. "That's why she sought you out."

Lea felt the tears freeze on her cheeks, the pain that crippled her escaping like so much ether. *This* was the secret Cray had discovered while he was alone in the Tank—the truth he would not confess to her.

"You *are* the Other."

Cray's resistance collapsed. The spires surrounding the core absorbed his loose energy, giving spontaneous rise to neural impulses and thickening the air with electricity. Those bursts then jumped the loop, higher and faster than Yin had managed, before coming back down on the extraction banks like pulse fire. Sparks exploded as Yin's mercs scrambled to contain the overload, but the man himself was undisturbed. He was too in awe of Cray to be concerned with anything else.

Avalon released Lea from her grip, then stepped forward and stood next to Yin.

"You'd be wise to observe him for a time before you proceed," the free agent said. "He may already have abilities that we don't know about."

Yin folded his arms. The mercs came over and gave him the

damage report. It was minimal—some fused circuits in the reception pool, nothing that couldn't be repaired in a matter of minutes. Yin waved them away to complete the job.

"The containment field will bring him down," Yin said. "As soon as he's in the freeze, we'll be able to control him."

"Are you certain of that?"

Two more mercs approached and took Cray by the arms. They led him over to the sarcophagus and placed him inside. An extraction team then moved in and began to hardwire his body with life support and fiber clusters. Cray went along blindly, his eyes almost catatonic.

"No question," Yin decided.

He strolled away from the free agent, over to where Lea was just getting to her feet. She was unsteady, still cradling her shoulder. The *Inru* closed in on her, moving at Yin's command, until they were close enough to fall on her with their fingernails and their fangs. Yin was waiting for the terror to appear on her face, but Lea had already resolved to deny him that. Instead, she kept her gaze leveled at *him*—seething with a violence that invited Yin to move closer, just so he could taste it for himself.

"Whatever you have in mind," she said, "you better make it quick."

Yin smiled. He had no such intentions.

CHAPTER

SIXTEEN

Yin granted Lea an unobstructed view, up in a glass booth that overlooked the core. A single row of control nodes lined the darkened space, linked to vital systems that ran throughout the facility and up into Point Eiffel. Reams of information poured out of virtual displays, assuming form as logical constructs that were monitored by a Japanese crew. From their tattoo scars, Lea had them pegged for *ronin*—disgraced gangsters who were denied the dignity of ritual suicide. Avalon methodically patrolled their stations, keeping a careful vigil. Hopped up on the same drugs as the *Inru*, the *ronin* looked like they had been down in it for some time.

"Still you shed tears."

It was Yin who addressed her, projecting his insincere charm. It was true her crying had never stopped. Lea just hadn't noticed—not until she saw her own likeness staring back at her.

"All for a man who would destroy you," Yin continued, shaking his head in pity as he came forward to join her. "Alden brought me countless heads in the time we worked together—but none he would have prized so much as yours. Heretic was his special project." A lewd smirk crept across his lips. "I see now that he was yours."

Lea stole a sideways glance at one of the displays. One of the partitions spouted out a stream of cryogenic stats, which supplied data to form a construct of the sarcophagus itself. The vessel was sealed, filling up with the liquid elements that would take Cray down. His respiration was already at half-normal and dropping fast—though brain wave activity was still off the charts. He was aware of every moment, even as his body slipped into stasis.

"Don't push your luck," Lea said, then turned around to face him. Tears evaporated under the heat of her resolve, a shift in the balance of power between them. "You can play your little games with the *Inru,* but don't you dare try it on me."

Yin was curious.

"What would you have me do?"

"Put a stop to this," Lea demanded. "You know as well as I do that the flash has no termination sequence. Once it's active in a living system, extraction is impossible."

"Precisely as it was intended," Yin explained. "The host genetic sequence must be irrevocably altered before flash-DNA can begin processing. Otherwise, the host would be dead in a matter of hours. We had hoped for a few more months of testing before actual deployment—but your friend Zoe altered the schedule." He leaned over the window to observe Cray, and remarked, "All things considered, it worked out remarkably well."

"Then why do this?"

Yin raised an eyebrow.

"I should have thought that obvious by now."

Yin had made no attempt to hide his design. He had, in fact, walked Lea straight through it—but only now did she realize what she had seen.

She whirled around in a panic, planting her hands against the window. Down in the core, sporadic pulses of energy were gathering around the sarcophagus, organizing themselves into tethers of coherent light. They traveled up and down the lengths of the spires, intertwining with one another in a delicate expression of intelligence, before returning to their point of origin and sinking back into a cryogenic void.

"It's beginning," Yin said.

Lea pushed past him, jumping onto one of the nodes. She grabbed some mixed packets of telemetry from the other stations and dumped them onto the virtual display. The resulting model clearly showed the corollary she had already worked out in her head:

the further Cray went down, the more powerful those pulses became. If it continued, the core would be generating a supernova of energy by the time Cray flatlined.

Going straight up through Point Eiffel.

Lea went numb.

"You're projecting him into the Axis."

Yin didn't acknowledge her, but it was all the confirmation Lea needed. Stars then rocked her vision, exploding from a steel vise that clamped down on her wounded shoulder. Cold breath creased the back of her neck, and Lea knew Avalon had her.

The free agent yanked her away from the node, then spun her around. Avalon hooked one hand into a claw, meaning to finish Lea with a single stroke.

"Wait," Yin commanded.

Avalon put Lea down, but held fast to both of her shoulders. She forced Lea to look at Yin, who approached with arms open and threatening. Lea knew what he wanted. She could smell it on him, that cheap anticipation.

"You can't do this," Lea warned. "A bionucleic matrix can't exist within the confines of logical space. The two will tear each other apart."

"Out of destruction comes salvation," Yin replied. His words were as slow and deliberate as the steps he took. "Once the structure of the Axis collapses, those impenetrable walls protecting the Assembly will come tumbling down. Within moments, those old men will be drowning in a flood of chaos logic."

Avalon pushed Lea to her knees.

"*Think* of it, Lea," he said. "A whole new order, forged from your creation."

Lea grimaced, twisting her expression into a defiant smile.

"With you," she observed, "waiting in the wings to assume control."

Yin shrugged modestly. "The burden of leadership must fall to those willing to serve. Order will have to be restored—but only after a suitable period of revolution."

"Sounds like a real party," Lea said, chewing on her pain. "Still, it's not the end you had planned. Is that why you took those little coffin trips down there? So you could pretend that *you* were the one bringing the Assembly down?" She laughed at him—a pitying laugh. "It must really hack you that Cray is down there making history, while you're sitting on your ass and watching."

Yin stopped. Lea had found his weakness: *envy*. That most human of failings.

"How does it feel," she goaded, "knowing that Zoe stole the only thing that ever mattered to you? Because I can tell you, it didn't mean a damn thing to her."

Yin's eyes went glassy, his hands clenched and quivering with rage. Slowly, deliberately, he held out one of those hands and demanded of Avalon:

"Quicksilver."

The free agent gave him the blade. Lea was enthralled by the play of light across the weapon's edge, as much as she was terrified of its singsong resonance. Yin raised it above her head, the clumsy move of a man who didn't care where the blade landed—only that it would kill.

He froze when the lights went out.

Alarms filled the closed space of the control booth, different alerts from different stations melding into a cacophony of urgent warnings. The displays all went blank, coming back up with static as they lost their connections to the vital subsystems.

Yin wrapped an arm around Lea's throat, clutching her against his body while his eyes tried to make sense of the dark. Everything moved in strobe, a crazy patchwork of images tied together by azure light erupting out of the core.

"What's happening?"

Avalon was an illusion in black. She vanished from Yin's side, a blur in the brilliance as she crossed the room to emerge at the security station. There, she hard-linked her sensuit to the node, using its power to deliver enough juice to run the display. Raw numerics came pouring out, which Avalon placed in context with her own subdural processors.

"Carrier breach," the free agent reported. "Multiple levels, media and interface layers. The local domain scrammed itself to quarantine the point of incursion."

Lea felt Yin's grip on her loosen.

"Where?" he breathed.

"Point Eiffel."

Yin shook his head in disbelief, his lips mouthing the word endless times before he finally got it out.

"*Impossible.*"

"Verified," Avalon assured him. "Without domain control, the transmitter will cycle down. Residual ice should give us a few minutes of cover, but after that we won't be able to contain our signature."

Yin breathed hard, the steam of his panic on the back of Lea's neck.

"Time," he said.

Avalon performed some calculations.

"Three minutes."

Tremors from the core reflected off the hollow spaces of the surrounding catacombs, pounding its foundations with steady waves. Cray was breeding energy, its glow flooding the entire complex in a deep ocean blue. Lea guessed that three minutes was optimistic. With nothing to restrain him, Cray was on the verge of becoming unbound. When that happened, his bloom would be visible to every Collective satellite in orbit over the continent.

"Fields collapsing," Avalon said. "Quarantine is breaking down."

Yin lowered the quicksilver, absently dicing the air as his mind wandered. His body trembled against Lea, an emulsion of sweat and heartbeat.

"Terminate cryogenic support," he ordered. "Shut everything down—*now.*"

Avalon tried, but the node wouldn't respond. The numerics on the display froze, and a feedback alert sounded. It was only a soft beep, accompanied by a flashing indicator that washed Avalon's face in crimson light—but in the utter silence of the booth, the sound was deafening.

The free agent removed her glasses, affixing her ruined eyes upon Yin.

"It's too late," she said. "They're already here."

Covalent explosive penetrated the vault door, seeping in between the microscopic spaces that ran along its perimeter. When it ignited, the force of the blast was so confined that it turned back *in* on itself— thousands of times in the space of a millisecond, creating an implosion of such magnitude that it generated temperatures equivalent to a fusion laser. The circular edge of the door sublimated into hot energy plasma, consuming itself as it expanded outward—but gravity fueled the most violent stage of the reaction. Five hundred metric tons of steel started to buckle under the stress of its own weight, releasing a groan into the catacombs as it broke free from the enormous pins that held it in place.

Everyone down in the core became still. It was a mirage at first, the bulge that appeared in the brushed surface of the door; but its growth was relentless, and brought several of the *Inru* closer to see. Their outlines appeared in silhouette against the glowing façade, motionless in spite of the white-hot embers that spilled out all around them. It was as if the dead on the other side had come calling, and the *Inru* could not resist the compulsion to answer.

The door collapsed in front of them.

A solid wall of heat advanced on the *Inru*. Their bodies burst into flame as they were overtaken—becoming ash in an instant, still standing in the positions they assumed in life. Then oxygen rushed out of the core to feed the voracious fire, pulverizing those figures before sucking them into the molten crater left by the fallen vault door.

That was when the ghosts of the catacombs appeared. Lea heard them before she saw them: a steady howl, coming up from the steam that rose out of the crater. Bone dust, impossibly thick and cold, blew in from the cathedral like a pyroclastic flow—a hurricane force that rushed back into the core to fill the momentary vacuum. The gray cloud snaked its way through the field of neural energy, responding to its flux and contours and assuming intelligent form as it descended upon the surviving workers. Lea caught glimpses of it in lightning flashes, but what she really tried to find was Cray. She was aware of him out in the confusion, a leader among the ghosts, and every bit as vengeful. But then he was gone, drawn back into the sarcophagus and his own physical being—and the cloud was left to play out the laws of physics.

Lea saw it coming. She closed her eyes.

The cloud smashed against the booth, shattering the windows like an explosive decompression. Lea lost her sense of everyone around her—everyone except for Phao Yin, who clutched her like a shield against the onslaught. They both stumbled backward against the full brunt of the wind, suddenly alone in the compressed reality that swirled around them.

Reaching backward, she cupped her hands around the sides of Yin's head and slapped down as hard as she could. Lea heard him scream. His arms fell away from her, and as they separated she steeled herself to take a breath. At the same time, she detected a sweet harmonic splitting the air between them—a swipe of the quicksilver blade, disjointed and fluttering as it tumbled out of Yin's hand. Lea made an instinctive reach, and caught the weapon by the handle before it could hit the floor.

She spun around, meaning to cut Yin and be on her way; but the dust was already clearing, and Avalon would be on her if she waited any longer. The open window was her only option. If she didn't take it immediately, there would be no second chance.

Lea jumped.

Yin quickly recovered. He forced himself to his feet, cradling his wounded head and feeling the blood trickle out of his ears. He had to shout to hear himself, but also to cover up his fear.

"Status!"

Yin didn't know who answered him, nor did he care. He only heard what he already knew, from the crackle of pulse fire that ripped into the core.

"Weapons discharge," one of the *ronin* yelled. "High confidence, attack dispersal. Coming right up through the main gate."

"Identify!"

There was a hit on one of the support pylons below the booth. Half of the nodes erupted in sparks, while the floor lurched downward. Yin grabbed the nearest console and held on, like a captain on the deck of a foundering vessel. Banks of equipment broke away from their mounts, crashing past him as the booth settled at an extreme angle. Somehow, the pylon held—but only as a gnarled mass, dangling on the verge of collapse.

Everyone was gone. Out through the broken windows, buried under piles of wreckage—all of them had disappeared. Yin struggled toward the only working node he could find, and bashed his hands against the interface until a flicker appeared on the display. All he could get was an audiograph, showing the spectrum of tactical frequencies utilized by Corporate Special Services. To Yin's horror, the image came alive with chatter. From Point Eiffel all the way down into the catacombs, their readings were everywhere.

Yin lost the image when another explosion blew the rest of his power. He dragged himself to the window, teetering over the side— and that was when he saw them. Dozens of them, outfitted in full combat gear and with enough weaponry to fight a small war. They poured in through the hole where the vault door once stood, the advance teams laying down a constant barrage of fire while the rear echelon prepared to occupy the space.

"Avalon!"

He shrieked her name. The free agent did not reply, and still Yin called out to her. Over and over again, until his throat burned and his voice cracked—the word came back to mock him and his ruined empire.

"Answer me!"

The floor beneath him folded. What was left of the support pylons gave way, and the booth plunged with them. Yin felt the walls compressing him, pushed on by the bellow of twisting steel—a primordial sound, not unlike the rage contained in the remains of his soul. It was all he could think about.

Alden . . .

In the midst of that torture, Yin could hear him laughing.

•   •   •

Lea flew.

She rode the adrenaline, her intellect displaced by chemical reactions and a need for flight. It translated to a kind of animal grace, strength, and momentum, which propelled her through the air as the heat of weapons fire carved up the atmosphere around her. Lea pivoted herself downward, going headfirst into a dive while her arms reached out for anything that could arrest her fall. Through a haze of dust, she found it—and wrapped her body around the jutting shaft like it was her only tether to life.

Lea slid.

Along one of the support pylons, away from the control booth, she hit the ground hard enough to crush bones—though in her jazzed state, that would not have stopped her. Lea just went on reflex, rolling with the impact and working out the pain after she got to her feet. She remained in a crouch, her eyes narrowing as she searched the chamber for the source of the attack that had saved her. Outside of Zone agents, there was only one kind of breed that hit this hard. When Lea spotted the line of troops moving in her direction, those fears were all but confirmed.

Special Services, she seethed. *They sent a fucking hit squad.*

The point man fired—though in the commotion, Lea doubted they even saw her. They were aiming with sensors, pulverizing anything that moved as they advanced on the core. Two of Yin's mercs were cut down where they stood, while the others scattered into the swelling *Inru* horde for protection. It did them no good. The troops unleashed pulse fire on widest dispersal, tearing into the crowd without discrimination.

It became a tangle of limbs and confusion. People fell to the left and to the right, with bright bolts of energy fusing flesh and oxygen into ozone. Lea tried to push her way out, but got slapped by a beam that passed only centimeters in front of her face. Another burst followed, which struck one of the spires and bounced off its surface—a ricochet that headed straight up into the base of the control booth. At that very moment, Lea looked up into a bloom of cinders that showered on her like hot hail.

Blinded, she got up and ran.

Pulse fire dogged Lea's every step. She went on instinct, urged by the crush of metal and the screams of those she left behind. She somehow made it to the bank of computers just outside the core and flopped behind one of them to take cover.

Lea wiped the soot from her eyes. Her vision turned liquid and surreal, putting distance between her and the surrounding chaos. She was the only person still inside the core, insulated from the weapons fire by waves of neural energy, everything around her taking on the shades of illusion. She watched the control booth, already in a violent plunge, ejecting bodies and machinery like it was trying to shake them out; but there was also the procession of *Inru,* drawn to the crumbling structure, who just *stood* there and watched, oblivious to the dangers above them and behind. A crossbeam fell on one and crushed him, after he made no move to save himself. Others became easy targets for CSS snipers, who picked them off one after the other.

The control booth pancaked as it struck the ground in front of them.

The crash consumed the dissonance of noise echoing throughout the chamber, then bled away into a disturbing silence. All the pulse fire stopped—but beneath the stillness emerged something far more ominous, in the way it gathered strength and synchronicity. It was slow and deliberate, the pace of a funeral march, but with a steady, military precision that made Lea assume the worst. She peeked out from her hiding place, waiting on the dust to clear and expecting to find columns of CSS advancing on her. She wanted to see if there was anywhere left to run—but then the marching passed right by her, away from the wreckage on its way to the cathedral tunnel.

Inru.

More than Lea had seen. More than Lea had imagined. As many of them had fallen, more had come in to take their place. They formed themselves along perfect lines, like pieces on a chessboard, moving forward in perfect unison. They stepped over their own dead, stopping only to pick up a stone or a brick or any other loose piece of debris that could be used as a weapon, and headed directly toward the CSS flank.

Their faces were vacant, distant—not the zombies they had been before. Those people had craved flesh. These were just a blank.

What the hell is this?

The CSS troops stood their ground as the crowd approached. They prepared to lay down a battery of fire that would turn the ground between them into a killing zone, but the *Inru* kept on coming. Any self-awareness they might have had was gone, replaced by a relentless push—like some unseen hand moving pawns across a chessboard.

Cray . . .

The thought grabbed Lea and spun her around. There, she found the sarcophagus alight with power. Not from the umbilicals, which had been severed at Yin's command, but from a perpetual source contained within. It was Cray, very much alive and very much aware. He had jacked the entire complex, and was playing the *Inru* to buy her time.

Get out of here, Lea.

His voice was an addiction, his words opiate. They summoned an escape tube, which sprouted from the ground near the center of the core. The door slid open and revealed a space big enough for a single person. Designed to accommodate the sarcophagus in the event of a disaster, it had become an escape route for Lea. Cray was showing her the way out.

While you still have the chance.

"Stop where you are!" the Special Services command officer shouted at the *Inru*. "Stop, or we will open fire!"

Lea turned toward them. They showed no signs of slowing down. Cray wouldn't allow them. She turned back.

"Don't do this, Cray."

No choice. This is the way Yin wants it, the way it has to be.

"You're better than that."

No, I'm not. But you are.

Lea felt a collective electricity, the energizing of heavy pulse cannons. It was beginning.

Survive, Lea. It's all you can do.

"The hell with it," she muttered, and made the run.

The first shot split the air and propagated outward, sonics shattering anything that still had a live electronic circuit. Lea ignored the ripple of explosions that followed in its wake, as she ignored the detached screams of the *Inru*. She also bypassed the escape tube, though a splinter of rational thought kept her eyes wandering back toward it. Cray read her thoughts and kept the pressure on. His barrage became so intense that it bordered on painful.

You can't help me, Lea. I'm past that now.

"They've already taken everything else," Lea said, fighting him off. She planted her hands on the smooth surface of the sarcophagus, brushing aside the frost that had caked on the glass. Cray was still in there, a vibrant apparition in the cold—both powerful and vulnerable as he cashed in the remains of his life. "They're not getting the rest of you."

Shots landed outside the core. Lea couldn't count how many—maybe a dozen, maybe more, small-arms fire combined with a volley of tactical artillery. CSS was taking the chamber apart. It wouldn't be long before they were through with the *Inru* and came for her.

Please, Lea.

"God knows what they'll do if I leave you here." Lea scanned the racks of equipment, trying to figure out how to reverse the cryogenic process. "We go, we go together."

None of that matters anymore.

"The hell it doesn't." A stray blast plowed into one of the computer banks. It exploded and fell over, knocking down the rest like a chain of dominoes. Lea struggled to keep her focus on Cray, but it was getting to be impossible. "Just tell me how to shut this damned thing off, will you? All this talk is making me jumpy."

One of the spires took a hit. Lea threw herself over the sarcophagus, as a surge of glittering particles settled over her like gold dust. Both matter and energy, they lighted on her only for a second before rising back into the air. Lea followed them, into a whirlpool that drew them around the other spires and formed a conduit that led straight into Point Eiffel. It was only visible for a moment, but Lea understood the significance. The fading ebb of Cray's neural pulse proved it.

He was pushing himself into the transmitter.

"*No!*" Lea shouted, beating her hands against the glass. She glared at the still life of Cray's visage, while a ghostly flood of St. Elmo's fire crawled in reflection along the surface of the spires. "Cray, the translink is *down*. You have no viable link to the Axis. If you don't stop, you'll project yourself into empty space."

Taking myself out of the equation, love.

"Don't you run out on me, Cray. Not like this."

Only way . . . to get . . . you to go.

He was only coming through in fragments, his manifestation weakening. Lea leaned in closer, trying to maintain her hold on him, but he was slipping. Too much of his mind had already passed, and what remained was locked on a single concept assembled out of incomplete data. Cray gathered the pieces and packed them into a tight stream, then broadcast them as he would utter words with his last breath.

—she's here she's here she's here she's here—

It was a warning. Lea read his intent, while a shock of adrenaline arced her system in a cold current. In the glass, she caught a hint of motion parting the fog behind her, a danger made all the more critical because she could not see it. Lea relaxed every muscle in her body and fell away from the sarcophagus—just ahead of a ferocious blow that split the window into a thousand spidering cracks.

Lea rolled away, into the exchange of fire between the *Inru* and Special Services. She jumped to her feet regardless, not caring about the pulse beams that seared the space between her and the core. In front of her there was only the enemy, which floated out of the mist like an angry revenant—more dead than living, eyes burning and fixed.

"Hello again," Avalon said.

Noises, out from the deep.

Collected and focused, down at the dark end of a tunnel—just beneath the surface, he could hear them: an amalgam of human voices passing back and forth, punctuated by the drumbeat of heavy-arms fire. The constant pounding awoke him and oriented him, plucking his senses out of the wreckage and giving him a place to reach. It fell into focus through broken slats of light, which he clawed at greedily. A connection with the above, he determined to seize it before it disappeared.

He broke the air, blinded by brightness and choking on dust. Pain displaced his awareness, and with it the flood of memories of what had happened. But his eyes remained open, and the images that rushed back in to fill the vacuum showed him a disaster far worse than he could have imagined.

The entire chamber lay in ruins. Smoke and flames obscured most of the destruction, but where the veil thinned he could see CSS troops finishing off what was left. The waves of *Inru* who had thrown themselves in front of the attack lay dead, scattered across the floor in bits and pieces, fresh bones to join the others in the catacombs. The few who survived seemed without direction and wandered about aimlessly until they were overrun. It was surreal, to watch them walk into their own deaths without any concern—but as he drank it all in, he realized he was no different. Buried in the debris of the control booth, he could do nothing but wait for the soldiers to come for him.

Out of sheer despair, he searched the chamber for any recognizable feature. He quickly settled on the core, where the seven spires remained intact. He thought it impossible that they should be untouched, and even more impossible that they were still active; yet there they were, conducting rhythms of light, a distinct bionucleic signature bound to a vortex of its own making. At first, the sight of it was beautiful and hypnotic. Then, slowly, he began to recognize latent patterns in the energy flow—a downcycle that was repeating itself at shorter and shorter intervals, heading toward an inevitable shutdown.

A full-scale memory dump was in progress. The core was wiping itself clean.

He reached out and willed for it to stop. When that didn't work, he reached even farther. One hand out in front, he pulled himself out of the wreckage. He didn't know how much of his body was still left, or if he even had the strength to make it to the core; his only thought was of Alden, of how *he* was the one responsible. With hatred pushing him, and fury shielding him, he snaked his way across the floor—one body amongst the many, writhing for every inch.

Phao Yin would not permit Alden the luxury of suicide. He would see him suffer an eternity first.

Lea barely saw it coming—a disconnected phase of precise motion, cause and effect. With dazzling speed, an approach so covert, the free agent's wake engulfed Lea just ahead of her hands. They stabbed out at her, fingers tearing flesh like talons, before retracting and spinning away. It was just a glancing blow, but the damage was done. Lea felt her blood spill before she felt any pain, and her legs collapsed beneath her.

Down on her knees, she pawed at her neck for the gash she knew was there. Instead, she found a slice running down the side of her left cheek. It bled profusely, but it was nowhere near a fatal wound. Avalon had missed her throat, by accident or by design—but none of that mattered. It was only a preview of things to come.

Shaking off her dizziness, Lea got up again. She raised her hands in a defensive posture, and looked up to find Avalon standing several meters off. The free agent had been *waiting* for her to recover, before she tried a second pass. To Avalon, it was nothing more than a game. That the chamber was falling down around them only made it more exhilarating.

"Strike one," the free agent said.

Lea looked over Avalon's shoulder, and saw the firefight winding down. Several squads of CSS fanned out to secure the rest of the complex, including one that headed straight for the core.

"Don't worry," Avalon told her. "I'll deal with them as soon as I'm finished with you."

Lea believed it. Hand to hand, she was doomed. Her only chance was the quicksilver—but only if she got Avalon close enough.

"Sure you're up to it?" Lea fired back. Her tone was mocking, meant to provoke the free agent. "You couldn't even get it up hard enough to do Cray."

Avalon grinned. Her right hand dripped with Lea's blood. Licking her fingertips clean, she locked them into a claw.

"Let's try that again," she said.

Then the free agent was gone, a pirouette shooting straight into the air. The force that propelled her was unimaginable, as were the physics behind her descent. Swooping back down, she curled herself into a ball and bounced off the floor, converting her downward trajectory into a forward rush. She then flipped over in midair, inverted as she made a grab for Lea's head.

Lea ducked. She was quick enough to avoid getting her neck snapped, but too slow to beat Avalon's punch. Agony penetrated her skull like a drill, compressing her vision into a tunnel filled with stars. When it cleared, Lea found herself stumbling back toward the core. One hand feebly clutched the quicksilver; the other capped the new wound on her forehead, stemming fresh blood that trickled down the front of her face.

Avalon stood where Lea had been only a moment before. She had yet to break a sweat.

"Strike two," she said.

Lea steadied herself against one of the fallen computer banks. The world around her wobbled, with only the pain keeping her conscious. Avalon wasn't playing anymore. Still, Lea eased her hand away from the quicksilver and kept it hidden. She wasn't ready to give up.

Not yet.

"What's the matter?" Lea asked. Her words were slurred, between heavy breaths. "Reflexes not what they used to be? I thought you were supposed to be bad."

Avalon turned her head slightly, toward the approaching squad. They were close, but veered off short of a direct attack. Instead, they dug themselves in at a distance and clustered their weapons for a combined assault.

"Come on," Lea invited. "What are you waiting for?"

A muzzle flash ignited behind Avalon, outlining her body in a stellar corona. She twisted to avoid the pulse beams, channeling them between her outstretched arms. Then she leaped into the air again, riding the heat in defiance of gravity, channeling her momentum into a spear. The shots tore up the floor at Lea's feet, but she didn't so much as twitch. She only saw the free agent, who pounced down on her like a gigantic bat.

And the brilliance of quicksilver.

Phao Yin struggled.

His disciples dead, he played the same when the soldiers stepped over him. He would then continue, pushing himself with broken legs and pulling himself with bleeding hands. By the time he reached the core, the pain was beyond comprehension—but so was the need, as great as any pleasure he had ever pursued.

Grabbing on to one of the computer banks, Yin pulled himself to his knees and rested there for one blistering moment. He then hoisted himself up, containing his screams long enough to roll onto his back. Yin had no idea what happened next. His eyes closed, he only remembered losing himself in free fall—then a sudden, horrid jolt as he crashed upon uneven ground. When he opened his eyes, he saw that he had fallen into the core. A frigid, dry mist clung to the floor, creating an eerie white calm that cleansed him of his agony. It renewed Yin's clarity of purpose and guided him to what should have been his destiny.

It was bleeding ice, from the disconnected hoses at its base. The crystals that settled on its surface sparkled like a thousand diamonds, beautiful in spite of the anger they inspired. Yin scrambled toward the sarcophagus, quickly because he did not know how long he could bear to look at it in his current state. He clawed at its surface, slipping time and time again while he tried to find a hold, finally throwing himself on top with a final, desperate lunge.

Embracing the thing, Yin squirmed his way up to the window. The shattered glass oozed cryogenic fluid between its cracks. Yin wiped away the viscous liquid with his bare hands, slicing his skin and freezing it at the same time. He didn't care. Nothing would stop him from confronting his enemy. Nothing would stop him from seeing his face.

A dense fog covered the glass from the inside. Yin leaned in closer and the fog cleared. Alden's features congealed out of the blue suspension that separated them. He had gone ashen—beyond the

porcelain texture of a frozen body, into the color of the dead. With
the seal breached, Alden's life had leaked out as easily as the cryogenic fluid.

"*No!*" Yin shrieked.

He pounded against the broken glass. Glittering shards descended
lazily through the fluid, settling around Alden's shoulders, but he remained still.

"*You can't die! Not until I say!*"

Alden wasn't interested.

"*I won't allow it!*" Yin cried, overcome with tears of impotent
rage. He kept beating his fists against the sarcophagus, weaker and
weaker with each blow. "You will *not* die! Not until I know!"

Alden just lay there, in taunting death.

"*You son of a bitch!*"

His eyes flew open.

Yin froze. He gulped one last, searing breath.

Then hands, the cold flesh of a corpse, breaking through the window. Fingers wrapped around his head, electric points penetrating
his skull, and Yin tasted the pain of a hard interface. He thrashed
about, trying to force himself off the sarcophagus, but the energy
from his body was fading. Alden had drained it as easily as he drained
Yin's thoughts.

Yin fell.

Into Alden's eyes, a space of light-years crossed in the breadth of a
nanosecond: shadow without black, light without substance. Particles and waves, they encircled Yin in a whirlpool of chaos and data
behaving as one—a logical singularity, tunnels branching out into infinite strings that behaved like water, collapsing on him only to reap-
pear in a million different permutations. The whole of the Axis
spread itself out before him, but it was only a microcosm of what lay
beyond. Like the stars in the sky visible from Earth, they parted to
reveal the universe as it truly was—expanding, unpredictable, infinite
combinations of exquisite complexity.

The first glimpse cleaved Yin's mind like a scalpel.

The bitstream condensed into a flat horizontal plane. Yin pierced
it, breaking the surface tension of the wave, but then discovered an

entire ocean underneath. His own logic failing him, he sank into the abyss and drifted through its currents—which he soon came to realize were the patterns of the dead. He listened to them all, their singing voices constant but out of tune, fragments of thought and emotion trapped in the Axis like the debris of consciousness.

Yin screamed. Nothing came out. Yin fought. His body was memory. He was already dead, to be permitted to walk among them. And the dead treated him as a father, returning to his brood after abandoning them. One by one, Yin assimilated them. And one by one, they feasted on the remains of his mind.

Alden, their host, savored the last bit for himself.

The blade guided Lea.

Even as she spun to avoid the kill, her hand knew where to go. The quicksilver just followed the lines of tracer fire that chased Avalon through the air, then made a delicate stab into her path. What happened next was illusion, a passage marked only by a quiver—but Lea knew the throb that traveled down the length of her arm, and the sound of the quicksilver when it drew blood.

Avalon tumbled.

The free agent slipped into the beams at a glancing angle, taking an indirect hit to her shoulder. The shot only grazed her, but its velocity magnified the effect tenfold. She flipped over and took a dive straight down, crashing into the computer stacks as the beams ripped into the floor around her.

Smoke rose. Debris fell.

An unnatural quiet settled over the chamber.

Lea heard shouts from the squad that fired on them, followed by a scramble of footsteps. They were coming again. She managed to pull herself up and shuffled into the dissipating mist that fled the core.

Avalon slid off the stacks, and was there to meet her. She was smoldering, hunched over and bleeding. Her left arm cradled the right, holding it up so that Lea could see the cauterized incision. The quicksilver had bitten right through Avalon's sensuit, just above her hand. The flesh around the wound had already started to mortify.

"Strike three," Lea said.

Avalon grimaced—her own version of a smile. Then she winced, a reaction to the isotopic toxins that crawled up her arm. She took a step back.

"You can't stop us," the free agent said. "The evolution will continue."

Lea followed, and took another step toward her.

"Maybe I just need to slow it down a little."

Avalon kept going, until she bumped against the sarcophagus. She was in considerable pain now, but maintained a defiant posture. She was through fighting—but her eyes, burned blue and black and more human than they had ever been, told Lea that there would be another time.

"Soon," Avalon told her. "Very soon."

She then dissolved, a flurry of incredible speed. When Lea caught up with her, the free agent was already in the escape tube. Avalon jacked the safety overrides, plugging in with her sensors and taking manual control of her descent. Lea launched herself at the tube, grabbing at the hatch before Avalon could close it—but the free agent was too far ahead of her. The hatch slammed shut.

Avalon, however, was not all there. Her wounded arm protruded from the lip of the hatch, which closed around it. Through the transparency of the tube, Lea could see the agony on the free agent's face, but she could also see the resolve. This was survival, pure and simple. Avalon was going to live, and this was the only way to do it.

Lea turned away before the arm sheared off.

And while Avalon dropped into the catacombs, Lea kept walking. Toward the sarcophagus and toward Cray, where she found the body of Phao Yin. He was facedown against the cracked window, his arms hanging limp off the sides of the cryogenic vessel—the very place where Lea had first seen him. She pulled Yin off and dumped him on the floor, his eyes wide-open in terror as they stared up at her.

Cray, in utter contrast, lay peacefully. Lea searched her thoughts for him, hoping to catch an echo, but she fell only on silence. She reached down and touched the broken glass, tracing the contours of his face with her hand.

"What now, cowboy?"

She barely acknowledged the group of soldiers forming a cordon around the core. They kept a cautious distance, treating Lea with the same awe the *Inru* had shown Cray.

"What now?"

EPILOGUE

Faces, just outside the glass.

An endless parade of them passing back and forth with no pattern or reason. Lea recognized some of them from her former life—hammerjacks who got burned trying to repeat her runs, old *Inru* comrades who didn't get out when she did—but mostly they were just *people*, common to each other only in their misery. Occasionally one would stop and press himself against the window, grimacing in despair—but mostly, they just stared. Permitted a glance into her luxurious world, they visited her with hatred, and used body language to promise revenge if they ever got her within reach of their hands. Then they would continue, the slow pace of the tortured and the enslaved, until they returned the next day to do it over again.

Lea tried to reason with them for the first few days. They didn't want to listen. There was a difference between her and them. The protective wall that separated them was only the beginning. Lea was a prisoner, but she was a *valuable* prisoner. It was precisely the message her jailers wanted to convey.

They despised her for that. After a while, Lea despised them equally.

She retreated to the rear of her cell, as far away from the glass as she could get. The food she had refused, she now accepted heartily. When asked what she wanted to drink, she requested the finest wine—and got it. The sparse accommodations she had started with gave way to plush furnishings and a feather bed that was sinful in its comfort. The Collective had upgraded her status to collaborator and made certain the entire population of the gulag knew it.

Lea didn't give a damn.

She would have known their purpose even if Cray hadn't warned her. She understood the rite of passage for what it was. Getting through it was the only way to get to the meat of what they *really* wanted—and so Lea served it up for them. By the time she was through, Lea was totally withdrawn into herself. She went through all the motions, but she was just living. Nothing kept her mind occupied, except the waiting. And when she had waited long enough, the window frosted to black and blocked the others out forever.

Trevor Bostic turned away from the monitor in the commandant's office, where he had watched the drama every day for the last six weeks.

"That's enough," he said.

They gassed her, a potent neuralstetic that rendered her unconscious for several hours. When she woke up, she was in an apartment—an opulent suite of rooms adorned in black and white marble, like something out of a dream. Rising out of bed, she realized she was dressed in a silk nightgown. Her skin had been delicately scrubbed and smelled of lilac. Through the windows in her room, the familiar skyline of Manhattan revealed itself, sparkling lights outfitted for the gathering dark. Then she realized she *had* dreamed about this place many times throughout the course of her life. It had been her oasis of peace—an art deco fantasy she had promised herself if she lived long enough to enjoy the rewards of her occupation.

Someone had plucked it out of her imagination and manufactured it for her.

Lea picked up a robe draped across a chair next to the bed and walked across the cool tile floor to the bedroom door. Opening it, she found an escort waiting for her on the other side. The man was dark, impeccably dressed in a silk suit—Japanese to the core. Lea knew he was a gangster the moment she saw him—probably a Special Services liaison. Spook masters used them for security when they didn't trust their own inner circle.

"Good evening, Miss Prism," he said, his tone businesslike—but latent with the threat of violence. "I've been assigned as shadow counsel for the duration of your deployment. Your presence has been ordered at corporate security headquarters—immediately."

Lea studied him for a moment and decided she had no choice.

"I'll be ready in a minute," she said.

They traveled by private pulser, off the Port Authority routes so there would be no record of transit. It was standard procedure for a mission that was off the books, which told Lea all she needed to know about how she got back to New York. Special Services had smuggled her in—a considerable risk, given the penalties for abetting a rogue hammerjack in the incorporated territories. It also meant Lea Prism no longer existed. All traces of her would be burned out of the Axis by now, with Heretic not far behind. There would be talk—but even that would soon dissolve into the fragments of legend. Just like Vortex, she would become a story and nothing more.

If they only knew, Lea thought—but they wouldn't. Some faction of the Assembly had already seen to it.

The rooftop was empty when they landed at CSS. There was no clearance, no armed escort—only Lea's shadow counsel, who bypassed approach control and slipped in during a programmed security downcycle. He whisked Lea over to a vaulted elevator, which took them several floors down to one of the executive levels. The doors opened upon an ornate suite, and her shadow stood aside to let her pass. Lea expected him to follow, but he remained behind. Apparently, it was to be a private meeting.

Lea entered without asking questions. She felt light-years away from that hole in the ground in Paris but still carried the dread that originated there. She hoped nobody else would notice.

"I trust that you slept well."

The owner of that voice descended a spiral staircase on the other side of the room. Like her shadow, the man was dressed to perfection—though his style was less modern and spoke of wealth as if it had always been a given. He had the look of a lawyer—the kind of man who gave orders but never got his own hands dirty. Lea disliked him on sight.

"Said the spider to the fly," she replied.

The man smiled.

"Dramatic," he observed as he stepped away from the stairs. He strolled over to the minibar and dropped some ice into a glass. "But it *does* convey an understanding of your position. That makes you somebody I can deal with."

"Who are you?"

"Trevor Bostic," he said, pouring himself a scotch. "I'm the reason you're still alive."

Lea raised an eyebrow.

"I stayed alive for a long time without your help," she said. "What makes you think I'm interested now?"

"Because you're smart," Bostic told her. He walked away from the bar and took a seat on a nearby couch. "Resourceful, cunning—all the qualities that make for a superb hammerjack. If you hadn't gotten mixed up in Alden's business, it's quite possible we never would have caught up with you."

"Yet here we are."

Bostic nodded.

"A situation we can put to our mutual advantage."

Bostic pointed her to the seat across from him. Lea ignored the offer, going instead to the bar. She selected a very fine cognac and poured herself a generous glass. Lifting the snifter to her lips, she allowed the alcohol to tease her senses before taking a sip.

"I have questions," she said.

"By all means."

She retreated to the window and looked a hundred floors down into the street. Even at this hour, the city was alive. Traffic passed along the traverse grid, back and forth into forever. Lea wondered how long it had been since she saw the light of day.

"How did you know?"

Bostic considered how much to tell her.

"We had a go team deployed in every incorporated sector, await-ing word on Dr. Alden," he said. "When we got the word on your location, we went in."

"Who told you?"

"We don't know that for certain," Bostic admitted. "The source was an anonymous transmission jacked into our private communica-tions band. It set off every intrusion countermeasure we have. Who-ever it was wanted to get our attention."

Lea didn't believe him.

"Just like that?" she asked, turning around to face him. "Some hammerjack drops a dime and you come running."

"Not quite," Bostic said. "A feedback trace isolated the source to somewhere in the research district—right in the vicinity of the Works."

Lea felt weak. That old fear revealed itself again—only now Bostic was around to see it. The game was up.

"Lyssa."

Bostic stood and joined her at the window. He was close, but not so close that he gave anything away. The lawyer danced along the edge of what he wanted, revealing only what was necessary.

"It's a possibility," he said, a bait for her interest. "Truth is, there's a lot we don't know about her. How she was connected to Alden is only one of those questions. The Assembly wants answers. That's where *you* come in."

Lea shook her head.

"No way," she said, and retreated to the bar.

"Alden was already working on the problem when all this started," Bostic said, his tone getting edgy. "He was the best we had—but even he didn't know a tenth of what you know about bionucleics. For Christ's sake, you *invented* the technology. You handed it over it to the *Inru*, not even caring what they did with it."

Lea's hands trembled as she put down her drink.

"That was a long time ago."

"The Assembly has a long memory," Bostic shot back. "They know a lot about your activities over the last few years. Alden mapped the whole thing out. You've been sabotaging them—as much as you've been sabotaging Collective research. You don't want anybody to have this thing."

"Then why the hell should I help you?"

"Because you can't stop it," he said. "And being close to it is the next best thing."

Bostic sounded desperate, even though he was trying to hide it. Lea closed her eyes, getting herself together so she could take the advantage. It was the hammerjack persona that came through when she faced him again—the Heretic the Collective had hunted and now needed so badly.

"They're afraid," Lea said. "Afraid of losing all that money they poured into bionucleics. But they're more afraid of the *Inru,* aren't they? *That's* why they want me. They're afraid this revolution of theirs will catch on."

"They have considered it."

"Why?" Lea asked. "Phao Yin is dead. His people are gone."

Bostic was quiet for a long while. It gave Lea time to think, and ponder the implications of his silence.

"What makes you think Yin was the only one?"

Lea went numb.

"There are as many factions as there are street species," he went on, "isolated cells that have only limited contact with one another. Yin's was, by far, the most advanced—but now he's dead, and his death has turned him into a martyr. Others will follow in his footsteps."

"And you think I can stop them?"

"You used to *be* one of them," Bostic pointed out. "Who better than you to finish what Alden started?"

Lea saw firsthand what that kind of life had done to Cray. It made him rich, but it landed him in purgatory—one that probably resembled the Midtown apartment where she had awakened. In the end, Cray had died rather than go back to it. How long would it be before Lea reached the same extreme?

"It's your choice," Bostic finished. "You can either go home to your place in Manhattan, or you can go back to prison."

The words came out easy, though the decision was not.

"When do you want me to start?"

• • •

The Works had transformed itself.

Work crews were still in the process of erasing all the damage, traces of which were still visible like scars from old wounds. The blood, however, was gone, and with it the pall that saturated these corridors and chased away the living. All that remained was the memory, which echoed throughout the building—but only for those who were willing to listen.

Then there was Lea.

Nobody recognized her. She passed through the security checkpoints without anyone giving her a second glance. The credentials Bostic supplied gave her unlimited access to all levels, so nobody asked any questions. She took her time, searching faces in every corner of the Works for somebody who might understand—but there was no one who had been here before Cray had arrived. They only knew Lyssa as a vague concept, not the living entity who spoke to her the moment she entered the research complex.

But that would change.

They would watch her go to the hundredth floor, into the laboratory few were allowed to see. They might wonder who she was, this woman with no name. And they would speculate about who sent her and why she was there. But they would never approach her—not after she went into the Tank, because after she emerged there would be no doubt.

She was a spook. That was all they needed to know.

Lea felt it even then, through layers of shielding as the entry door closed behind her. She heard it in their breathing and whispers that escaped with the hissing air when the chamber pressurized. It had been the same for Cray, whenever they had seen him coming: that apprehension, coupled with uncertainty—as if he were there to deliver or destroy them. In a way, Lea supposed it was true.

Technology has superseded itself to become the new religion.

It wasn't her own thought—just a familiar voice, broadcasting out of the dark as the door to the Tank opened. Then the lights came on, slowly at first, rising to a dim invitation. Lea stepped inside and sensed that the vibe had shifted, as if her presence was the catalyst;

but then she saw the colors, red shifting to blue as galaxies had done since the beginning of creation, moving ever outward toward that day they would oscillate back in on themselves.

And Lea knew.

Before she reclined in the interface chair, she knew. Before electrodes delivered his presence to her cortex, she knew. More than anything, it was the power that had drawn her here, infused by the simple memory of what Cray had told her: *Survive, Lea. It's all you can do.*

She then rose, away from the chair because she no longer needed it. Hands reaching the surface of the Tank, Lea watched the swirling patterns react to her touch and gather form. She smiled, and the elements smiled back.

With the soul—and the face—of a man behind the glass.

"Hello, Vortex," Lea said to him.

ABOUT THE AUTHOR

MARC D. GILLER wrote his first science-fiction novel at the tender age of sixteen, with the certainty of fame and riches before him. When that plan didn't work out he went to college, earning a bachelor of science degree in journalism from Texas A&M University.

Never cured of the writing bug, he tried a few other genres—horror, thriller, historical fiction—when a script he wrote for *Star Trek: The Next Generation* earned him a chance to pitch stories for the show.

Though none of those stories aired, that experience made him more determined than ever to keep writing. He fired off a few more novels and screenplays until *Hammerjack* finally caught the attention of Bantam Spectra. This is his first published work.

Over the years, Marc has worked as a photographer, producer, computer trainer, and even had a one-night stint as a television news reporter. For the last five years, he has been manager of information systems for a Tampa law firm.

Marc makes his home in the Tampa Bay area of Florida, where he lives with his wife, two children, and a furry golden retriever.

Think you've reached the end?

This is only the beginning . . .

Read on for a special sneak peek at the next

thrilling read from Marc D. Giller

PRODIGAL

Coming Summer 2006

From Bantam Spectra

PRODIGAL

on sale summer 2006

Lea Prism took measure of herself the way she always did—in fleeting glimpses, caught by accident, off some reflective surface that obscured her face in shadow. Tonight it was a window, her face flanked by pinpoint stars and glowing LEDs, the flood of virtual monitors elongating her features in a trick of the light. As much as she avoided herself, when caught like this she would always pause to consider the person staring back at her. It was a mission ritual—a sideways glance, just to see how much she had changed since the last time.

Outwardly, there wasn't much. An *Inru* blade had grazed Lea's neck some months ago, leaving a thin scar that trailed along her jaw line, but everything else was the same. With her long blond hair pulled back into a ponytail and her green eyes narrowed to a scowl, the scar made her appear harsh—which was why she had decided against having it removed. Inwardly, however, that scar concealed some deeper wounds, not the least of which was the memory of what she had done to the *Inru* bitch who cut her. That day had marked the beginning of the spiral—and Lea's first realization of how far down she would have to go.

That's how they get you, a trusted voice had once warned her. *You just wake up one morning and you're one of them. After that, you can't go back.*

Worse still, Lea now understood that she didn't even have the will to try. The life was the only thing that stirred her passions. The job was her only purpose.

And the kill, she added. *What are you when that's your only kick?*

A spot of turbulence jolted her out of that thought. Lea grabbed the nearest handhold out of reflex, so accustomed was she to the bucking of the deck beneath her feet. It seemed like she had already spent a lifetime in the air—most of it aboard heavy transports like this, sealed within cramped quarters rife with the taste of adrenaline. After more than fifty combat drops, she had developed a serious taste for it.

"CIC," Lea heard her pilot say, the message conveyed by her earpiece. "We're crossing the Old Federation border now. Estimate thirty minutes to target."

"Acknowledged," she replied. "Keep it dark up there, guys. You know the drill when we're operating outside of jurisdiction."

"When are we ever *in* jurisdiction?"

Lea smiled. Even though Russia was technically part of the Incorporated Territories, there were still a lot of military freelancers in the former republics who made sport out of shooting down stray aircraft. "Just do the flying and let me worry about the travel arrangements," she said gamely.

"Next time, maybe the bad guys will hole up someplace nicer."

"Roger on that, Skipper."

Lea closed off the channel, turning around to confront the intense but controlled activity in the Critical Information Center. At one time an empty cargo hold, the space was now crammed with rows of interface consoles, tracking nodes, and communications equipment: everything required to coordinate a complex mobile insertion. Manning the stations was a small crew of men and women wearing the black and gold uniform of Technical Branch. Independent of Corporate Special Services, T-Branch was an elite unit comprised of personnel selected by Lea herself—a hedge against the split loyalties and infighting that plagued other security agencies. That autonomy had also spared her from having to deal with the layers of civilian bureaucracy at CSS—not to mention an entrenched command structure that still viewed her as an enemy.

For that reason, among others, Lea eschewed the uniform, even though she held the commissioned rank of major as a condition of her job. She had always been wary of working with the big guns, based on her own experience with the kind of mercenaries CSS employed; and it had taken her a while to recruit people who fit into her command style, which prized careful thought over blind obedience. In time, though, Lea had come to think of the team as an extension of herself—which included her cunning, her instincts, and sometimes even her rage. It was their work, more than anything, that had assured her reputation as a corporate spook.

You mean your reputation as an Inru *nightmare.*

Lea studied the glint of her quicksilver blade. A non-regulation weapon, it had saved her life at one time—and since then, she had never entered battle without it. She stowed the blade in the leg compartment of her body armor, then headed toward a rising fracas at the back of the CIC. There, five members of her advance team were engaged in a game of breakneck poker, their voices rising and falling in a familiar chorus as the cards flew around a pile of money that had accumulated on the deck. Epithets seared the air like a volley of pulse fire, back and forth with the turning of each card, while the players fell one by one. Not even their own armor could protect them from the dealer—a skinny kid with fast hands and kinetic eyes, who radiated a confidence that didn't know when to quit.

"Hey, Pallas," Lea told him. "Just make sure the house gets ten percent, okay?"

The kid flashed her a knowing grin.

"With this bunch," Pallas scoffed, "you'll have to wait until payday."

Lea shook her head, barely concealing her affection for him. Alex Pallas was a natural hammerjack: cool and creative, but too cocky to appreciate danger when it was staring him in the face. That he was fleecing five armed commandos was a case in point. It was the same attitude that had gotten him kicked out of MIT, after the board of regents discovered he had been looting the university's research budget to finance his high-stakes gambling excursions. That Pallas had turned a handsome profit didn't impress the disciplinary board, but it had impressed Lea. The kid may have been a liar and a thief, but his game was always honest.

Pallas dealt out a quick hand of five-card stud, while Lea heard a baritone voice growling behind her. "One of these days," it said, "that boy is going to get himself launched ass-first out of the back of this transport."

Lea looked back to find the last member of the advance team sauntering up to her. Eric Tiernan was pure T-Branch: tall and angular, with a seasoned toughness that telegraphed his rank even more than his lieutenant's bars. As squad commander, he was in charge of the tactical aspects of the team's missions. He was also Lea's executive officer.

"Relax, Tiernan," she said. "He's going easy on them."

Pallas threw down an ace to match the other one he had showing.

"I can see that," the lieutenant replied.

Lea brushed off Tiernan's remark, but also took that as her cue. "Stations, people," she ordered. "Pre-op briefing in one minute."

The advance team jumped into action, throwing their cards down and scooping up what was left of their money. They then filed over to the weapons lockers, where they loaded up on all the gear Tiernan had speced out—pulse rifles, flash grenades, stun pistols, plus the integrators Lea had designed for this mission. Their rowdy swagger had disappeared, replaced by the cool professionalism of a combat unit.

Pallas, meanwhile, remained sitting on the deck. As Lea looked back at him, she saw his head shaking mournfully.

"You really know how to hurt a guy, boss," he said.

"You have no idea," Lea retorted.

She helped Pallas up, and walked with him toward an imaging station at the center of the CIC. Pallas plugged himself into the interface, and within moments a three-dimensional map of Ukraine sublimated out of the hazy mist that hovered over the console. A red line cut a slash across the country, following the transport's approach from the Black Sea. A blinking graphic showed their current position near the city of Cherkasy, while a blue arrow pointed out their projected course—straight toward the upper bend of the Dnipro River. Their target was a restricted zone near the southern border of Belarus, an area of rolling hills that grew larger on the display as Pallas zoomed in on it.

Lea gave her people a few moments to absorb the image as they gathered. Tiernan assumed his place at her side, while the rest of the advance team formed a circle around the display.

"Patch in latest orbital pass," she told her hammerjack, who jacked into a satellite feed of the target area and positioned it over the display. High-res images assembled into a mosaic of visual and thermal elements, smeared by the telltale blur of creeping radiation.

"Twelve hours ago," Lea began, "we received some intel that points to significant *Inru* activity. It seems that after prolonged conflict with our team, their operational cells are starting to get a little desperate."

That statement brought a wave of approval from her audience. From the start, Lea had been single minded in her dealings with the anti-technology cult—a pursuit that bordered on obsessive. Using a more extreme approach than her predecessor, she had pounded their infrastructure with virtual attacks, drying up their finances and material support. After that, she went after the *Inru* leadership itself, targeting them personally in a series of relentless strikes. In a matter of months, Lea had effectively decapitated the major cells, pushing them even further underground where they could do little but stir up some minor trouble. As for their leaders, most of them were now either dead or rotting in some Collective gulag.

Most, she reminded herself, *but not all.*

Lea chewed on that thought before continuing. "Analysis based on my information points to an *Inru* summit. Some kind of high-level gathering of the surviving leadership—probably to discuss a new, larger strategy against the Collective. CSS has been wondering when they might pool their remaining resources to mount some kind of counterstrike. If what we're hearing is true, they could be very close to making that happen."

"What's the source of this intel?" one of the commandos asked.

Lea hesitated for a moment before giving her answer.

"Intercepted communications," she said evasively.

An exchange of muttered comments arose around the table, a familiar reaction on the squad's part. Lea was always secretive about how she got her information, choosing to compartmentalize intelligence operations to the non-tactical members of her team. She knew it spooked them—not because of her methods, but because she was almost never wrong. In their view, Lea was almost clairvoyant when it came to the enemy.

If they only knew.

"SIGINT has been pretty flaky for a while," Tiernan pointed out. "The *Inru* have been putting out a lot of false information since they got wind we compromised their networks. What are the chances this is just comm chatter designed to throw us off?"

Lea gave Pallas a nod, and allowed him to go first.

"We picked up some weird inclusions in Axis traffic," the hammerjack said, seeming to enjoy himself. "Most secure communications are condensed into proprietary tokens, which means you can backtrace them to their source by parsing the routing code. CSS keeps a record of these codes, so they can listen in on pirate traffic, unauthorized exchanges, whatever pisses them off. Lea happened to notice a couple of stray tokens originating from some Port Authority nexus, so she had me check them out. Turns out they're not stray after all—they're *repeating* at regular intervals, using some custom algorithm designed make it look random."

"Burst communications," Tiernan decided.

"Give the man a cigar," Pallas said. "The *Inru* were using the North American Pulser Grid as a transmission medium—modulating photons into carrier streams, then encoding their messages with some routing key I'd never seen before."

"How did you crack the key?"

Pallas tossed a sideways glance at Lea.

"I found it while running some permutations through a CSS computer," she said—an honest answer, though not even close to the whole story. "After a couple of cycles, it came up with a mathematical constant: the decay rate of heliox emissions."

The squad responded with muted laughter. Tiernan resisted the urge to do the same, though Lea knew the lieutenant shared their sentiment. That kind of attention made her uneasy—and not just because he was her second-in-command. In a life with so many secrets, that was the price she paid. Trust was hard to come by, even with a man who had risked his life for her.

"*Shit*, Major," one of them chuckled. "That must be one hell of a crystal ball you have back at the office."

"Just because you're good," Lea said, "doesn't mean you can't get lucky."

She paused. "Our objective is in the wastelands of northern Ukraine," she continued, while Pallas augmented the image. The profile of a small city appeared in silhouette, its dimensions extrapolated into a graphic that showed a cluster of buildings surrounding a large technical complex near the center of town. "The Old Federation abandoned the area a long time ago, for logistical and safety reasons—which means there are no military outposts anywhere nearby. Then there's the radiation endemic to the region, which scrambles the ability of sensors to pick up electronic signatures. Put it all together, you've got a pretty good place to hide."

"What's the target?" one of the commandos asked.

Lea pointed at the shadow city, dark as the night of a new moon.

"Chernobyl," she said.

The low flurry of discussion fell into an abject silence. Even now, over a century after the disaster that happened there, the sound of that name inspired a dry fear, like dust settling in a catacomb. It was the last place on Earth anybody would want to look.

Pallas used the interface to overlay a sixty-kilometer circle on the map, with Chernobyl at the center. "Within this border is the so-called 'dead zone' around the city," Lea explained. "This is where radiation from the old nuclear accident is still high enough to make long-term exposure dangerous. Nobody has lived within the perimeter since the late twentieth century, although the roads and structures within the zone are largely intact."

She motioned toward a satellite image of the reactor complex. Pallas zoomed in on the ancient facility, its lone cooling tower still jaggedly pointing toward the sky. Time had ravaged the power plant even more than the explosion that had blown the lid off the number four reactor, releasing untold amounts of deadly radiation into the atmosphere—radiation that still lurked in the buildings and forests of Chernobyl.

"A sarcophagus of steel and concrete encases the damaged reactor,"

Lea continued. "The decaying core is nominally contained inside, but over time the materials have become brittle and unstable. That's why our mission profile calls for a remote insertion." Pallas highlighted a section of road about twenty clicks inside the dead zone. "That's our spot, right there. The distance minimizes the risk of disturbing the ruins and attracting attention, but it's close enough for us to roll the rest of the way in our APC."

"A personnel carrier on an empty road makes a juicy target," Tiernan said. "What about a more stealth approach through the woods?"

Lea shook her head. "Too dangerous in the countryside. All those trees soak up radiation like a sponge. More than one hour in there and you'll get cooked, even with protective gear. The road is the only safe way in or out."

Tiernan sighed. "Well, at least we won't have to worry about electronic surveillance," he observed. "If background rads are too much for our sensors, the *Inru* won't be able to use them either."

"Which means we can get them before they even know we're there." Lea then directed Pallas to focus on one of the taller buildings in town, which stood a few blocks away from the power plant. "This is where we believe the *Inru* are holed up. It's an old apartment complex, full of places to hide. Blueprints show the place has a basement, which is the most logical place for them to go. There's cover from thermal satellite sweeps, plus enough shielding to protect them from the radiation."

"A party right under our noses," the lieutenant said, impressed. "So what's the protocol?"

Lea handed the briefing over to Novak. "I've prepared your body armor with dual layers of specially resistant pollyalloys," the GME said, as a lecturer would address her students. "This *should* offer you limited protection from background radiation, increasing your safe exposure times. All the same, I wouldn't recommend a leisurely stroll. I'd keep my activities limited to what's absolutely necessary, if I were you."

The members of the advance team swore under their breath. They bitched about every mission, because that was what soldiers were supposed to do—but in this case Lea understood perfectly. Even though she could never express it in front of the others, she felt the same way about this place. Chernobyl didn't want them there. The city didn't want *anybody* there.

"What kind of levels are we talking about?" one of them asked.

"Anywhere from 20 to 2,000 roentgens, depending on where you are," Novak noted dryly.

"Which is why it's advisable to watch your step. Should you chance to walk into a rather robust dose, I'm afraid there won't be much I can do for you."

"The most toxic zones are mapped out on the integrators I programmed for this mission," Lea said, as those areas appeared in red on the display. "They're also equipped with radiation detectors, so you'll know your levels every step of the way. The primary danger, of course, is from the damaged reactor—but there's also the park adjacent to the plant, and the town cemetery. The graphite core is buried there, so don't set foot inside under *any* circumstances."

"Not unless you want to glow in the dark," Pallas added.

Novak leveled an icy stare at him. A green line, meanwhile, twisted between the red zones, following a convoluted path through town that terminated at the apartment building.

"This corridor provides the least exposure," Lea said, "so that's our path."

Tiernan examined the approach and frowned doubtfully. "There's a lot of kill zones along the way, Major," he warned, pointing to a number of tight squeezes between structures—perfect places to get boxed in with no way out. "We get caught in there, our backs are against the wall." He looked at Lea in earnest, something he did when he was searching her for clues. "What kind of contingency do we have?"

The way he looked at her made Lea anxious. It wasn't the first time—but it was certainly the first time in front of the team.

"We fight," she said evenly, "even if we have to pull the town out from underneath them."

Tiernan raised an eyebrow. Lea knew she would hear more from him later, but for now she just barked out commands. "We're talking about an opportunity to *end* this thing, tonight. That's why I need this to go by the numbers, people. We do this right, the *Inru* won't get a second chance. Everybody understand?"

The advance team nodded in agreement, and slapped one another on the shoulder in a show of swelling bravado. Lea knew they prized the hunt as much as she did, in spite of the dangers—especially when the entire game was at stake. In stoking each other, they were smelling *Inru* blood, which was just what Lea wanted.

"Stations," she ordered.

The team disbanded to their landing positions, while Pallas left the display to assume control of the tactical interface. At the same time, Novak rounded the table and fixed Lea with a stare—the kind that was all business, no bullshit.

"Fifty roentgens," the GME said in no uncertain terms. "That's your limit. More than that and you'll back away, promise me."

"Don't worry," Lea assured her with a weak smile. "I know what I'm doing."

"I'm sure you do, my dear. They *all* do—particularly the ones who don't come back."

With that parting shot, Novak left her alone with Tiernan. He hung back for a time, while Lea busied herself with the display of the town, absorbing its risks and its dimensions with the same cool detachment that had served her so well as a hammerjack. Lea missed the unbridled certainty of that world, where her victims had been virtual, the manifestation of some soulless corporate entity. Flesh and blood, as she had discovered, was a different proposition. As easy as it was to kill, it was much harder to watch people die—especially when those people were her own.

Absently, she checked her armor compartments one last time, running down her list of weapons and supplies. She paused for a moment over her medikit, counting out the ampoules of antirad elixirs and stims—including the speedtec doses she had requisitioned for just this mission. The amber liquid glinted at Lea, the fascination of a deadly poison.

"You're loaded for bear," Tiernan observed, in the worn tones of someone who knew her better than she would have liked. "You think she'll be there tonight, don't you?"

Lea snapped the medikit shut and stowed it back in her armor. She hated justifying herself to him, but always felt a compulsion to do just that. Tiernan was, after all, her XO—but Lea knew that his position had little to do with how she felt.

"I'm not taking any chances," she replied, turning back toward him. Lea read the fine lines in his face, his expression showing that same latent concern he always had when he looked at her. "She's one of the few senior commanders the *Inru* has left, so it makes sense that she would be involved. Besides," she added, letting more emotion slip than she intended, "this operation has her fingerprints all over it."

"You should know. You developed the Avalon profile."

Avalon. Her shadow was so omnipresent, and still it sounded strange to hear her name spoken out loud. That Tiernan had mentioned it was meant to provoke a response, but Lea didn't take the bait. Instead, she raised a curious eyebrow at her executive officer.

"You don't need to tap dance around me, Eric," she said evenly. "If you have concerns about this mission, just tell me."

"I've never been worried about the *mission*," Tiernan reassured her. "You know this team would follow you anywhere, Lea—and that includes me." He then lowered his voice before continuing, "I just want to be clear about our objective. We're about to drop into some seriously hazardous territory, and that means tough choices. I can't make that call unless I know what's important—neutralizing the *Inru* or putting Avalon's head on a spike."

"At this point, I'd say they were one and the same."

"Maybe they are—but where your head is makes a big difference." He leaned in close. "If it comes down to saving one of us or taking Avalon out, which one is it going to be? You better make that decision right now, because in the field you might not get the chance."

Lea narrowed her eyes at him, but Tiernan didn't flinch.

What was worse, she knew he might be right. In the entire time she had been working as a corporate spook, not *once* did Lea come close to finding Avalon. The former free agent had been too sly, too cautious—dark matter in the Axis, leaving no patterns to trace, no trails to follow. But the *Inru* bore Avalon's signature, in the boldness of their attacks and their unwillingness to abandon their jihad. In reality, all the leads Lea had chased down—and all the victories she had gained from them—had been incidental to her pursuit of the one target that still eluded her.

Avalon.

"I'm aware of that, Eric," Lea answered quietly. "I'm also aware of my responsibilities."

"I know you are," Tiernan said. "If I had the slightest doubt about that, we wouldn't be having this conversation. But I won't allow a personal vendetta to jeopardize the safety of my team, Lea. If I see that happening, I *will* pull the plug."

Lea forced down a swell of anger—but only because she didn't want to create an incident in the middle of the CIC. From Tiernan, however, she hid nothing. Telegraphing her point with an intense glare, Lea made certain he knew that he had stepped over the line.

"That isn't your decision to make, *Lieutenant*," she seethed. "If you have a problem with that, you can stay back here with the support crew."

Tiernan got the message, and backed off.

"I go where my people go," he said, submitting but not submissive.

"They're not just your people, Eric."

"I know that," he said, softening a little. "I just don't want to be in a situation where one of us gets between you and Avalon."

"That won't happen," Lea told him without the least bit of irony, "if you stay out of my way."

That ended the conversation—not on the note Lea wanted, but in a way that served her purposes nonetheless. She then turned back to her work, looking back up only when she knew Tiernan was gone. It was cruel, but to do anything less would have risked opening the discussion even further, in directions she couldn't go.

It's for his own good, she told herself. *He doesn't want to know you that way.*

What frightened her was the thought that he already did.

A full moon illuminated the night sky as the transport started its descent, the ungainly lines and jutting angles of its airframe traced in a panoply of vaporous light. Electronic countermeasures had, up until then, obscured the signature of the bulky craft, protecting it from the various missile installations that dotted the countryside below; but as it broke the heavy cloud cover over the Chernobyl dead zone, the pilot disengaged the ECMs and took refuge in the permanent layer of radiation that blanketed the wastelands like an invisible haze. By the time the forest loomed in the cockpit window, the leaden clouds had rendered the terrain almost completely dark, visible only as a green and black mosaic through the pilot's infrared goggles.

Lea, meanwhile, monitored the approach from inside the armored personnel carrier. The vehicle was parked on the aft cargo ramp of the transport, which opened into the frigid air as they neared the landing area. She was seated up front with her driver, and watched the unwelcoming landscape roll by on a dashboard monitor that carried a feed from the cockpit. As the wind howled outside her window, what struck her most was the utter *lack* of human activity. In a world where urban metroplexes covered half a continent, around here not a single light burned to curse the darkness.

"Talon, this is Wanderer," she heard Pallas say over her earpiece, his message peppered by light static. "We're about one minute out. You guys ready?"

Lea glanced over at her driver, who nodded affirmatively.

"We're all set, Wanderer," she reported. "Sounds like your signal is dropping out. What's the story?"

"We're picking up some interference from stray radiation. I was afraid of this, Skipper. Our coded channels operate in the same bands, so it's only going to get worse the closer we get to the source. That could mean we'll have problems monitoring the mission from here."

"What about the lower bands?"

"Hold on." After a moment, Pallas came back on and said, "Those are marginal for data, but good enough for voice. Of course, in this dead spectrum any open transmissions will stick out like a sore dick."

"Then we'll maintain radio silence as long as we can," Lea said. "Do your best with the passive feed, but no active bursts unless it's an emergency."

"Affirmative, boss. Thirty seconds. Prepare to disengage."

"Acknowledged. Talon out." Lea got out of her seat and poked her head into the rear of the APC, where all six members of the advance team were crammed. With all their weapons and gear, everyone was packed pretty tight. "Looks like we're going in dark, people. Hyperband is spotty, so we'll be on uncoded channels. That means we stay close—use the comm gear only when necessary. We don't want to alert the *Inru* to our presence before we're ready to take them down."

The team made the necessary switch to their personal transmitters. A round of comm checks crackled in their earpieces as each of them strapped a helmet on, their features illuminated in a pale red glow beneath their visors. Tiny columns of information appeared in the heads-up display in front of their eyes, keyed to sensors placed throughout their body armor. Lea studied the readings carefully as she flipped her visor down, paying the closest attention to the radiation counter. Already it was ticking at 30 microroentgens per hour—and that was within the confines of the APC's shielded plates. Even now, the transport was starting to kick up plumes of radioactive particles.

"Twenty meters," Lea heard Pallas say.

She strapped herself back into the passenger seat, listening in silence with the others as Pallas counted the distance until landing. She rubbed her gloved hands together, unable to wipe the sweat of her palms or slow the urging of her heart, which made her body feel alive and restrained at the same time.

"Contact," the hammerjack said.

There was a horrendous jolt when they touched down. Lea's driver instantly threw the APC into gear, bouncing everyone around as the vehicle lurched down the landing ramp and into the open air. The hulking outline of the transport filled the thin slats of the forward windows, but only for a moment; as soon as the APC rolled away, the transport lifted off again and was gone. When the roar of the turbines faded, all that was left was a cloud of settling dust.

And a lonely highway that stretched into forever.

"Let's move," Lea said.